A WOLF AT THE DOOR
AND OTHER RARE TALES

PUBLISHER'S
ACKNOWLEDGEMENTS

Immanion Press would like to thank Jeremy Brett and his staff at the Cushing Memorial Library & Archives, Texas A&M University, for providing scanned archive copies of many of the stories in this book, which made its compilation so much easier. Thanks also to Allison Rich, who administers Tanith Lee's online bibliography 'Daughter of the Night', for her assistance in sourcing the stories and proof-reading the finished book.

Author's Notes are included in this volume when they accompanied the original stories.

A Wolf at the Door
and Other Rare Tales

Tanith Lee

IMMANION
PRESS
Stafford England

Cover Art by John Kaiine
Cover Design by Danielle Lainton
Interior layout by Storm Constantine
Illustrations: pages 4, 28, 56, 84, 128: Storm Constantine; pages 142,
270: Danielle Lainton

Set in Garamond

ISBN 978-1-912815-04-3

IP0155

Author Site:
Daughter of the Night: An Annotated Tanith Lee Bibliography:
http://www.daughterofthenight.com/

Facebook Page for Tanith Lee's readers: Paradys Forum - Daughter
of the Night - Tanith Lee

An Immanion Press Edition
http://www.immanion—press.com
info@immanion—press.com

CONTENTS

Introduction by Storm Constantine 7

Huzdra 9

A Wolf at the Door 29

Venus Rising on Water 33

The Puma's Daughter 57

The Return of Berenice 85

Sea Wharg 93

Table Manners 111

The Werewolf 129

The Janfia Tree 143

Tiger I 159

Pinewood 171

Nightshade 177

Why Light? 271

About the Author 290

Publishing History of the Stories 291

Books by Tanith Lee 292

INTRODUCTION

Storm Constantine

In the year before Tanith Lee died, she and I talked of future anthologies of her work, some of which Immanion Press would publish. Tanith had the idea for them to be themed – for example, all her werewolf stories in one book, all her dragon stories in another, and yet another for all her vampire tales. She'd written so many stories and was also prepared to write new ones to fill a collection, so it didn't seem these volumes would be difficult to compile. Sadly, her final illness, when it came, was sooner than perhaps even she expected. Novels she'd planned to write (or had even begun) would now never be realised, nor all the stories that continually poured through her.

Immanion Press, along with Tanith's husband John Kaiine, are committed not only to keeping her legacy alive but to fulfilling – as far as we are able – the plans she'd had for her work. As many of Tanith's stories appeared only in magazines, online or in anthologies that included other authors' work, some of which were obscure, it was – and still is – difficult for her fans to track down all her work. It is John's aim to have all Tanith's stories available in collections of her own work. For these reasons, the new volumes published by Immanion Press focus upon releasing her rare or uncollected stories.

Another independent press, Telos, published a vampire-themed collection, in *Blood 20* (2015), which included many of Tanith's vampire stories – but not all of them (including *The Janfia Tree* and *Why Light,* which appear in this book). But for us it proved difficult to gather enough stories for werewolf and dragon collections, mainly because the most pertinent stories have already been widely anthologised or have appeared recently in other collections dedicated solely to Tanith's work. We didn't want to present a volume half-filled with stories easily available elsewhere, as this would defeat our aim with these collections and, in our opinion, be unfair to Tanith's fans. Surely, they'd prefer stories new to them rather than those – even if they were favourites – they'd read many times before? As we can no longer rely on new tales to fill a book, we realised with regret we couldn't stick exclusively to the themes Tanith had talked about.

However, dragons and were-creatures can take many forms and be metaphors for human emotions and circumstances. In the previous volume of stories, *Love in a Time of Dragons*, we remained faithful to the theme – what the dragon can symbolise – while including stories featuring creatures other than dragons. Similarly, the wolf at the door in this collection isn't simply a wolf, or even a shape-shifting werewolf, although you will find these beasts among the stories.

'A wolf at the door' implies hidden threat – until the door is open, we don't really know what lies beyond. It can also refer to misfortune, seen coming from a distance, when all you can do is hide within your home, ineffectual weapons at the ready. And now the beast is upon you, scratching at the wood, its hot breath steaming on the step. Will you survive the encounter? Will the dawn save you – that good fortune you've longed for? The phrase is used to describe rapacious creditors – people to whom money is owed that cannot be paid. By implication, the wolf is hunger, the depletion of finances with no hope of replenishment, the end of the line. The wolf might also be a metaphor for madness, another kind of predator that may creep towards a person unseen. Perhaps, once the door is opened, what you might have thought to be a savage predator turns out to be something else entirely. But of course, it could also be a werewolf…

HUZDRA

Author's Note:

*With what glee I wrote this tale, in my late twenties, and new into the glory
and pleasure of being a professional writer - at last. As with many of my
ideas, it simply came, and drove itself with simple complexity through my
fingers and pen, lovely black scribble only I or my mother could read. And
I have always liked justice.*

It was the sunset of Midwinter's Eve. Black-haired Mirromi, the
wife of Count Fedesha, sat before the eastern window of the great
house, as she had sat by the same window, at the same hour, on the
same day, for the past six years. The window was made up of
alternating squares of blue and cochineal glass, all but the single
clear pane through which Mirromi looked. This pane being, in fact,
a lens of highly magnified crystal, it gave a fine and detailed view of
the snowy countryside beyond the walls, and the highway which cut
through it, and of any traffic that journeyed there.

And there was considerable traffic on Midwinter's Eve,
everything going one way: north toward the city, for the festival.
The sun was almost down, the snow darkening from white to lead,
and still several carts and wagons were visible, trundling along the
road, and a couple of rich men's carriages with outriders.

Countess Mirromi watched intently, just as she always watched
at this moment, when the pale crimson winter sun plunged nearer
and nearer the brink of the land. The carriages galloped away; the
carts vanished on their iron wheels. The road was for an instant
empty. And then (Mirromi smiled) two new figures appeared. The
larger was a man, walking slowly and doggedly, and he held the
other, a young girl, bundled in his arms.

Mirromi rose. No need to watch any longer. As in the past six
years, her cunning and her magic had not failed her. And though
she was not surprised at her cleverness, it did her good to see the
proof of it.

Countess Mirromi's hair, under its net of jewels, was black as oil;
her velvet gown, under its goldwork, was blacker. And her heart
and soul and mind blacker than either of them.

A track ran from the highway to the walls of the great house. This track the man and the girl he carried took without a second's hesitation, as if they had been invited, or as if they had been summoned there.

There were large gates in the wall, but they swung grindingly open as the travellers advanced, though who or what opened them remained unseen. Beyond the wall lay a grim garden, rather like a graveyard, with peculiar statuary poking from the snow, and an avenue of snow-fringed cypresses leading up toward the house. The house itself was a bizarre amalgam of tapering roofs and overhanging stories, with three gaunt towers, one of which faced directly to the east, and had a high window set in it of blue and blue-red glass.

Presently, the man and girl went on. Reaching the door, and finding this did not widen of itself, the man rapped with the knocker. It was shaped like a child's head, this knocker, with the ears of a rabbit – a silly yet rather unnerving object, especially when you saw the face of the child properly, and its malevolent grin of unherbivorous pointed teeth.

The girl rested her head on the man's shoulder, as if she were very weary. The man waited stolidly for an answer to his knock. He was quite unremarkable, except for his bigness and his obvious strength. He had an overall wind-tanned, weather-beaten look that seemed to have washed his skin and his clothes and his hair in the same brownish-greyish uncolour. His eyes were large and pallid, and appeared not as strong as the rest of him, for he stared at things in a dim, uncertain way. The girl was another matter, for though she also was clad in the drab garments of the poor, her fair skin was beautifully clear, almost transparent, like that of some rich man's daughter kept much from the sun. And her hair was a wonderful soft pale shade of reddish blond.

The door was opened abruptly.

Inside the doorway loomed a large, black-bearded man in a suit of dark scarlet velvet, with rings and chain of gold, and a pearl in his left ear. He laughed aloud at the two visitors.

"Come, don't be startled. You expected a servant, no doubt, not the master of the house. I am Count Fedesha, and you are welcome to my home on this night of Midwinter's Eve."

"We are unlucky travellers, my lord," said the man outside. "We were on our way to the city for the festival, but a strange thing happened to us. As the sun turned to the west, we passed between two old dead trees on either side of the road, and no sooner had the shadow of the western tree fallen on us than our poor little horse dropped dead in the shafts. Of course, a wagon is no use without a horse to draw it, and we were forced to leave it where it stood and come seeking help. Yours is the first dwelling we have seen on the road, and such a fine one I hardly dared approach. Yet I thought perhaps, out of your generosity, you might send a groom to aid us. My sister's a cripple, sir," he added, almost as if in excuse. "I have carried her all this way."

"But tell me," said the Count, still extraordinarily jovial, "did no others pass you on the road who might have helped you?"

"Indeed yes," the man replied, with a slow, puzzled air. "Many that we called out to, though none of them stopped. Perhaps they thought us robbers, yet it seemed they never saw us, almost, you might say, as if we had grown invisible – a carriage nearly rode me down. But there's no telling. It was most odd, my lord."

Count Fedesha laughed again, or rather, he giggled. He reached and chucked the tired beautiful cripple girl under the chin. "Such pretty hair," he said, "should not be out in the cold."

He led them inside.

Within was a vast hall, pillared in stone, and hung by tapestries that winked with gold thread in the firelight of the tall hearth; a thousand candles lit the room where the fire did not. Before the hearth lay a white bear fur with a head, and rubies in the eyes. Just beyond that, near the room's centre, a mosaic was set in the floor, a curious design of circle and star, and the twelve shapes of the zodiac.

"Please, put your sister in the chair beside the fire, sir. You take the other," cried Count Fedesha.

"My lord, you are too kind," faltered the big man.

"Not at all. Tonight is the night of the festival, the turning away of the Old Beast, Winter. If we can't be kind to each other on such a night, why, God help us. There, put the maid down, and I'll bring you wine." Count Fedesha waved his ringed hand at a table near the hearth. "Will you have the white wine in the silver jug, or the rose wine in the gold? Or would you prefer the red rum of the Westlands? Or maybe some apricot cordial, in that yellow bottle

11

there? You must be surprised that I wait on you," added the Count, "but it's our custom, the Countess's and mine, to send our servants away to the city on Midwinter's Eve. So they may enjoy the festival, you understand."

The big man had placed his burden in the chair. The girl sighed, and smiled at him, and at the Count, who handed her a goblet of cordial. Her eyes, the Count observed, were an amber shade, like her hair. It really was a great pity... but it was foolish to speculate. Even though her innocence and grace appealed to him, there could be no leisure to dally.

Count Fedesha gave the big man rum and made him take the other chair.

"I'm sorry we can send no one to retrieve your wagon until tomorrow, when the servants return," the Count went on, "but you shall be our guests tonight, eat well and sleep soft."

The big man gaped at him. They always did, and sometimes the women did too, but usually the women were more trusting than the men, and more greedy for a brief taste of good living. Some had smiled winningly at the Count, hoping to prolong their stay.

Count Fedesha watched the two of them drink from their goblets. Everything was going most smoothly, and would go more smoothly now than ever, because of the black herb Mirromi had mixed ready in the cups. But it had gone smoothly for six years. This was the seventh year, and this the seventh occasion – the last occasion, if his clever Mirromi was right, and when had she ever been wrong? – and this the seventh pair of travellers brought here by the spells Mirromi had left on the road to waylay them. Count Fedesha remembered the first time, seven years before. How afraid he had been, eaten alive with terror. But Mirromi had gone up to the Tertiary Tower, and when she had come back, she had been smiling. Before dawn of Midwinter's Eve, she had slipped out and marked the occult symbols on the two dead trees half a mile off, next, left her potent magics on the highway, the track, the walls of the house, the gates. And ever since, each year on this dreary night of Midwinter's Eve, Mirromi had reactivated the spells. Cunning, uncanny spells they were, that would select only two travellers, a man and a woman, cause them some accident – a loosened wheel, a dead horse – that would then exert a drawing influence to pull the elected two toward the great house, rendering them the while quite invisible, inaudible, intangible to any passers-by who might otherwise aid them. Indeed, Mirromi and he, thought Count Fedesha, they were an ingenious and wondrous couple; they deserved their victory.

Still, a shame this girl was so pretty; she did not look so common as the rest, not a peasant type at all, though the brother was as rough and ready as they came. The Count giggled again, softly, into his wine. Odd to recall how afraid he had been at the beginning, those seven years ago. And here he was, almost complacent.

And now came the naming of names.

Neither of his guests had offered him their names as yet, the girl too timid, the man too bemused. If they had tried, Fedesha would have forestalled them. It was important that their own names be set aside, and thus, until the moment when the atmosphere must be altered, Fedesha would give then nicknames. Having drunk the sorcerous herb, overawed in any case and eager to please, the travellers always accepted these titles. And there had been some wicked ones he had invented in the past: 'Primrose' for the woman with the sallow yellow skin, and 'Camel' for the man with the humped back, and 'Biter' for the man with but three black teeth in his head. Now the Count looked his guests over and said: "I'm going to call you 'Quick', my fellow, because you move so fast. I hope you won't mind my eccentricity."

The big man gave a slow sheepish grin. Obviously, he took the point of the joke with the true yokel's lack of resentment. For the girl, the name was easy, and for once complimentary. "The pretty lady I shall call 'Amber', for her hair and her eyes."

The girl lowered these eyes. She seemed to blush, but it might only be the firelight shining on her pale face. The Count wondered idly if she had been crippled from birth, or in some mishap. Probably her spine was weak, a frequent enough ailment among the poor, the result of childhood malnutrition.

A door opened behind a drapery.

The Count heard the step of his Countess on the mosaic floor and turned to see her glittering there in her black-and-gold gown, and with her raven's-wing hair poured in a net of jewels. At the centre of her white forehead hung a scarab beetle of black jade on a silver chain. Fedesha recollected how she had sent a demon to rob the tomb of a dead queen for it.

"Ah, the stranded travellers!" cried Mirromi. At this point no one had ever questioned, and did not now, that the Countess apparently knew everything, without having been told. "How pleasant to have guests on this night, though with our servants all away."

It had been very convenient that it had *been* this night, of all the nights of the year, on which the trouble had begun. What better excuse than to say their servants had been sent by a benign master and mistress to the festival in the city? When in reality, of course, their servants fled the house and neither promise of reward nor threat of pain could persuade them to remain here on Midwinter's Eve.

Suddenly, Fedesha heard the sound. Despite his complacence, what he had boasted of to himself, he became for a moment icy with returning fear. Even Mirromi stood motionless as a stone, her eyes darting. As for the big man, the man Fedesha had nicknamed Quick, he raised his shaggy slow head, and gazed about in puzzlement. Then the amber girl cried aloud.

The big man lumbered to her. "Don't be frightened."

The girl clung to his hand, but it was at Fedesha she stared. "It was a fly, a great black fly."

She had not spoken before. Her voice, Fedesha thought, was not as pleasing as the rest of her – thin and breathy, and rather flat, even in her fright.

"Oh, there are sometimes flies here, even in winter," he coaxed her. "They sleep in the crevices of the house, and the warmth of the fire draws them out."

Buzz. Buzz. The fly, large as the scarab ornament Mirromi had stolen from the queen's tomb, crawled along the hearth, the flames glinting on its poison-coloured wings. It seemed oblivious of the season, the heat. Oblivious of the lunge the traveller made to stamp on it.

"No!" Fedesha shouted. He dragged the big man back from the hearth, and the monstrous fly droned up toward the shadowy rafters of the hall, its noise going with it.

Mirromi spoke sweetly, reasonably. "You must forgive us. We consider it unlucky to kill flies upon Midwinter's Eve."

When they had drunk together, the Countess and the Count, unsparing hosts, led them upstairs into another story, and into a passage where a series of splendid bedchambers were to be found behind mahogany doors.

"This room shall be yours, mistress Amber," said the Countess, beckoning the brother to carry his sister inside.

Again, as ever at this juncture, there was fresh staring. The girl's face was full of marvel as a child's.

The fat white candles shone on the silk hangings of the bed; the coverlet was of velvet trimmed with ermines' tails. You could not see through the oval window, for it was a picture done in coloured glass of a maiden plucking red fruit from a green tree – she had a disturbing girdle, like an elongated golden rat. Here and there, pomanders of blue and lavender pottery sent up a rare fragrance.

"Here is a silver basin, and the water is yet warm in it and scented with violet petals," said the Countess. "And here," she flung open an upright closet, "here is a dress that you shall wear tonight."

Then the brother and sister saw another unlikely thing. For in the closet were hung six or seven dresses of black velvet embroidered over with a thick tracery of gold. Each dress was in a different size – some would fit buxom women, and some would fit skinny ones, and one was just right for the slender cripple girl. And each dress, moreover, was an exact replica of the dress the Countess wore.

"Madam," whispered the girl, "it is too fine. And surely…"

"Nonsense," said the Countess. "As for the resemblance to my own garment, you are quite correct. You must permit us our eccentricities, my dove, really you must. And what harm will it do for you to be a Countess for one night? I will even give you my jewels to go with the gown, even my black scarab to wear on your forehead."

Though the big man had set his sister on the fur stool before the bedchamber hearth, she shivered now, but she did not argue.

The Countess smiled and smiled. "I will even dress you myself."

"No, lady," said the girl's brother. "I can do it. I'm used to helping her." He came near to the Countess and spoke low. "She does not like others to see her. She's shy, being crippled."

"Oh, very well," said the Countess, granting him a vast favour. "But don't forget, your own chamber is next door to this, and there are red velvet suits laid out there, one of which will fit you. For if your amber sister is to be a Countess for our Festival of Midwinter's Eve, then you are to be a Count."

"Why must that be?" asked the big man, hesitantly.

"Why not, pray?" inquired Mirromi. "Come," she added to her

husband, who had begun to giggle again. "Give master Quick your chain and your rings and let us leave our guests their privacy. I shall be back to fetch you to supper in one half of an hour," she murmured, putting Fedesha's jewellery into Quick's unprotesting wooden hand.

The Count and his lady adjourned outside and closed the heavy door. At the far end of the passage a flight of fifty steps led up into another room, hung this time with black silks and with a window of blue and cochineal glass – the eastern window of the Tertiary Tower.

The Countess drew aside a silk hanging on the wall to reveal two round spy holes equipped with magnifying lenses. By means of skilfully angled tubes and the strategic mirrors placed in them, these spy holes gave a view into the rich bedchamber Countess Mirromi had allotted the cripple girl. A similar tube, once Mirromi had twisted open its amplifying valves, rendered audible any conversation which took place in the room. The Countess and the Count applied their eyes to the lenses, looked and listened.

The girl and her brother, in drugged obedience, had already dressed themselves in the velvet reproductions of their hosts' clothing. Now Amber sat on the bed in an attitude of dejection. The brother, Quick, stood before the fire.

"I'm afraid," said the girl. "Could we not leave, before they come back? Such a great lady, but to act this strangely. Oh, I am afraid."

"Yes," said the brother. "I don't care for it. Yet, perhaps, as they said, it's merely some prank, some jest to celebrate Midwinter's Eve – though the mighty are not usually so liberal to such as we. Then, again... if they mean us harm, we should not get far, I having to carry you. And though I am strong, I'm not fast, my sister, nor very clever. And suppose they have guards here after all, hidden somewhere? It is a large mansion. Who knows?"

The girl buried her face in her hands, and her shoulders shook. She whispered: "Go without me, then. I know I should slow you. I would rather suffer myself than see you hurt."

The big man knelt by her and patted her with gentle awkwardness. "Hush, don't cry. How could I leave you? You're all my life, little sister. Besides, truly, I believe I must remain. I think we may be under a spell."

The black action of a large fly flickered over the rooms, the corridors, the staircases of the great house; the air vibrated with its buzzing. But the Count and Countess paid it little heed as they clad themselves in homespun and rags for supper.

Quick carried Amber into the hall, preceded by the Countess, who now wore, in sharp contrast to the finery of her guests, a shapeless grey gown, rough wooden shoes and knitted stockings. Her black hair was bound in a tattered scarf. Amber's hair glowed under the net of gems the Countess had confined it in, and the black jade scarab rested on her forehead.

A long table had been set near the hearth over the design of the zodiac. At one end of the table, two places had been laid with plate of silver and fine cut-glass goblets. Close to these were a variety of generous roasts, vegetables and hot pastries, piles of costly winter fruit, candies and sweetmeats, and many jugs and bottles of liquor. At the opposite end of the table were a couple of earthenware plates and mugs, a jar of beer and an ewer of water, a loaf of coarse black bread.

The Count, in labourer's garments, waved Quick to the elegant portion of the table, seated the Countess and himself before the earthenware dishes. "Now, no protests," said the Count. "This is how it is. My wife and I are able to enjoy luxury on every other night of the year. On this one night, we choose to live humbly and let our guests play our parts, don our velvets and jewels, eat of our fare and sup our wine."

The brother and sister sat down. They gazed uneasily at the rich food, the laden plates. Perhaps they were pondering, if all the servants were supposedly gone to the city, who it could be who had prepared this dinner. Surely not the Countess? Despite her impoverished clothes, her hands were white and her nails dyed flawless crimson. The Countess broke off a piece of the coarse bread and ate it, drank some water. She did not require cooks to provide an elaborate meal. She could summon up others who could do as well as a human cook, and better.

"Eat, drink," encouraged the Count. He rose, carved meat for the visitors, heaped their silver platters, poured them wine. There was no pearl earring in his ear now, just a small hole where it had been.

The brother and sister began to pick at their food.

The darting of a fly, the intermittent buzz it made, had become so familiar now, it was scarcely remarkable, like the ticking of a clock. Then, abruptly, the darting buzzing stopped.

The Countess glanced up; the Count paused over his mug of beer. An instant's silence in the wide and well-lit hall.

The amber girl moaned and shrank back in her chair.

Something was hopping on the table.

It hopped between the silver salt cellars, the gold cellars of spice. It hopped into the mound of fruit, setting the apples and the peaches rolling. It was like a warty, shiny, grey-green fruit itself. It hopped, this warty fruit, into the dish of the cripple girl, and its upraised round eyes, the colour of yellow sourness, glittered and glared at her. It froze to the immobility of marble, still glaring.

"It's only a toad. A pathetic harmless toad," said the Countess. "Surely you are not afraid of a poor ugly toad?"

"Don't strike out at it," added Count Fedesha, somewhat nervously, to the man he called Quick. But Quick had made no move at all. Seeing this, the Count elaborated: "There is an old legend, isn't there, that in some cases a beast slain reproduces and multiplies itself? Tread on a fly and there are two flies. The skin of the dead toad lets out two more toads."

The toad hopped from the girl's plate. It bounded onto the knee of Quick, and then away into the shadow beyond the hearth. They heard its croaking there, and presently from another place, and then another.

The Count quaffed down his beer. For an instant he had looked afraid, and he had lost much of his blandness. The Countess Mirromi, however, was calm, and regarded the brother and sister with satisfaction. Their faces had taken on the vacant stupid expression of people half-asleep. Though they had eaten hardly any of the food, the drugs she had mixed in it were powerful ones.

Mirromi left her chair and crossed to the tall candle branch beside the hearth. Each candle was of fractionally differing length from its fellows; the shortest was burned out, others were scarcely begun: it was a means of telling time.

"How long?" asked Count Fedesha. He giggled, but his mouth was pale and dry in the black beard.

"A little longer," said Mirromi. "Though I think possibly the moment has come to give our friends their proper titles."

"Ah, yes," said Fedesha. He seemed to recover his spirits. He got to his feet, and lifted his mug of beer, toasting the listless guests.

"Here's health to you, Count and Countess."

"Health, Count and Countess, and a happy life," added Mirromi, raising her own mug of water.

Fedesha and Mirromi drank.

Quick spoke thickly and falteringly, peering through his myopic eyes, obviously trying to throw off the effects of Mirromi's drug – to no avail. "Why name us so? Count and – Countess?"

"A whim," said Mirromi.

"A foible," said Fedesha.

From five or six separate parts of the hall, the toad croaked. The light gleamed fitfully on its knotty skin as it shuffled and hopped, now across the mosaic floor, now along the back of a chair.

"A piece more meat, Count?" Fedesha inquired.

"A plum, Countess?" Mirromi offered.

They both laughed this time.

"Do you have it to hand?" Fedesha asked his wife.

"In my sleeve. As always."

"This is the last year," Fedesha said. "Then the trouble is done with."

"What could defeat my magic?" Mirromi said. She smiled and patted his face. "Foolish of you ever to doubt me."

Fedesha glanced at the crippled girl, whose gaze had grown huge with a sort of glazed anguish.

"A pity, though..."

The croaking of the toad ceased.

Fedesha gripped his wife's arm.

Quick writhed mutely in his chair, and the girl Amber whimpered.

Between the table and the hearth, something darkening on the bearskin, not smoke, not shadow. Gradually a black dog came visible. It was thin as a stick, every bone showed through its hide. Its eyes were filmed yet burning, its tongue lolled. Its body was faintly iridescent, and where its spit dripped down it flamed and then vanished.

Fedesha shook and his eyes started. Mirromi's smile became more of a snarl.

The dog did not snarl, nor growl, nor make any sound. It moved by them, along the side of the table. It sniffed at the velvet gown of the crippled girl and at her brother's velvet cuff, and then it padded away and straight through the tapestried wall as if the wall were not there.

"Now!" cried Mirromi. There was a brittle triumph in her voice. She resumed her seat and struck the table with her white hand. The brother and sister turned to her as if she mesmerised them. "As it is festival night," said Mirromi, "we will tell you a story, most worthy Count and Countess. Are you ready? Good. The story concerns a *huzdra,* which, as you may or may not know, is a kind of curse invented by the primitive folk of the Eastlands."

"A very effective curse," Fedesha said. He shivered and licked his lips. "Surprisingly so."

"But to begin at the beginning," Mirromi said, "for we must make certain the Count and Countess understand everything.

"It was the chill dawn of Midwinter's Eve seven years ago. The sun was just coming up, when someone commenced knocking on the gates. Occasionally I leave my bed before dawn, for there are particular herbs that can be gathered only at sunrise and on selected days in order that they retain their potency. The porter, knowing I was about, soon brought me word that a desperate peasant girl was at the gate, begging for shelter and food, offering her service at any form of work in exchange. I instructed the porter to bring the wench to me, and this he did. She was a pitiful sight indeed, filthy and ragged, half dead of the cold and almost starved. She told me her name; it was some barbaric Eastlands foolishness. I called her 'Pebble' instead, for she was aptly as dirty, as uncared-for and as common as one. She was brought nourishment and wine. I foresaw a use for her but did not reveal to her what it was to be, saying that she must consult my husband later. I could tell she was strong, this Pebble, despite her deprivations. She kissed my hands and feet and swore she would serve me till death, but she was not so tractable afterward.

"Now you must hear, dear Count and Countess, something of my husband and myself. I am of humble stock, though you would never guess it; my husband, whose title he has given you, master Quick, wed me for my beauty, and also for certain magic powers that I possess. Accordingly, I gained the title I have given you, mistress Amber, while by my powers, my husband became a deal wealthier and more influential than before, which was to our mutual pleasure. You should realise, this magic involves traffic and trade with demons, hobgoblins and elementals. These delightful creatures will do business willingly with humankind if they are summoned correctly and paid a fee. We had learned, my spouse and

I, of an ancient treasure to the north; in order to gain access to it there was one infallible demon which could aid us. And the fee this demon demands is to drink the blood of a living maiden. You will understand, then, how opportune was the arrival of Pebble. None knew her, she was a stranger from the Eastlands, dull-witted, and a maid to boot. For our servants, they would dare tell no one – they respect my gifts too much for that. So it was arranged that Pebble's blood should entice the demon, and accordingly, at sunset, I took her to the Tertiary Tower, where everything was laid out in readiness. No sooner did the wretch learn her fate, than she began to scream and struggle. I subdued her, as I am able to do. The demon was called, answered, brought us what we wished to have, and took his payment gladly. A space before midnight, when all was finished, we instructed our menials to carry Pebble away. We thought her dead, as well we might, but somehow she had clung to life, and as the servants lifted her she opened her eyes, and staring at me and at my husband, she said: 'Fine Count and fine Countess, your fine food and your fine clothes and your fine spells shall avail you nothing. I have put my *huzdra* on you both. One year beyond this night you may take your ease. But next Midwinter's Eve, look for death, and for Hell after it.' Then she did die. We witnessed her buried as midnight struck and thought ourselves rid of her.

"You may suppose," went on Mirromi, "her puny threat would be forgotten as the year passed, but this was not the case. As the months elapsed, we found we brooded more and yet more upon Pebble's words. At length, a month before Midwinter's Eve should dawn again – the anniversary of Pebble's death – I conjured one up by my magic that is wise in curses and questioned it. And thus we discovered the nature of a *huzdra*.

"The *huzdra* is effected through some personal item belonging to whoever lays the curse. It may be something as mundane as a shoe, a scarf, a ring. Though once *huzdra* is laid on it, it assumes weird attributes – the shoe runs on its own as if a foot were in it, the scarf wriggles like a snake, the ring grows large as a noose. The object of *huzdra* is ultimately to kill those on whom the curse has been set. It is a thing of antique Eastlands sorcery, and very strong, for it is always sealed with hate. It is difficult, even for one as well versed in magic as myself, to evade this curse, for in such an instance, even the most agile demons grow uneasy. They will advise but may not intervene. In the east, *huzdra* is feared worse than the

White Plague, by simpleton and mage alike.

"As my conjuration assured me, our first concern was to find which item of Pebble's belongings had become the *huzdra*. She had brought nothing with her to the gate; all she possessed had been her rags. My husband and I were forced to go by night to the spot where we had had the girl buried, dig up the grave, and search her body. It was not difficult to recognize the *huzdra*. Little remained in the earth that was distinguishable, except for one thing: a bracelet she had worn high on her forearm, hidden by her sleeve. It was very old, the bracelet, crudely fashioned, discoloured by age and by lying in the ground. The band was black copper, with seven pendants of reddish, greenish stone or black stone, chipped and dirty. I brought the bracelet to the Tower, and recalled the elemental wise in such matters, and made it tell me all I must know, though it was afraid.

"The strength of Pebble's *huzdra* was sevenfold, because of its seven pendants. Even if we could thwart the curse on the first anniversary of her death, the *huzdra* would yet be activated six more years, seven in all, and each successive year the power of it would grow. However, though the seventh year, the seventh anniversary, would be the most terrible, it would also be the last. After that, the strength of the *huzdra* was exhausted. Though who could expect to hold off such a bane for so long?"

Mirromi glanced aside at the time-telling candles by the hearth, and broke off the story to say, "One moment, honoured Count and Countess, with your indulgence."

Then she and Fedesha rose from their chairs and withdrew across the hall to stand beneath a tapestry of gold and ruby thread.

The brother and sister, silent all this while, lay in their chairs like discarded dolls. Only their eyes blinked and strained, and their hands twitched.

There came a sound from the fire. A hissing, spurling sound. Out of the fire bowled a bone-white wheel. It was ten feet in diameter, and though it looked solid it had no substance. It passed straight through the table, it rolled once, twice, about the cripple girl and her brother. Flames gushed from its spokes. It hurtled away into nothing and sparks faded on the air.

Mirromi said to Fedesha: "Success, as ever. The wheel has marked them out, and not us. We have won, and this the last year of the curse."

"My wondrous witch-wife," Fedesha said, kissing her hand,

licking his lips, which had grown red and healthy once again.

"Now I will show them," said Mirromi. She returned to the table, and sliding something from her arm beneath her sleeve, laid it before the brother and sister on the damask cloth.

It was a bracelet of black copper, with seven pendants of greenish, reddish or black stone, chipped, grimy and very old.

"Here is the *huzdra*," said Mirromi. "See the little figures? First the fly; he generally appears before the rest. Next, the toad; he usually comes second. There is the dog, tonight's third visitor. And see, there the fourth thing, the fiery wheel, though its spokes are clogged with dirt. These manifestations are warnings, heralds, preparations for the ultimate terror. Whatever else, this is the final omen, this tilted pitcher. You have not seen it yet, but you shall. It will appear, as it always does, when that candle there has burned out. Then we shall have had all the warnings, and only death need come. Death is represented by these last two figures on the bracelet. Observe closely, so you shall recognise them."

It was hardest of all to make out these last figures of the bracelet. This was the seventh occasion Mirromi had displayed them, the seventh year that two travellers, brought here by magic and drugged by occult herbs, had peered down with horror scrawled on their stupefied faces, trying to see.

One figure was of a man. In his head and on his chest little glass scintillants winked like many eyes. The second figure was female, except that below her waist her body grew into a single coiled thing, like a worm.

"It was a clever *huzdra*," said Mirromi. "That the demon man and the demon woman should be part of it, two for two, a man and woman as my husband and I are man and woman. Clever of that wretched Pebble; it made the curse doubly powerful. But," said Mirromi, "as you notice, we live. I will tell you how we cheated the *huzdra*, and how we shall cheat it tonight, the seventh and last night it can seek us.

"By my peerless spells, I have drawn to this house, each Midwinter's Eve, two wanderers from the road. Some have been brash, some sly, some foolish, though none, I think, so innocent and so stupid as you, my doves. Really the curse, while being a mighty one, is also naive. It relies upon the fear of the victim, and on his ignorance.

"The canny elemental advised me well. Never destroy the object of the *huzdra,* for to destroy it doubles its vitality, unleashing its force from the earthly materials which form it and loosing them entirely into the spirit world, where they become invincible. Destroy the bracelet, and you could never be rid of its potency. Nor must you use violence against the apparitions – the buzzing fly, the croaking toad, the black dog. They cannot be harmed but absorb fresh energy from every blow which is dealt them. No, let them roam freely, and cherish the *huzdra.*

"Now, the *huzdra* can only match whoever works it. Though Pebble's hate was ferocious, she was an imbecile. By employment of certain incantations, runes, auras, by dressing the two strangers in our garments and our jewels, by setting before them the riches of our house, our foods and wines, by addressing them by our titles of Count and Countess, we have made them into replicas of ourselves. When Pebble hated us, she hated only the symbols – velvet clothes, silver plate, a name. And thus it is that the *huzdra* and its hate fall similarly on the appearance, the effigy, the name. In six years, twelve strangers have taken our places, become our scapegoats, and the vengeance of the *huzdra* has claimed them, and we have survived royally. It is a dreadful death that comes. There are screams and raucous cries, and when midnight strikes, the hour of Pebble's burial, and we are able to return safely into the chamber, we find our jewels scattered about, and otherwise merely clean bones. For sure, too, the curse has gained strength each year. The first year the apparitions were faint, the death very swift at its predestined time. But, as the years pass, the apparitions are more solid, appear for longer periods and in a different order, though always the wheel and the pitcher are the last. The two entities which bring death have no ability to kill until the exact moment when Pebble's curse was spoken – and do not arrive before, being powerless. But even here there is a change. The shrieks of agony in the locked room are more prolonged, the bones are more thoroughly picked and drained of marrow. This is the final year, when you, my pair of ducks, are to take our place and remove the *huzdra* for ever from our house and our lives. No doubt, it will be very awful. I even ask myself if they will leave your bones intact on this occasion.

"You may ponder why I have told you all this, and in such detail. You will understand when I say that I do it to inspire you with terror. For nothing lures the *huzdra* toward you so well as your absolute fear. And now," added Mirromi to Fedesha, "it's time we took our guests to their chamber."

Up the great flights of steps to the Primary Tower, to the pitch-black, dank and windowless room, whose door of stone was opened only once a year to admit terror, and to contain terror, until the stroke of midnight should end it.

Up those flights, as once every Midwinter's Eve in the past six years, two strangers dressed in velvet were propelled, their eyes running and their limbs water. This year the girl seemed to have fainted. Fedesha carried her, she felt boneless already, and escaped strands of her amber hair trailed after them on the steps. The big man stumbled forward, his hands outstretched as if he were blind.

Up to the door, the key in the brass lock. The door opened.

On the black nothingness of the tower chamber a shining pitcher had formed, tilting slowly, slowly, until from its narrow lip poured a stream of thick, red and smoking blood.

Fedesha flung the girl into the room, thrust the big man after her. As in the past six years, he banged the stone door shut, and Mirromi locked it.

As in the past six years, Fedesha and Mirromi held their breaths, waited.

As in the past six years, there came a broken wild screaming inside the locked chamber, and then a man's screams, deeper, and without pause.

Mirromi and Fedesha smiled.

Hand in hand, like two happy children, they went smiling down toward the hall, to wait for midnight, as in the past six years.

Word gets around, even in Hell.

For six years, the *huzdra* had been negated by the stroke of midnight because the components of *huzdra* believed its victims had been claimed, the curse accomplished. Yet, as each year progressed, the knowledge that Countess Mirromi and Count Fedesha still lived, and boasted of their guile, had roused the *huzdra* to reactivate itself again upon the next Midwinter's Eve.

A curse is not a thinking thing as such. Like the spear, it homes to its target when a marksman aims it. And yet, each year cheated, each following year reawoken, and each year *stronger*, some element of the *huzdra* began to reason. The warning apparitions of the curse began to rearrange themselves, to appear for longer periods, to deviate. There was no law which bound them to materialise only in an exact order, or for any exact period. Once the sun began to sink, they were free to manifest themselves as the instinct moved them. Nor were they bound to vanish at midnight; they had merely done so from the sense that the work was completed.

And yet the work had never been completed.

Somewhere the ghost of the Eastlands girl, cruelly nicknamed Pebble for her dirt and her common, uncared-for person, somewhere that ghost roared in its limbo, unsatisfied and unappeased.

At last, the notion came aware in the midst of the unthinking but oddly reasoning entity of the curse that what deprived it of its intended victims must be a scapegoat insertion of two others, as innocent and beguiled as Pebble had been.

This, the seventh year, which brought the *huzdra* to the climax of its power, brought it also the solution to the deception.

Mirromi's magic runes on the ancient dead trees by the highway, registering two travellers journeying in any case toward the great house, selected no others, since the Countess had no requirement for more than two, a man and a woman, to enter her doors.

The travellers were like several others of the twelve who had gone before, poor and uneducated. They had much the same tale to tell, of the dead horse, the abandoned wagon, how no one had stopped to aid them. Yes, these two travellers were very like those who had gone before, except, perhaps, more pliable than they. And even in the bedchamber, having put on the fated velvet garments, they had spoken to each other in such a desolate, pathetic way. Almost as if they had known about the hidden lenses and the amplifying tube, known that the Count and Countess would listen and watch, and had wanted to convince the Count and Countess that all was going, for the seventh time, exactly to plan...

It was safe to return to the tower room after midnight had struck, absolutely safe.

The only occasion when it would not have been safe would have been if, by some extraordinary oversight, two flesh-and-blood scapegoats had not been left there after all.

Count Fedesha and Countess Mirromi returned a few minutes following the stroke. The Count carried a lamp, the better to inspect what lay about. Neither he nor his Countess was squeamish. They had been inflicting negligent torture and death on innumerable droves of men and women for sufficient years that raw bones were no trouble to them. Indeed, they were rather curious, rather intrigued, to observe this last scene of the doltish *huzdra*, this last proof of their triumph.

The stone door, unlocked, swung open.

The Countess gasped; the Count grunted.

For there, quite unharmed, were the brother and his crippled sister.

A couple of heartbeats, a couple of wild inner questionings.

Then the melting of the illusion of velvet clothes and of homespun, of gem and of poverty. Of humanity.

A brown man, seeing clearly now he was naked, not only through the two large eyes in his head, but out of the several glinting eyes in his breast, which blinked, and which opened and closed, and which finally focused with great intensity. And by him, no longer a cripple who could not walk, an amber-haired woman, who reared upright from the sinuous flexible column of a serpent's tail.

Now it was the brother and sister who were smiling, with sharp, sharp teeth, while they raised their long-nailed hands as if in welcome.

And the Count and the Countess began to scream.

A WOLF AT THE DOOR

It was summer during the Ice Age, so Glasina wasn't at school. She spent her holidays with her father and mother in a large house by the sea, whose water in summer unfroze and turned to liquid, although the shore was still deep in snow. The sea and the sky were blue in summer, and the ice cliffs behind the house shone and sparkled. The tall trees in the snowfields put out leaves like glass, which tinkled. They had changed over the centuries of the Ice Age in order to survive, and their trunks were like thick sticks of hard, green sugar. Lions lived along the shore near the house, and they had had to change, too. The lions had developed long, heavy, grayish fur, and huge orange manes (to show they were still fierce), which from the front made them look like chrysanthemums.

For the first fortnight of the summer holidays, Glasina's mother, who was a teacher, was still away teaching in the south. But Glasina's father was an artist, and he always worked at home in the house by the sea.

On the fifth day of her holiday, Glasina was walking along the snowy shore by the dark blue sea. She had her camera and took pictures of the seals playing in the water, and of the lions, some of whom were fishing off the ice floes. The lions were used to Glasina, since she and her parents fed them sometimes.

After she had walked about a mile, and taken about twenty photographs, Glasina sat down on a snowdrift, and simply smiled and sighed at the joy of being on holiday. Then, when she turned her head, she saw a black wolf was trotting along the sea's edge, toward her.

Now Glasina knew that wolves were not often dangerous; if you acted sensibly, they would never attack you unless they were starving. But this wolf could be hungry, for it looked very thin, and its pale eyes gleamed. Glasina stood up and pointed her camera at the wolf, who might not be sure what it was.

"Stay where you are," said Glasina, "or I'll shoot."

"Shoot away," said the wolf carelessly. "Though I don't look my best."

Glasina lowered the camera. Because of the Ice Age, to help them survive most of the animals had learned how to talk, but usually they could only manage a few words. For example, the lions could only say things such as, *Hallo, wot ya got?* and *More!* This wolf, though, was different.

"How are you?" Glasina therefore said politely.

"Fine," said the wolf. "And that's a lie."

"Yes," said Glasina. "Have you had a difficult winter, wolf?"

"Terrible," said the wolf. It came and sat down nearby. "Is that your house?" it inquired.

"Well, it's my parents' house, but I live there."

"Wow," said the wolf "Do you mean you're still at school? I thought you were at *least* eighteen."

Glasina was fourteen, and she wasn't silly, either. The wolf was obviously trying to get on her good side. On the other hand, her father and mother would expect her to be kind to the wolf, and considerate.

"If you'd like to come with me," said Glasina, "my father or I can get the food machine to make you something to eat."

"Oh, wonderful," said the wolf, rolling over in the snow with delight. "And I'd give *anything* for a bath! Do you know," it went on, hurrying at Glasina's heels, "I haven't slept in a proper bed for weeks."

"How's the wolf today?" asked Glasina's father three mornings later.

"Still in bed," said Glasina, "with the covers up over its ears. It's spilt coffee on the sheets again, too, and last night it left the bath taps running. The housework machine's still clearing up."

"I'm not happy about this," said Glasina's father, whose hands were red and blue from his latest painting. "And your mother won't like it at all when she gets home."

Glasina had already taken a photo of the wolf in bed in the guest room, in case it left before her mother returned, and her mother didn't believe what had happened, and how it had broken two coffee mugs and two teacups, and about the egg stain on the living room wall – the wolf had been explaining how it had run away from some polar bears and brought down its foot in the fried eggs for emphasis. There were also some T-shirts the wolf had wanted to wear, one of which was Glasina's mother's favorite, and the wolf had torn all the T-shirts across the back when it was dancing to Glasina's music tapes, leaping and waving its paws.

"What shall we do?" said Glasina uneasily.

"To be honest," said her father, "I don't know. I mean," he added later as they walked along the shore to avoid the horribly loud way the wolf was by then playing their music centre (it always found the tapes they liked the least and said it liked those the best). "It seems to have wandered for miles across the snow, hungry and lonely and forlorn. It doesn't seem to have any family, or any friends... although, I must say, I'm not all that amazed by *that*. Its behavior as a human being is dreadful, but it doesn't seem to know how to be a wolf." He frowned. "Which is what worries me the most."

"I've been thinking about that, too," said Glasina.

"You hear these stories," said her father.

They stood and stared out to sea gloomily. It was a beautiful day, sunny and bright, and the water looked like sapphire jelly, but this didn't cheer them up. Nor did the sight of one of the lions standing on the ice at the sea's edge. The lion, too, seemed anxious, or only bored. She was a lioness, so she didn't have a mane and didn't look like a chrysanthemum.

"It's such a responsibility," said Glasina's father. "And, besides, what about you?"

"I wanted to go to college," said Glasina sadly.

"Of course, he couldn't claim you for at least three years..."

Glasina felt like crying, but she bravely didn't. Her father, however, rubbed red and blue paint all over his face without realising it.

What they were afraid of was that the wolf was really a young man under a spell. According to the stories, if Glasina kissed the wolf, the spell would break, and it would become a young man again. But if he was as annoying as a human being as he was as a wolf, Glasina wasn't keen on the idea. She would, naturally, as his rescuer, be expected to fall in love with him and set up house with him in due course, in the correct tradition. It always happened like that in the stories. And Glasina hadn't planned her life this way. She wanted to learn things, travel, teach, and paint and take pictures. On the other hand, how could she allow a young man to go on being trapped in a wolf body once she'd guessed what was wrong?

"I suppose," said Glasina at last, "I'll have to do it."

"I'm so sorry," said her father. "I wish I could think of another way. Perhaps we should wait until your mother gets here…"

But just then there was a crash of crockery from the house as another coffee mug dropped from the wolf's clumsy paws.

"At least if he's a young man," said Glasina, "he'll be able to hold a mug properly. I'd better go and kiss him now."

The wolf was coming out of the house as they arrived. It was wearing a Walkman, although the earpieces didn't fit in its ears, and any minute everything seemed likely to fall off into the snow and get broken.

Glasina strode up to the wolf, with her father marching behind. Behind him loped the lioness, who had recognised them and kept saying insistently, "Hallo, wot ya got?"

"Wolf," said Glasina, "I've considered carefully, and you'd better understand I don't want to. But I will."

"And just you watch yourself when she does," shouted her blue-and-red-faced father angrily at the wolf.

"Wot ya got?" the lioness put in and barged past them.

Glasina kissed the wolf on the cheek.

The lioness kissed the wolf on the other cheek.

The Walkman fell off and got broken.

The wolf disappeared.

Glasina and her father looked round nervously, and there was a lion with a chrysanthemum mane, gazing at the lioness in surprise. "Funny," it said. "I thought I was meant to be a human being – oh, well. Knew I had friends here somewhere. Confused by the spell… anyone can make a mistake." Then it trod on the Walkman, nuzzled the lioness, and said fiercely to Glasina's father, "Hallo, wot ya got?"

"I'll get you a lovely big steak," said Glasina's father, beaming.

"And I'll take your photo," said Glasina. To her relief, both lions only looked puzzled.

VENUS RISING ON WATER

Like long hair, the weeds grew down the façades of the city, over ornate shutters and leaden doors, into the pale green silk of the lagoon. Ten hundred ancient mansions crumbled. Sometimes a flight of birds was exhaled from their crowded mass, or a thread of smoke was drawn up into the sky. Day long a mist bloomed on the water, out of which distant towers rose like snakes of deadly gold. Once in every month a boat passed, carving the lagoon that had seemed thickened beyond movement. Far less often, here and there, a shutter cracked open and the weed hair broke, a stream of plaster fell like a blue ray. Then, some faint face peered out, probably eclipsed by a mask. It was a place of veils. Visitors were occasional. They examined the decaying mosaics, loitered in the caves of arches, hunted phantoms through marble tunnels. And under the streets they took photographs: one bald flash scouring a century off the catacombs and sewers, the lacework coffins, the handful of albino rats perched upon them, caught in a second like ghosts of white hearts, mute, with waiting eyes.

The dawn star shone in the lagoon on a tail of jagged silver. The sun rose. There was an unsuitable noise – the boat was coming.

"There," said the girl on the deck of the boat, "stop there, please."

The boat sidled to a pavement and stood on the water, trembling and murmuring. The girl left it with a clumsy gracefulness and poised at the edge of the city with her single bag, cheerful and undaunted before the lonely cliffs of masonry, and all time's indifference.

She was small, about twenty-five, with ornately short fair hair, clad in old-fashioned jeans and a shirt. Her skin was fresh, her eyes bright with intelligent foolishness. She looked about, and upward. Her interest clearly centred on a particular house, which overhung the water like a face above a mirror, its eyes closed.

Presently the boat pulled away and went off across the lagoon, and only the girl and the silence remained.

She picked up her bag and walked along the pavement to an archway with a shut, leaden door. Here she knocked boldly, as if too stupid to understand the new silence must not yet be tampered with.

Her knocking sent hard blobs of sound careering round the vault of greenish crystal space that was the city's morning. They seemed to strike peeling walls and stone pilasters five miles off. From the house itself came no response, not even the vague sense of something stirring like a serpent in sleep.

"Now this is too bad," said the girl to the silence, upbraiding it mildly. "They *told* me a caretaker would be here, in time for the boat."

She left her bag, (subconscious acknowledgment of the emptiness and indifference), by the gate, and walked along under the leaning face of the house. From here she saw the floors of the balconies of flowered iron; she listened for a sudden snap of shutters. But only the water lapped under the pavement, component of silence. This house was called the Palace of the Planet. The girl knew all about it, and what she did not know she had come here to discover. She was writing a long essay that was necessary to her career of scholastic journalism. She was not afraid.

In the façade of the Palace of the Planet was another door, plated with green bronze. The weed had not choked it, and over its top leaned a marble woman with bare breasts and a dove in her hands. The girl reached out and rapped with a bronze knocker shaped like a fist. The house gave off a sound that after all succeeded in astonishing her. It must be a hollow shell, unfurnished, half its walls fallen...

These old cities were museums now, kept for their history, made available on request to anyone, not many – who wished to view. They had their dwellers also, but in scarcity. Destitutes and eccentrics lived in them, monitored by the state. The girl, whose name was Jonquil Hare, had seen the register of this place. In all, there were 174 names, some queried, where once had teemed thousands, crushing each other in the ambition to survive.

The hollow howling of her knock faded in the house. Jonquil said, "I'm coming in. I *am*." And marched back to her bag beneath the leaden gate. She surveyed the gate, and the knotted weed which had come down on it. Jonquil Hare tried the weed. It resisted her strongly. She took up her bag, in which there was nothing breakable, seasoned traveller as she was, and flung it over the arch. She took the weed in her small strong hands and hauled herself up in her clumsy, graceful way, up to the arch, and sat there, looking in at a morning-twilight garden of shrubs that had not been pruned in a hundred years, and trees that became each other. A blue fountain shone dimly. Jonquil smiled upon it and swung herself over in the weed and slithered down, into the environ of the house.

By midday, Jonquil had gone busily over most of the Palace of the Planet. Its geography was fixed in her head, but partly, confusedly, for she liked the effect of a puzzle of rooms and corridors. Within the lower portion of the house a large hall gave on to a large enclosed inner courtyard, that in turn led to the garden. Above, chambers of the first story would have opened onto the court, but their doors were sealed by the blue-green weed, which had smothered the court itself and so turned it into a strange undersea grotto where columns protruded like yellow coral. Above the lower floor, two long staircases drew up into apparently uncountable annexes and cells, and to a great salon with tarnished mirrors, also broken like spiderwebs. The salon had tall windows that stared through their blind shutters at the lagoon.

There were carvings everywhere; lacking light, she did not study them now. And, as suspected, there was very little furniture – a pair of desks with hollow drawers, spindly chairs, a divan in rotted ivory silk. In one oblong room was a bedframe with vast tapering pillars like idle rockets. Cobwebby draperies shimmered from the canopy in a draught, while Jonquil succeeded in opening a shutter in the salon. A block of afternoon fell in. Next door, in the adjacent chamber, she set up her inflatable mattress, her battery lamp and heater, some candles she had brought illegally in a padded tube. Sitting on her unrolled mat in the subaqueous light of a shuttered window which refused to give, she ate from her pack ol food snacks and drank cola. Then she arranged some books and notepads, pens and pencils, a magnifier, camera and unit, and a miniature recorder on the unfolded table.

She spoke to the room, as from the start she had spoken consecutively to the house. "Well, here we are."

But she was restless. The caretaker must be due to arrive, and until this necessary procedure had taken place, interruption hung over her. Of course, the caretaker would enable Jonquil to gain possession of the house secrets, the holostetic displays of furnishings and earlier life that might have been indigenous here, the hidden walks and rooms that undoubtedly lay inside the walls.

Jonquil was tired. She had risen at 3:00 a.m. for the boat, after an evening of hospitable farewells. She lay down on her inflatable bed with the pillow under her neck. Through half-closed eyes she saw the room breathing with pastel motes of sun and heard the rustle of weed at the shutter.

She dreamed of climbing a staircase which, dreaming, seemed new to her. At the foot of the stair a marble pillar supported a globe of some aquamarine material, covered by small configurations of alien landmasses, isolate in seas. The globe was a whimsical and inaccurate eighteenth-century rendition of the planet Venus, to which the house was mysteriously affiliated. As she climbed the stairs, random sprinklings of light came and went. Jonquil sensed that someone was ascending with her, step for step, not on the actual stair, but inside the peeling wall at her left side. Near the top of the stair (which was lost in darkness) an arched window had been let into the wall, milky and unclear and further obscured by some drops of waxen stained glass. As she came level with the window, Jonquil glanced sidelong at it. A shadowy figure appeared, on the far side of the pane, perhaps a woman, but hardly to be seen.

Jonquil started awake at the sound of the caretaker's serviceable shoes clumping into the house.

The caretaker was a woman. She did not offer her name, and no explanation for her late arrival. She had brought the house manual and advised Jonquil on how to operate the triggers in its panel – visions flickered annoyingly over the rooms and were gone. A large box contained facsimiles of things pertaining to the house and its history. Jonquil had seen most of these already.

"There are the upper rooms, the attics. Here's the master key."

The woman showed Jonquil a hidden stair that probed these upper reaches of the house. It was not the stairway from the dream, but narrow and winding as the steps of a bell tower. There were no other concealed chambers.

"If there's anything else you find you require, you must go out to the booth in the square. Here is the code to give the machine."

The caretaker was middle-aged, stout and uncharming. She seemed not to know the house at all, only everything about it, and glanced around her disapprovingly. Doubtless she lived in one of the contemporary golden towers across the lagoon, which, in the lingering powder of mist, passed for something older and stranger that they were not.

"Who came here last?" asked Jonquil. "Did anyone?"

"There was a visitor in the spring of the last Centenary Year. He stayed only one day, to study the plaster, I believe."

Jonquil smiled, pleased and smug that the house was virtually her own, for the city's last centenary had been twenty years ago, nearly her lifetime.

She was glad when the caretaker left, and the silence of the house did not occur to Jonquil as she went murmuring from room to room, able now to operate the shutters, bring in light and examine the carvings in corners, on cornices. Most of them showed earlier defacement, as expected. She switched on, too, scenes from the manual, of costumed, dining and conversing figures amid huge pieces of furniture and swags of brocade. No idea of ghosts was suggested by these holostets. Jonquil reserved a candlelit masked ball for a later, more fitting hour.

The greenish amber of afternoon slid into the plate of water. A chemical rose flooded the sky, like colour processing for a photograph. Venus, the evening star, was visible beyond the garden.

Jonquil climbed up the bell tower steps to the attics.

The key turned easily in an upper door. But the attics disappointed. They were high and dark – her flashlight penetrated like a sword – webbed with the woven dust, and thick with damp, and a sour cloacal smell that turned the stomach of the mind. Otherwise, there was an almost emptiness. From beams hung unidentified shreds. On one wall a tapestry on a frame, indecipherable, presumably not thought good enough for renovation.

Jonquil moved reluctantly through the obscured space, telling it it was in a poor state, commiserating with it, until she came against a chest of cold black wood.

"Now what are you?" Jonquil inquired of the chest.

It was long and low, its lid carved over with a design that had begun to crumble... Curious fruits in a wreath.

The shape of the chest reminded her of something. She peered at the fruits. Were they elongate lemons, pomegranates? Perhaps they were meant to be Venusian fruits. The astrologer Johanus, who had lived in the Palace of the Planet, had played over the house his obsession and ignorance with, and of, Venus. He had claimed in his treatise closely to have studied the surface of the planet through his own telescope. There was an atmosphere of clouds, parting slowly; beneath, an underlake landscape, cratered and mountained, upon limitless waters. "The mirror of Venus is her sea," Johanus wrote. And he had painted her, but his daubs were lost, like most of his writing, reputedly burned. He had haunted the house alive, an old wild man, watching for star-rise, muttering. He had died in the charity hospital, penniless and mad. His servants had destroyed his work, frightened of it, and vandalised the decorations of the house.

Jonquil tried to raise the lid of the chest. It would not come up.

"Are you locked?"

But there was no lock. The lid was stuck or merely awkward. "I shall come back," said Jonquil.

She had herself concocted an essay on the astrologer, but rather as a good little girl writes once a year to her senile grandfather. She appreciated his involvement – that, but for him, none of this would be – but he did not interest her. It was the house which did that. There was a switch on the manual that would conjure acted reconstructions of the astrologer's life, even to the final days, and to the rampage of the vandals. But Jonquil did not bother with this record. It was to her as if the house had adorned itself, using the man only as an instrument. His paintings and notes were subsidiary, and she had not troubled much over their disappearance.

"Yes, I'll be back with a wrench, and you'd just better have something in there worth looking at," said Jonquil to the chest. Doubtless it was vacant.

Night on the lagoon, in the city. The towers in the distance offered no lights, being constructed to conceal them. In two far-off spots, a pale glow crept from a window to the water. The silence of night was not like the silence of day.

Jonquil sang as the travel-cook prepared her steak, and, drinking a glass of reconstituted wine, going out into the salon, she switched on the masked ball.

At once the room was over two hundred years younger. It was drenched in gilt, and candle-flames stood like flowers of golden diamond on their stems of wax, while the ceiling revealed dolphins and doves who escorted a goddess over a sea in a ship that was a shell. The windows were open to a revised night hung with diamanté lamps, to a lagoon of black ink where bright boats were passing to the sound of mandolins. The salon purred and thrummed with voices. It was impossible to decipher a word, yet laughter broke through, and clear notes of the music. No one danced as yet. Perhaps they never would, for they were creatures from another world indeed, every one clad in gold and silver, ebony and glacial white, with jewels on them like water-drops tossed up by a wave. They had no faces. Their heads were those of plumed herons and horned deer, black velvet cats and lions of the sun, and moon lynxes, angels, demons, mer-things from out of the lagoon, and scarabs from the hollows of time. They moved and promenaded, paused with teardrops of glass holding bloodlike wine, fluttered their fans of peacocks and palm leaves.

Jonquil stayed at the edge of the salon. She could have walked straight through them, through their holostetic actors' bodies and their prop garments of silk, steel and chrysoprase, but she preferred to stay in the doorway, drinking her own wine, adapting her little song to the tune of the mandolins.

After the astrologer had gone, others had come, and passed, in the house. The rich lady, and the prince, with their masks and balls, suppers and recitals.

The travel-cook chimed, and Jonquil switched off two hundred elegantly acting persons, one thousand faked gems and lights, and went to eat her steak.

She wrote with her free hand: *Much too pretty. Tomorrow I must photograph the proper carvings.* And said this over aloud.

Jonquil dreamed she was in the attic. There was a vague light, perhaps the moon coming in at cracks in the shutters, or the dying walls. Below, a noise went on, the holostetic masked ball which she had forgotten to switch off. Jonquil looked at the chest of black wood. She had realised she did not have to open it herself. Downstairs, in the salon, an ormolu clock struck midnight, the hour of unmasking. There was a little click. In the revealing darkness, the lid of the chest began to lift. Jonquil knew what it had reminded her of. A shadow sat upright in the coffin of the chest. It had a slender but indefinite form, and yet it turned its head and Jonquil saw the two eyes looking at her, only the eyeballs gleaming, in two crescents, in the dark.

The lid fell over with a crash.

Jonquil woke up sitting on her inflatable bed, with her hands at her throat, her eyes raised toward the ceiling.

"A dream," announced Jonquil.

She turned on her battery lamp, and the small room appeared. There was no sound in the house. Beyond the closed door the salon rested.

"Silly," said Jonquil.

She lay and read a book having nothing to do with the Palace of the Planet, until she fell asleep with the light on.

The square was a terrifying ruin. Hidden by the frontage of the city, it was nearly inconceivable. Upper stories had collapsed onto the paving, only the skeletons of architecture remained, with occasionally a statue, some of them shining green and vegetable (the dissolution of gold) piercing through. The paving was broken up, marked by the slough of birds. Here the booth arose, unable to decay.

"There's a chest in the attics. It won't open," Jonquil accused the receiver. "The manual lists it. It says, one sable-wood jester chest."

The reply came. "This is why you are unable to open it. A jester chest was just that, a deceiving or joke object, often solid. There is nothing inside."

"No," said Jonquil, "some jester chests do open. And this isn't solid."

"I am afraid you are wrong. The chest has been investigated, and contains nothing; neither is there any means to open it."

"An x-ray doesn't always show…" began Jonquil.

But the machine had disconnected.

"I won't have this," said Jonquil.

Three birds blew over the square. Beneath in the sewers, the colony of voiceless rats, white as moonlight, ran noiselessly under her feet. But she would not shudder. Jonquil strutted back to the house through alleys of black rot, where windows were suspended like lingering cards of ice. Smashed glass lay underfoot. The awful smell of the sea was in the alleys, for the sea came in and in. It had drowned the city in psychic reality, and already lay far over the heads of all the buildings, calm, oily and still, reflecting the sun and the stars.

Jonquil got into the house by the gate-door the manual had made accessible, crossing the garden where the blue fountain was a girl crowned with myrtle. Jonquil went straight up over the floors to the attic stair and climbed that. The attic door was ajar, as she believed she had left it.

"Here I am," said Jonquil. The morning light was much stronger in the attics and she did not need her torch. She found the chest and bent over it.

"You've got a secret. Maybe you're only warped shut, that would be the damp up here... There may be a lining that could baffle the x-ray."

She tried the wrench, specifically designed not to inflict any injury. But it slipped and slithered and did no good. Jonquil knelt down and began to feel all over the chest, searching for some spring or other mechanism. She was caressing the chest, going so cautiously and delicately over it. Its likeness to a coffin was very evident, but bones would have been seen. "Giving me dreams," she said.

Something moved against her finger. It was very slight. It was as if the chest had wriggled under her tickling and testing like a sleeping child. Jonquil put back her hand – she had flinched – and reprimanded herself. At her touch the movement came again. She heard the clarity of the *click* she had heard before in the dream. And before she could stop herself, she jumped up, and stepped backward, one, two, three, until the wall stopped her.

The lid of the chest was coming up, gliding over, and slipping down without any noise but a mild slap. Nothing sat up in the chest. But Jonquil saw the edge of something lying there in it, in the shadow of it.

"Yes, it is," she said, and went forward. She leaned on the chest, familiarly now. Everything was explained, even the psycho-kinetic activity the dream. "A painting."

Jonquil Hare leaned on the chest and stared in. Presently she took hold of the elaborate and gilded frame, and got the picture angled upward a short way, so it too leaned on the chest.

The painting was probably three centuries old. She could tell that from the pigments and disposition of the oils, but not from the artist. The artist was unknown. In size it was an upright oblong, about fifteen metres by one metre in width.

The work was a full-length portrait, rather well executed and proportioned, lacking only any vestige of life, or animation. It might have been the masterly likeness of a handsome doll – this was how the artist had given away his amateur status.

She looked like a woman of about Jonquil's age, which given the period meant of course that she would have been far younger, eighteen or nineteen years. Her skin was pale, and had a curious tint, as did in fact the entire scene, perhaps due to some corrosion of the paint – but even so had not gone to the usual brown and mud tones, but rather to a sort yellowish blue. Therefore, the colour scheme of clothing and hair might be misleading, for the long loose tresses were yellowish blonde, and the dress bluish grey. Like the hair, the dress was loose, a robe of a kind. And yet, naturally, both hair and robe were draped in a particular manner that dated them, as surely as if their owner had been gowned and coiffured at the apex of that day's fashion. She was slender but looked strong. There was no plumpness to her chin and throat, her hands were narrow. An unusually masculine woman, more suitable to Jonquil's century, where the sexes often blended, slim and lightly muscular – the woman in the painting was also like this. Her face was impervious, its eyes black. She was not beautiful or alluring. It was a flat animal face, tempered like the moon by its own chill light, and lacking sight or true expression because the artist had not understood how to intercept them.

Behind the woman was a vista that Jonquil took at first for the lagoon. But then she saw that between the fogbank of blued-yellow cloud and the bluish-greenish water, a range of pocked and fissured mountains lurched like an unearthly aqueduct. It was the landscape of Johanus's Venus. The artist of the picture was the mad astrologer who had invested the house.

How could it be that the authorities had missed this find?

"My," said Jonquil to the painting. She was excited. What would this not be worth in tokens of fame?

She pulled on the painting again, more carefully than before. It was light for its size. She could manage it. She paused a moment, close to the woman on the canvas. The canvas was strange, the texture of it under the paint – but in those days three centuries before, they had sometimes used odd materials. Even some chemical or experimental potion could have been mixed with the paint, to give it now its uncanny tinge.

A name was written in a scroll at the bottom of the picture. Jonquil took it for a signature. But it was not the astrologer's name, though near enough it indicated some link. *Johnina.*

"Jo-*nine*-ah," said Jonquil, "we are going for a short walk, down to where I can take a proper look at you."

With enormous care now, she drew the picture of Johnina out of the chest, and down the narrow stair toward the salon.

Jonquil was at the masked ball. In her hand was a fan of long white feathers caught in a claw of zircons, her costume was of white satin streaked with silver veins, and her face was masked like a white-furred cat. She knew her hair was too short for the day and age, and this worried her by its inappropriateness. No one spoke to her, but all around they chattered to each other (incomprehensibly), and their curled powdered hair poured out of their masks like milk boiling over. Jonquil observed everything acutely, the man daintily taking snuff (an addict), the woman in the dress striped black and ivory, peering through her ruby eyeglass. Out on the lagoon, the gleaming boats went by, trailing red roses in the water.

Jonquil was aware that no one took any notice of her, had anything to do with her, and she was peevish, because they must have invited her. Who was she supposed to be? A duke's daughter, or his mistress? Should she not be married at her age, and have borne children? She would have to pretend.

There was a man with rings on every finger, and beyond him a checkered mandolin player, and beyond him, a woman stood in a grey gown different from the rest. Her mask covered all her face; it was the countenance of a globe, perhaps the moon, in silver, and about it hair like pale tarnished fleece, too long as Jonquil's was too short, was falling to her pelvis over the bodice of the gown.

A group of actors – yes, they were only acting, it was not real – intervened. The woman was hidden for a moment, and when the group had passed, she was gone.

She was an actress, too, which was why Jonquil had thought something about her recognisable.

Jonquil became annoyed that she should be here, among actors, for acting was nothing to do with her. She turned briskly and went toward the door of the chamber that led off from the salon. Inside, the area was dark, yet everything there was visible, and Jonquil was surprised to see a huge bedframe from another room dominating the space. Surely Jonquil's professional impedimenta had been put here, and the inflatable sleeping couch she travelled with? As for this bed, she had seen it elsewhere, and it had been naked then, but now it was dressed. Silk curtains hung from the pillars, and a mattress, pillows, sheets and embroidered coverlet were on it. Rather than the pristine appearance of a model furnishing, the bed had a slightly rumpled, tumbled look, as if Jonquil had indeed used it. Jonquil closed the door of the room firmly on the ball outside, and all sound of it at once ceased.

To her relief, she found that she was actually undressed and in the thin shirt that was her night garment. She went to the bed, resigned, and got into it. She lay back on the pillows. The bed was wonderfully comfortable, lushly undisciplined.

Johanus's house was so silent – noiseless. Jonquil lay and listened to the total absence of sound, which was like a pressure, as if she had floated down beneath the sea. Her bones were coral and pearls her eyes... Fish might swim in through the slats of a shutter, across the water of the air. But before that happened, the door would open again.

The door opened.

The doorway was lit with moonlight, and the salon beyond it, for the masked ball had gone. Only the woman with the silver planet face remained, and she came over the threshold. Behind her, in lunar twilight, Jonquil saw the lagoon lying across the salon, and the walls had evaporated, leaving a misty shore, and mountains that were tunnelled through. The bed itself was adrift on water, and bobbed gently, but Johnina crossed without difficulty.

Her silver mask was incised, like the carvings in the house corners, the globes that were the planet Venus. The mask reflected in the water. Two silver discs, separated, drawing nearer.

Jonquil said sternly, "I must wake up."

And she dived upward from the bed and tore through layers of cloud or water and came out into the actual room, rolling on the inflatable couch.

"I'm not frightened," stated Jonquil. "Why should I be?"

She turned on her battery lamp and angled the light to fall across the painting of Johnina, which she had leaned against the wall.

"What are you trying to tell me now? In the morning I'm going to call them up about you. Don't you want to be famous?"

The painting had no resonance. It looked poorly in the harsh glare of the lamp, a stilted figure and crackpot scenery, the brushwork disordered. The canvas was so smooth.

"Go to sleep," said Jonquil to Johnina, and shut off the light as if to be sensible with a tiresome child.

In the true dark, which had no moon, the silence of the house crept closer. Dispassionately, Jonquil visualised old Johanus padding about the floors in his broken soft shoes. He thought he had seen the surface of the planet Venus. He had painted the planet as an allegory that was a woman, just like the puns of Venus the *goddess* in marble over the door, and on the ceiling of the salon.

Jonquil began to see Johanus in his study, among the alchemical muddle, the primeval alchemical chaos from which all perfect creation evolved. But she regarded him offhandedly, the dust and grime and spillages, the blackened skulls and lembics growing moss.

Johanus wrote on parchment with a goose quill.

He wrote in Latin also, and although she had learned Latin in order to pursue her study, this was too idiosyncratic, too much of its era, for her to follow. Then the words began to sound, and she grasped them. Bored, Jonquil attended. She did not recall switching on this holostet, could not think why she had decided to play it.

"So, on the forty-third night, after an hour of watching, the cloud parted, and there was before me the face of the planet. I saw great seas, or one greater sea, with small masses of land, pitted like debased silver. And the mountains I saw. And all this in a yellow glow from the cloud..."

Jonquil wondered why she did not stop the holostet. She was not interested in this. But she could not remember where the manual was.

"For seven nights I applied myself to my telescope, and on each night, the clouds of the planet sensuously parted, allowing me a view of her bareness."

Jonquil thought she would have to leave the bed in order to switch off the manual. But the bed, with its tall draped posts, was warm and comfortable.

"On the eighth night it came to me. Even as I watched, I was watched in my turn. Some creature was there, some unseen intelligence, which, sensing my appraisal, reached out to seize me. I do not know how such a thing is possible. Where I see only a miniature of that world, it sees me exactly, where and what I am, every atom. At once I removed myself, left my perusal, and shut up the instrument. But I believe I was too late. Somehow it has come to me, here, in the world of men. It is with me, although I cannot hear it or behold it. It is the invisible air; it is the silence of the night.

What shall I do?"

The holostet of Johanus was no longer operating. Jonquil lay in the four-poster bed in the room that led from the salon. The door was shut. Someone was in the room with her, beside the bed. Jonquil turned her head on the pillow, without hurry, to see.

A hand was stroking back her short hair; it was very pleasant; she was a cat that was being caressed. Jonquil smiled lazily. It was like the first day of the holidays, and her mother was standing by her bed, and they would talk. But no, not her mother. It was the wonderful-looking woman she had seen – where was that, now? Perhaps in the city, an eccentric who lived there, out walking in the turquoise of dusk or funeral orchid of dawning, when the star was on the lagoon. Very tall, a developed, lithe body, graceful, with the blue wrap tied loosely, and the amazing hair, so thick and blonde, falling over it, over her shoulders and the firm cupped line of the breasts, the flat belly, and into the mermaid V of the thighs.

"Hello," said Jonquil.

And the woman gave the faintest shake of her lion's head in its mane. Jonquil was not to speak. They did not need words. But the woman smiled, too. It was such a sensational smile. So effortless, stimulating and calming. The dark, dark eyes rested on Jonquil with a tenderness that was also cruel. Jonquil had seen this look in the eyes of others, and a *frisson* of eagerness went over her, and she was ashamed; it was too soon to expect – but the woman was leaning over her now, the marvel of face blurred and the mane of hair trickling over Jonquil's skin. The mouth kissed, gently and unhesitatingly.

"Oh, yes," said Jonquil, without any words.

The woman, who was called Johnina, was lying on her. She was heavy, her weight crushed and pinned, and Jonquil was helpless. It was the most desired thing, to be helpless like this, unable even to lift her own hands, as if she had no strength at all. And Johnina's hands were on her breasts somehow, between their two adhering bodies, finding out Jonquil's shape with slow smooth spirallings. And softly, without anything crude or urgent, the sea-blue thigh of Johnina rubbed against Jonquil until she ached and melted. She shut her eyes and could think only of the sweet unhurried journey of her body, of the hands that guided and stroked, and the mermaid tail that bore her up, and the sound of the sea in her ears. Johnina kissed and kissed, and Jonquil Hare felt herself dissolving into Johnina, into her body, and she could not even cry out. And then Jonquil was spread-eagled out into a tidal orgasm, where with every wave some further part of her was washed away. And when there was nothing left, she woke up in the pitch-black void of the silence, with something hard and cold, clammy, but nearly weightless, lying on her, an oblong in a gilded frame, the painting which had dropped over on top of her and covered her from breast to ankle.

She flung it off and it clattered down. She clutched at her body, thinking to discover herself clotted with a sort of glue or slime, but there was nothing like that.

She was weak and dizzy, and her heart drummed noisily, so she could not hear the silence anymore.

"Let me speak to the house caretaker," snapped Jonquil at the obtuse machine. Outside the booth, the ruin of the great square seemed to sway on the wind, which was violent, ruffling the lagoon in flounces, whirling small scraps of coloured substances that might have been paper, rags, or skin.

"The caretaker is not available. However, your request has been noted."

"But this picture is an important find – and I want it removed, today, to a place of safety."

The machine had disconnected.

Jonquil stood in the booth, as if inside a spacesuit, and watched the alien atmosphere of the city swirling with bits and colours.

"Don't be a fool," said Jonquil. She left the booth and cowered before the wind, which was not like any breeze felt in civilised places. "It's an old painting. A *bad* old painting. So, you're lonely, you had a dream. Get back to work."

Jonquil worked. She photographed all the carvings she had decided were relevant or unusually bizarre – Venus the goddess riding the crescent moon, a serpent coiled about a planet that maybe was simply an orb. She put these into the developer and later drew them out and arranged them in her room beside the salon. (She had already moved the painting of Johnina into the salon – she felt tired, and it seemed heavier than before – left it with its face to the wall, propped under the mirrors. It was now about twenty-five metres from her inflatable bed, and well outside the door.)

She went over the house again, measuring and recording comments. She opened shutters and regarded the once hive-like cliffs of the city, and the waters on the other side. The wind settled and a mist condensed. By mid-afternoon the towers of modernity were quite gone.

"The light always has a green tinge – blue and yellow mixed. When the sky pinkens at dawn or sunset the water is bottle green, an apothecary's bottle. And purple for the prose," Jonquil added.

In two hours it would be dusk, and then night.

This was ridiculous. She had to face up to herself that she was nervous and apprehensive. But there was nothing to be afraid of, or even to look forward to.

She still felt depressed, exhausted, so she took some more vitamins. Something she had eaten, probably, before leaving for the city, had caught up with her. And that might even account for the dream. The dreams.

She did not go up into the attics. She spent some time out of doors, in the grotto of the courtyard, and in the garden, which the manual showed her with paved paths and carven box hedges, orange trees, and the fountain playing. She did not watch this holostet long. Her imagination was working too, and too hard, and she might start to see Johnina in a blue-grey gown going about between the trees.

What, anyway, *was* Johnina? Doubtless Jonquil's unconscious had based the Johanus part of the dream on scraps of the astrologer's writings she had seen, and that she had consciously forgotten. Johanus presumably believed some alien intelligence from the planet he observed had made use of the channel of his awareness. For him it was female, (interesting women then were always witches, demons; he would be bound to think in that way), and when she suborned him, in his old man's obsession, he painted her approximately to a woman – just as he had approximated his vision of the planet to something identifiable, the *pastorale* of a cool Hell. And he gave his demoness a name birthed out of his own, a strange daughter.

Jonquil did not recollect, try as she would, reading anything so curious about Johanus, but she must have done.

He then concealed the painting of his malign inamorata in the trick chest, to protect it from the destructive fears of the servants.

Only another hour, and the sky would infuse like pale tea and rose petals. The sun would go, the star would visit the garden. Darkness.

"You're not as tough as you thought," said Jonquil. She disapproved of herself. "All right. We'll sit this one out. Stay awake tonight. And tomorrow I'll get hold of that damn caretaker lady if I have to swim there."

As soon as it was sunset, Jonquil went back to her chosen room. She had to pass through the salon and had an urge to go up to the picture, turn it round, and scrutinise it. But that was stupid. She had seen all there was to see. She shut her inner door on the salon with a bang. Now she was separate from all the house.

She lit her lamp, and, pulling out her candles, lit those too. She primed the travel-cook for a special meal, chicken with a lemon sauce, creamed potatoes, and as the wing of night unfolded over the lagoon, she closed the shutter and switched on a music tape. She sat drinking wine and writing up that day's notes on the house. After all, she had done almost all that was needed. Might she not see if she could leave tomorrow? To hire transport before the month was up and the regular boat arrived would be expensive, but then, she could get to work the quicker perhaps, away from the house... She had meant to explore the city, of course, but it was in fact less romantic than dejecting, and potentially dangerous. She might run into one of the insane inhabitants, and then what?

Jonquil thought, acutely visualising the nocturnal mass of the city. No one was alive in it, surely. The few lights, the occasional smokes and whispers, were inaugurated by machines, to deceive. There were the birds, and their subterranean counterpart, the rats. Only she alone, Jonquil Hare, was here this night between masonry and water. She alone, and one another.

"*Don't* be silly," said Jonquil.

How loud her voice sounded, now the music had come to an end. The silence was gigantic, a fifth dimension.

It seemed wrong to put on another tape. The silence should not be angered. Let it lie, move quietly, and do not speak at all.

Johanus wrote quickly, as if he might be interrupted; his goose pen snapped, and he seized another, ready cut. He spoke the words aloud as he wrote them, although his lips were closed.

"For days, and for nights when I could not sleep, I was aware of the presence of my invader. I told myself it was my fancy, but I could not be rid of the sensation of it. I listened for the sounds of breathing, I looked for a shadow – there were none of these. I felt no touch, and when I dozed fitfully in the dark, waking suddenly, no beast crouched on my breast. Yet, it was with me, it breathed, it brushed by me, it touched me without hands, and watched me with its unseen eyes.

"So passed five days and four nights. And on the evening of the fifth day, even as the silver planet stood above the garden, it grew bold, knowing by now it had little to fear from me in my terror, and took on a shape.

"Yes, it took on a sort of shape, but if this is its reality I cannot know, or only some semblance, all it can encompass here, or deigns to assume.

"It hung across the window, and faintly through it the light of dusk was ebbing. A membraneous thing, like a sail. It did not move, no pulse of life seemed in it, and yet it lived. I shut the door on it, but later I returned. In the candle's light I saw it had fallen, or lowered itself, to my table. It had kept its soft sheen of blue. I touched it, I could not help myself, and it had the texture of velum – that is, of skin. It lay before me, the length of the table, and under it dimly I could discern the outline of my books, my dish of powders, and other things. I cannot describe my state. My terror had sunk into a sort of blinded wonderment. I do not know how great a while I stood and looked at it, but at length I heard the girl with my food, and I went out and locked up the room again. What would it do while I was gone? Would it perhaps vanish again?

"That night I slept, stupefied, and in the morning opened my eyes and there the thing hung, above me, inside the canopy of the very bed. How long had it been there, watching me with its invisible organs of sight? Of course, its method had been simple: it had slid under the doors of my house – my house so long dressed for it and named for its planet in the common vernacular.

"What now must I do? What is required of me? For clearly I shall become its slave. It seems to me I am supposed to be able to give it a more usual form, some camouflage, so that it may pass with men, but how is that possible? *How* render such a thing ordinary, and attractive?

"The means came to me in my sleep. Perhaps the being has influenced my brain. There is one sure way. It has noticed my canvases. Now I am to stretch this skin upon a frame and put paint to it. What shall I figure there? No doubt, I shall be guided in what I do, as it has led me to the idea.

"I must obscure my actions from my servants. They are already ill at ease, and the man was very threatening this morning; he is a ruffian and capable of anything – it will be wise to destroy these papers, when all else is done."

Jonquil turned from Johanus and saw a group of friends she had not communicated with in three years, gliding over the lagoon in a white boat. They waved and shouted, and Jonquil knew she had been rescued, she would escape, but running toward the boat she heard a metallic crash, and jumped inadvertently up out of the dream into the room, where her candles were burning low, fluttering, and the air quivered like a disturbed pond. The silence had been agitated after all. There had been some noise, like the noise in the dream, which woke her.

She sat bolt upright in the lock of fear. She had never felt fear in this way in her life. She had meant to stay awake, but the meal, the wine...

And the dream of Johanus – absurd.

Outside, in the mirrored night-time salon, there came a sharp screeching *scrape*.

Jonquil's mind shrieked, and she clamped her hand over her mouth.

Don't be a fool. Listen! She listened. The silence. Had she imagined...?

The noise came again, harsher and more absolute.

It was like the abrasion of a rusty chain dragged along the marble floor.

And again...

Jonquil sprang up. In her life, where she had never before known such fear, the credo had been that fear, confronted, proved to be less than it had seemed. Always the maxim held true. It was this brainwashing of accredited experience which sent her to the door of the room and caused her to dash it wide and to stare outward.

The guttering glim of the candles, so apposite to the house, gave a half-presence to the salon. But mostly it was black, thick and composite, black, watery and uncertain on the ruined faces of the mirrors. And out of this blackness came a low flicker of motion, catching the candlelight along its edge. And this motion made the sound she had heard and now heard again. Jonquil did not believe what she saw. She did not believe it. No. This was still the dream, and she must, she *must* wake up.

The picture of Johnina, painted by the astrologer on a piece of membraneous bluish alien skin, had fallen over in its frame, and now the framed skin pulled itself along the floor, and, catching the light, Jonquil saw the little formless excrescences of the face-down canvas, little bluish-yellow paws, hauling the assemblage forward, the big balanced oblong shape with its rim of gilt vaguely shining. Machine-like, primeval, a mutated tortoise. It pulled itself on, and as the frame scraped along the floor it screamed, toward Jonquil in the doorway.

Jonquil slammed shut the door. She turned and caught up things – the inflatable bed, the table – and stuffed them up against the doorway. And the mechanical tortoise screamed twice more – and struck against the door, and the door shook.

Jonquil turned round and round in her trap, as the thing outside thudded back and forth, and her flimsy barricade trembled and tottered. There was no other exit but the window. She got it open and ran onto the balcony, which creaked and dipped. The weed was there, the blue-green Venus weed that choked the whole city. Jonquil threw herself off into it. As she did so, the door of the room gave way.

She was half-climbing, half-rebounding and falling down the wall of the house. Everywhere was darkness, and below the sucking of the water at the pavement.

As she struggled in the ropes of weed, tangled, clawing, a shape reared up in the window above her.

Jonquil cried out. The painting was in the window. But something comically macabre had happened. In rearing, it had caught at an angle between the uprights of the shutters. It was stuck, could not move out or in.

Jonquil hung in the weed, staring up at Johnina in her frame of gilt and wood and plaster and night. How soulless she looked, how without life.

And then a convulsion went over the picture. Like a blue amoeba touched by venom it writhed and wrinkled. It tore itself free of the golden frame. It billowed out, still held by a few filaments and threads, like a sail, a veil, the belly of something swollen with the hunger of centuries...

And Jonquil fought, and dropped the last two metres from the weed, landing on the pavement hard, in the box of darkness that was the city.

She was not dreaming, but it was like a dream. It seemed to her she saw herself running. The engine of her heart drove her forward. She did not know where or through what she ran. There was no moon, there were no lights. A kind of luminescence filmed over the atmosphere, and constructions loomed suddenly at her, an arch, a flight of steps, a platform, a severed wall. She fell and got up and ran on.

And behind her, *that* came. That which had ripped itself from an oblong of gilding. It had taken to the air. It flew through the city, between the pillars and under the porticos, along the ribbed arteries carrying night. It rolled and unrolled as it came, with a faint soft snapping. And then it sailed, wide open, catching some helpful draught, a huge pale bat.

Weed rushed over Jonquil and she thought the thing which had been called Johnina had settled on her lightly, coaxingly, and she screamed. The city filled with her scream like an empty gourd with water.

There were no lights, no figures huddled at smouldering fires, no guards or watchmen, no villains, no one here to save her, no one even to be the witness of what must come, when her young heart finally failed, her legs buckled, when the sailing softness came down and covered her, stroking and devouring, caressing and eating – its tongues and fingers and the whole porous mouth that it was – to drink her away and away.

Jonquil ran. She ran over streets that were cratered as if by meteorites, through vaulted passages, beside the still waters of night and death. It occurred to her, (her stunned and now almost witless brain), to plunge into the lagoon, to swim toward the unseen towers. But on the face of the mirror, gentleness would drift down on her, and in the morning mist, not even a ripple...

The paving tipped. Jonquil stumbled, ran, downward now, hopeless and mindless, her heart burning a hole in her side. Down and down, cracked tiles spinning off from her feet, down into some underground place that must be a prison for her, perhaps a catacomb, to stagger among filigree coffins, where the water puddled like glass on the floor, no way out, down into despair, and yet, mockingly, there was more light. More light to see what she did not want to see. It was the phosphorus of the death already there, the mummies in their narrow homes. Yes, she saw the water pools now, as she splashed through them, she saw the peculiar shelves and cubbies, the stone statue of a saint barnacled by the sea-rot the water brought into a creature from another world. And she saw the wall also that rose peremptory before her, the deadend that would end in death, and for which she had been waiting, to which she had run, and where now she collapsed, her body useless, run out.

She dropped against the wall, and, in the coffin-light, turned and looked back. And through the descending vault, a pale blue shadow floated, innocent and faithful, coming down to her like a kiss.

I don't believe this, Jonquil would have said, but now she did. And anyway she had no breath, no breath even to scream again or cry. She could only watch, could not take her eyes off the coming of the feaster. It had singled her out, allowed her to bring it from the chest. With others it had been more reticent, hiding itself. Perhaps it had eaten of Johanus, too, before he had been forced to secure it against the witch-hunting servants. Or maybe Johanus had not been to its taste. How ravenous it was, and how controlled was its need.

It alighted five metres from her, from Jonquil, as she lay against the death-end wall. She saw it down an aisle of coffins. Touching the water on the floor, it rolled together, and furled open, and skimmed over the surface onto the stone.

She was fascinated now. She wanted it to reach her. She wanted it to be over. She dug her hands into the dirt and a yellow bone crumbled under her fingers.

The painting of Johnina was crawling ably along the aisle. There was no impediment, no heavy frame to drag with it.

Sweat slipped into Jonquil's eyes and for a moment she saw a blue woman with ivory hair walking slowly between the coffins, but there was something catching at her robe, and she hesitated, to try to pluck the material away.

Jonquil blinked. She saw a second movement, behind the limpid roll of the Venus skin. A flicker, like a white handkerchief. And then another.

Something darted, and it was on the painting, on top of it, and then it flashed and was gone. And then two other white darts sewed through the blueness of the shadow, bundling it up into an ungainly lump, and two more, gathering and kneading.

The painting had vanished. It was buried under a pure white

jostling. And there began to be a thin high note on the air, like a whistling in the ear, without any emotion or language. Ten white rats of the catacombs had settled on the painting, and with their teeth and busy paws they held it still and rent it in pieces, and they ate it. They ate the painted image of the Venus Johnina, and her background of mountains and sea, they ate the living shrieking membrane of the flesh. Their hunger too had been long unappeased.

Jonquil lay by the wall, watching, until the last crumb and shred had disappeared into dainty needled mouths. It did not take more than two or three minutes. Then there was only a space, nothing on it, no rats, no other thing.

"Get up," Jonquil said. There was a low singing in her head, but no other noise. She stood in stages and went back along the aisle of dead. She was very cold, feeble and sluggish. She thought she felt old. She walked through the water pools. She had a dreadful intimation that everything had changed, that she would never be the same, that nothing ever would, that survival had sent her into an unknown and fearful world.

A rat sat on a coffin overseeing her departure, digesting in its belly blueness and alien dreams. The walls went on crumbling particle by particle. Silence flowed over the city like the approaching sea.

Author's Note: I've written several novels about vampires, or types of vampire, and quite a lot of short stories of various lengths. Vampirism, to me, is one of those themes where somehow another idea or twist is always making itself known to me. The subject seems limitless, perhaps because the vampire seems somehow to have woven itself among the human psyche.

'Venus Rising on Water' came initially from a fascination with Venice. It's about the clash between the future and the past – although the denouement, however odd or apparently fortuitous, demonstrates the hold everyday Real Life can get on the strangest matters.

THE PUMA'S DAUGHTER

1. The Bride

Since he was eight years old, Matthew Seaton understood he was betrothed to a girl up in the hills. As a child it hadn't bothered him. After all, among the Farming Families, these early handfastings were quite usual. His own elder brother, Chanter, had wed at eighteen the young woman selected for him when Chanter and she were only four and five.

Even at twelve, Matt didn't worry so much. He had never seen his proposed wife, nor she him – which was quite normal too. She had a strange name, he knew that, and was one year younger than he.

Then, when he was thirteen, Matt did become a little more interested. Wanted to know a little more. Think of her, maybe, just now and then.

"She has long gold hair," his mother told him, "hangs down to her knees when she unbraids it."

Which sounded good.

"She's strong," his father said. "She can ride and fish and cook, and use a gun as handily as you can, it seems."

Matt doubted this, but he accepted it. Up there, certainly, in the savage forested hills that lay at the feet of the great blue mountains, skills with firearms were needed.

"Can she read?" he had asked, however. *He* could, and he liked his books.

"I've been told," said Veniah Seaton, "she can do almost anything, and finely."

It wasn't until the evening of his fourteenth birthday that Matt began to hear other things about his bride.

Other things that had nothing to do with skills and virtues and were not fine at all.

Matt was seventeen when he rode up to *Sure Hold*, now his brother's house, wanting to talk to Chanter.

They sat with the coffeepot before a blazing winter hearth. No snow had come yet, but in a week or so it would. Snow always closed off the outer world for five or six months of each year, and Chanter's farm and land were part of that outer world now, so far as Veniah's farm was concerned. This was the last visit, then, that Matt could make before spring. And his wedding.

For a while they talked about ordinary things – the crops and livestock, and a bit of gossip – such as the dance last leaf-fall, when the two girls from the Hanniby Family had run off with two of the young men from the Styles. Disgrace and disowning followed; it went without saying.

"I guess I'd fare the same way, wouldn't I, Chanter, if I just took to my heels and ran?"

"I guess you would," Matt's brother replied, easy, only his eyes suddenly alert and guarded. "But why'd you run anyhow? Have you seen someone you like? Take up with one of the farmgirls, boy. She'll get it out your system. And you'll be wed in spring."

"To Thena Proctor."

"To Thena Proctor."

"I've never met her, Chant."

"No, you haven't, boy. But others have on your behalf. She's a good-looking lady. Our pa wouldn't ever pick us any girl not fit. Take my wife. Pretty as a picture and strong as a bear."

Matt looked off into the fire with his blue eyes full of trouble.

Chanter waited.

Matt said, "Did you ever hear – a tale of the Proctor girl?"

"Yes." Chanter grinned. "Gold hair, waist narrow as a rose stem, and can wrestle a deer to the ground."

"How does she do that, then, Chant?"

"How the heck do I know, Matt?"

Matt's eyes came back from the hearth and fixed like two blue gun-mouths on Chanter's own.

"Does she perhaps leap on its back, sink in her claws, fangs in its neck – drag it to the earth *that* way?"

Chanter winced. And Matt saw he wasn't alone in hearing stories.

Matt added, slow and deadly, "Does her long hair get shorter, yet cover her all over? Do her *paws* leave pad-marks on snow? Are some of her white front teeth pointed and long as my thumb?"

Chanter finished his coffee. "Where you hear this stuff?"

"Everywhere."

"You must see it, sometimes men get jealous – our pa is rich and so we'll be too – some men want to fright you. Malice."

"Chant, you know I rather think these fellers were set – not to scare – but to *warn* me."

"Warn you with horror tales."

"*Are* they tales? They said..."

Chanter rose, angry and determined.

So Matt got up too. By now they were almost the same height. They stood glaring at each other.

Chanter said, "They told you old man Proctor is a shape-switcher. He sheds his human skin of a full moon midnight and runs out the house a mountain lion."

"Something like that. And she's the same."

"Do you think our pa," shouted Chanter, "would handfast you to a..."

"Yes," said Matt, cool and hard and steady, though his heart crashed inside him like a fall of rocks. "*Yes*, if the settlement was good enough. Enough land, money. The Proctors are a powerful Family. Yet no one else made a play for Thena."

"Because they knew we Seatons would ask for her."

Matt said, "This summer, late, about three weeks back, I had to ride up that way, through the forests! Let me tell you, brother, what I saw *then*."

That evening Matt hadn't been thinking at all of the Proctors. Some cattle had strayed, so he and his father's hands rode into the woods above the valley. The landscape here was like three patterns on a blanket: the greener trees, birch, maple, oak, amberwood, with already a light dusting of fall red and gold beginning to show; next up, the forests on their higher levels, spruce and larch and pine, dark enough a green to seem black in the levelling sunlight; last of all the mountains that were sky-colour, etched in here and there by now with a line of white.

In less than two hours it would be sunfall. Once the cattle had been found, on the rough wild pasture against the woodland, they minded to make camp for the night and ride back to the Seaton farm the next day.

Matt had known most of these hands since boyhood. Some were his own age. They joked and played around while the coffee boiled on the fire. Then Ephran remembered a little river that ran farther up, where the first pines started. He and Matt and a couple of others decided on some night fishing there. It would be cooler, full moon too, when the flap-fish rose to stare at the sky and were easy caught.

After supper, going to the river, it was Ephran who spoke to Matt. "I guess you know. Joz Proctor's place is all up that way."

Matt said, "I suppose I did." It was perhaps strange he hadn't recalled. But then, he'd never been exactly certain where the Proctor farm and lands began. Hadn't ever tried to learn. Never been tempted to come up and see. It seemed to him right then, as they walked on into the darkness of the forest, he hadn't cared to, nor even wanted to remember now. He added, lightly, "Ever been there, Ephran?"

"Not I. It's all right, Matt. We're at least ten miles below the place."

"Think old man Joz would reckon I was out to spy on him otherwise, to see what I was getting? Run me off?"

"No. Not that."

They walked in silence for a while after this. The big moon was rising by then, leftward, burning holes between the trees.

Ephran, who was eighteen now, had never been one of the ones Matt had heard muttering about Joz and his golden daughter. The first time, when he had been fourteen, Matt had felt he *overheard* the mutters, anyhow. Later, though, he'd wondered if they meant him to, less from spite or stupidity than from that idea of forewarning – just as he was to say to Chanter.

What had the men said?

"…Bad luck for the boy. He don't know no better. But Veniah Seaton should've."

"By the Lord, so he should."

And the lower, more sombre voice of the old man in the corner of the barn: "Not a wife he'll get, but a wild beast. A *beast* for a bride. God help him."

There'd been other incidents through the years after that. In front of Matt even, once or twice – given like a piece of wit: "Proctor, that old puma-man…"

"Joz *Puma's* Farm . . ."

Matt took it all for lies. Then for games. Then…

Then.

The river appeared.

It was slender and coiling, moonlit now to sparkling white.

The other men went on, and Ephran paused, as if to check his line.

"Listen up, Matt," said Ephran, "you don't want to worry too much. About her."

"Why's that?" said Matt, again light and easy.

"Because there are ways. Do your duty by her. There'll be no hardship there. Do that and let her keep her secrets. Then when the time's right, you can be off. Not leave her, I don't mean that, Seatons and Proctors have a union, you'll have to stay wedded. But big place, the Proctor lands. Plenty to do. Just let her be. Don't – try an' rule her or get on her bad side – jus' do as you want and let her do as *her* wants. That's the bestest way."

Matt said, "So you think it's true?"

Ephran scowled. "I don't think no thing at all."

"She's a shape-twist."

"I never said…"

"And her daddy before her."

Ephran glared in his face. "Don't you put words in my mouth. You may be the boss's second-born but I'm freer 'an you. *I* can go off."

Matt had the urge to punch Ephran in the mouth. So instead he nodded. "Fair enough. Let's go fish."

They fished. And the moon and the fish rose high. They laid the slim silver bodies by for breakfast, and not another word was spoken of the Seaton handfast or the Proctor house not ten miles away above, beside the forest.

It was when they had enough catch and were making ready to go back down to the camp.

Matt glanced up, and there across the narrow river, less distance from him than the other men, it stood, pearl in moonlight, and looked at him.

He hadn't seen one alive. In fact, only the drawn one in the book of pictures, when he was schooled.

They haunted the forests and the lower slopes of the mountains. But they were shy of men, only slipping from the shadows of dawn or dusk, once in a while, to kill them. The last occasion one of their kind had killed one of Matt's had been in his childhood, about the time, he thought, he had seen the book-picture. Puma.

None of the other men seemed to have noticed. They were busy stringing the fish.

For the strange moment then, he and it were alone in utter silence, total stillness, unbroken privacy, eye to eye.

Its eyes were smoky and greenish, like old glass, and they glowed. Its coat was smooth and nacreous, glowing too.

Matt thought it would spring at him, straight over the water for his throat or heart. Yet this didn't quite matter. He wasn't afraid.

He could smell the musky, grassy-meaty odour of it.

It opened its red mouth – red even by moonlight – and for a second seemed to laugh – then it sprang about, and the long thick whip of its tail *cracked* the panes of the night apart like glass as it sped away.

All the men whirled round at that and were staring, shouting. Old Cooper raised his gun. It was Ephran bellowed the gun down.

Like a streak of softest dimmest lightning, the racing shape of the great cat slewed off among the pines, veering, vanishing; behind it, it left a sort of afterimage, a kind of *shine* smeared on the dark, but that too swiftly faded.

None of them spoke much to Matt as they trudged down to the pasture. In the camp, each man quickly settled to rigid sleep. Matt lay on his back, staring up at the stars until the moon went all the way over and slid home into the earth like a sheathed knife.

"So I wondered to myself," said Matt to his brother Chanter in *Sure Hold* now, "if that was Thena Proctor, I mean, or her daddy, come down to take a look at me."

Chanter strode to the fire and threw on another log. "You pay too much mind to the chat of the men. Are you sure you even saw that big cat?"

"Oh, I did. All of us did. Ephran was white as a bone. He stopped Cooper shooting it. Could it even have died, though, I wonder?"

Then he left off because he saw Chanter's face, and it had altered. He had never seen Chanter like this before. Not in a good humour, or in a rage, nor with that serious and uneasy expression he had whenever he had to pick up a book, or the daft, happy smile he gained if he glanced at his wife. No, this was a new Chanter – or maybe a very young one, how Chanter had been perhaps when *he* was only a child.

"Matt, I don't know. How can I know? I know our pa meant well by us – both. But I think – I think he never thought enough on this. Probably it's all crazy talk and damn foolery. Those upland Families – they go back a great way, hundreds of years, deep into the roots of the Old Countries... What you saw... what Joz Proctor is – and she, the girl – I've only ever gotten sight of a little sketch someone made of her. Good-looking as summer. But Pa met her. He liked her mightily. Uncommonly fine, he said."

"The puma," said Matt on a slow cold sigh, "was beautiful. Silk and whipcord. Pearl and – blood."

"God, Matty. Thena Proctor's a human girl. She has to be. She *must* be. Human."

Matt smiled. He said, softly, "*Puman*."

2: The Marriage

A spring wedding.

The valleys and hills were still wet with the broken snows, rivers and creeks thick and tumbling with swelled white water. The scent of the pines breathed so fresh, you felt you had never smelled it before.

In the usual way among the Families, neither bride nor groom had been allowed to look at each other. That was custom. The old, humorous saying had it this was to prevent either, or both, making off if they didn't care for what they saw.

None had the gall to try that in the prayer house. Well, they said, ha-ha, only a couple of times, and those long, long ago.

And Matt? He hadn't taken to his heels. He had left off asking questions. He simply *waited.*

No one around him among the Seaton clan acted as if anything abnormal went on. Even Chant didn't, when he and his Anne came to call. He didn't even give Matt a single searching glance.

Matt had anyway grasped by then that he was quite alone.

He'd dreamed of it, the mountain cat, two or three times all through the winter. Nothing very awful. Just – glimpsing it among trees by night, or up on some high mountain ledge, its eyes – *male* – *female* – gleaming.

They drove, trap horses burnished and a-clink with bells, to the prayer house, done up in their smartest, Matt too, bathed and shaved and brushed, the white silk shirt too close on his neck.

What did he feel? Hollow, sort of. Solid and strong enough on the outside, able to nod and curve his mouth, exchange a few words, be polite, not stammering, not stumbling, not in a sweat. His mouth wasn't dry. He noticed his mother, in her new velvet dress, haughty and glad. And Veniah, like a person from a painting of A *Father: The Proud Patriarch...*

They are stone-cut crazy. So he thought as they drove between the leafing trees and into the prayer house yard. *They don't know what they've done.* And along with the hollow feeling, he had too a kind of scorn for them all, which helped, a little.

Inside the building there were early flowers in vases, and all the pewter polished, and the windows letting in the pale clear light. Everyone else, the representatives of the Families, were well dressed as turkeys for a Grace-giving Dinner.

He stood by the altar facing forward, and the minister nodded to him. Then the piano-organ sounded in the upper storey, and all the hairs on Matt's head and neck rose in bristles. For the music meant that here she was, his bride, coming toward him. He wouldn't turn and look to see – a mountain cat in human form and wedding gown, on the arm of her father, the other human mountain cat.

She wore a blue silk dress.

That he *did* see from the corner of his eye, once she stood beside him.

She had only the kind of scent he would have expected, if things were straightforward, cleanness and youngness, expensive perfume from a bottle.

When they had had their hands joined, hers was small and slender, with clean short nails, and two or three little scars.

"And now, say after me…"

He had to look directly down at her then. Not to do so as he swore the marriage vows would have been the action of an insulting dolt – or a coward. So he did. He looked.

Thena Proctor, now in the very seconds of being made over as Thena Seaton, was only about three inches shorter than he.

She was tanned brown, as most of the Farm Family daughters were, unless kept from learning on the land – brown as Matt. Her eyes were brown too, the colour of cobnuts.

She was attractive enough. She had a *thinking* face, with a wide, high forehead, arched brows, straight nose, a full but well-shaped mouth with white teeth in it. Not that she showed them in a smile.

She met his eyes steadily with her own.

How did *she*, then, reckon all this? Oh, marry him for the Scaton-Proctor alliance, the benefit of extra land and power for her clan. And then, when bored, kill him one night out in the fields or forest, with a single swift blow of her puma paw – pretend after, with help from her pa, some other thing had done for him.

Matt had shocked himself.

He felt the blood drain from his face.

That was when her cool hand, so much smaller than his own, gave his the most fleeting squeeze. She shut her right eye at him. So quick – had he imagined – she *winked?*

Taken aback, yet she'd steadied him. He thought after all she was real. Or was it only her animal cunning?

Her hair was arranged in a complicated fashion, all its gilded length and thickness braided and coiled, part pinned up and part let fall down – like corn braids made for Harvest Home.

Matt liked her hair, her eyes, the way she had winked at him. He liked her name, the full version of which the minister had said – Athena. Matt knew from his books *Athena* was the wise warrior goddess of the Ancient Greeks. It might have been fine, really fine, if everything else had been different.

They ate the Wedding Breakfast in the prayer house Goodwill room, among more bunches of flowers.

Here Matt finally met Joz Proctor, an unextraordinary, rangy, dark-haired man, who shook Matt's hand, and clapped him on the back, and said he had heard only worthy and elegant things of Matthew Seaton, and welcome to the Upland Folk.

There was wine. Matt was now like a pair of men. One of whom wasn't unhappy, kept glancing at his new young wife. One of whom, however, stood back in hollow shadows, frowning, tense as a trigger.

Joz had given them a house, as the head of each Family generally did with the new son-in-law. Chanter's house was like that too, gifted by his Anne's father. So after the Breakfast, under a shower of little coloured coins of rice paper, Thena and Matt climbed into a beribboned Proctor trap, and Matt snapped the whip high over the heads of the beribboned grey horses, and off they flew up the hill, in a chink of bells and spangle of sunlight. Just he and she. They two.

"I guess you'd like to change out of that."

This was the first real thing she said to him since they'd been alone – really since they'd met by the altar.

"Uh – yeah. It rubs on my neck."

"And such smooth silk too," she said, almost... playful.

But anyhow, they both went up the splendid wooden staircase and changed in separate rooms into more everyday clothing.

When he came down, one of the house servants was seeing to the fire, but Thena, *Athena,* was lighting the lamps. The servant seemed not to mind her at all. But then, even wild animals, where they had gotten accustomed to people, might behave gently.

They ate a late supper in candlelight.

"Do you like your house, Matthew?" she asked him, courteously. This was the very first she had spoken his name.

"Yes."

"My father spent a lot of thought on it." A lot of money too, obviously.

"Yes, it's a generous and magnificent house."

"I'd like," she said, "to alter a few small things."

"I leave that to you, of course."

"Then I will."

The servant girl came around the table and poured him more coffee, as Maggie would have at home. But *this* was home, now.

"Tomorrow I'll ride out, have a word with the men, take a look at the land," he said in a businesslike way.

"No one expects it, Matthew, not on your first day..." She broke off.

Indeed, nobody would, first morning after the bridal night.

He said, "Oh, well, I'd like to anyhow. Get to know the place."

He had already seen something of the grand extent of it as he drove down in the westering light. Cleared from the surrounding woods and forest, miles of fields awaiting the new-sown grain, tracts of trees kept for timber, cows and sheep and goats. Stables and pigpens, orchards with the blossom flickering pink. The house was called *High Hills.*

There was an interval after the brief discussion. A log cracked on the hearth. But the servants had gone and let them be. Over the mantel, the big old clock with the golden sun-face gave the hour before midnight.

"Well," she said, rising with a spare seamlessness, "I'll go up."

Then she made one flamboyant gesture. She pulled some central comb or pin from her braided hair and it rushed down around her, down to the backs of her knees, as promised. As it fell, it frayed out of the braids like water from an unfrozen spring and seemed to give off sparks like the fire.

She turned then to look at him over her shoulder.

"No need for you to come up to me yet, Matthew Seaton." She spoke level as a balance. "Nor any need to come upstairs at all. If you'd rather not."

"Oh, but I…" he said, having already lurched to his feet as a gentleman should.

"*Oh, but.* Oh, but you don't want me, that's plain enough. I have no trouble with *you*. You're a strong, handsome man, with very honest eyes. But if you have trouble with me, then we can keep apart."

And so saying she left him there, his mouth hung open.

It was nearly midnight, his coffee cold on the table and the candles mostly burned out, when he pushed back his chair once more and went after her up the stair.

At her door, he knocked. He thought perhaps she was asleep by now. Did he hope so? But she answered, soft and calm, and he undid the door and went in.

The big bedroom, the very bed, were of the best. White feather pillows, crisp white linen sheets, a quilt stitched by twenty women into the patterns of running deer and starry nights.

Thena sat propped on pillows. Her hair poured all around her like golden treacle. She was reading a book. She glanced at him. "Shall I move over and make room, or stay put?"

Matt shut the door behind him.

"You're a splendour," he said, colouring a little at his own words. "All any man'd want. It isn't that."

She looked at him, not blinking. In the sidelong lamplight her eyes now shone differently. He had seen a precious stone like it once – a topaz. Like that.

"Then?" she quietly asked.

What could he say?

Something in him, that wasn't him – or was more him than *he* was – took a firm sudden grip on his mind, his blood, even perhaps his heart. He said, "I'd like it goodly if you would move over a little, Thena Seaton."

While he took off his boots, she lowered the lamp. And in the window he saw the stars of the quilt had gotten away, and were returned safely to the midnight sky.

3: The Wife

Summer came. It came into the new house too, unrolled over the stone floors in transparent yellow carpets, sliding along the oak banister of the stair, turning windows to diamonds.

Outside, the fields ripened through green to blond. In the orchard, apples blazed red. The peach vine growing on the ancient hackwood tree was hung with round lanterns of fruit.

He got along well with the hands, some of whom were Joz Proctor's, some the roving kind that arrived to work each summer for cash but were known and reliable for all that. Once they were sure Matt knew his business with crops and beasts, they gave him their respect with their casual helpful friendliness. None of them had anything to say about Joz Proctor but what you'd expect, seeing they dealt here with Joz's son-in-law.

None of them seemed at all uneasy either. Even when their tasks kept them near the house. And none of them had a strange look for Thena – save now and then, on seeing her, one of the newer younger boys coloured up or smiled appreciatively to himself.

Every night when Matt went home to the house, the big, cool rooms, well swept and polished, would light with lamps as the day went out. Coming in he might hear Thena too, playing the old pianotto in the parlour. She played quite brilliantly, though she never sang. Sometimes she persuaded Matt to do that. He had a good tenor voice, she said, true to the note. Otherwise, when the meal was done, they'd sit reading each side the fire, which even in summer was generally needed once the sun went down. She might read something out to him, some story from a myth, or piece of a play by some old dramatist or poet. He might do the same. But they seldom went up late to bed. They told each other things besides about their childhood – how he had hitched his first dog to a cart, and ridden over the fields, pretending he was a charioteer from Roman times; how she had seen a falling star once that was bright blue, and no one believed her, but Matt said he did.

She wasn't one for chores, darning or sewing, left all that to the house girls. But frequently she drove them laughing out of the kitchen and cooked up a feast for him. Some days they rode out together along the land, debating the state of this or that.

Did he love her by then, so fast? He couldn't say. But he was glad to come back to her, glad to be with her, always. Thought of her often in the day, especially when he was far off on the outskirts of the mountains and wouldn't see her or lie at her side that night.

And she. Did *she* love *him*?

A woman did, surely, if she acted to you as Thena did to Matt. The other girls he had known who had definitely loved him, at least for a while, had acted in similar ways, though none so intelligently and wonderfully as she. She was like a young princess, regal in her generous giving, strict only with herself, and even in that never cold.

How had he ever been wary, been afraid of her? Why hadn't he known that the stupid tales were only that, just what Chant had warned him of, jealousy and empty-headed gossip? Aside from all else, five full moons had by then gone by. She had been in his arms on each of those nights and never stirred till morning.

For Matt's wife was no more a were-beast, a shape-twister, than the sun was dead when it set.

It was getting on for leaf-fall, and the farm busy and soon to be more so with harvest.

That night they went upstairs directly after supper, around nine by the sun-clock, for Matt needed to be away with the dawn.

He was brushing her hair. His mother had let him do this too, when he was much younger. It had fascinated him then, did so now, the liveness of a woman's hair, its scents and electric quiverings, as if it were another separate animal…

"When will you be home again?" Thena asked, her eyes shut as she leaned back into the brush. Any woman might ask this of her young husband.

"Oh, not for a night, I'd say. More's the pity."

"I see," she said. She sounded just a touch – what? Unhappy? He was glad to hear.

"Maybe," he said, "I *can* get back tomorrow, very late – would that do better?"

"No, Matt," she said. "Don't hurry home."

Something in him checked. He stopped the brushing.

As if joking, he said, "Why, don't you want me home if I can be?

Would I disturb you so much arriving in the little hours? You don't often mind when I wake you."

She put out one of her slim calloused hands and covered his wrist. "Come home if you want, Matt. It's only, if you do, I may be from the house."

The pall cleared from his brain. Of course. There was a baby about to be born, several miles off at the next big farm. Joz's other kin, one of the Fletcher Family. Probably they had asked Thena, now a married woman, to help out when the time came.

"Well I'll miss you. I hope Fletcher's wife is swift in delivery, for her sake – and mine."

"Oh, Matt, no, I'm not going there. That child's not due till Honeymass."

Again taken aback, he left off brushing completely. He stepped away, and with a mild *Thank you*, she gathered all her hair in over her right shoulder like a waterfall. She was going to braid it and he wanted to stop her. He loved her hair loose in their bed. But he said nothing of that now. He said, "Then why won't you be at home at our house, Thena?"

Her hands continued braiding. He couldn't see her face. Matt moved around her and seated himself across from her in the large carved chair in the corner. He could still tell nothing from her face. Nor did she reply.

He said again, very flat, "Do you want me to think you have some fancy lover you like better'n me? If not, say where you're going."

Then she answered promptly. "Into the forest."

The bedroom lamps were trimmed and rosy. None of them went out. But it was as if the whole room – the house – the land outside – plunged down into a deeper, *darker* darkness.

All these months he had disbelieved and nearly forgotten his earlier fears. Yet instantly they returned, leaping on him, sinking in their fangs, their claws, lashing their tails to break the panes of night and of his peace.

"The forest? *Why?* No, Thena. Look at me. And tell me the truth."

She let go of the braid.

She raised her head and met his eyes with her topaz ones, and abruptly he knew that no woman's eyes, even in sidelong lampshine, ever went that colour.

As if she simply told him the price of wheat, she said to him, "Because I have a need now, sometimes, to be that other thing I am. The thing not human, and which once you saw, when I came down from the woods to look at you as you fished, by the river in the moon."

Matt shook from head to foot. He could barely see her, she seemed wrapped in a mist, only her eyes burning out at him. "No…" he said.

"Yes," she said. "It's how it is with me. It isn't at full moon I have to change, nor any other time, not in that way. But sometimes – as another woman might want very much to wear a red dress, or to eat a certain food, or travel to a certain house or town – like *that*. I have a choice. But I want to and *choose* now to do it."

He saw in his mind's eye what she had chosen then – as another chose to visit or wear red: the mountain cat with its pelt of dusk. The puma. *The shape-twist.*

"No, Thena… no, no."

She left him immediately. She walked out of the bedroom, and went to the other little bedroom, and shut the door. And Matt went on sitting in the carved chair. He sat there until four in the morning, when anyway he must get up for the dawn ride.

Afterward he never recalled much about what he did that day. It was to do with the stock, fences, something of that sort. But though he dealt with it, it was never him. And by sunfall he and the men were up along Tangle Ridge, the black forests curling below, and the house he shared with Thena far away.

He always thought of her. But today he had thought of nothing else.

Matt kept asking himself if he had heard her rightly. Had she truly said what he recollected? Or was he losing his wits? But even though he couldn't fully involve himself in his work, he knew he had seen to it. And what he had heard the other men say to him had been *logical* and *coherent*. While everything he'd looked at was what you would reckon on. The sun hadn't risen in the north, and now it didn't sink in the east. So he hadn't gone mad, nor had the world. What she had said, therefore, she had said. He'd not imagined it.

He did wonder – why? for it scarcely mattered – how she had known he was fishing that past night at the river. But it seemed to him, uneasily, the puma side of her had sharper senses – perhaps she had picked up the *scent* of him, found him in that animal way. *Tracked* him.

Or was she only *lying*?

Was it *all* some damned lie, meant to throw him, scare him – yet why'd she do that? She loved him – maybe she didn't.

Maybe she hated his guts and it was all a plan to be shot of him, or else *send* him crazy and get rid *that* way.

By sundown his head ached.

He wanted only to go to sleep, off beyond the fire, solid rock under him, and the stars staring back in his eyes.

But instead, having let the horse rest herself a while, and having shared a meal without appetite, Matt swung again into the saddle. The men laughed at him, just a bit, not unkindly. He and his wife had been wed less than six months. No wonder he'd want to ride home through the night.

The horse picked her way off the ridge, and an hour later, delicate and firm-footed, in among the pines.

The trees had the tang of fall already on them, and the streams were shallow as they trickled downhill.

Every glint of moonlight, every deeper shadow, took on the form for him of topaz-green-glass eyes, a slink of four-legged body, round ears, pointed teeth...

But it never was.

The moon was only a little thing, thin and new and curved. Like the shed claw-case of a cat.

Three more hours he rode down through the forest, into stands of larch and oak and amberwood. In the end he must have fallen asleep, sitting there on the sure-footed mare. But the horse knew the way, the way home.

Matt reached the house before sunrise. By the time he went into the bedroom, he was thinking in a sort of dream. He thought she would be there, asleep, her gold hair on the pillows. But she wasn't there. And in the house no one was about, and outside the man who had come to stable the horse, old Seph, was the same as he always was. Not a sign anyplace that anything was wrong. Except the empty bed and, when Matt tried the door, the other smaller room was also empty. He slept in there anyway, in the smaller room.

When he woke again it was full day and everything going on at its usual pace. And when he went down, Thena was in the parlour, helping one of the girls to clean some silver, both of them laughing over something. And Thena greeted him apparently without a care and came over to kiss his cheek. And murmured, "Don't upset the girl. Make pretend all's well."

So he did. And having had his breakfast, he went out to the fields.

They didn't meet, after that, he and Thena, till supper.

Silence had come back with him. It made a third at the table. When the servants left them, there they were, the three of them: he, Thena, the silence.

In the end he spoke.

"What shall I do?"

He had thought of all sorts of things he might say – demands, threats, making fun of it even. Or saying she had made a fool of him because he'd believed her.

But all he said was that. *What shall I do?*

She answered him straight back. "Come out with me tonight."

"...come out..."

"Come out and see for yourself. Oh," she added, "I don't think you'll faint away, will you, Matthew Seaton? Or *run* away. I think you'll take a book-learned scientific interest in it. Won't you?"

"To see you change..."

"To see me change into my other self."

"My God," he said. He gazed at the plate, where most of his food lay untouched. "Is it true?"

"You know it is. Or why this fuss?"

"Thena," he said.

He put his head into his hands.

At last she came and rested her own hand, cool and steady, on his burning neck. How human it felt, this slim hand with its scars, human and *known*, and kind.

"In God's world," she said, "so many wonders. Who are we to argue with such a wise magician as God? Midnight," she whispered, as if inviting him to an unlawful tryst. "By the old door."

Then, she was gone.

The old door led from the cellar. You got down there by way of the kitchen, but only Thena and he had a key to the cellarage. Going to meet her there he partly feared, his distress so overall he barely felt it, that already she would be... *in that other shape.* But she wasn't. She was just Thena, her hair roped round her head, and dressed as she did to go riding.

Together they slipped out into the soft cold of an early fall night.

Stars roared like silver gunshot in the black. No moon was up, or else it had come and gone; Matt couldn't recall what the moon did tonight, only that it wasn't full, was in its first quarter, and that the moon had no effect on her. To *alter* was her *choice.* Puman...

They didn't take the horses. They strode from the house and farmland, up through the tall tasselled fields, reached the woods and went into them.

Again, silence accompanied them all this while.

Then, all at once, Thena turned and caught his face lightly in both hands and kissed his mouth.

"This is mountain country, Matt, it isn't the Valley of the Shadow."

And *then* – she was darting away among the trees, and he too must run to keep her in sight.

The trees flashed by. Stars flashed between. The mountains lifted beyond, very near-seeming, very high, a wall built around everything, keeping everything in. Was it possible to climb right up those mountains? Get over them to the other side? Tonight it seemed to him nothing *lay* on the other side. For here was the last border of the world, what the ancients had called *Ultima Thule.*

She stopped still in a glade, where already the rocky steps showed that were the first treads of the mountain staircase. A creek ran through, and Thena pulled off her clothes, everything she wore, and loosed her hair out of its combs as she had that very first night. Clothed now quite modestly in the striped dapple of the starlit pines, she lay down on her knees and elbows and lapped from the stream, as an animal did.

He couldn't see her clearly. Couldn't see... Only how the shadows shifted, spilled. Fell differently. She was a young woman drinking from the water, then a creature neither woman nor beast – and next, in only half a minute – or half a year, for that was how slow it seemed to him – she was the puma in its velvet pelt, raising its muzzle, mouth dripping crystal from the creek, its eyes marked like flowers, and tail slowly lashing.

This... my wife.

They stared at each another. To his – almost angry –

astonishment Matt felt no particular fear. He was terrified and yet beyond terror. Or rather all things were so terrible and fearful and Thena and the puma only one slight splinter dazzling from the chaos.

And dazzled he was. For too – so beautiful.

The puma – was beautiful.

It slinked upright and shook away the last beads of water.

When it spun about, it moved like quicksilver, mercury in the jar of darkness… It. *She.*

He couldn't follow her now. He would never catch her, as she had become. How curious. There was suddenly, to all of it, a sense only of the *normal.*

Matt sat down by the creek, where her clothes sprawled in a heap as if dead. Idiotically he had the urge to pick them up, spread them, perhaps fold them in a tidy way. He didn't.

He tried to decide now what to do, but in fact this seemed redundant. There was no urgency. Was he tired? He couldn't have said. He selected pebbles and dropped them idly in the water.

When she came back, which was perhaps only two hours later, she brought a small slain deer with her, gripped in her jaws. He was not shocked or repelled by this. He had expected it, maybe. It had been neatly and swiftly killed by a single bite to the back of the neck. Matt had seen even the best shots among the hands, even Chant, who was a fine hunter, sometimes misjudge, causing an animal suffering and panic before it could be finished. When she, the puma, sat across the carcass from him, watching him, he thought he was sure that what Thena said to him, if wordlessly, was, *See, this is better.*

And it was. All of it – was.

They slept by the stream, he and the cat, a few feet between them – but when he stirred in sleep once, they were back to back, and her warmth was good. She did him no harm. Though he couldn't bring himself to touch her with his hands, this was less nervousness than a sort of respect. She smelled of grass and balsam from the pines, of cold upper air, of stars. And of killing and blood.

He hadn't meant to sleep. Somehow, he hadn't been able to make himself understand.

But in the sunrise when he wakened, the trees painted pink along their eastern stems, Thena was there as a woman. She had dressed and set a fire, portioned the deer, and was cooking it slowly. The glorious savour of freshest roasting meat rose up on a blue smoke.

"Well," she said.

"Did I dream it?" he said.

"Maybe you did too."

"No, I didn't dream. Oh, Thena... what's that *like?* To be – *that?*"

"It's wonderful," she answered simply. "What else?"

"But you knew me, even then?"

"I know you all. It isn't I cease to be myself. Or that I forget. Only I'm another kind of *me*. The true one, do you think?"

After they ate the meat and drank from the stream, they lay back on the pine needles. If until then he hadn't quite loved her, now he did. That was the strangest part of it, he thought ever after. That he *loved* her fully then, once he had seen her puma-soul. And he believed, that day, that nothing now could destroy their union. He had confronted the terror, and it was *no* terror, only a great, rare miracle, the blessing of God. And there was magic in the world, as the myths and stories in books had always told him.

4: The Beast

Years on, when he was older, Matthew Seaton sometimes asked himself if this was, precisely, what was at the root of his reaction – magic. Sorcery – a spell. She had put some sort of hex on him, bewitched and made him her dupe.

It hadn't felt like that. Rather, it had felt like the most reasonable *natural* thing. And the love – that too.

Surely something wicked might inspire all types of wrong emotion, such as greed or cruelty or rage. But it wouldn't bring on feelings of pure happiness. Or such a sense of rightness, harmony. Hope.

This then was the worst of it, in one way.

Yet only in one.

They did talk afterward, after the night in the forest. She let him ask his questions, answered them without hesitation. The substance of it was that her shape-switching had begun in infancy. It was the same, she implied, for her father, and when young he had often taken cat form – but it seemed with age he turned to it less and less. Nor had she ever seen it happen. None had. It was for him a private thing. He only told *her* when he became aware that she also had the gift. And *gift* was how he termed it, comparing it as she grew older to her talent for the pianotto. He said he had heard his great-grandmother had powers of a similar sort. He never revealed who told *him* about that.

As to whether Thena had been afraid when first she found what she could do, she replied no – only, perhaps oddly as she was then a child, she had known intuitively to keep it hidden from others. Yet something had prompted her to tell Joz. But it had *frightened* her not at all. It had seemed always merely what *should* happen, as presumably it had when she had learned to walk and talk, and presently to read. She said that some of the commonplace human changes that occurred in her body as she became a woman had alarmed her far more.

Again, much later, Matt – looking back at it – was startled by his calm questions and her frank answers. He could remember, by then stunned and oppressed, that at that time nothing about her 'gift' anymore disquieted him. Indeed, he left her to indulge in her *other* life, felt no misgiving, let alone horror. And this of course *was* horrible. Horrible beyond thought or words.

Stranger too – or not strange, not at all given the rest – was how he began almost to lose interest in her uncanny pursuit, leaving her to solitary enjoyment, just kissing her farewell on such nights, letting her go without a qualm. As if she only went on a visit to some trusted neighbour.

It had seemed to him then that everyone in the house called *High Hills*, and on their land, knew what Thena did. They must see her come and go but were reassured they need fear nothing from her. Perhaps even the very cattle and sheep that grazed the slopes saw her pass in her shadow-shape, the blood of deer on her breath, and never even flicked an ear. Thena would not prey on her own. Thena, even when puma, stayed mistress and guardian.

Besides, anyhow, by the time the first snows began to arrive, she had told Matt *they* had something far more important on their hands. She was pregnant. He and she were to have a child.

Thena withdrew into herself in the last months of her pregnancy. Some women did this. Matt had seen it with his own mother, when the younger children came. Rather daunted by the idea of fatherhood, he already treated her with a certain awed caution. Still he was happy, and as the good wishes of the hands poured over him, pleased with himself.

Once the snow eased away, the Family visits began. The Seaton clan was followed by Proctors and Fletchers. He saw people young and old he'd met once at the wedding and barely once since. Joz was just as he recalled, well humoured and approving of both the baby, and the running of the farm. But he too was remote somehow, as he had seemed before. It came to Matt, though he scarcely considered it then, that this ultimate remoteness belonged in Thena too. However close and connected he and she might become, some part of her stayed always far off, behind her eyes, beyond the mind's horizon. As with her father, the puma part of her? The sorcerous and elemental part...

As the fields greened with new summer, Thena told Matt she believed the baby might come a little early.

Soon heavy with the child, she hadn't, from her fourth month, gone off anymore at night. They did not discuss it. It seemed to him only sensible that she didn't indulge the shape-switch at this time. Though she had done it, he realised at the beginning of her pregnancy, perhaps not yet aware she carried. What effect would such an action have on the growing being inside her? He never asked her that and never himself fretted. He trusted Thena. Again, in the future, he would remember that. And curse himself as blind.

Now and then, on certain nights, he did find her at a window, gazing out toward the forests and mountains. He noticed, when she gazed – he liked to see it – one of her hands always rested protectively on her swelling stomach.

Thena was right. The child was nearly two weeks premature.

He was away the day her labour started. Returning he found the house moving to a kind of ritualistic uproar. The doctor's trap stood in the yard, women ran up and down the staircase. No one, however, forgot Matt's comforts. Hot coffee and fresh water stood waiting. The bath had been drawn. His evening meal, he was assured, was in preparation.

When urgently he asked after his wife, they tried to keep him from her. The doctor was there, and two of the Proctor-Fletcher women. Finally, he let them see his anger – or his nerves – and they allowed him to go up too.

Thena was in the bed, blue rings round her eyes, but smiling gravely. "Brace up, Matthew," she told him. "Within the hour I'll have it done."

Then they shooed him out again, the women. And twenty minutes after he heard Thena give a loud savage cry, the only violent noise she had made. He dropped the china coffee cup and bounded up the stair, where the doctor caught him. "All's nicely, Matt. Listen, do you hear?" And Matt heard a baby crying.

"My wife...!" he shouted.

But when they let him go in again Thena lay there still, still gravely smiling, now with the child in her arms.

The baby was a girl. He didn't mind that, nor the fact the fluff of hair on her head was dark, not golden. And he praised the baby, because that was expected, and too, if he didn't, some of them might think he sulked at not receiving a son. But really, he hardly saw it – her, this girl, if he were honest. She was just an object, like a dear little newborn lamb, useful, attractive – unimportant. All he cared about was that Thena had come through the birth and held out her hand to him.

Fatherly feeling might have found him later. He didn't seek it. More than all else, as the month went on, he felt a sort of confusion. For now another was with them. He and Thena – and the child. Three of them. Like the silence that had been with them that other time, he and she, and it.

He had a dream one night, and for a while on other nights. Always the same. There was no definite image, only vague shiftings of shade and moonlight in what might be forest. And an unknown voice, not male or female. Which said quietly to him in his sleep, "Thena." And then, "The puma's daughter." And this upset him in the dream, as if he didn't know, had never heard even a rumour of shape-twisting, let alone *seen* her change, lain back to back with her in that form, eaten of her kill, loved her better for all of it.

There was a piece of music Thena had sometimes played. Matt couldn't ever remember the composer; he'd never liked it much. Beginning softly and seeming rather dull to him, so his thoughts wandered, then abruptly it changed tempo, becoming a ragged gallop full of fury and foreboding, ending with two or three clashing chords that could make you jump.

The sun-clock showed the days and nights as they went by. The farm's work-journal showed the passage of weeks and months. The seasons altered in their ever changing, ever unalterable fashion. As did the moon.

People came and went as well, in their own correct stages of visit, hire, service.

It wasn't so long, anyhow. Far less than a year. Far more than a century.

In this space they grew apart, the husband and his wife. Like two strong trees, one leaning like a dancer to the breeze, the other bending at a tilt in the earth, backward, sinking.

It was Matt who sank and looked backward. He tried to recapture what they had been before the child came. Or what he believed they'd been. But the child was always there somewhere, needing something. Present – if not in the room, then in the house – and a woman would appear to fetch Thena, who left her cooking or the pianotto, or put down her book, and went away.

But then Thena too began to go away on her own account. There was a nurse at such times, for the child. The notion was that this allowed Matt and Thena a night together. But on those nights, she didn't remain with Matt. It was the forest she went to, like a lover.

For she never said to him now, *Come with me.* And he never offered her company. She wouldn't want it, would she? She had company enough, her own.

How thin, he thought, *her profound patience must be wearing with her child.* She was its slave. *He* must let her go.

The baby was starting to toddle and was due to be God-blessed soon at the prayer house, and there was to be a big party. Spring was on the land again also, calling up sap, and extra work, and memory.

And a night fell when Matt was exhausted, sleeping as hard as if he were roping cows or tying the sheaves. Yet he woke. Something wakened him.

He lay on his back in their bed and wondered what it was – and then saw the moon burning in the window, full and white as a bonfire of snow.

The room was palest blue with light, and in a moment more he saw Thena was gone from the bed. Putting out his hand, he felt that her side of the mattress was cold.

Nor was this a night for the nurse to watch the baby. It must be lying in the cot in the corner and would wake and begin it – her – loud lamb's bleating for Thena – and Thena wasn't there. So Matt sat up and looked at the cot, and it was empty. Empty as the bed, and as anything meant to hold something else safe, when a theft has happened.

If never before had the child meant anything to him, now suddenly she did.

Her name, at the God-blessing, was to be declared as Amy.

Matt called it aloud, "*Amy! Amy!*" and sprang from the covers. He rushed to the small room, where the nurse slept when the cot was moved there – but no one was there now, not the nurse, never Thena and the child. He'd known this would be so.

Matt flung on his clothes, his boots. He dashed down through the house. Nobody was about. Not even out in the stable. He slung the saddle on his horse and galloped away, straight through the young-sown fields, cleaving them.

He knew where she'd gone, Thena, his wife.

His heart was pounding in his brain, which was full too of one terrible picture. He thought of the old religious phrase: *And the scales drop't from mine eyes.*

Blind – blind fool. She was a *beast*, daughter of a *beast*. A mountain cat – and she had taken his child with her up into the wilderness of pines and rocks under the glare of the bitter, burning moon.

Oh, the picture. It lit his mind with terror as the wicked moon the world. A puma running with its red mouth just ajar on a thing held clamped within its jaws, a small bundle, with a fluff of darkish hair, faintly crying on a lamb's lost bleat.

It was as he entered the first mass of the trees, looking up, he saw. Bright-lighted on a shelf of stone above, trotting through from one tree line to another. The silver puma with the little bundle, exactly as he saw it in his head, gripped in by the sparkle of white teeth.

He pulled the horse's head round so sharply she swerved and almost unseated him. Frozen, he clung there, staring up at his baby in the fangs of death.

Peculiarly none of this had made a sound or attracted the attention of the cat. The child didn't cry. Could it be – *she* had already killed it?

Then the pines reabsorbed them, those two joined figures, and the hex broke from him and he floundered from the horse and left her, and ran, *ran* up the chunky side of the mountainous forest, with his hunting rifle in his hand.

In any myth, or tale like that, he must have located them. In reality it wasn't likely. He knew it and took no notice. Matt was *living* in a legend. And this was finally proven, when at last he ran to the brink of the cold blue moonlight. And there they were, on the ice-blue grass, Thena and her baby. And they...

They were playing. But not as a human mother and her human infant ever play. For Thena was a mountain lion, and Amy was her cub. No room was ever shined up by a lamp so light to show Matt, clear as day, the sleek puma mother, rolling and boxing with the energetic cub, it carelessly nipping her, and she gentle and claw-sheathed, while both their dusken pelts gleamed from moon-powder, and their crimson mouths were open, the mother to mimic growls, the infant to spit back and warble as best she could. Open-mouthed, they seemed to be both of them, laughing. But when the play ended and the puma lay down to lick the cub for a bath, her hoarse purr was louder in the night than any other sound.

Matt stood by the tree that hid him. He thought after, they should surely have known he was there, only their total involvement with each other and themselves shut out his presence. Hidden as if invisible, he might have ceased to exist.

So he watched them for a while. And when the moon passed over, and the edge of the forest was no longer a flame of light, but a shattered muddle of stripes and angles, he was yet able to watch one further thing. And this was how both creatures changed, quick and easy, back into their human form. Then there she was, Thena. And her baby. And Thena picked up the child, and kissed her, and humanly laughed and held her high, laughing, proud and laughing with joy, and the little child laughed back, waving at the night her little hands which, minutes before, had been the paws of a cat.

She had never been his. Neither of them. Not Thena. Not Thena's daughter. No, they came of another race. The shape-twisting kind. *Him* she had used. And could Thena harm her baby? Never. Thena loved her. *Knew* her. They were to each other all and everything and needed no one else on earth.

He'd wondered in the before-time, if it was possible to ride all the way up to some mountain pass, and so cross the mountains and get over to the other places, where other people were. Human people. Ordinary.

That night Matt Seaton, with only his horse and his gun, and the clothes he stood in, climbed up the side of the world, and combed the ridges until he did find some way through. He left all behind him. His kinfolk, the Seaton-Proctor alliance and the Families, his property, himself. His marriage and his fatherhood he didn't leave, they'd been stolen already. Stolen by his jealousy. By his cheated humanness, and his lonely human heart.

Author's Note:

The Beastly Bride [the anthology in which this story first appeared] is a very evocative title. From it I got the instant idea of a reverse of the usual 'Beauty and the Beast' scenario – this time the reluctant and alarmed young man going uneasily to wed an unknown and supernaturally beastly young woman.

(Of course, sometimes one forgets, in any strictly arranged marriage sight unseen, there may well be severe qualms on both sides.)

Then I needed to decide what kind of beast. I chose the puma (or mountain lion) because though I've always loved its beauty, its cry, heard by me in a movie when I was about eleven, seemed terrifying. (Strangely, that cry is the one pumaesque attribute not mentioned in this tale.) With the puma settled on, its natural habitat was also immediately there, less a backdrop than a third main character: a parallel North American Rockies, probably around 1840.

THE RETURN OF BERENICE

Author's Note: Since my early teens, I was interested in Poe. At sixteen, a friend lent me a huge Collected Works. In this was Berenice. *I read the story and couldn't understand the basic, if horrifying, scenario. One night I read it again and thought, with darkest horror, so that's it! My friend, an intelligent young woman, hadn't got it at all. I've been haunted by the tale for years.*

Proprium humani ingenil est odisse quern laeseris.
(It is part of human nature to abhor the one you harm.)
— *Tacitus*

Only some while after the events I shall recount, did I learn of them, and only then, too, was I told – in that kind of secrecy, the seal of which demands, finally, to be broken – of the concluding scenes of the tragedy of the man known solely to me as Egaeus, and his cousin Berenice.

The Family was immensely rich, and not, in itself, unpowerful. But for their male relative, Egaeus; he was a scholar and a recluse. He had no interest, it seemed, in outer things. He dwelled within the House, among his books and personal fascinations. Something of an invalid, he appeared himself to have confessed that his observation and character were actually obsessive, perhaps to the point of slight mania. An eccentric, then, yet he did no harm and caused his Family neither distress nor shame. Until, alas, the last acts of his life.

The Family records have it that some while before that time, he had become engaged to marry his cousin, who also lived in the House. Initially the arrangement had seemed to be completely to her liking, and to his, although his generally remote manner did not evince an especially passionate delight. She was, however, a lovely young woman, gently vivacious, slender, pale and clear as a lily, seeming ideal in all forms. What else could such a sensitive aficionado of the Fine, indeed the *Perfect,* as Egaeus, tolerate. Dynastically, and in other ways, their match suited their House exactly.

Most unfortunately nevertheless, and with no warning, a malady of incalculable proportions then struck down Berenice, she who had been the hale and able-bodied partner of the cousins. Far more ill than Egaeus the misfortuned girl became, shocking all, and her ailment, both mysterious and intransigent, had, it turned out, no negotiable cure.

While Egaeus reportedly declared: "I knew her not – or knew her no longer as Berenice."

The disease involved, additionally, a form of what is detailed as epilepsy, whose fits could induce a deathlike trance. Although her recoveries from these attacks were 'startlingly abrupt'.

Perhaps it might go without saying, in the atmosphere of this, Egaeus's own sickness grew worse. Which brought on additionally an increase in his *morbid* exaggeration of attention to the most ordinary matters and objects. He would lose himself nights long in staring at the flame of a lamp, or whole days lost in the scent of some plant. He considered these obsessions 'frivolous'.

Naturally, one may not be amazed by any of that, given what had fallen on Berenice.

Yet while feeling perhaps mostly aesthetic distress for his cousin, he began to be obsessive over the physical changes he noted in her...

Let it be said too, rather repellently, he now admitted to never having loved her, and indeed that he had already come to regret the inevitable tradition of marriage that would normally join them forever, and was like a shackle to him.

There arrived instead a period, then, during which, perhaps predictably, he saw Berenice in a fresh and feverishly repulsive light. It seemed to him her dark hair had gone yellow; *had* it so? Her unlustred eyes had lost both *pupils* and colour. Last of all, he noted the *teeth* of Berenice. They, unlike the remainder of her vanquished frame, looked to have grown uniquely and flawlessly long, white and obdurate. He dwelled then upon them, both when viewing them, and in subsequent reverie. They represented to him now a separate Power, and a very strong one, where Berenice was no longer humanly vital in the least. They seemed to him, as it were, independent beings in their own adamantine right.

Not so long after the revelation of her teeth to him, his cousin abruptly died, amid a terrible outcry that shook the House like an earthquake.

Her own destiny, her destination now, could only be the doors of the grave, and presently the burial was performed in the grounds of the House, and the doors of the Sarcophagus shut fast as the frozen lids of two dead eyes. Following which all else too certainly might have been expected desolately to calm and to decay.

But, for Egaeus at least, it did not.

On the exact evening of her interment, he awakened in the library, where he sat so very often.

He afterwards alluded to feelings both of wild excitement and vague horror. But he could, apparently, make nothing comprehensive of his own mood. Yet he seemed, even so, to hear the shrieking of a female voice on and on in his head. He had, he thought, 'done a deed' – but what?

A small box lay on the table by him, rather oddly, and it made him shudder, if again in utter ignorance as to why.

This blissful ignorance was not to linger.

In another while, a servant crept into the room. The man was plainly in an agony of fear. It seemed a shrieking had indeed occurred, cracking wide the vaulted silence of the night. This had sent the entire Household, (aside, evidently, from the self-locked Egaeus himself), in the direction of the unholy noise: which, it transpired, was the now-violated tomb of Berenice.

The servant next, shivering and wan, pointed out to Egaeus that Egaeus's clothes were filthy with damp earth and soil, and – far worse – thick with blood. The servant in sequence indicated a muddied spade left leaning on the library wall. Only at this did Egaeus reach out and grasp the strange little box on the table, then uncontrollably dropped it at once. Thus he beheld how it broke in bits. And from it, with a rattling note, there flew out the brutal and cruel instruments of dental surgery. Plus thirty-two 'small, white and ivory-looking substances' that were cast all about the floor.

It would appear that even at such a juncture, Egaeus did not immediately identify them as teeth; the perfect and vital teeth of his dead cousin, Berenice.

I have to confide here that what amazed me when initially informed of all this, was Egaeus's total and continuing, likely genuine, unawareness and misunderstanding of what he had actually done – which was, evidently, to break into his cousin's Sarcophagus and rip and cut, by means of the dental implements he had somehow acquired, every exquisite, long, white tooth from her head. He appeared to persist in believing he had effected this admittedly, at least, in a sort of trance, surely one as intense as any of her own during her sickness, solely because of his insane obsession with minute details. But it goes really without saying, does it not, why he was driven to carry out so vile and disgusting a deed? He had plainly become aware, in some annex even of his convoluted mind, that Berenice had become, although by what means he did not know, nor do any, it seems, a vampire. And in order to save others, not to mention the denizens of his ancestral House, he had gone at once to deprive her of her major weapon, her piercing fangs. That he brought them back with him, perhaps, is in itself curious and disturbing. But then, he would, that way, have them with him, a proof of her disarming. If any further proof of the fact – and the efficacy – of the action is demanded, the awful shrieking that resulted in the tomb unarguably furnished it. The truly dead do not shriek. That are dead. But Egaeus's cousin was Un-dead. And by his peculiar and frankly alarming singlemindedness, he rendered, or attempted to, a great service to the rest of the area.

The history of this, then, might end here. But it does not. For subsequent occurrences take the dreadful affair farther, unless one does not at all in any way credit the rest of the report which was rendered me. We are all the judges and arbitrators of our own opinions, or we should be. Each then must draw his conclusion, as it seems apt to him.

The House did not expose Egaeus to any external or public justice. They did not desire, no doubt, such an exposure themselves. Instead they kept him, as ever, a rare and useless flower, in his tropic case, and in addition, their own unofficial prisoner now. He kept his few favourite rooms and was denied meanwhile any access to the outer environs, including the remainder of the Mansion. Let alone did he retain any social unity with members of his Family Tribe. Servants, choicelessly selected, two particular men, exclusively waited on him, servitors and jailers. They seldom spoke to him beyond the barest phrase. Very likely he would not have minded this at all. He had never been garrulous, nor desirous of intimacy, when in the mode of his original life. He was fed, kept in clean linen, awarded minor comforts and all necessities. He was 'forgotten', erased from thought.

Some months passed through various dismal seasons towards a sunless summer. Beyond the gracious windows of the blinded, shadowy building, the park of trees hung thickly massed with heavy and leaden leaves, as if packs of whispering creatures had gathered on their boughs, to watch and monitor, savagely and mockingly, the goings on of human things.

Apparently, it was a nocturnal of full moon, white rifts of glare flung like bolts of bleached flame across and over the grounds and the House, making distorted patchwork most deceptive to the clearest eye.

As usual, Egaeus was not abed, although it was well past the second hour of the morning. In the library he sat. At that same table. The spade and the fatal box, with its contents, had, naturally, seasons before, been removed. There was by then no physical clue to history, even for him.

In what he expressed later, it seems he said, first and foremost: "It was as formerly. Without preface or omen, she appeared again before me, in vacillating and indistinct outline. And, exactly as before, if now with entire astonishment, a freezing chill ran through me, sole to crown."

The old 'consuming curiosity' he at once felt also, seemingly, if one would say most strangely, given such circumstances.

A vast exaggeration, nevertheless, had been added to the vision. If when yet, previously, she lived, the emaciation of her ruined body had attained for him so extreme and livid a pitch, she had at the time stayed as some vestige still of Berenice. Now not so. She was currently most like a skeleton and clad only in part-translucent flakes of her shroud, and the thinnest, least textural gauze of a partly transparent skin. Through this inadequate veil her bones themselves, it seemed to him this night, or so he averred, were themselves half transparent, thin as milky and discoloured water.

Her eyes, he said, were now as well *entirely* empty of any ocular feature. They were quite white, lacking, it would seem, all ability to see. And yet she did, for she advanced towards him, weightlessly as something blown, and stood on the opposite side of the table on which, so much earlier, her severed teeth had sat bleeding in their tiny prison-box.

Before, of course, he had noted primarily the *presence* of those teeth in her mouth. Now, in a ghastly parody of remembrance, Berenice, or whatever remnant of Berenice here remained, opened wide her colourless lips to reveal the colourless and shrivelled vacant gums. Not one fang had been left embedded there. He had been scrupulous, after all.

And then, he said, and those that later wrote down his trembling and enfeebled words, agreed that he seemed to faint even as he voiced them, "And then my cousin spoke to me."

She spoke some while. He made no try, during his recital, to describe her voice. Conceivably her vocality was now quite beyond analysis, or connection. She did not at first, nor at any point in her monologue, which I was not surprised he made no attempt to interrupt, either for a question or a mere exclamation, to outline how she had come to her vampiric Fate. Instead she set upon Egaeus, at once and completely, the razor edges of an awful and diabolically resentful wrath.

"I had loved you," it seems she said. "You were to be my husband and my lord. For this I had waited patiently and for so very long. But when events befell me, you treated me with such an evil and Satanically indifferent cruelty, that I cannot comprehend it. Nor can or could I ever forgive it."

Berenice told Egaeus that what he had done to her, in the matter of her dentition, was nothing less than the most sordid and granite-hearted injustice he might have coined. For, having become what then she was, how else was she to sustain her altered 'life' – it would seem too, that 'life' was how she referred to the Un-dead fix in which she had found herself. Dependent on her teeth, Egaeus had robbed her of them, and so left her in an abyss of remedyless pain and despair. This then, the final gift of her reluctant husband. Thereafter, toothless, she had persisted in a limbo of wilting, writhing desuetude, unable either to maintain herself or to cease to be. Dead, she could not die. She languished in Hell, in extremes of torture, those physical enough still, and highly cognitive, aside, of course, from her rage and suffering at his ineffable and indifferent malice and 'spite'.

After these stanzas, a silence fell in the library, or so Egaeus afterwards recalled. He lay back, he said, barely conscious in his chair. But in those moments, once more startling and terrifying him, her skeletal wraith slid lightly up onto the table-top, with the ease of a swimming imp.

He found then, to his utmost dread, this too astounding him – since he thought he had reached the limit of his responsive endurance, she leaned forward to him, closer and ever closer, until her vile and barely viewable face had slipped near enough he feared indeed that she might place her shrivelled lifeless lips on his. But no doing that, she arched up her frightful neck, like that of a greyish snake. And from this neck, once lovely and now outside every boundary of both the real and the describable, a phalanx of what appeared to him to be, for several frenzied nightmare moments, long, spiny *teeth* protruded after all, not from her lips, but out of her very *throat*.

Before he could do anything, even to cry aloud in terror, these fang-like protuberances elongated further, and with vast ease, or so it looked to him, in a moment or so more, they had gained and *touched* his own throat, and its vital vein.

He was aware instantly of a drawing, which he had, now and then previously experienced on being medically bled by a physician. But all about, the darkling room dimmed suddenly, as would a window in the stormy curtain-fall of deepest night. The very last words she spoke to him, or so he believed, were these: "But for my kind, dear husband, there *are* other ways. What an obscure slow numbskull you always were, and have remained."

After which Egaeus knew no more, until he woke, late the morning after. By then it transpired, he was dying. He had been leached of most of his blood.

Through some massive intransigence of will, which very seldom before had he demonstrated, save maybe on the night he unwittingly drew the fangs of Berenice, he gave his final statements and avowals to the two cold, unwilling and, by now, frenziedly revolted servants. Others also, however, witnessed the testament. It is their report which has come into my possession.

Egaeus died writhing with an icy fever, screaming sometimes, not more than five hours following this. He left an ultimate menu of instructions, which one at least faithfully, or perhaps merely in pure fearfulness, had also, and conceivably inaccurately, written down. This read, when translated from the jumble of the dying, wrecked mind: "When deceased, every tooth in my head, every bone in my frame, must be smashed like broken bottle-glass. My heart must be pierced, my head, perhaps, disassociated from my neck. I must be burned, and the ashes interred in some deep vault."

There was no more after this, *nor perhaps was any needed.*

As I have stated, you, or any other, will believe my account, or not. For myself, I am uncertain even as to what, thereafter, was finally concluded upon by the great Family. Let alone any alternative authority. Besides, could any creature rest, if ever so dealt with?

The House has long since fallen, stone on stone. The trees are dead and lie in ranks. Those Sarcophagi remaining in the grounds have also lost their shape and meaning. Maybe, whatever Power may briefly oust him, and itself drive the chariot of poor, helpless Man, when once it lets go, this is always ultimately the result. Creatures of air and wind, we: vehicles, playthings of the gods.

SEA WARG

One dull red star was sinking through the air into the sea. It was the sun. But eastward the October night had already commenced. There the water was dark green and the air purple, and the old ruinous pier stood between like a burnt spider.

Under the pier was a ghostly blackness, holed by mysterious luminous apertures. Ancient weeds and shreds of nets dripped. The insectile, leprous, wooden legs of the pier seemed to ripple, just as their drowning reflections did. The tide would be high.

The sea pushed softly against the land. It was destroying the land. The cliffs, eaten alive by the sea, (smelling of antique metal, fish odour of Leviathan, depth, death), were crumbling in little pieces and large slabs, and the promenade, where seasiders had strolled not more than thirty years ago, rotted and grew rank. Even the *danger* notices had faded and in the dark were only pale splashes, daubed with words that might have been printed in Russian.

But the sea-influencing moon would rise in a while.

Almost full tonight.

Under the pier the water twitched. Something moved through it. Perhaps a late swimmer who was indifferent to the cold evening or the warning *danger – keep out.* Or nothing at all maybe, just some rogue current, for the currents were temperamental all along this stretch of coast.

A small rock fell from above and clove the water, copying the sound of a rising fish.

The sun had been squashed from view. Half a mile westward the lights of hotels and restaurants shone upward, like the rays of another world, another planet.

When the man had stabbed him in the groin, Johnson had not really believed it. Hadn't *understood* the fountain of blood. When the next moment two security guards burst in and threw the weeping man onto the fitted carpet, Johnson simply sat there.

"Are you OK? *Fuck.* You're not," said the first security guard.

"Oh. I'm—" said Johnson. The next thing he recalled, subsequently, was the hospital.

The compensation had been generous. And a partial pension, too, until in eighteen years' time he came of age to draw it in full. The matter was hushed up otherwise, obliterated. Office bullying by the venomous Mr. Haine had driven a single employee – not to the usual nervous breakdown or mere resignation – but to stab reliable Mr. Johnson, leaving him with a permanent limp and some slight but ineradicable impairments both of a digestive and a sexual nature.

"I hope you won't think of us too badly," said old Mr. Birch, gentle as an Alzheimer's lamb.

"Not at all, sir," replied Johnson in his normal, quiet, pragmatic way.

Sandbourne was his choice for the bungalow with the view of the sea that his own dead father had always wanted, and never achieved.

Johnson wasn't quite certain why he fitted himself, so seamlessly, into that redundant role.

Probably the rundown nature of the seaside town provided inducement. House prices were much lower than elsewhere in the southeast. And he had always liked the sea. Besides, there were endless opportunities in Sandbourne for the long, tough walks he must now take, every day of his life if possible, to keep the spoilt muscles in his left leg in working order.

But he didn't mind walking. It gave extra scope for the other thing he liked, which had originally furnished his job in staff liaison at Haine and Birch. Johnson was fascinated by people. He never tired of the study he gave them. A literate and practiced reader, he found they provided him with *animated* books. His perceptions had, he was aware, cost him his five-year marriage: he had seen too well what Susan, clever though she had been, was up to. But then, Susan wouldn't have wanted him now anyway, with his limp and the bungalow, forty-two years of age, and two months into the town-city and walking everywhere, staring at the wet wilderness of waters.

"I see that dog again, up by the old pier."

"Yeah?" asked the man behind the counter. "What dog's that, then?"

"I tol' yer. Didn' I? I was up there shrimping. An' I looks an' it's swimming aroun' out there, great big fucker, too. Don' like the looks of it, mate. I can tell yer."

"Right."

"Think I oughta call the RSPCee like?"

"What, the Animal Rights people?" chipped in the other man.

"Nah. He means the RSPCA, don't ya, Benny?"

"'S right. RSPCee. Only it shouldn' be out there like that on its own. No one about. Just druggies and pushers."

The man behind the counter filled Benny's mug with a brown foam of coffee and slapped a bacon sandwich down before the other man at the counter. Johnson, sitting back by the cafe wall, his breakfast finished, watched them closely in the way he had perfected, seeming not to, seeming miles off.

"An' it's allus this time of the month."

"Didn't know you still had them, Benny, times of the month."

Benny shook his head, dismissing – or just missing – the joke. "I don' mean that."

"What *do* ya mean, then, pal?"

"I don' like it. Great big bloody dog like that, out there in the water when it starts ter get dark and just that big moon ter show it."

"Sure it weren't a shark?"

"Dog. It was a dog."

"Live and let live," said the counter man.

Benny slouched to a table. "You ain't seen it."

After breakfast Johnson had meant to walk up steep Hill Road and take the rocky path along the clifftop and inland, through the forest of newish high-rises, well-decked shops, and SF-movie-dominated cinemas, to the less fashionable supermarket at Crakes Bay.

Now he decided to go eastwards along the beach, following the cliff line, to the place where the warning notices were. There had been a few major rockfalls in the 1990s, so he had heard; less now, they said. People were always getting over the council barricade. A haunt of drug-addicts, too, that area, 'down-and-outs holing up like rats' among the boarded-up shops and drown-foundationed houses farther up. Johnson wasn't afraid of any of that. He didn't look either well-off or so impoverished as to be desperate. Besides, he'd been mugged in London once or twice. As a general rule, if you kept calm and gave them what they wanted without fuss, no harm befell you. No, it was in a smart office with a weakened man in tears that harm had happened.

The beach was an easy walk. Have to do something more arduous later.

The sand was still damp, the low October sun reflecting in smooth, mirrored strafes where the sea had decided to remain until the next incoming tide fetched it. A faintly hazy morning, salt-smelling and chilly and fresh.

Johnson thought about the dog. Poor animal, no doubt belonging to one of the drugged outcasts. He wondered if, neglected and famished, it had learned to swim out to sea, catching the fish that a full moon lured to the water's surface.

There were quite a few other people walking on the beach, but after the half mile it took to come around to the pier-end, none at all. There was a dismal beauty to the scene. The steely sea and soft grey-blue sky featuring its sun. The derelict promenade, much of which had collapsed. Behind these the defunct shops with their look of broken toy models, and then the long, helpless arm of the pier, with the hulks of its arcades and tea-rooms, and the ballroom, now mostly a skeleton, where had hung – so books on Sandbourne's history told one – sixteen crystal chandeliers.

Johnson climbed the rocks and rubbish – soggy pizza boxes, orange peels, beer cans – and stood up against the creviced pavement of the esplanade. It looked as if bombs had exploded there. Out at sea nothing moved, but for the eternal sideways running of the waves.

At the beginning of the previous century, a steamboat had sailed across regularly from France, putting in by the pier, then a white confection like a bridal cake. The strange currents that beset this coast had made that the only safe spot. The fishing fleet had gone out from here too, this old part of the city-town, the roots of which had been there, it seemed, since Saxon times. Now the boats put off from the west end of Sandbourne, or at least they did so when the rest of Europe allowed it.

Johnson wondered whether it was worth the climb, awkward now with his leg, over the boarding and notices. By day there were no movements, no people. They were night dwellers very likely, eyes sore from skunk, skins scabrous from crack. And by night, of course, this place would indeed be dangerous.

As he turned and started back along the shore, Johnson's eye was attracted by something not the cloud-and-sea shades of the morning, lying at the very edge of the land. He took it at first for some unusual shell or sea-life washed ashore. Then decided it must be something manufactured, some gruesome modern fancy for

Halloween, perhaps.

In fact, when he went down the beach and saw it clearly, lying there as if it had tried to clutch at the coast, kept its grip but let go of all else, he found it wasn't plastic or rubber but quite real. A man's hand, torn off raggedly just behind the wrist bone, a little of which stuck out from the bloated and discolouring skin.

Naturally he thought about it, the severed hand.

He had never, even in London, come across such an item. But then, probably, he'd never been in the right (wrong) place to do so.

Johnson imagined that one of the down-and-outs had killed another, for drugs or cash. Maybe even for a burger from the Alnite Caff.

He did wonder, briefly, if the near-starving dog might have liked to eat the hand. But there wasn't much meat on a hand, was there?

That evening, after he had gone to the supermarket and walked all the way back along Bourne Road, he poured himself a Guinness and sat at his table in the little 'study' of the bungalow and wrote up his find in his journal. He had kept a journal ever since he started work in Staff Liaison. Case-notes, histories... *people* – cameos, whole bios sometimes.

Later he fried a couple of chops and ate them with a green salad. Nothing on TV. He read Trollope until 11:36, then went to bed.

He dreamed of being in the sea, swimming with great strength and ability, although in reality he had always been an inadequate swimmer. In the dream he was aware of a dog nearby but was not made afraid by this. Instead he felt a vague exhilaration, which on waking he labelled as a sort of puerile pleasure in unsafety. Physically he had long outgrown it. But there, deep in his own mind, perhaps not so?

The young man was leaning over his motorbike, adjusting something apparently. The action was reminiscent of a rider with his favourite steed, checking the animal for discomfort.

Johnson thought he had seen him before. He was what? Twenty-five, thirty? He had a thick shock of darkish fair hair, cut short the way they did now, and a lean face from which the summer tan was fading. In the sickly glare under the streetlight his clothes were good but ordinary. He had, Johnson thought, very long fingers, and his body was tall and almost athletic in build.

Tanith Lee

This was outside the pub they called in Sandbourne the 'Biker Inn'.

Johnson didn't know the make of the bike, but it was a powerful model, elegant.

Turning off Ship Street, Johnson went into *The Cat in Clover*. He wasn't yet curious as to why he had noted the man with the bike. Johnson noted virtually everyone. An hour into the evening he did, however, recall where he had twice seen him before, which was in the same launderette Johnson himself frequented. Nice and clean then. Also perhaps, like Johnson, more interested in coming out to do the wash than in buying a machine.

During the rest of the week Johnson found he kept seeing the man he then named, for the convenience of the journal, Biker. The rather mundane region where Johnson lived was one of those village-in-city conurbations featured by London journalists writing on London – like Hampstead, for example, if without the dosh. You did get to be aware, indirectly, sometimes, of the locals, as they of you, perhaps. Johnson believed that in fact he wasn't coincidentally and now constantly 'bumping into' Biker, but that he had become *aware* of Biker. Therefore, he noticed him now each time he saw him, whereas formerly he had frequently seen him *without* noticing, therefore without consciously *seeing*.

This kind of thing had happened before.

In the beginning, when in his teens, Johnson had thought it meant something profoundly important, particularly when it was a girl he abruptly kept on seeing – that was, *noticing*. Even in his thirties he had been misled by that idea, with Susan. He had realised, after their separation, that what had drawn him to her at first wasn't love or sex but her own quirkiness and his observation of it. She had worked it out herself, eventually. In the final year of their life together she came to call those he especially studied (including those at Haine and Birch) his 'prey'. "Which of your prey are you seeing tomorrow?" she would ask playfully.

Now grasping that it was some type of acuity in him that latched on to certain others in this fashion, Johnson had not an instant's doubt that he had reacted differently to Biker.

So what was it, then, with Biker? *What* had alerted Johnson there under the streetlamp on that moonless night?

During the next week, Johnson took his washing to the launderette about 6 p.m., and there Biker sat.

Biker was unloading his wash but raised his eyes. They were very long eyes, extraordinarily clear, a pale, gleaming grey.

"Cold out," said Johnson, dumping the washing.

"Yeah," said Biker.

"Damn it, this machine isn't working."

"Yeah," said Biker. He looked up again. "Try kicking it."

"You're joking," said Johnson placidly.

"No," said Biker, and he came over quite calmly, and did something astonishing. Which was he jumped straight upward with enormous agility and power, and fetched the washer the lightest but most expressive slap with his left foot. Landing, he was like a lion – totally co-ordinated, unfazed. While the machine, which had let out a rattling roar, now gulped straight into its cycle. Biker nodded and returned to his wash.

"Wow," said Johnson. "Thanks."

"Don't mention it."

"I owe you a drink. The girlfriend's refused to come round till I get these bloody sheets done."

Biker glanced at him.

Johnson saw there was neither reluctance nor interest in the smooth, lean face, hardly any expression at all. The eyes were only mercury and white china.

"I'll be in *The Victory*," he said.

Once Biker left, Johnson, not to seem too eager, stayed ten minutes with his washing. He had chosen the crank machine on purpose. And what a response he had got! Biker must be an acrobat. At the very least a trained dancer.

Perhaps, Johnson thought, he shouldn't indulge this. Perhaps it was unwise. But then, he usually did indulge his observation. It had never led to anything bad. Except once.

Had being stabbed and disabled made him reckless? He thought not. Johnson *wasn't* reckless. And he could afford the price of a couple of drinks.

When he got into the pub, the place was already full. The music machine filled the air with huge thuddings, while on every side other machines for gambling flashed like a firework display.

He looked round, then went to the bar and ordered a drink, whisky for the cold. He could already see Biker wasn't there.

Which might mean *he* had distrusted Johnson, or that something else had called him away. Or anything, really.

Johnson was not unduly disappointed. Sometimes *not* knowing was the more intriguing state. Besides, going out of the door he heard a man say, as if signalling to him, "Yeah, there's something out by the old pier sometimes. I seen it too. Big animal. Dolphin p'rhaps. But it was dark."

Yet another week after the exchange with Biker, Johnson was leaving the smaller Sainsbury, near the Odeon, when he glimpsed his quarry, bikeless, driving by in a dark blue BMW.

Johnson knew he would thereafter keep his eyes open also for the car, whose number plate he had at once memorised. He was sure, inevitably, that he had often seen the car as well. He was struck by an idea, too, that Biker, in some strange, low-key way, wished to be visible – the bike itself, the car, the habit of the launderette. And that in turn implied (perhaps) a wish to be less visible, or non-visible, on other occasions.

With his groceries Johnson picked up one of the local papers. He liked to glance at it; the doings of the city of Sandbourne amused and puzzled him. Accordingly, he presently read in it that another late-season holidaymaker had gone missing. There had apparently been two the previous summer, who vanished without a trace. Keen swimmers, they were thought to have fallen foul of the wild currents east of the town. The new case, however, one Alice Minerva McClunes, had been a talented lady from New York. On the southeast coast to visit a niece, she had gone out with her camera and sketchpad and failed to return. "She wanted to stay on the beach," the presumably woebegone niece reported, "till moonrise. It was the full moon." Alice was, it seemed, known for her photography of moonlight on various things.

This small article stayed intransigently with Johnson for the rest of the evening. He reread it twice, not knowing quite why.

Johnson the observer had made no friendships in Sandbourne, but he had by now gained a few acquaintances to say 'hello' to.

He went to the local library the next day, then to the fish market above the beach. There, in between the little shops, he met the man he knew as Reg. And then Biker appeared walking along from the east end of the town, from the direction actually of the eldritch pier. And Reg called out to him, "Hi, mate. OK?" And Biker smiled and was gone.

As one might, Johnson said, "You know him? I've seen him around – nice bike. Drives a car, too, doesn't he?"

"Yes, that's Jason. Don't know his other name. Lives in one of the rock-houses. Got a posh IT job in London – only goes up a couple of times a week. Oh, and once a month, three days and nights in Nores." Reg pronounced this neighbouring, still parochial, town in the proper local way as *Nor-ez*. "Bit of money, yes."

"A rock-house? They're the ones built into the cliff, aren't they?"

"Yep. Caves in back with pools of seawater. Pretty trendy now. Not so good when we get a freak high tide. Flooded out last year, all of 'em. Only, he was off at Nores – three days every time. Thought he might come back to see the damage, but he never did. When I saw him, he just says, 'I'll just buy a new carpet'. OK for some."

"Yes," said Johnson regretfully.

But his mind was busy springing off along the last stretch of habitable Sandbourne, mentally inspecting the houses set back into the cliffs. Smugglers had put them to good use in the 1800s. Now renovated and 'smart', they engaged the wealthy and artistic. He was curious (of *course* he was) as to which house was Jason's – Jason, who, after all, must be rich. He thought of the pools of sea that lay behind the facades, and the great stoops of bending cliff that overhung them. Johnson had seen photographs of these structures in *History of Sandbourne*.

He visualised acrobatic Jason leaping straight down into a glimmering, glittery, nocturnal pool, descending like a spear, wriggling effortless and subtle as an eel out through some pipe or fissure, and so into the black-emerald bowel of the sea. He pictured those cold silver eyes under the glazes of blind green water, and the whip of the two legs, working as one, like a merman's tail. But somehow, too, Johnson pictured Jason as a sort of dog – hairy, unrecognisable, though swimming – as if there had been a dream of this, and now he, Johnson, recalled. As gradually he had remembered, was remembering all the rest, the sightings in launderette, car – all, everything.

Turquoise, blood-orange daylight snagged the drips of nets under the skeletal arm of the pier. Bottle-green light gloomed through rotted struts, shining up the mud, debris, the crinkle of water like pleated glass...

And the day lifted to its zenith and folded away. It was November now. Behind the west end, the sky bled through paintwork themes of amber and golden sienna. The sea blued. Side lit, long tidal runners, like snakes with triangular pale indigo heads, swarmed inward on the land. Darkness began to stir in the east.

They forgot, people, how the dark began there, eastward, just as light did. The sun, the moon, rose always from the east. But so did night.

Never mind that. Soon the moon would be full again.

Under the pier, the mind was lying in its shell of skull. As dark filled in on dark, dark was in the brain, smooth and spontaneously ambient as the ink of a squid.

Under the pier.

Overhead the ruin, and the ancient ballroom, which a full moon might light better than sixteen chandeliers.

Something not a wave moved through the water.

Perhaps a late swimmer, indifferent to the cold.

Jason lived in the house behind the courtyard. It had high gates that were, most of the time, kept shut and presumably locked. A craning tree of a type unknown to Johnson grew up the wall, partly hiding with its bare, twisted slender branches an upper-storey window. Johnson discovered the correct house by knocking at another in the group, asking innocently for Jason, the man with the bike. An uninterested young woman said the man with the bike lived at the one with the courtyard. She didn't want to know Johnson's business. Johnson guessed the BMW would be parked in one of the garages above that corresponded with the rock terrace. The bike, according to the woman, was kept in the yard.

Having walked past the relevant house, he walked back and up Pelling Road to the clifftop. He sat on a bench there, looking down at the winter shore and the greyling sea. From here, away along the saucer curve of the earth, he could make out the pier like a thing of matchsticks. They said any storm destroyed always another piece of it. And yet there it still was, incredibly enduring.

He had visited the library again, looking at back numbers of the local papers. There had been a few disappearances mentioned in those past years he had viewed. But he supposed only taxpaying citizens or visitors would be counted. The coast's flotsam might well vanish without a trace.

That night the moon came up like a white plate in the tree at the end of the bungalow's small fenced garden.

The disk wasn't yet full but filling out; in another couple of nights it would be perfect.

Johnson put down the Graham Greene novel he was reading and went out into the dusk.

Sea-influencing, blood-influencing, mind-influencing moon.

He thought of Jason, perhaps in his rich man's house just above the beach, behind the high gates and the yard, inside stone walls with the sea in the back of them.

By midnight Johnson was in bed asleep. He dreamed clearly and concisely of standing inside the cliffs, in a huge cave that was pearl white, lit by a great flush of brilliance at either end. And the far end opened to the sea, long thick rollers combering in, and where they struck the inner floor of the cave, white chalk sprayed up in the surf. But then out of the sea a figure came, riding fast on a motorbike. He was clad in denim and had short and lustrous hair, but as he burst through the cave, brushing Johnson with the rush of his passage, anyone would have noticed that the biker had the face of a dog, and in his parted jaws, rather delicately, he held a man's severed hand.

Waking from this, Johnson found he had sat bolt upright.

There was a dull, groaning ache in his lower gut and back, which he experienced off and on since the stabbing. He was barely aware of it.

Johnson was thinking of the changes the moon brought. And how something so affected might well share an affinity with the lunar-tidal sea. But also Johnson thought of an old acquaintance of his, fussy Geoffry Prentiss, who had been fascinated by the sightings, detailed in papers, of strange fauna, such as the Beast of Bodmin. He'd coined a term for such a phenomenon: *warg*. An acronym, WARG stood for Weird Animal Reported Generally.

With a slow, inevitable movement, not really disturbing, Johnson got up, went into the bathroom, and presently returned to put on his clothes and boots.

By the time he reached St. Luke's, the clock showed ten minutes to 3 a.m. There had been almost no one on the upper streets, just a young couple kissing. Soon though, a surreal distant pounding revealed the area of the nearest nightclubs, and outside *The Jester* a trio of youths were holding up another, who was being impressively sick. Compared to London, Sandbourne was a mild place. Or so it had seemed.

He wondered, when he turned east along the promenade, under the high lamps already strung with their Christmas neons of holly and stars, if he were sleepwalking. He considered this with complete calm, analytically. Never before had he taken his study of others to such an extremity. Had he in fact had a breakdown, or in more honest words, gone mad?

But the night was keen. He felt and smelled and saw and *experienced* the night. This was not a dream. He walked in the world.

The moon had vanished westward in cloud, as if in pretence of modesty. Beyond the line of land, the sea was jet black under jet black sky, yet the pale fringes of wavelets came in and in. Constant renewal. Repetition of the most elaborate and harmonious kind. Or the most *relentless* kind.

In the end, the seas would devour all the landmasses of the earth. The waters would cover them.

Several elderly men, drunk or drugged, sprawled on a bench and swore at him as he passed, less maliciously than in a sort of greeting for which, by now, they lacked other words.

Gulls, which never slept, circled high above the town, lit underneath translucently by the lamps.

Johnson went down the steps and into the area where the fishing fleet left its boats and sheds. The sand, the sheds, the boats, were sleeping. Only a tiny glow of fire about fifty feet away showed someone there keeping watch, or dossing.

The shadows clung as he passed the fish shops and turned into the terraced street above the shore. The lamps by the rock-houses were greenish and less powerful. They threw a stark quarter-glow on the stone walls, then on the many-armed tree, the two high gates. One of which stood ajar.

Jason, the acrobat with metallic eyes. And the gate was open.

Inside, the yard had been paved, but the bike wasn't to be seen. Instead a single window burned yellow in the lower storey, casting a reflected oblong, vivid and unreal as if painted there, on the ground.

Johnson accepted that it was impossible not to equate this with a trap, or an invitation, and that it was probably neither.

He hesitated with only the utter silence, the silence of the sea, which was a sound, to guide him. Such an ancient noise, the clockwork rhythm of an immortal god that could never cease. No wonder it was cruel, implacable.

He went through the gate and stepped softly over the yard until he reached the window's edge.

The bright room was lit by a powerful overhead source. It showed banks of computers, mechanical accessories, a twenty-first-century nerd's paradise. And there in the middle of it Jason kneeled on the uncarpeted floor. He was dressed in jeans, shirt, and jumper. He was eating a late supper.

A shock passed through Johnson, quite a violent one.

Afterwards, he was slightly amazed at his own reaction.

For Jason was not dining on a severed hand, not on anything human at all, and yet... Yet the *way* he ate and *what* he ate – a fish, evidently raw and very fresh, head and scales and fins and tail and eyes and bones all there, tearing at them with his opened jaws, eating, gnawing, swallowing all, those metal eyes glazed like those of a lion, a *dragon*... This alone. It was enough.

Not since London had Johnson driven, but his licence was current and immaculate. Even his ironic leg, driving, gave him no problems.

He hired the red Skoda in town. It wasn't bad, easy to handle.

On the afternoon of the almost full moon, having waited on the Nores Road for six and three-quarter hours, he spotted Jason's blue BMW instantly. Johnson followed it on through forty minutes of country lanes, between winter fields and tall, bare trees, all the way to a small village known as Stacklebridge. Here, at a roundabout, the BMW turned around and drove straight back the way it had come.

Johnson, however, drove on to Newsham and spent an hour admiring the Saxon church, sheep, and rush-hour traffic going north and south. He had not risked the obvious move of also turning and tracking the other car homeward. Near Sandbourne, he was sure, Jason would park his vehicle in concealment off the road, perhaps in a derelict barn. Then walk, maybe even *sprint* the last distance, to reach his house or the pier before moonrise.

The nature of his studies had often meant Johnson must be patient. He had realised, even before following the blue car, that he could do nothing now, that was, nothing *this* month; it was already too late. But waiting was always part of watching, wasn't it? And he had been stupidly inattentive and over-confident only once, and so received the corrective punishment of a knife. He would be careful this time.

He didn't need to dream about it now. He was forewarned, forearmed.

But the dream still occurred.

He was in the pier ballroom, and it was years ago because the ballroom was almost intact, just some broken windows and holes in the floor and walls, where brickwork and struts and darkness and black water showed. But the chandeliers burned with a cold, sparkling lemon glory overhead. All about were heaps of dancers, lying in their dancing clothes, black and white and rainbow. They were all dead and mutilated, torn, bitten, and rotted almost to unrecognisability.

Jason came up from under the pier, directly through the floor, already eating, with a savage hunger that was more like rage, a long white arm with ringed fingers.

But his eyes weren't glazed now. They were fixed on Johnson. They *knew* Johnson. And in ten seconds more Jason would spring, and as he sprang, would become what he truly was, even if only for three nights of every month. The nights he had made sure everyone who knew of him here also thought he spent in Nores.

Johnson reacted prudently. He woke himself up.

He had had dreams about other people, too, which had indicated to him some psychological key to what was troubling them, far beyond anything they had been able to say. Johnson had normally trusted the dreams, reckoning they were his own mechanism of analysis, explaining to him. And he had been very accurate. Then Johnson had dreamed that gentle, tearful Mark Cruikshank from Publicity had come up to him on the carpark roof at Haine and Birch and stuck a long, pointed fingernail through his heart. The dream was so absurd, so out of character, so *overdramatic* that Johnson dismissed it as indigestion. But a couple of days later Mark stabbed him in the groin, with the kind of knife you could now buy anywhere in the backways of London. For this reason, Johnson did not think to discount the dreams of Jason. And for this reason, too, Johnson had known, almost at once, exactly what he was dealing with.

Christmas, personally irrelevant to Johnson for years, was much more important this year. Just as December was, with its crowds of frantic shoppers – not only in the festive, noisy shops, but in their cars racing up to London and back, or to Nores and back.

Moonrise on the first of the three nights (waxing full, declining to gibbous) was earlier in the day, according to the calendar Johnson had bought. It was due at 5:33 p.m.

Not knowing, therefore, if Jason would set out earlier than he had the previous month in order to beat the rush-hour traffic after four, Johnson parked the hired Skoda in a layby just clear of the suburbs, where the Nores Road began.

In fact, the BMW didn't appear until 3.30. Perhaps Jason had been delayed. Or perhaps, as Johnson suspected, a frisson of excitement always ruled the man's life at this time, adding pleasure to the danger of cutting things fine. For, once the moon was up, visible to Jason and to others, the change must happen. (There were plenty of books, fiction and non, to apprise any researcher of this point.)

On this occasion, Johnson only followed the blue car far enough to get out into the hump-backed country lanes. Then he pulled off the road and parked on a narrow, pebbly shoulder.

He had himself to judge everything to within a hair's breadth.

To begin the manoeuvre too soon would be to call attention, and therefore assistance and so *dispersal*. Indeed, the local radio station would doubtless report it, and so might warn Jason off. There were other places after all that Jason, or what Jason became, could seek refuge in.

Probably Jason always turned round at the Stacklebridge roundabout, however. It was the easiest spot to do so.

Johnson kept his eye on his watch. He had made the trip twice more in the interim, and it took consistently roughly eighty minutes to the village and back. But already there was a steady increase in cars buzzing, and frequently too quickly, along the sea-bound lane.

At ten to four the sun went. The sky stayed a fiery lavender for another thirteen minutes.

At 4.25, Johnson, using a brief gap in traffic, started the Skoda and drove it back fast onto and across the narrow road, simultaneously slamming into reverse. A horrible crunching. The car juddered to a permanent halt.

He had judged it on his last trip: stalled and slanted sidelong across the lane, the Skoda blocked the thoroughfare entirely for anything – save a supermodel on a bicycle.

Johnson got out of the car and locked the doors. He made no attempt to warn the next car whose headlamps he could see blooming. It came bounding over the crest of the lane, registered it had about twenty yards to brake, almost managed it, and tapped into the Skoda with a bump and screech. Belted in, the driver didn't come to much harm. But he had buckled a headlight, and the Skoda's bodywork would need some repairs, aside from its gearbox. The driver scrambled out and began to swear at Johnson, who was most apologetic, describing how his vehicle had gone out of control. They exchanged details. Johnson's were the real ones; he saw no need to disguise them.

As they communicated, three more cars flowed over the crest and, not going quite so fast, pulled to a halt without mishap. Meanwhile two other cars coming from the direction of Sandbourne were also forced to stop.

Soon there was quite a crowd.

The police must be called, and the AA, plus partners and others waiting. Lights from headlamps and digital gadgets flickered and blazed. Mobiles were out all along the verges, chattering and chiming and playing silly tunes under the darkling winter trees.

All the while, the backup of trapped cars on either side was growing.

Covered by this group event, Johnson absented himself carefully, slipping off along the tree-walled hem of the fields, making his way back up the static vehicular line towards Stacklebridge.

People asked him if he knew what had happened, how long help would be in coming. He said some idiot had crashed his gears. He said the police were on their way.

It was full dark, 5.15, eighteen minutes to moonrise, when he noted Jason's BMW. It was boxed in on all sides, and people were out of their cars here, too, shouting, making calls, angry, frustrated, and only Jason still there, poised over the wheel, staring out blankly like something caught in a cage. *He* didn't look angry. He wasn't making a call. Standing back in darkness under the leafless boughs, Johnson observed Jason and timed the moon on his luminous watch.

In fact, the disk didn't come up over the slope to the left until the dial showed 5:41. By then the changes were well advanced.

Afterward, Johnson guessed no one else had noticed much what happened *inside* the BMW. It was the Age of Solipsism. You cared only for yourself and what was yours. The agony of another, unless presented on celluloid, was missed.

But Johnson saw.

He saw the flurry and then the frenzy, planes of half-light and deep darkness fighting with each other like two vultures over a corpse. And he heard the screams.

And when the creature – and by then this was all one could call it – burst out, straight out the side of the BMW, none of them could ignore that they might have to deal with it.

Jason had become his true self. He – it – was about seven feet tall and solidly built, but as fluid in movement as an eel. The head and face, chest and back and arms were heavily hairy, covered in a sort of pelt through which two pale, fishlike eyes and a row of icy teeth glared and *flamed*. The genital area was also sheathed in fur, but under that the legs were scaled like those of a giant snake or fish. When the huge clawed hands rose up, they, too, had scales, very pallid in the blaze of headlights. It snarled, and it stank, rank, stale, *fishy*. This anomalous thing, with the face of a dog and the eyes of a cod, sprang directly against the crowd.

Johnson, cool, calculating, lonely Johnson, (to whom every human was a type of study animal), had deemed casualties inevitable, and certainly there were a few. But then, as he, student of humanity, had predicted, they *turned*.

Subsequent news broadcasts spared no one who heard, saw, or read them the account of how a mob of already outraged people had ripped the monstrous beast apart. Questioned later, they had been nauseous, shivering, crying, but at the hour, Johnson himself had seen what they did, and how they stood there after, looking down at the mess smeared and trampled on the roadway. Jason of course, given half a chance, would have and had done the same to them. And contrary to the myth, he did not alter back in death to human form, to lie there, defenceless and accusing. No, he, it, had retained the metamorphosis, to puzzle everyone for months, perhaps years, to come. Naturally, too, it hadn't needed a silver bullet, either. Silver bullets were the product of legends where the only strong metal, church candlesticks, was melted down to make suitable ammunition. If Johnson had had any doubt, Jason's own silvery eyes would have removed it.

That night, when the howling tumult and the flying sprays of blood had ceased, Johnson had stood there under the trees. He had felt quite collected. Self-aware, he was thinking of Mark Cruikshank, who had stabbed him, and that finally he, Johnson, for once in his bleak and manacled life, had got his own back on this bloody and insane world of aliens – werewolves, *human beings*.

TABLE MANNERS

The moment I saw him I knew. I suppose any one of us would, by now. We're so used, via movie and novel, to the nature and ways of The Vampire (capital letters intended), we can – or ought to – spot one at two hundred paces. And go grab ourselves a sharpened stake...

Or, of course, not...

I had been sent, that is *persuaded*, to attend the October Ball at the Reconstruct Mansion, by my father, Anthony. He said, and here I quote: "You'll find it interesting, I think."

"Why?" I had demanded. For this wasn't how I wished to spend the first five days of the month.

"Because the world is full of people like the Kokersons. If you like, Lei, put this down as the final part of your education. You'll learn how such people tick."

"Tick in the sense," I said, "of clock or bomb?"

"Either," replied my elegant, lovely, and infuriating father.

October is fall. Time of flaming, *falling* leaves, of mists and dreams, before Halloween and winter close in. I'd had my own plans, but there you go. Dad knows it all. (The trouble is, as far as I can tell, he usually does.)

And so I accepted the Kokerson invite and packed my bags and caught the train to Chakhatti Halt, and then took a cab driven by a very sweet guy, who looked and spoke just like a really jolly Tyrannosaurus Rex (I do not lie) in (quasi) human form.

I call the castle Reconstruct Mansion, did so from the very start, the moment I read in a newspaper that they had imported the edifice, once a huge old castle-type house from someplace in Eastern Europe, and were having it rebuilt stone by stone, in a vast parkland some other place, well outside the small town of Chakhatti. The Kokersons, obviously, are very rich. One of them won a lottery about twenty years back. I had seen photos of them. I really didn't want to go. But go there, Anthony thought, I must.

In case this makes my dad sound like a manipulative monster, I have to state right here and now that is the very opposite of what he is. As I said, it's just – he seems to know about... everything. But then, that's how he is.

My name is Lelystra. It's a family name, only usually I have myself called Lei by those who are my friends: "Call me Lei, all right?"

"Oh! You should have called – we would have sent a car! And you are Lelystra? What a delicious name! Oh, we wouldn't *dream* of mangling it down to Lei!!!"

So they greeted me, the Kokersons. A never-ending family, only lacking a father (had he run away? I might have). Toothy, bronzed sons and toothy, bleached daughters, and boisterous aunts, and an uncle like a dark satanic Bill, (his name), and the mother, Mrs. Kokerson, or Ariadne, as I was told to call her. She was sixty going on fifteen. That is, she was sixty, but had somehow stayed fifteen in all the *wrong* ways. I felt an immediate requirement to look after her, steer her away from the cocktails – she was *much* too young to even taste one – and perhaps introduce her to some youthfully elderly male.

I flew upstairs with wings of worry on my feet and leapt into the cover of a bright white bedroom, with a bed the size of a softball field.

I tried to put through a call to Anthony. Cunningly he was in a meeting. I left a message. "Dad, I am going to kill you."

Let me describe the reconstruct castle.

An apparent ascending thousand feet of coal-blue stone, with towers, cupolas, balconies, verandas, staircases inside and out like static stepped waterfalls, and some of them just as slippery. The window glass is lightly polarised. From outside the windows look like smoky eyeglasses. Inside they colour day sky green, and night sky purple, with pink stars. The landscape all around is private and full of trees, lake, and deer. October stags bellowed from the woods all night, waking me regular as a fire alarm roughly every thirty minutes.

It was all a gigantic theme park.

The *theme,* presumably, was the Kokersons, or their fantasy about themselves. The feel of fake antiquity and illusory age was so intense it was quite serious.

And we all had to dress in the clothes they provided, females in flowing gowns, males in Gothic tailoring, nothing later than 1880, or earlier than 1694. We were like refugees from a muddled movie set. Even the house was like that.

Two days, two bellowing nights passed.

The day of the ball, everyone (or the Young People, at least) spent all morning and afternoon compulsorily in hot tubs, being massaged, creamed, pedicure-manicured, topped off by shampoo and styling (as if for a cat show). Then came the dressing up in the most extreme clothes yet.

I yawned and yawned, blaming it on the wake-up calls of the noisy stags.

My dress, which Ariadne had chosen me, was white. (Ariadne: "So perfect with your lovely pale hair.") My hair is natural, but somehow the hairdresser had gotten it to go even paler – scared it, maybe. My skin is white too. I like the sun but never take a tan. In the white dress I vanished without meaning to, became a sort of plaster statue figure lacking any features, apart from my eyes which, thank the Lord, are very dark grey.

I thought, *I shall attend, play their silly game, dance a few of the minuets and waltzes,* (anything modern was absolutely out), *and retire graciously as soon as I can, later saying I was still there all the while.* I'm good at that sort of thing.

Either that is selfishly self-protective, or my kinder side not wanting to offend or hurt. I have no idea which and I don't care. It works. I escape, others aren't upset.

So I descended the indoor glass-slippery, glass-slipper stair, and entered the ballroom, (like the outside of a bridal cake, icing sugar and gilding, with grapevines of chandeliers). I glanced around.

And that was when I saw him. And knew him. Or rather, knew what he *was*.

And all along my spine, rising upward, ran the kind of prickly electricity that on a cat reveals itself as the fur standing on end.

Ariadne sailed by, right on cue.

Me, casually: "Who is that? I *do* like his costume."

"Yes, isn't it glorious? But I'm sure you notice that he's *very* handsome too," she enthused at me.

I answered calmly. "Yes. Quite a good face."

"And *perfect* masculine physique. Strong, like a dancer's. And his hair…"

"Is it really so long or is that a piece?"

"No. It's all his own. It's only that usually Anghel ties it back. How romantic he looks, doesn't he? I'm not surprised you'd pick him out. But I have to warn you, Lelystra, he's cold as snow. Cold as…" She fought for an even more cryogenic noun.

"As very *cold* snow?" I helpfully suggested.

"Well, er, yes. The *coldest* of cold snow. We're all quite crazy over him, and my two daughters are besotted, but he's only ever polite. But then, Anghel has escorted *movie stars*. Always in demand. He only arrived an hour ago."

"Really."

"He's been offered parts himself in so many movies…"

"But always coldly and politely refused," I supplied. I tried to keep all trace of irritation from my voice. *Obviously*, he wouldn't take a part in any film. You only had to look at him to see it – this one would never be up at the crack of dawn and out on location in the blazing sun.

He was A Vampire.

Someone called Ariadne then, and she floated off on a sea of people dancing polkas.

Anghel (a name to conjure with) might be any age from twenty to six hundred. Or more. He looked about twenty-two. His hair was black as if he had washed it in the night outside. His eyes were blacker. He was pale, paler no doubt than I was. It wasn't any kind of make-up. He had a handsome – no, a beautiful – and cruel face. It was his mask, evidently, to keep all of us just far enough away – or if near then suitably nervous and/or impressed – while he chose his victim for that night, maybe for the weekend. It wouldn't be more, because also evidently he hadn't *killed* anyone by drinking their blood. His dates might keep quiet or be made to 'forget' what had gone on, but surely word would have gotten around if none of them ever went home? His quaint costume was that of some European nobleman of the eighteenth century. All black, need I add, and embroidered, the tall black boots flittering with quills of steel and his coat with wild lace cuffs of sheerest snow white (to match his manner, perhaps).

He was unmistakable!

I felt I should have known he'd be here, been *warned*. Maybe I took my ignorance too much to heart.

Yet my – almost *outrage* – made me linger after all. None of the rest of them, it seemed, could figure him out, and put their fascination down only to his looks. I had to assume too that now and then, if only after dark, he had been spotted in everyday garb where, frankly, even if his hair *was* tied back, and he wore jeans and a baseball cap to advertise the Chakhatti Arrows, he would stick out like an eagle in an aviary of pigeons.

I am not ashamed of what I next did. I felt it was my right and duty. If everyone else was blind, I wasn't. Oh, I'm nothing so gallant as a vampire-slayer, not me. Sorry if you hoped that was the next bit. No, I am just a nosy eighteen-year-old woman who sometimes – OK *often* (thank you, Dad) takes herself a tad too seriously, and who *hates* to be beaten once she wakes up to a challenge. So, well... Reader, I *followed* him.

Back on the glacial dance floor, a thousand feet pounced, pranced, and stumbled, and the band played and the chandeliers shone.

And I slid like a panther, all right a *white* one, through the mob, spying on wicked Mr. Anghel whose second name no one seemed to know. (I had asked again, here and there, about him.)

First off, he danced a waltz with a dazzled girl, who almost swooned and then was non-swooning and dis-dazzled when he abandoned her for another. (Later in the evening, I came across knots of unsettled young women fuming or sighing or even sobbing – or plotting how to lure him back.)

He went through about ten girls in ten dances. He was picky, wasn't he? Of course, his partners, did they but know, were better off *not* being the selected maiden for the night's feast.

I did note he could dance stunningly well. Wondered briefly if he'd be as good in a club, decided he would be, as the vampire kind are simply wired to move well, in whatever context. It comes with the territory.

He never actually spotted *me*. I took care he didn't. I've said I'm pretty brilliant at seeming to be there when I'm not. I'm pretty good at doing the reverse too. But now and then he glanced around, looking for a split second slightly uneasy. He was A Vampire. He realised that *someone* was on his track. But I could see too he didn't truly reckon anyone was or could be. His madly *apparent* vampiricness was the camouflage. He was like an actor in the *role* of The Vampire. He *wants* to convince he is exactly that. The true vampire would cut his hair, dress in rags, and keep in the shadows.

All this anyhow, he centre stage, me stalking unseen, went on for about two hours.

Then, *he found her.*

I was startled, and then less so. She was completely loud in clothes and make-up, with gold neon for hair. Quite pretty but mainly like a flag. The ideal choice. She thought she was the Star of the Night. She had convinced a lot of other people too that she was. Few therefore would doubt *he* thought so.

The target of some, by now, seventy-odd distracted jealousies, he drew her smoothly off the floor, and next they melted away onto another flight of watery stairs, and so down and out and in between the velvet curtains of the night.

It was rather more challenging hunting them now, in all my white shimmer, for the dark was *dark* even if a half moon was rising on the lake. Yet here too, I could hide. A slant of moonlight through the shrubs, a blond deer slipping from tree to tree – a trick of the eyes. That was me. (I'd better own up. Anthony taught me these skills, though I did have natural talent.)

He and she were fairly unoriginal in their choice of resting place, but then, I suppose, if you have a vast lake like a polished silver tray, and everywhere else the backdrop of darkness, you simply *have* to perch at the edges of both. Which means, presumably, Anghel The Vampire was a romantic? He must have bought into his own legend in a big way.

I watched them a while, as they sat on a bench at the brim of the water. They talked, he speaking low and she... well, she had a kind of high and penetrating voice. "Oh, wow!" she kept saying, and, "What did you do then?" I could catch his words too – my hearing is fine – but they sounded like sort of movie dialogue. Quite *good* movie dialogue, but. He was telling her about his harsh life, and the novel he wanted to write, and sometimes he quoted a little poetry (Byron, Keats), and though when most guys do that they come over as truly useless, when he did it, it was quite impressive. But it was all a show, a sham. It was him being The Vampire, in the movie *role* he had invented, and for which he'd coined this well-written script.

I wondered if he even made himself sleep, by day, in some sort of *tomb.* If so, probably a really comfortable one, with a crystal goblet of bottled water on the side...

And then, quite abruptly, for somehow – even knowing it had to – I hadn't foreseen exactly when it would happen, he was bending toward her.

I thought, *Is she honestly so dumb she thinks this is just going to be a kiss?*

Sure. The idea of vampires is romantic. But not when you actually think about what they do. They bite you. Which, if that wasn't what you wanted, or expected, is an *assault* in anyone's book. And then – they steal your blood. Because again, unless you genuinely desire to nourish them in this way, it's *theft*. So what do those two procedures demonstrate a vampire to be? Shall I say: A mugger.

When he moved, so did I. I darted forward and burst out on them, white as vanilla ice cream. I made my voice even higher and more piercing than hers – which took some doing.

"Oh, hi! Am I *interrupting? Sorry!* But I'm just completely *lost* – and this is such a HUGE place, isn't it? Oh, do you mind if I sit down on your bench? I've been wandering around for over an hour. I mean, where *is* that castle? You wouldn't think, would you, you could lose a place that HUGE, but…" And down I flopped, with the sigh of a woman who just is not going to move for a while.

They were both gaping at me. She looked furious too. He, more as if he had just gotten the answer to a question that had been bothering him for hours. I had no doubt the answer was: *Yes! This plaster-of-Paris person* is *the one who was following me!*

I let a few moments pass, but neither she nor he spoke. Anyone else but the character I pretended to be would have grasped, however miles-thick they were, that *monsieur et mademoiselle* wished to be *left alone*.

Not I.

"What *ever* do you think of the ball?" I sparkled at them. "Isn't it too divine?"

"Then why," he said, in a low, dark, *awful* tone, "don't you go back to it?"

I'd tempted him from cover.

"I just said, you see," I replied. "I'm lost."

"I doubt that," he said. "If you walk up that path there, the path you just came down, I guess, you can see the house. You can't miss the house."

"Oh, really?" I gasped, and right then the neon girl clutched his arm, so for a second he scowled at her. She was in fact too thick herself to realise how terrible this scowl was. She said angrily, "Come on, Ang," (she pronounced that to rhyme with *hang*) "let's just get outta here."

And this was when the stag came shouldering from the woods about twenty feet away along the shore, noiseless and then *extremely* noisy, as branches went rushing and snapping out of the way of its great-antlered head, lit silver by the moonlight. Its eyes flashed electric green – and it bellowed.

That sound, from far off, had been devastating. Being close to it could cause total panic. I'd hoped so anyhow, when I was mentally coaxing the stag – that is, *one* of the stags – to come find us by the lake. This first-class animal had obliged. Neon spurted to her feet. Her eyes – her hair – had gone insane. She shrieked – and *ran*. She left us, him too, and bolted away, around the water and then off into the woods.

He, of course, didn't move.

Nor did I.

The stag though snorted down its gorgeous Roman nose, pawed the grass once as if to say, *You owe me, Lei,* then turned and sauntered back among the shadows.

He spoke once more. "So you can do that too."

"Excuse me?"

He sighed deeply, stood up, and turned his elegant black velvet back to me. His black hair swung. "This is set in concrete, then," he said. "You are to be my downfall."

"Er," I fluted, "my name's Lei."

"Let's not play games. I know you judged me at once, in the house. So, Lei. When do the heavies arrive?"

He had set his baleful eyes on me again. To my annoyance I found I wasn't ready for them. I should have been, shouldn't I? I wasn't a complete dope, like Neon.

"Why don't you sit down," I said.

"And let's talk it over? Very well."

But he stood there. Right next to me. I found too I was uncomfortably over-aware of him, but I should have been able to cope with that, because I already *knew* the power he had, and in my case, prepared as I was, that power really could not and would not be having an effect.

For quite a while, then, we stayed, in silence.

The moon silvered the lake, shining it up like an old dollar.

Finally, I glanced sidelong at him. He looked magnificently and broodingly sad. Then, just sad. Like a child whose dog died, and he never forgot, even ten years later, the way you *don't* ever forget the ones you love. Things like that.

"Shall I tell you how I came to be – how I got like I am?"

This was what he eventually said. I'd already heard most of what I took to be his 'line'. Obviously, nothing to do with vampires, but ancient feuds and some curse of his 'ancestors' he hadn't believed. He had been born on the borders of France, in a mountain region. His family were aristocrats who had lost everything way back in the 1790s. He had escaped them, and now lived in one room, out here in Chakhatti, (the sticks), an impoverished writer who worked nights waiting tables and pumping gas. But of course this mixture of Vampire Angst and modern day necessity was all baloney (as Dad might say).

I hazarded a guess. "Your family is well off, something in big business maybe. They live here and you were born here. You were also well-educated, went to a top-grade college – but left on discovering your true... how shall I say, vocation? Your family meanwhile still support you financially, because you tell them you are teaching yourself to be a writer."

He threw me a swift glare. "Not bad. Actually, I received a legacy – enough money to survive. That was from an aunt of mine. They always thought she was crazy, but she was – what *I* am. She was…"

"A vampire," I said.

"I have to assume," he said, flexing his hands, (perhaps practicing how he would strangle me), "you don't believe vampires exist. That is, in the mythic sense. You just imagine I'm dangerous."

"Wrong again. I know true vampires are quite real. And I know, Mr. Anghel, you belong firmly among them."

"Usually people dismiss my *interests* as... a fantasy."

I gazed hard at the lake. He was much too distracting. "The only thing that's a fantasy here," I answered, pleased at my own crisp tone, "is your total misunderstanding of what *being* a vampire entails."

"Some secret society – a code known only to the few…" he solemnly said.

"No. Frankly, the opposite," He had turned and I felt him stare at me. It was compelling but I didn't allow myself to react. To the lake alone, I added, "You need to talk to someone. If you're as messed up as I think you are, you need some *help*."

He gave a bitter, quite violent laugh. "Sure. You mean a shrink."

"You need," I continued, "to speak to my father."

"Your – your *what*?"

"Father." I opened the tiny white glitzy evening purse I'd been given, and pulled out one of Anthony's cards, and handed it to him.

He stared at that, now. "This is some joke, right?"

"No joke, Mr. Anghel…"

"Will you quit that *Mister* stuff – how fucking old do you think I am?"

"You could be a thousand. But no joke. This is for real. If you prefer, I can start you off on the road to redemption by just asking you nine straight questions. All *you* need do is reply and be honest."

Finally, our eyes met.

I thought – well. I thought in one big golden blank. To my relief my voice came out again, not in a husky squeak, but crisp now as very dry toast. I was at my most businesslike, and that was how I asked those nine questions.

"First question: Do you reflect in mirrors or reflective surfaces?"

"I don't look anymore. Obviously I don't. I'm undead. My soul – or whatever – that's gone. So, no reflection. The night I realised I threw any mirrors away. And yes, I've learned to shave by touch. I'm good at that, dextrous. It seems to be part of what I am, what I can do, now. The same as I can seem to vanish, even on an empty sidewalk… that kind of thing."

"OK. Second question. Do you go out by day?"

"You *are kidding me*. What do *you* think? Do I look like a case from a burns unit? Yeah, I did once make a mistake. Last winter. I was walking around in broad daylight for one half hour. I was blistered so bad, even inside my clothes, I had to hide for three nights. My *skin*, bits of it, fell off in patches. No. I *don't go* out in sunlight. Sunset is dawn for my kind."

"Question three: How old *are* you?"

"Twenty-two this fall. Next week in fact. I suppose I'll live forever, but I only got started on this *thing* about sixteen months ago."

"Question four…"

"Wait a minute…"

"Question four…" I paused, but he didn't interrupt again. Just looked. With his sorrowful dark eyes. "Do you take and drink human blood? Is that your food?"

"Yes. You know that already. That was what you broke up back there. Me, trying to take and drink and feed on *blood.*"

"Question five."

(He sighed. Nothing else.)

"Do you otherwise eat and drink?"

"No. Oh, water's OK – a glass of wine. Even a beer or a Coke. Fluids seem to digest. I don't risk anything else."

"So your last meal was…"

"Sixteen months ago. I threw it right up."

"So blood is your only sustenance. Which leads us to question six: How often do you do this?"

"Once a week. Roughly. I can go a month without, if I have to. But if I don't, it's… all I can think of."

"Rather like partying with a so-called recreational drug, yes?"

"I wouldn't know," he said icily. "I never tried those."

"Fine. Question seven: Do you shapeshift? I mean, can you seem to become another thing, an animal, say, or even an inanimate object?"

"Yes." (He sounded almost embarrassed, as if he boasted and hadn't wanted to.) "A wolf. Mostly. But once I… I kind of made myself kind of like a phone booth."

I couldn't help it. I burst out laughing. "Did anyone try to – get inside and *make a call?*"

He grinned.

Oh. The grin was beautiful too.

"Yeah. But the door stayed shut."

I pulled us back to grim reality. "Question eight: Ever killed anyone, Anghel?"

"My God – no. No. I don't… I'm careful. It's bad enough being – what I am. I don't want to be a murderer as well."

We were both standing up now. I wasn't sure when I did.

I said, "Question nine, then. And this is the last one. How did you find out you'd become a vampire?"

"How did I…? Look, I'd had suspicions before that we – my family – had the gene for it. I suppose it *is* a gene. Like some families having the gene for red hair, or a particular allergy. I know how it is in books, movies. Someone does it to you, takes your blood and makes you a vampire, just like they are. It didn't happen that way. I said my aunt… I came to realise she was… she was a vampire. She'd just seemed to think she was mad. Everybody put everything weird about her down to that – avoiding sunlight, not eating, that stuff. By the time I connected it all up, she'd been dead two years. And she had left me the legacy. Like she knew I would be the same. So I put it together. I still didn't believe it at first. I said, I want – *wanted* to be a writer. So I started to *write* about it, about my life if I had been, if I was, a vampire. I was trying to sort it out.

"Then I met a girl at some party in Manhattan. And she'd read a story of mine, a pretty lurid one, in some magazine and she… she wanted to act it out with me. Scared me. But when I'm scared – then sometimes I have to do it. Prove to myself I can. So, we did. I didn't hurt her. It's important to me you understand that. She loved every minute, and I had a real difficult time putting her off after. But for me…something changed. Something changed when I took the blood. It was…" He hesitated, looking out at the lake and the moon. "It was like finding something in your own self, *meeting* who you really are – and I wasn't who I'd ever thought. And I was… not better… but I *fit*. And when I went out of the apartment, everything – the street, the city – it was *alive,* and I was *alive,* in a way it and I had never been, not until then. Do you begin to see? I can't explain it. I can write with words, use them, make them work. But with this, I can't *find* the words. It was like I'd walked out – not of a room, but of a dark *cave.* My whole world had only *been* a cave – but now the lights were on and the true world was there all around me, and inside me, forever.

"So, I've answered all your questions, and now I guess your wonderful father and his men arrive and finish me off. Right, Lei? That name on the card though, that's a lie, isn't it? Only one thing puzzles me. Shouldn't it read Anthony *Van Helsing*?"

I shook my head. "*Oh* no, it surely should not. That name on the card is a family name. It's mine too."

He looked quizzical. Sad and quizzical and courageous, all ready to meet some horrible bloodthirsty anti-vampire end of sharpened stakes and villagers with flaming torches ready to burn him alive.

It must have been that that made me feel protective and want to put my arms around him.

But anyhow that was when he laughed again, a very different silky, inky laugh – and then he was gone. There instead stood a great black wolf, the height of a mastiff dog, with eyes like rubies. The wolf too seemed to be laughing. But the next second it sprang away and dove along the lake shore and into the trees.

And *my* next move? I stood there cursing myself.

I knew he wasn't headed for the house, or the town. He had vanished not only from his human shape but out of the life of anyone who'd recently known him. Though everything he said, I was certain, was honest and true, with my artful, smug little plans I'd cornered him, and blown the whole thing. I'd lost him. And worse than that, I had lost him also his own chance of living free and safe in this mad world he had only properly come to see sixteen months before. Oh, Lei. Clever, cunning, know-it-all, stupid, dumb damn Lei.

My father is a physician. He deals with sickness of the psyche and the mind. He has endlessly various patients. He is *good.*

He went into this line of work, as he would be the first to say, because he had already cured both himself, and another member of his family, of a pretty dire life-destructive mental illness. His name, which is real enough, is quite a talking point, but he's found, as I have on the whole, it causes startled amusement rather than giving anything away. It's like that thing about camouflage I mentioned earlier.

Vampirism isn't a disease. It isn't a possession or an evil spell or the devil's work. *It's a way of evolving.* Because the human race did and does evolve. Superman, Batman – they're already around out there. If they keep a low profile, do you *blame* them? A vampire, or what's come to be called a vampire, (the word seems to come from ancient Turkey, and means something like *magician*), is just one more variety of this evolving super-race, the one we watch on screen and read about in books, but which most of us seldom think may just have sat there next to us on the subway.

Vampires are this: They grow up but stay young for a very long while (centuries sometimes). They don't need food or drink, though they *can* eat and drink a little, if they want. Taking another person's blood can bring out awareness of themselves and what they are. But that is only because they have already bought into the idea. That is, they *think* it will, so it does. And in fact where they can come to awareness of the truth *without* assault and robbery, they come to it better and more fully, and with far less damage to themselves. Put it this way: They only go after that blood because they have the notion they are, on some level, vampires. So taking the blood isn't needed. What *is* needed is just facing up to the facts.

Feeding on or drinking blood is – *redundant*. People are *not* the allotted prey, and blood is *not* the essential food. *No vampire on Earth has to have blood.* Just as they don't have to have ordinary food or fluid either. So the Blood Feast made so popular in stories only has value (if that is the right word) in sometimes shocking them into focus for themselves. And believe me, it also hurts them on some deep level too. If you aren't a vampire, though, grabbing blood won't do a darn thing for you. I mean you won't be able to shapeshift or apparently disappear, let alone live to three hundred and forty-nine. Oh, and no vampire can turn anyone else into one by taking their blood. Unless, of course, they already were one to start with.

So, the meaning of blood for vampires is basically a misunderstanding. It has nothing to do with drink or food, with goblets and dishes and the dining table of the world. It is bloodlines – it's genes – as Anghel said. And if you've gotten that gene, you have it. You are a vampire, a Being of the Blood. And one day you'll wake up, and *know,* even if it takes till you're fifty and you look in a mirror (yes, I did say mirror) and think – *I only look twenty-two still. How can this be?*

Because vampires *do* reflect in mirrors, in all reflective surfaces. They cast shadows too. They can even go out all day long in the blazing summer sun. No tan, sure. But the sun won't fry you. Unless, of course, brainwashed by hundreds of years of legendary propaganda, you *believe it will.*

You see, all that stuff is a psychosomatic illness. It *seems* real, so real you'll have the symptoms, as can happen with any major psychosomatic sickness. And in fact a vampire's own abilities can turn against him to reinforce the myth. A vampire *can* seem invisible – so in that looking glass, he is. So you come up in blisters too, and seek a big box to sleep in, and hunt down innocent people and mug them for blood. You can even throw up at the smell of garlic or pass out at a powerful religious symbol. But it isn't for real. It is a kind of *guilt trip.* The vampire knows he is superior. That frightens him. So, unconsciously, he tries to keep himself chained up. No one can be harder on us than we are ourselves, once we've gotten started. Otherwise, a vampire can live forever, maybe. But you don't need a stake or fire to kill him. You can just shoot a vampire dead, and you won't need a special bullet. Vampires are long-lived, not invulnerable. What they can also do are things like seem to be other creatures, vanish, sometimes fly, and, obviously, call animals to them and ask *them* to do things – like a stag, for example. We don't abuse these gifts. Not when we grasp what we are and why. But then, some of us are lucky. I grew up in a partly vampiric family. I knew by age three what I was, and when I found on my tenth birthday I could turn into a fox, my Dad took a photo of me like that. I still have that picture. Yes, cameras can catch us too.

My father does look remarkably young. He puts it down, to his patients, as the vitamins he takes. And his name – our family name? Draculian. Anthony Draculian. Lelystra Draculian. But no, we're not from that famous branch of our kind (the Romanian one, brought to public attention in the 1800s by clever Mr. Stoker). Though, if you trace bloodlines back far enough, we are related.

And there, you see, these were all the things I should have said to poor, handsome, unhappy Anghel. And instead I'd been flustered and messed up.

I had to stay another two days with the Kokersons. I did it and it was hell. But then, there wasn't much point in running back to Dad two days early, howling about my dismal failure. Anghel was gone. I knew I'd never see him again; I knew I could have helped and instead I only helped make his life worse.

I did put one call through to Dad. But he was with a patient. Oh, let it wait then till I was home. I'd have all the rest of my days after all, to blame myself, and to regret.

Anthony has his office way across town. We live in a big russet brownstone on the corner of Dale and Landry. It's a nice area.

I'd tried to call him again from the cell phone booth on the train, but he was back in another eternal meeting. No one was home.

I dumped my bags and then took the little elevator up to our roof garden. It's only a little garden, a kind of outdoor living room. The last roses were dying on the walls, but the grapevine had big purple grapes. I took some off and ate them, gazing down over the parapet at the sun deciding to sink, as it always does, west of the city.

I had never felt I had to go rob someone of their blood. Lucky in that, I said. Lucky me. I'd had it all very easy. Only when Mom died – I was fifteen then. That had been hard. She wasn't like us, Dad and me, or my uncle. She didn't have the gene. I knew they'd talked about – when she was older, how they would handle that... But it never happened, a truck in town saw to that. It killed her. And we, Dad and me, we wouldn't be immune to that either.

The sky was rose gold. Birds were flying like scribbles over it. The city made its noises of trains and cabs and people, but I knew the moment my father came back in the house I would sense it, I always did. And then the oddest idea went through my mind. It made me straighten up and hold my breath a moment. This strange thought was – had my father, my clever amazing father who seemed always to know everything – had he known too Anghel was due to be at the Kokersons' weird ball? Had he known I would see what Anghel was – might try to alter things – even think I'd be the one to save Anghel from the dark he'd stumbled into? If that was it, how much more awful it was going to be, telling Anthony that I *hadn't*...

And this was when I picked up what must *be* Dad, that silent step of his I can always hear, just inside the door below. And next the elevator rising.

I was horrified. Not of Dad – of the thing I'd have to say. I braced myself, with the taste of the grapes in my mouth. And out onto the roof he walked. But it wasn't Anthony. It was Anghel.

I froze. Like the biggest fool, (the one who wins the Oscar for idiocy), I said, "Whuh?"

And he grinned.

His hair was tied back, a long, long black tail falling down his back. He wore jeans, a shirt, a light leather jacket. Even this way, as I had predicted, you couldn't miss he was something else. Different, astonishing.

He said, "It's OK, Lei. I have a pass for the door. Your father gave it to me. He trusts me. Can you?"

Anthony only ever trusts those who really can be trusted. But I'd been kidding myself, hadn't I? It wasn't just I felt I'd messed up, let Anghel, a *patient,* down. It was me I was unhappy for. I hadn't been able to stop thinking of him. I thought I had lost him for good. But here he was.

Very coolly I said, "It's early for you to be out, isn't it? I mean, the sun's not down yet, is it."

"He said – Anthony said – take it slow but try a few new things.

So, I do. Just an hour after sunrise, an hour before sunset. And look…" He was close now, holding out his strong, elegant hands. "Not a single burn."

I swallowed. "So you *are* my father's patient."

"Since yesterday. I've made great strides, yes?"

"Yes. Good." Lamely I studied the buttons on his shirt. They were fine, for buttons. It was better than looking up into his eyes.

"Lei," he said quietly, "thank you."

So then I had to look. When I did, those hands reached out and gently took mine. His touch was fiery, but what else? Something in his eyes had altered too. They weren't less overpowering exactly, but – there was something else in them now. I could see – *Anghel.* That is, I think I mean I could see who he truly was. A man not cruel or mean or a robber, never stupid, rich in possibility, brave, yes, *gallant*… only wanting to find his way.

"I apologise for the wolf stuff – the shape-shift," he said to me. "I was – confused. Had to sort it out. As you see, though, I didn't lose the card. And I called Anthony, and I saw him yesterday. He's OK, your father."

"Yes, he is."

He still held my hands. "Lei," he said, and then, very softly, "Lelystra…" And for the first time in my entire life my name sounded wonderful to me, as if I'd never *heard* it before. "Lelystra, you saved my skin. You saved my sanity. You stopped me becoming something I'd never want. And I don't want – I can't make you any promises or ask for any. Not yet. Not until I *know* I'm really *there*, where I have to be. Where *you* are. But if I make it, then…"

The whole roof was glowing now, the walls, the vines, the grapes, blood-red from the sunfall. And in the blood-red light Anghel leaned forward and kissed my mouth. It was a marvellous kiss, weightless yet profound. As gently as he, I gave it back to him. There in the sunset light as red as blood.

THE WEREWOLF

The house overhung a corner of the heath, where the columns of the trees climbed up into the lanes and streets above. The building was like an outpost, for no other houses were on the road for half a mile, and the streetlights were few. An occasional car passed by on its speeding way to somewhere else. The house was sometimes noted, for it was Gothic in design and had a high tower, turrets, and tall windows fruited with coloured glass. No one approached, and certainly no one was near enough, on nights of the full moon, to catch the screams within the house of the werewolf as he was translated into his bestial shape.

It was a hot summer, and at night a low mist lay along the earth. The treetops were clear, and high above the house stood the smudged white plate of the moon. About eleven, something dark might be seen slinking grotesquely down the outer stairway of the house, between the shrubs.

This was the manner in which the werewolf descended to the heath. The heath was his hunting ground. But not always did he locate prey there, and then not always human – the kind for which he lusted. It was the moonlight night between the trees which drew him primarily, perhaps more than the severe hunger for blood. In the form of such a thing as he became, he could not stay inside the walls of a house, even the Gothic house on the slope.

The heath by night was like a frame of the past. The werewolf's beast eyes did not see the litter of chocolate wrappers, cans, cigarettes and condoms. The beast existed in a world of primal timelessness. The beast did not think – or have a need to.

Now and then, the remains of the werewolf's feasts had been uncovered, and had given rise to an ongoing legend of unsolved murder cases, loosely known by the title of The Heath Hacker.

Though unnatural they were not rated as *super*natural, and though once or twice over the years police had called at the isolated house, its occupant had never been under suspicion.

He was a small, mild, fussy man of late middle age, the antithesis of anything dramatic, and obviously without the physical strength the murders had required.

Generally, bodies were not found, the very little that had been left of them trampled or buried in leaf mould, under boulders, or rolled into deep bushes. Dogs too were inclined to avoid these kills. They ran to their owners with their tails down and their eyes full of green horror.

The dogs knew what the travellers and the questing police did not.

"There is a werewolf on the heath," said Constant to Vivienne.

"What rubbish," said Vivienne, a slender white girl of twenty with maroon hair. And, after a pause, "Why do you say such things?"

"Because of the bones. Look." And bending gracefully he picked up a long stick of creamy grey. "A tibia. And over there another. The third evidence I've seen this afternoon."

"Even if it is a bone," said Vivienne, swinging her heavy rufous hair, "it's animal. Picked clean. A fox, maybe."

"Not of a fox or by a fox. I've noticed none of these bones, therefore none of the carcasses, were dragged into a lair. Normally you'd expect animals to polish off the leftovers, whoever caused them, but these they've left strictly alone."

"Terrified by the taint of wolf."

"Not wolf. *Were*wolf. You mustn't confuse the two."

"But I thought," said Vivienne, "that a werewolf was someone who turned into a wolf."

"In a way," said Constant, elusively. He infuriated her subtly, which was the other reason, aside from his handsome foreignness, which attracted Vivienne to him.

"Well," she said, "we're quite safe by daylight, aren't we? It's only at night that werewolves walk, or stalk, or whatever they do."

"The three nights of the full moon. The full moon affects all of us to some extent. It moves the tides of the sea, and the tides of the water, which makes up so much of the human composition. How could we not be affected? But to a werewolf the tidal urge draws up its inner nature."

They crossed one of the many tracks of the woodland and came out in a great meadow lit by flowers and sun.

"What a lovely summer," said Vivienne. "And no people."

"This is the advantage of a weekday," said Constant. "At night, of course, people do come here."

"For illicit sex," said Vivienne, primly, having made love with

Constant not two hours before.

"And other darker things," said Constant, looking about.

"Murder and evil," said Vivienne.

"You're right," said Constant, "to separate the two concepts. Evil is by itself."

"And the werewolf hunts here," said Vivienne, "over the moonlit grass, chasing the sly rapists and skulking muggers."

"Of course."

"You really believe what you say," accused Vivienne.

They left the meadow and were under the trees again.

"This is a fearful place," said Constant, "a sink of ancient crimes. You can only see the yellow flowers and hear the birds singing. At night everything is black and white. The birds hide, the flowers close fast."

"And the werewolf bounds between the trees."

Constant stopped.

Vivienne stopped also and turned to see.

Above the wood the ground ran upwards.

"That's the way onto South Heath Road."

"That house," said Constant.

"Oh that – it's marvellous, isn't it," said Vivienne. "You can see it further up on the heath too, by Walworth Lane. But here's best. I used to come and draw it years ago."

"You were most unwise," said Constant.

"Nonsense," said Vivienne. "There were six or seven of us used to come here in a group. Once we saw the funny man who lived there. He came out and sort of hippity-hopped down that stair to put something out over the garden wall."

"I hope you didn't go to see what it was."

"Joanie did. It was a great mound of awful old curtains. There was a place where things were burnt. He was obviously going to burn them sometime."

"And this man with the curtains," said Constant, "what was he like?"

"About five feet five, slim in a plump, weak sort of way, with a round pudding of a face. He had thin hair and baggy trousers and a cardigan, and he wore slippers."

"What a good memory you have," said Constant slowly.

"I wonder if he still lives there?" pondered Vivienne. "I should think so."

They were walking up through the wood towards the house. Its wall and flight of steps hung over them through the poles of the trees and the garlands of thick green leaves.

"There's the burning place," said Vivienne. "And look, something's smouldering there now. Naughty, in this heat."

"He would find fire attractive," said Constant, "in his human form. Things that sparkle. Fire, water, jewels."

"Oh yes?"

"One of the oldest ways to hypnotise his kind," said Constant, "a diamond in a bowl of water. Or a ruby under a candle. In the human form only. Once transmogrified, nothing can reach him. He is all beast."

"You think the funny pudding man in slippers is your werewolf?"

"Look at the house," said Constant. "The coloured bright windows, the dark tower."

"Isn't it just too apt?"

"Your reasoning is overly sophisticated," said Constant. "You're dealing here with something very simple, and utterly terrible."

"Brr," said Vivienne. "Can we come back at full moon and see?"

"Tonight is full moon."

"Is it? Well, then. We can lie in wait. Catch him out."

"You don't understand, Vivienne. It's he who would catch you. He would tear you in pieces and devour you."

"Nasty. Then I'd need a silver bullet."

"A silver bullet isn't necessary. Is useless."

"Now you should know," said Vivienne, "you can't kill a werewolf without one."

"It's just a misunderstanding," said Constant. "Usually such executions were carried out by villages in remote places where ammunition was scarce or obsolete. The bullet was made from some holy object melted down, a cross from the church, say, or the replica of a saint. It's the faith of the hunter which assures the shot. Otherwise a werewolf is impossible to kill."

"You mean you must have faith in God."

"Yes, I mean exactly that. Faith in something other than the power of evil."

"I wouldn't be any good, then," Vivienne said seriously, after a silence.

"I know. You're too young, Vivienne, and your culture is too young."

"Oh really? Well, you're no better."

"My country to yours," he said, "is an old bowed man. And I'm far older, Vivienne, although not in years."

"Then you can kill the werewolf?" she asked, mockingly, as they stood among the trees below the Gothic house, and the birds sang in the sunlight.

"I believe in God," said Constant. "Perhaps I could kill the werewolf. But who said I was going to try?"

By the late afternoon a golden glow filled the heath, and the dark amber of the shadows lay thickly twisted on the ground between the trees. The things of the day fed and played and darted in the last spaces of sunlight. Everything busied itself, for now time was running out.

The westering sun worked tricks too with the windows of the house, finding in them long daggers of rose red and Egyptian green.

The door was of oak, with a black iron knocker of an imp's head. Constant, standing alone in the porch, considered the knocker; and then used it decisively.

There was an extended interval between the knock and any sound inside the house, but Constant did not knock again. He knew the house's inhabitant was obedient and law-abiding and would come to answer the summons. Presently there was a faint shuffling from beyond the door. It opened.

"Good afternoon," said Constant.

"Yes?" asked the inhabitant of the house. He was the height Vivienne had described and had to look up half a foot into Constant's face. Though slim, his body was composed of curves, and a little round tummy pushed at his poplin shirt and fawn trousers. His head was also round, and in the round countenance two fish-pale eyes gazed, not unfriendly, into Constant's own. It was a mild creature, shy but trusting. "How can I help you?"

"It was your wonderful house," said Constant.

"My house."

"I was wondering if you would object if I took some photographs? Only for my own personal record. I am intrigued by architecture."

Constant put out his left hand and readjusted the camera case he was holding. Something glittered. The man's eyes shifted and came to rest there. As Constant put down his hand again, the man's eyes followed it avidly.

"No, no objection, of course. Please feel free."

Constant thanked the obliging householder, who stood and watched him as he went back down the steps and retreated a little way along the slope. Here he removed from the camera case an impressive looking Nikon, set it up on a monopod, and began apparently to frame a shot.

After Constant had taken two or three photographs of the façade of the house, the man went back inside. Maybe he would watch from windows, between the screens of coloured glass.

Constant went about the building slowly, sometimes ascending the slope, now and then kneeling in the grass.

On the smallest finger of his left hand the diamond flashed in his father's ring, a piece of jewellery which Constant did not normally wear.

After perhaps fifteen minutes, the front door of the house reopened. The man came out and stood watching Constant take a long-angled shot of the tower.

"Have you finished? I didn't want to disturb you. I wondered if you'd care for a cup of tea."

English tea, probably from teabags, and with milk, had never appealed to Constant, but now he nodded enthusiastically. He returned to the house, having closed up the camera in its case and telescoped the monopod.

"That's very kind of you."

"I thought you might like to see something of the inside as well."

"I would," Constant said.

From a black and white chequerboard floor a stair curved up, a carved indulgence, and highly polished – someone must come in, presumably in the mornings or early afternoons, leaving, in winter, long before it got dark. Above the stair a huge window of crimson lilies and Nile water showered the hall, and their skins, with tinted lights like some beautiful disease.

His host led Constant into a drawing-room. There were two more windows, each with an ornate female figure, perhaps Muses, for they were classically adorned, and with Burne-Jones hair, rather like Vivienne's in colour. Otherwise the room was stuffed full of elderly furniture, bulging couches and chairs and a plethora of small tables. The ceiling was a carousel of plaster shapes, fruits and vines, echoed in a gilt mirror above the fireplace. Despite the attentions of the help, there was an aura of dust, weightless as the deepening sunlight.

They sat down, and the man poured out the tea in a careful, feminine way. Constant took his without milk and was pleased to note the werewolf had used leaves.

"I hope you got the pictures you wanted."

"I hope so too; the light's a little undependable at this time."

"Yes, the evening draws on. I like this hour of day. I find it restful."

Constant smiled politely and raised his cup.

"Forgive my saying so, but I'm quite fascinated by your ring."

"A family heirloom," said Constant. "It belonged to my father. Would you like to see it more closely?" He slipped off the ring and handed it to the little man in the poplin shirt. Who grasped it, *absorbed* it, and taking it over to the light, *played* with it, turning it this way and that, over and over, to make it glitter.

Constant surreptitiously timed him. It was a full six minutes before the werewolf turned and said, regretfully, "An excellent stone. I confess I'm drawn to such things – as you are to houses. I have a small collection, some rubies, a diamond."

Constant retrieved the ring from reluctant fingers and got up. "Thank you for the tea."

"But stay a little longer," said the werewolf looking at him with luminous lonely eyes. "I can show you over the house."

"That's remarkably kind of you, but unfortunately I have to be in Walworth by seven."

"Meeting a young lady perhaps," said the werewolf, playfully.

"No, actually. Then again I sometimes walk the heath at dusk, the quietest time, I find. Perhaps I could call on you again."

The eyes of the werewolf gave off a peculiar stony flash. Had no one ever noticed this before, police questioning after murders, shopkeepers, the weekly help? It was the beast part of the subconscious brain incoherently communicating. For there were nights like tonight when the full moon rose at dusk. Perhaps it would be possible to add this diamond to the collection? Off what bitten and ravaged fingers, ears and throats had the other trophies come?

"Of course, feel free to knock. I may not answer unless I can be sure it's you. I'm sensibly rather nervous of callers after dark."

He took Constant back across the chequered floor where the

colours of the window had deepened to blood and chartreuse.

They parted at the door with expressions of mutual friendliness, having not exchanged their names.

Outside on the mellow heath, Constant studied his watch. Two hours before dark.

The light perished in stages. Birds quartered the sky, sank and vanished into the high coronas of the trees. A deft rustling in the undergrowth signalled the passaging of other daylight entities to their holes and burrows. A few people came walking along Walworth Lane, heading out of the woodland towards the traffic lights and busy high street of Walworth, one mile off along the road.

Constant sat on a fallen tree beside the lane. Behind him, still partly concealed in bushes, was his motorbike. As the flame began to leave the sky, he drew the bike out and walked it up the steep incline. He stood among the tree trunks, looking down across the umbra of the heath.

To the naked eye, the towered house a quarter of a mile away was quite visible, small and perfect as a model above the trees. It stood in a bowl of gold, the last traces of the sunset. A pale ghost, caught on the rim of the light, the moon had already risen.

The heat of the sky went to ashes.

Constant set the camera on the monopod and attached the powerful zoom lens. He set his sights for the outer stairway of the house.

The image leapt towards him. He could see the brickwork on the wall, flower heads on the shrubs. As the afterglow faded, the sullen marble stare of the moon took over, a cold blind eye.

He saw now in black and white.

Constant waited.

After ten minutes something dark appeared on the stairway. It might have been anything, perhaps a large dog let out. It passed between the shrubs, and paused, and the moon came over the house, so everything was lit up in a cool white searchlight. The thing on the stairway raised its head. Constant saw it through the lens.

It was black like a ball of shadow. The skull was a little too large for the body so that in form it was like a boar; heavy-headed, powerful in the shoulder. The black head was something like a wolf's, with a great ruff of black hair. The mouth came open and all the teeth appeared in the muzzle, not the teeth of a wolf but each pointed, the canines enormous, and between them the movement of a thick black tongue.

Constant touched the button of the camera, and the head swung. Across a quarter mile of dusk and sudden silence, the eyes of the thing on the stair met Constant's eye within the lens. The eyes were red even in moonlight, with a sheen like oil. They held a thousand years of awareness but not a single thought. They were not the eyes of a wolf, but of some creature older and unremittingly terrible, inimical to yet entirely belonging with man. The eyes of a monster not a beast.

Constant depressed the button of the camera.

The tiny click echoed sheer and sharp across the sloping valley. It was the only sound.

The werewolf heard.

Its muzzle wrinkled and its soulless eyes became two pits of blood. Constant heaved the camera free and thrust it and the lens into their case, folded up the monopod, and slung them on the bike.

Mounting the bike, he gunned the engine into life.

In his vision was the image of the werewolf pouring suddenly over down the stair like a bolt of black liquid.

The motorbike cannoned into motion. It swerved down the hill between the trees and skated out onto the road. Bearing left, it burst forward and the pillars of the trees became a blur. Ground erupted beneath the wheels and was gone.

The bike could outrace death. As he rode between the shadows, Constant murmured a few words of thanks, in Latin.

He was almost off the lane when he made out the two figures walking towards him along the edge of the road.

Constant jammed the bike to a standstill.

He waved at them, the two young men in denims and T-shirts, walking hand in hand until they saw him coming, not pleased to encounter him.

"Don't go onto the heath."

"What's he say?" one of them asked the other.

"A member of the moral majority," said this other; and grinned.

"There is a wild animal loose," said Constant. "There is danger."

"He's nuts," said the first boy.

"Piss off," said the second boy to Constant.

They shrugged him away and strolled on along the lane, the black shade of the trees coming down to smother them. The low mist was forming in veils.

Constant shouted after them once. It was useless. What could he tell them they would believe? They would have to take their chances along with the other creatures of the night. Perhaps something might distract the werewolf, it might take a different path. It could not have seen the camera, though it had looked straight at it, and the sound of the button might have been anything. To the thing it was, a camera anyway was senseless.

Constant raced the motorbike on and came to the lights, the intersection, the brink of the high street, its shops, and cars in flight. Only there, hesitating a moment, did he seem to hear a distant noise, far back among the trees. It might have been a squeal of brakes, the call of a night bird, or a human cry, stripped of all meaning but fear.

"What have you been doing all afternoon?" asked Vivienne.

"Developing some film."

"Let me see."

"No, there's nothing that would interest you," said Constant.

"You've been back to that house," said Vivienne, shaking her sea green beads. "What did you find?"

"Which house?" said Constant.

"Did you know, there's been another murder on the heath? Not The Hacker. Did you read about it?"

"I never read newspapers," said Constant.

"It was very gory," said Vivienne. "But a jealous lover; they think. The man was gay. Torn in pieces."

"Just one," said Constant. The other must have run, perhaps been felled in another place, more thoroughly devoured, or hidden.

"The heath is horrible," said Vivienne petulantly.

"I would advise you then to avoid it," said Constant. "For now."

The black iron imp knocked against the oak door with especial force, and birds in the neighbouring trees took fright.

Constant attended on the knock as he had done before. And after some while, as before, the door was dutifully opened.

Late afternoon light fell slanting on the curves of the gentle face, the innocent belly. This time the shirt was of grey rayon.

"Good afternoon," said Constant. "Do you remember? I took some photographs of your house and you were kind enough to give me tea."

"Ah, yes," the man said. "I do indeed remember."

"I thought," said Constant, "you might care to see the pictures." With his diamonded left hand, he tapped a folder.

"Oh yes, oh yes indeed."

The door was opened wide, and Constant admitted. Familiar, rose and green fell from the window. In the drawing-room the two Muses were at their stations. A faint cobweb floated high up in the plaster carousel of the ceiling. Peach-coloured, the light leaned on the mirror above the fireplace.

They sat down. One by one, Constant handed the householder his views of the house. Of the tall façade, the windows and the steps, the angled tower.

"These are really quite splendid," said the man, admiringly. "A true professional job. The hour is rather later today; can I offer you a sherry?"

Constant, who did not like sherry, professed pleasure.

The man brought two small glasses of gold and set them on the table where the pictures lay.

"There's one more I should like to show you," Constant said. "It was taken from across the heath, and the sun had gone down. Infrared film. The quality is rather grainy, I'm afraid."

The little man took the photograph and stared at it. He stared a long time. "But what is this?"

"A view of the outer stairway."

"Yes, I see – but…"

"You notice something on the steps?" said Constant.

"Surely," said the werewolf, "only a strange shadow."

"Do shadows have eyes?"

The man laughed uneasily. He took a sip of his sherry. "What can it be, I wonder?"

"Perhaps you own a dog?" said Constant, helpfully.

The man blinked. "No. No dog. I've never been able to get on with animals."

"I wonder what it is, then," said Constant. "It looks like an animal, doesn't it?"

"Yes... very like one. How odd." The windows were clouding, the peach ray was gone from the mirror. "Possibly, some light..." The man went to a series of lamps and switched them on one by one. The room lit up and the windows turned blue. "Once the sun goes down," said the werewolf, "this house grows very dark."

"The moon was shining when I took the photograph," said Constant. "A full moon, very bright."

The werewolf lifted up the photograph a second time and peered at it short-sightedly. "Probably I should fetch my glasses. I can't make it out at all. What do you think it is?"

"Oh," said Constant, "*I* think it's a photograph of you."

"Of me?" The werewolf raised his head.

All at once there was a suggestion of heaviness to his skull and shoulders, something ape-like, and the eyes were flat and thoughtless, some instinct struggling to pierce to their surface. Failing.

"If I had come back last week," said Constant, "there would have been no doubt. But of course the nights of the full moon are over until next month, aren't they?"

"But this isn't human," said the man resentfully.

"Not human? Would you say it was a wolf?"

"Maybe," said the man, cautiously, almost bashfully.

"No, it isn't a wolf," said Constant. "That is a misnomer. The wolf is a clean animal whose eyes are like a man's. What eyes does this thing have? Like the Devil. Perhaps the superstitions of wolves, the lies, what men fear when they hear the cry of a wolf: That. But this is a beast from the swamp at the bottom of man's soul. A beast from the id. Solely man's. Completely human."

Constant got up and drew something else out of the folder. He unwrapped it quickly. It was a steak knife from Selfridges.

"No," said the man, moving backwards, judging his route, through long proximity, between the bulky furniture.

"There is another way, of course, to see the change," said Constant. He ran forward and stuck the knife into the werewolf's round belly, until only the handle protruded.

The werewolf gave a scream and fell on to the floor. His blood splashed round him. He tried to pull out the knife and did not have the strength.

Constant watched.

Outside was the shadow of a moonless dusk, but in the room the lamps fully illuminated the death-throes. Then they illuminated the long after-spasms as the body altered, the clothes splitting and the skin heaving, the great muscles pumping up and the hair swarming out like a dark forest. Halfway through, the transmogrification ceased, unable to sustain itself without life. What was left on the carpet was a thing one third a man and two thirds some sort of beast, unlike anything yet reminiscent of a wolf. From the guts of this Constant plucked his knife, wrapped it, and replaced it with the photographs in his folder. What the police would say when they were called by the help was a matter for conjecture.

Constant left the lights burning and went out through the hall. The window cast on him a last meteor shower. The rest of the house hung dark and silent in a void. He closed the door with care and walked away over the heath in the night.

THE JANFIA TREE

Author's Note:

There are many marvellous legends of tree spirits. The darkness of my version has to do, I think, with the fearful danger of projection. Life can be what you make it. Beware.

After eight years of what is termed 'bad luck', it becomes a way of life. One is no longer anything so dramatic as unhappy. One achieves a sort of state of what can only be described as de-happiness. One expects nothing, not even, actually, the worst. A certain relaxation follows, a certain equilibrium. Not flawless, of course. There are still moments of rage and misery. It is very hard to give up hope, that last evil let loose from Pandora's box of horrors. And it is always, in fact, after a bout of hope, springing without cause, perishing not necessarily at any fresh blow but merely from the absence of anything to sustain it, that there comes a revulsion of the senses. A wish, not exactly for death, but for the torturer at least to step out of the shadows, to reveal himself, and his plans. And to this end one issues invitations, generally very trivial ones, a door forgetfully unlocked, a stop light driven through. Tempting fate, they call it.

"Well, you do look tired," said Isabella, who had met me in her car, in the town, in the white dust that veiled and covered everything.

I agreed that perhaps I did look tired.

"I'm so sorry about…" said Isabella. She checked herself, thankfully, on my thanks. "I expect you've had enough of all that. And this other thing. That's not for a while, is it?"

"Not until next month."

"That gives you time to take a break at least."

"Yes."

It was a very minor medical matter to which she referred. Any one of millions would have been glad, I was sure, to exchange their intolerable suffering for something twice as bad. For me, it filled the quota quite adequately. I had not been sleeping very well. Isabella's offer of the villa had seemed, not like an escape, since that was impossible, yet like an island. But I wished she would talk about something else.

Mind-reading, "Look at the olives, aren't they splendid?" she said, as we hurtled up the road.

I looked at the olives through the blinding sun and dust.

"And there it is, you see? Straight up there in the sky."

The villa rose, as she said, in the hard sky above; on a crest of gilded rock curtained with cypress and pine. The building was alabaster in the sun, and, like alabaster, had a pinkish inner glow where the light exchanged itself with the shade. Below, the waves of the olives washed down to the road, shaking to silver as the breeze ruffled them. It was all very beautiful, but one comes in time to regard mortal glamours rather as the Cathars regarded them, snares of the Devil to hide the blemishes beneath, to make us love a world which will defile and betray us.

The car sped up the road and arrived on a driveway in a flaming jungle of bougainvillea and rhododendrons.

Isabella led me between the stalks of the veranda, into the villa, with all the pride of money and goodwill. She pointed out to me, on a long immediate tour, every excellence, and showed me the views, which were exceptional, from every window and balcony.

"Marta's away down the hill at the moment, but she'll be back quite soon. She says she goes to visit her aunt, but I suspect it's a lover. But she's a dulcet girl. You can see how nicely she keeps everything here. With the woman who cooks, that's just about all, except for the gardeners, but they won't be coming again for a week. So no one will bother you."

"That does sound good."

"Save myself of course," she added. "I shall keep an eye on you. And tomorrow, remember, we want you across for dinner. Down there, beyond those pines, we're just over that spectacular ridge. Less than half a mile. Indeed, if you want to, you can send us Morse signals after dark from the second bathroom window. Isn't that fun? So near, so far."

"Isabella, you're really too kind to me."

"Nonsense," she said. "Who else would be, you pessimistic old sausage?" And she took me into her arms, and to my horror I shed tears, but not many. Isabella, wiping her own eyes, said it had done me good. But she was quite wrong.

Marta arrived as we were having drinks at the east end of the veranda. She was a pretty, sunlit creature, who looked about fourteen and was probably eighteen or so. She greeted me politely, rising from the bath of her liaison. I felt nothing very special about her, or that. Though I am often envious of the stamina, youth and health of others, I have never wanted to be any of them.

"Definitely, a lover," said Isabella, when the girl was gone. "My God, do you remember what it was like at her age? All those clandestine fumblings in grey city places."

If that had been true for her, it had not been true of me, but I smiled.

"But here," she said, "in all this honey heat, these scents and flowers. Heaven on earth – Arcadia. Well, at least I'm here with good old Alec. And he hands me quite a few surprises, he's quite the boy, now and then."

"I've been meaning to ask you," I said, "that flowering tree along there, what is it?"

I had not been meaning to ask, had only just noticed the particular tree. But I was afraid of flirtatious sexual revelations. I had been denied in love-desire too long, and celibate too long, to find such a thing comfortable. But Isabella, full of intrigued interest in her own possessions, got up at once and went with me to inspect the tree.

It stood high in a white and terracotta urn, its stem and head in silhouette against a golden noon. There was a soft pervasive scent which, as I drew closer, I realised had lightly filled all the veranda like a bowl with water.

"Oh yes, the fragrance," she said. "It gets headier later in the day, and at night it's almost overpowering. Now, what is it?" She fingered dark glossy leaves and found a tiny slender bloom, of a sombre white. "This will open after sunset," she said. "Oh Lord, what *is* the name?" She stared at me and her face cleared, glad to give me another gift. "Janfia," she said. "Now I can tell you all about it. Janfia – it's supposed to be from the French, *Janvier*."

It was a shame to discourage her. "January. Why? Does it start to bloom then?"

"Well, perhaps it's supposed to, although it doesn't. No. It's something to do with January, though."

"Janus, maybe," I said, "two-faced god of doorways. You always plant it by a doorway or an opening into a house? A guardian tree." I had almost said: a tree for good luck.

"That might be it. But I don't think it's protective. No, now isn't there some story...? I do hope I can recall it. It's like the legend of the myrtle – or is it the basil? You know the one, with a spirit living in the tree."

"That's the myrtle. Venus, or a nymph, coming out for dalliance at night, hiding in the branches by day. The basil is a severed head. The basil grows from the mouth of the head and tells the young girl her brothers have murdered her lover, whose *decapitum* is in the pot."

"Yum, yum," said Isabella. "Well, Alec will know about the Janfia. I'll get him to tell you when you come to dinner tomorrow."

I smiled again. Alec and I made great efforts to get along with each other, for Isabella's sake. We both found it difficult. He did not like me, and I, reciprocating, had come to dislike him in turn. Now our only bond, aside from Isabella, was natural sympathy at the irritation each endured in the presence of the other.

As I said goodbye to Isabella, I was already wondering how I could get out of the dinner.

I spent the rest of the afternoon unpacking and organising myself for my stay, swimming all the while in amber light, pausing frequently to gaze out across the pines, the sea of olive groves. A little orange church rose in the distance, and a sprawling farm with Roman roofs. The town was already well lost in purple shadow. I began, from the sheer charm of it, to have moments of pleasure. I had dreaded their advent but received them mutely. It was all right, it was all right to feel this mindless animal sweetness. It did not interfere with the other things, the darkness, the sword hanging by a thread. I had accepted that, that it was above me, then why trouble with it?

But I began to feel well. I began to feel all the chances were not gone. I risked red wine and ate my supper greedily, enjoying being waited on.

During the night, not thinking to sleep in the strange bed, I slept a long while. When I woke once, there was an extraordinary floating presence in the bedroom. It was the perfume of the Janfia tree, entering the open shutters from the veranda below. It must stand directly beneath my window. Mine was the open way it had been placed to favour. How deep and strangely clear was the scent.

When I woke in the morning, the scent had gone, and my stomach was full of knots of pain and ghastly nausea. The long journey, the heat, the rich food, the wine. Nevertheless, it gave me my excuse to avoid the unwanted dinner with Isabella and Alec.

I called her about eleven o'clock. She commiserated. What could she say? I must rest and take care, and we would all meet further along the week.

In the afternoon, when I was beginning to feel better, she woke me from a long hot doze with two plastic containers of local yoghurt, which would apparently do wonders for me.

"I'll only stay a moment. God, you do look pale. Haven't you got something to take for it?"

"Yes. I've taken it."

"Well. Try the yoghurt, too."

"As soon as I can manage anything, I'll try the yoghurt."

"By the way," she said, "I can tell you the story of the Janfia now." She stood in the bedroom window, looking out and down at it. "It's extremely sinister. Are you up to it, I wonder?"

"Tell me, and see."

Although I had not wanted the interruption, now it had arrived, I was oddly loth to let her go. I wished she would have stayed and had dinner with me herself, alone. Isabella had always tried to be kind to me. Then again, I was useless with people now. I could relate to no one, could not give them any quarter. I would be better off on my own.

"Well, it seems there was a poet, young and handsome, for whose verses princes would pay in gold."

"Those were the days," I said idly.

"Come, it was the fifteenth century. No sewers, no antibiotics, only superstition and gold could get you by."

"You sound nostalgic, Isabella."

"Shush now. He used to roam the countryside, the young poet, looking for inspiration, doubtless finding it with shepherdesses, or whatever they had here then. One dusk he smelled an exquisite fragrance, and, searching for its source, came on a bush of pale opening flowers. So enamoured was he of the perfume that he dug up the bush, took it home with him, and planted it in a pot on the balcony outside his room. Here it grew into a tree, and here the poet, dreaming, would sit all afternoon, and when night fell, and the moon rose, he would carry his mattress onto the balcony, and go to sleep under the moon-shade of the tree's foliage."

Isabella broke off. Already falling into the idiom, she said, "Am I going to write this, or are you?"

"I'm too tired to write nowadays. And anyway, I can't sell anything. You do it."

"We'll see. After all the trouble I had with that cow of an editor over my last…"

"And meantime, finish the story, Isabella."

Isabella beamed.

She told me; it began to be noticed that the poet was very wan, very thin, very listless. That he no longer wrote a line, and soon all he did was to sit all day and lie all night long by the tree. His companions looked in vain for him in the taverns and his patrons looked in vain for his verse. Finally, a very great prince, the lord of the town, went himself to the poet's room. Here, to his dismay, he found the poet stretched out under the tree. It was close to evening, the evening star stood in the sky and the young moon, shining in through the leaves of the Janfia tree upon the poet's white face which was now little better than a beautiful skull. He seemed near to death, which the prince's physicians, being called in, confirmed. "How," cried the prince, in grief, "have you come to this condition?"

Then, though it was not likely to restore him, he begged the poet to allow them to take him to some more comfortable spot.

The poet refused. "Life is nothing to me now." he said. And he asked the prince to leave him, for the night was approaching and he wished to be alone.

The prince was at once suspicious. He sent the whole company away, and only he returned with stealth, and hid himself in the poet's room, to see what went on.

Sure enough, at midnight, when the sky was black and the moon rode high, there came a gentle rustling in the leaves of the Janfia. Presently there stepped forth into the moonlight a young man, dark-haired and pale of skin, clothed in garments that seemed woven of the foliage of the tree itself. And he, bending over the poet, kissed him, and the poet stretched up his arms. And what the prince then witnessed filled him with abysmal terror, for not only was it a demon he watched, but one which performed acts utterly proscribed by Mother Church. Eventually overcome, the prince lost consciousness. When he roused, the dawn was breaking, the tree stood scentless and empty, and the poet, lying alone, was dead.

"So naturally," said Isabella, with relish, "there was a cry of witchcraft, and the priests came, and the tree was burnt to cinders. All but for one tiny piece the prince found, to his astonishment, he had broken off. Long after the poet had been buried, in unhallowed ground, the prince kept this little piece of the Janfia tree, and eventually thinking it dead, he threw it from his window out into the garden of his palace."

She looked at me.

"Where it grew," I said, "watered only by the rain, and nurtured only by the glow of the moon by night."

"Until an evening came," said Isabella, "when the prince, overcome by a strange longing, sat brooding in his chair. And all at once an amazing perfume filled the air, so mysterious, so irresistible, he dared not even turn his head to see what it portended. And as he sat thus, a shadow fell across his shoulder on to the floor in front of him, and then a quiet, leaf-cool hand was laid upon his neck."

She and I burst out laughing.

"Gorgeous," I said. "Erotic, Gothic, perverse, Wildean, Freudian. Yes."

"Now tell me you won't write it."

I shook my head. "No. Maybe later, sometime. If you don't. But your story still doesn't explain the name, does it?"

"Alec said it might be something to do with Ianus being the male form of the name Diana – the moon and the night. But it's tenuous. Oh," she said, "you do look so much better."

Thereby reminding me that I was ill, and that the sword still hung by its hair, and that all we had shared was a derivative little horror story from the back hills.

"Are you sure you can't manage dinner?" she said.

"Probably could. Then I'd regret it. No, thank you. Just for now, I'll stick to that yoghurt, or it to me, whatever it does."

"All right. Well, I must dash. I'll call you tomorrow."

I had come to the villa for solitude in a different climate, but learned, of course, that climate is climate, and that solitude too is always precisely and only that. In my case, the desire to be alone was simply the horror of not being so. Besides, I never was alone, dogged by the sick, discontented and unshakable companions of my body, my own restless mind. The sun was wonderful, and the place was beautiful, but I quickly realised I did not know what to do with the sun and the beauty. I needed to translate them, perhaps, into words, certainly into feelings, but neither would respond as I wished. I kept a desultory journal, then gave it up. I read and soon found I could not control my eyes enough to get them to focus on the pages. On the third evening, I went to dinner with Isabella and Alec, did my best, watched Alec do his best, came back a little drunk, more ill in soul than in body. Disgraced myself in private by weeping.

Finally, the scent of the Janfia tree, coming in such tides into the room, drew me to the window.

I stood there, looking down at the veranda, the far away hills beyond described only by starlight, the black tree much nearer, with here and there its moonburst of smoky white, an open flower.

And I thought about the poet, and the incubus that was the spirit of the tree. It was the hour to think of that. A demon which vampirised and killed by irresistible pleasures of the flesh. What an entirely enchanting thought. After all, life itself vampirised, and ultimately killed, did it not, by a constant, equally irresistible, administration of the exact reverse of pleasure?

But since I had no longer any belief in God, I had lost all hopes of anything supernatural abroad in the universe. There was evil, naturally, in its abstract or human incarnations, but nothing artistic, no demons stepping from trees by night.

Just then, the leaves of the Janfia rustled. Some night breeze was passing through them, though not, it seemed, through any other thing which grew on the veranda.

A couple of handsome, shy wild cats came and went at the villa. The woman who cooked left out scraps for them, and I had seen Marta, one morning, leaving a large bowl of water in the shade of a cypress they were wont to climb. A cat then, prowling along the veranda rail, was disturbing the tree. I tried to make out the flash of eyes. Presently, endeavouring to do this, I began to see another thing.

It was a shadow, cast from the tree, but not in the tree's shape. Nor was there light, beyond that of the stars above the hills, to fashion it. A man, then, young and slender, stood below me, by the

Janfia, and from a barely suggested paleness, like that of a thin half-moon, it seemed he might be looking up towards my room.

A kind of instinct made me move quickly back, away from the window. It was a profound and primitive reaction, which startled me, and refreshed me. It had no place on the modern earth, and scarcely any name. A kind of panic – the pagan fear of something elemental, godlike and terrible. Caught up in it, for a second, I was no longer myself, no longer the one I dreaded most in all the world. I was no one, only a reaction to an unknown matter, more vital than sickness or pessimism, something from the days when all ills and joys were in the charge of the gods, when men need not think, but simply *were*.

And then, I did think. I thought of some intruder, something rational, and I moved into the open window again, and looked down, and there was nothing there. Just the tree against the starlight.

"Isabella," I said to her over the telephone, "would you mind if I had that tree carried up to my bedroom?"

"Tree?"

I laughed brightly. "I don't mean one of the pines. The little Janfia. It's funny, but you know I hadn't been sleeping very well – the scent seems to help. I thought, actually in the room, it would be about foolproof. Non-stop inhalations of white double brandies."

"Well, I don't see why not. Only, mightn't it give you a headache, or something? All that carbon monoxide – or is it dioxide? – plants exude at night. Didn't someone famous suffocate themselves with flowers? One of Mirabeau's mistresses, wasn't it? No, that was with a charcoal brazier…"

"The thing is," I said, "your two gardeners have arrived this morning, after all. And between them, they shouldn't have any trouble getting the urn upstairs. I'll have it by the window. No problems with asphyxia that way."

"Oh well, if you want, why not?" Having consented, she babbled for a moment over how I was doing and assured me she would 'pop in' tomorrow. Alec had succumbed to some virus, and she had almost forgotten me. I doubted that I would see her for the rest of the week.

Marta scintillantly organised the gardeners. Each gave me a narrow look. But they raised the terracotta and the tree, bore them grunting up to the second floor, plonked them by the window as requested. Marta even followed this up with a can of water to sprinkle the earth. That done, she pulled two desiccated leaves off the tree with a coarse functional disregard. It was part of the indoor furnishings now and must be cared for.

I had been possessed by a curious idea, which I called, to myself, an experiment. It was impossible that I had seen anything, any 'being', on the veranda. That was an alcoholic fantasy. But then again, I had an urge to call the bluff of the Janfia tree. Because it seemed to me responsible, in its own way, for my mirage. Perhaps the blooms were mildly hallucinogenic. If so, I meant to test them. In lieu of any other social event or creative project, an investigation of the Janfia would have to serve.

By day it gave, of course, very little scent; in the morning it had seemed to have none at all. I sat and watched it a while, then stretched out for a siesta. Falling asleep, almost immediately I dreamed that I lay bleeding in a blood-soaked bed, in the middle of a busy city pavement. People stepped around me, sometimes cursing the obstacle. No one would help me. Somebody – formless, genderless – when I caught at a sleeve, detached me with a good-natured, "Oh, you'll be all right."

I woke up in a sweat of horror. Not a wise measure anymore, then, to sleep by day. Too hot, conducive to the nightmare... The dream's psychological impetus was all too obvious, the paranoia and self-pity. One was expected to be calm and well-mannered in adversity. People soon got tired of you otherwise. How not, who was exempt from distress?

I stared across the room at the Janfia tree, glossy with its health and beauty. Quite unassailable it looked. Was it a vampire? Did it suck away the life of other things to feed its own? It was welcome to mine. What a way to die. Not messily and uncouthly. But ecstatically, romantically, poignantly. They would say, they simply could not understand it, I had been a little under the weather, but *dying*... So very odd of me. And Isabella, remembering the story, would glance at the Janfia fearfully, and shakily giggle the notion aside.

I got up and walked across.

"Why don't you?" I said. "I'm here. I'm willing. I'd be – I'd be only too glad to die like that, in the arms of something that needed me, held, in pleasure – not from some bloody slip of a careless uncaring knife, some surgeon with a hangover, whoops, lost another patient today, oh dear what a shame. Or else to go on with this bloody awful misery, one slap in the teeth after another, nothing going right, nothing, nothing... Get out, to oblivion hopefully, or get out and start over, or if there's some bearded old damnable God, he couldn't blame me, could he? Your honour, I'd say, I was all for keeping going, suffering for another forty years, whatever your gracious will for me was. But a demon set on me. You know I didn't stand a chance. So," I said again to the Janfia tree, "why not?"

Did it hear? Did it attend? I reached out and touched its stems, its leaves, the fruited, tight-coiled blossoms. All of it seemed to sing, to vibrate with some colossal hidden force, like an instrument still faintly thrumming after the hand of the musician has left it, perhaps five centuries ago.

"Christ, I'm going crazy," I said, and turned from the tree with an insulting laugh. *See*, the laugh said, *I know all that is a lie. So, I dare you.*

There was a writing desk in the room. Normally, when writing, I did not employ a desk, but now I sat at it and began to jot some notes on the legend of the tree. I was not particularly interested in doing this, it was only a sort of sympathetic magic. But the time went swiftly, and soon the world had reached the drinks hour, and I was able with a clear conscience to go down with thoughts of opening a bottle of white wine. The sun burned low in the cypress tree, and Marta stood beneath it, perplexed, a dish of scraps in her hand.

"Cats not hungry today?" I asked her.

She cast me a flashing look. "No cats. Cats runs off. I am say, Where you go give you better food? Mrs Isabella like the cats. Perhaps they there. Thing scares them. They see a monster, go big eyes and then they runs."

Surprising me with my surprise, I shivered. "What was it? That they saw?"

Marta shrugged. "Who's know? I am see them runs. Fat tail and big eyes."

"Where was it?"

"This minute."

"But where? Down here?"

She shrugged a second time. "Nothing there. They see. I am go along now. My aunt, she is waits for me."

"Oh yes. Your aunt. Do go."

I smiled. Marta ignored my smile, for she would only smile at me when I was serious or preoccupied, or ill. In the same way, her English deteriorated in my presence, improved in Isabella's. In some fashion, it seemed to me, she had begun to guard herself against me, sensing bad luck might rub off.

I had explained earlier to everyone that I wanted nothing very much for dinner, some cheese and fruit would suffice, such items easily accessible. And they had all then accordingly escaped, the cook, the cats and Marta. Now I was alone. Was I?

At the third glass I began to make my plans. It would be a full moon tonight. It would shine in at my bedroom window about two in the morning, casting a white clear light across the room, the desk, so that anything, coming between, would cast equally a deep shadow.

Well, I would give it every chance. The Janfia could not say I had omitted anything. The lunar orb, I at the desk my back to night and moon and tree. Waiting.

Why was I even contemplating such a foolish adolescent act? Naturally so that tomorrow, properly stood up on my date with delicious death, I could cry out loudly: The gods are dead! There is nothing left to me but *this,* the dunghill of the world.

But I ought to be fairly drunk. Yes, I owed the situation that. Drink, the opening medicine of the mind and heart, sometimes of the psyche.

The clean cheeses and green and pink fruits did not interrupt the spell of the wine. They stabilised my stomach and made it only accommodating.

Tomorrow I would regret drinking so much, but tomorrow I was going to regret everything in any case.

And so I opened a second bottle, and carried it to the bath with me, to the ritual cleansing before the assignation or the witchcraft. I fell asleep, sitting at the desk. There was a brief sea-like afterglow, and my notes and a book and a lamp and the bottle spread before me. The perfume of the Janfia at my back seemed faint, luminous as the dying of the light. Beginning to read, quite easily, for the wine, interfering itself with vision, made it somehow less difficult to see or guess correctly the printed words; I weighed the time once or twice on my watch. Four hours, three hours, to moonrise.

When I woke, it was to an electric stillness. The oil lamp, which I had been using in preference, was burning low, and I reached instantly and turned down the wick. As the flame went out, all the lit darkness came in about me. The moon was in the window, climbing up behind the jet-black outline of the Janfia tree.

The scent was extraordinary. Was it my imagination – it seemed never to have smelled this way before, with this sort of aching, chiming note. Perhaps the full moon brought it out. I would not turn to look. Instead, I drew the paper to me and the pen. I wrote nothing, simply doodled on the pad, long spirals and convolutions; doubtless a psychiatrist would have found them most revealing.

My mind was a blank. A drunken, receptive, amiable blank. I was amused, but exhilarated. All things were supposed to be possible. If a black spectre could stalk me through eight years, surely then phantoms of all kinds, curses, blessings, did exist.

The shadow of the Janfia was being thrown down now all around me, on the floor, on the desk and the paper: the lacy foliage and the wide-stretched blooms.

And then, something else, a long finger of shadow, began to spill forwards, across everything. What was it? No, I must not turn to see. Probably some freak arrangement of the leaves, or even some simple element of the room's furniture, suddenly caught against the lifting moon.

My skin tingled. I sat as if turned to stone, watching the slow forward movement of the shadow which, after all, might also be that of a tall and slender man. Not a sound. The cicadas were silent. On the hills not a dog barked. And the villa was utterly dumb, empty of everything but me, and perhaps of this other thing, which itself was noiseless.

And all at once the Janfia tree gave a little whispering rustle. As if it laughed to itself. Only a breeze, of course only that, or some night insect, or a late flower unfolding…

A compound of fear and excitement held me rigid. My eyes were wide, and I breathed in shallow gasps. I had ceased altogether to reason. I did not even feel. I waited. I waited in a type of delirium, for the touch of a cruel serene hand upon my neck… For truth to step at last from the shadow, with a naked blade.

And I shut my eyes, the better to experience whatever might come to me.

There was then what is known as a lacuna, a gap, something missing, and amiss. In this gap, gradually, as I sank from the heights back inside myself, I began after all to hear a sound.

It was a peculiar one. I could not make it out.

Since ordinary sense was, unwelcome, returning, I started vaguely to think, *Oh, some animal, hunting*. It had a kind of coughing, retching, whining quality, inimical and awesome, something which would have nothing to do with what basically it entailed – like the agonised female scream of the mating fox.

The noises went on for some time, driving me ever further and further back to proper awareness, until I opened my eyes, and stood up abruptly. I was cold and felt rather sick. The scent of the Janfia tree was overpowering, nauseating, and nothing at all had happened. The shadows were all quite usual, and, rounding on the window, I saw the last of the moon's edge was in it, and the tree like a cut-out of black and white papers. Nothing more.

I swore, childishly, in rage, at all things, and myself. It served me right; fool, fool, ever to expect anything. And that long shadow, what had that been? Well. It might have been anything. Why else had I shut my eyes but to aid the delusion, afraid if I continued to look I must be undeceived.

Something horrible had occurred. The night was full of the knowledge of that. Of my idiotic invitation to demons, and my failure, their refusal.

But I really had to get out of the room; the scent of the tree was making me ill at last. How could I ever have thought it pleasant?

I took the wine-bottle, meaning to replace it in the refrigerator downstairs, and, going out into the corridor, brought on the lights. Below, I hit the other switches rapidly, one after the other, flooding the villa with hard modern glare. So much for the moon. But the smell of the Janfia was more persistent, it seemed to cling to everything... I went out onto the western veranda, to get away from it, but even here on the other side of the house the fragrance hovered.

I was trying, very firmly, to be practical. I was trying to close the door, banish the element I had summoned, for though it had not come to me, yet somehow the night clamoured with it, reeked of it. What was it? Only me, of course. My nerves were shot, and what did I do but essay stupid flirtations with the powers of the dark? Though they did not exist in their own right, they do exist inside every one of us. I had called my own demons. Let loose, they peopled the night.

All I could hope for now was to go in and make a gallon of coffee, and leaf through and through the silly magazines that lay about, and stave off sleep until the dawn came. But there was something wrong with the cypress tree. The moon, slipping over the roof now in pursuit of me, caught the cypress and showed what I thought was a broken bough.

That puzzled me. I was glad of the opportunity to go out between the bushes and take a prosaic look.

It was not any distance, and the moon came bright. All the night, all its essence, had concentrated in that spot, yet when I first looked, and first saw, my reaction was only startled astonishment. I rejected the evidence as superficial, which it was not, and looked about and found the tumbled kitchen stool, and then looked up again to be sure, quite certain, that it was Marta who hung there pendant and motionless, her engorged and terrible face twisted away from me. She had used a strong cord. And those unidentifiable sounds I had heard, I realised now, had been the noises Marta made, as she swung and kicked there, strangling to death.

The shock of what had happened was too much for Isabella and made her unwell. She had been fond of the girl and could not understand why Marta had not confided her troubles. Presumably her lover had thrown her over, and perhaps she was pregnant – Isabella could have helped, the girl could have had her baby under the shelter of a foreign umbrella of bank notes. But then it transpired Marta had not been pregnant, so there was no proper explanation. The woman who cooked said both she and the girl had been oppressed for days, in some way she could not or did not reveal. It was the season. And then, the girl was young and impressionable. She had gone mad. God would forgive her suicide.

I sat on the veranda of the other villa, my bags around me and a car due to arrive and take me to the town, and Alec and Isabella, both pale with convalescence, facing me over the white iron table.

"It wasn't your fault," said Alec to Isabella. "It's no use brooding over it. The way they are here, it's always been a mystery to me." Then, he went in, saying he felt the heat, but he would return to wave me off.

"And poor poor you," said Isabella, close to tears. "I tell you to come here and rest, and this has to happen."

I could not answer that I felt it was my fault. I could not confess that it seemed to me that I, invoking darkness, had conjured Marta's death. I did not understand the process, only the result. Nor had I told Isabella that the Janfia tree seemed to have contracted its own terminal disease. The leaves and flowers had begun to rot away, and the scent had grown acid. My vibrations had done that. Or it was because the tree had been my focus, my burning-glass. That would reveal me then as my own enemy. That powerful thing which slowly destroyed me, that stalker with a knife, it was myself. And knowing it, naming it, rather than free me of it, could only give it greater power.

"Poor little Marta," said Isabella. She surrendered and began to sob, which would be no use to Marta at all, or to herself, maybe.

Then the car, cheerful in red and white, came up the dusty road, tooting merrily to us. And the driver, heaving my luggage into the boot, cried out to us in joy, "What a beautiful day, ah, what a beautiful day!"

TIGER 1

The drive through the desert was a long one, taking most of the day. I had keyed the coordinates into the car myself, but I was still unsure I would get there. It might be some trick, or an error. They might take me only to the middle of nowhere.

In the fall sunshine, the landscape was smoky pink, with occasionally a rusted mesa rising up, and the distant mountains, maroon fading back into the blue of the sky. It might have been another planet. Only the confines of the car kept off agoraphobia.

I went over my plans: if I don't find it, if it isn't there, I can sleep in the car. I've done that before. Drive back in the morning. Give my source a black mark and don't use him again.

I imagined the desert by night, the sky crowded and rife with stars. Things howling. Or an utter silence.

About four o'clock the car took a right off the road, and headed up among the burned slopes, under amber rock stacks. The adapted tires failed to cushion all the jolts.

For eight hours I hadn't seen the trace of any living thing, not even the white trail of a plane across that pure hot sky.

I had spent the long deep summer with my lover, revelling in the crowds that gently swept against us like a warm sea, meaning no harm.

Then, from the crowd, one stepped out and took my lover away, and now I did not care for people, much.

Yet the desert was too empty. It was not an alternative.

Just then the car came around the rocks and directly ahead, borne up in the heart of them, it was. The house and the oasis of garden, exactly as they had been described to me.

I stopped, and the car coordinator flicked up its light, congratulating itself on bringing me to the proper place.

The house was, as he had said, my source, dramatic, theatrical. Tall and white, with curving arches of a dull turquoise green, and terra-cotta roofs. Colours flashed from windows. And below, the garden descended, a series of green terraces, lush with broad trees, spiked palms and tunnelled vines. Only the faintest shimmer in the air at the base of this paradise revealed an electric wall.

She would need protection. Even if it wasn't true – and of course, it wasn't. More so for that reason, perhaps.

I shut down the car, got out, and switched on the guard, for all the world as if I stood on a busy avenue.

I thought, I too must be guarded. And she – what would she be? Would she even let me in?

The walk up to the gate in the invisible wall was posted with warnings, 'KEEP OUT. DON'T TOUCH. GO AWAY', in diplomatic legal phrases.

On the gate was a name in small clear letters: SATTERSLEY. The right name. There was a little panel with a button, which I pressed quickly, staring through the ripple of the wall at a tapestry of grapes hanging so close but out of reach, like the apples of Eden.

After five minutes, I pressed the button again.

This time a light bloomed in the panel. A message came up: PLEASE WAIT.

And then a woman's voice, low, musical and husky, like the voice of an actress who smoked. "Mary Sattersley. Can I help you?"

She was so courteous. Almost to a fault. I hadn't expected that. Why should I? I had begun to be wary of strangers.

"I'd like to come in."

"And who are you?" she asked, calm, lucid, almost playful.

I told her. I expected she would repulse me at once and for that reason had not first given my name and calling. A foolish ruse. One must always unmask eventually. I could have lied. But that seemed mediocre. She would scent the lie, somehow. I had been counselled; she was intelligent.

She said. "Oh." And then, "The gate will chime, then it will open. Come up by the path. You're not afraid of large animals?"

"Will they attack me?"

"Oh, no."

"I trust you," I said, frivolous.

She laughed. "I'm afraid you must, for the moment. A machine will meet you on the veranda."

The panel darkened, and immediately after, the gate gave off a fluting noise. It opened, and I went through, and the gate shut behind me.

I was in the jungle now. All around, the green grapes on the basketwork of their arches, and huge flowers, white and purple. The path ascended quite primly through all the abundance, and it was kept clear as only a mechanical gardener could do it. I had heard that Mary Sattersley had service robots, the kind you saw on TV, the kind that wait only on the very rich.

I climbed through her garden. Long ago I had got over my envy of the rich. I didn't want their comforts. What would I do with them?

Birds sang, nightingales among the rest. They might have been machines too.

Nothing happened until the third terrace. There was a dark green pool there, with magnolias that had pale green flowers. A lynx rose from the bank and looked at me. I nodded, and the lynx lay down again. This could have been anything. Her animals were supposed to be used to human company, and quite tame.

On the fourth terrace were two tigers. They had been playing, and now stood up. Their beauty was painful. They looked at me with lemon daiquiri eyes.

"Mary, Mary, quite contrary," I said, "how does your garden grow?"

Both sets of toy ears moved.

Then I said, "In the forests of the night."

Then I had gone past them, and around the flames of the rhododendrons three white steps ran up to the paved veranda. The tigers did not pursue me.

I stood in the open sunshine among her orange trees, looking at the turquoise arches, from which hung dishes of Praetorian red valerian. A glass door opened with a subtle hiss, and a metal creature glided out. It was not like a man or a woman, but a sort of globe on runners. There were no light displays, nothing like a mouth or eyes. A sceptic's robot, without concessions.

Yet it spoke.

"Mary says to bring you to the drawing room."

What was this reminiscent of? A good child.

"Thank you," I said, stupidly, as one does in the clichés.

But there, it expected my idiocy. It turned and glided back through the glass door, and I followed.

The hall was wide and cool, having a massive floor with red tiles, white walls with skulls on them of desert beasts, and one old painting in a shell of gold.

The robot led me through into a big green room, where plants had been trained up on to the glass ceiling.

Outside was a yard with a raised pond, thick with lilies. A cheetah, yellow as a banana, sat on the rim.

Looking at that, I did not see for a moment Mary Sattersley, as she walked towards me.

She's of medium height, and she was wearing a long, dark blue dress, in the style they call Venetian. Of course she wasn't tanned, but her skin had a kind of flush, a glow. My source had told me she was forty-seven years of age, and her hair was mostly grey. Grey eyes to go with that. She was fully pregnant. The belly was the largest thing about her. But, like Titania's favourite, she *sailed*.

She said, directly, "Probably my last. I didn't anticipate it. I'm menopausal. One last gift."

I swallowed, and said, "I suppose they are gifts?"

"My God, yes." She laughed again. "But you want proof."

"I'd just like to talk to you."

She sat down on one of the green couches, and motioned me to do the same. I did.

The robot came back with a tray of drinks, everything from gin and geneva to Appelite. And a crystal vase of ice.

"Just tell it what you want," she encouraged me.

I chose two fingers of vodka with orange juice. Mary took a glass of transparent champagne. Obviously, she was one of those expectant mothers who believe a little alcohol can do the baby no ill.

"Are you working for the journals now?" she inquired, as the robot slid away. "Or is it a TV magazine?"

"Neither. This is just – I wanted to meet you, Ms. Sattersley."

"Mary," she said. "Let's pretend we know each other."

I drank the vodka, which was African and very good.

"It was very generous of you to see me," I lamely said.

"You didn't think I would."

"No."

"A number of people have approached me," she said, "over the last twenty years. Once word got out. That was Francis. He couldn't keep quiet. And no one thought it was true. That can be very boring. I'm sure you understand."

"But I don't think it's true," I said.

"No, naturally you don't. You're curious as to what kind of madness drives me. However, you're a woman."

"You mean," I said, "I have a womb. This makes me more sympathetic."

"Perhaps," she said, "or not. It makes you more recognisable. To me."

The vodka had loosened my tongue. But there again. I wanted to be direct, possibly to shock or surprise her. It was her party. Who likes that? The world revolves around *us*.

"But you enjoy men," I said, "apparently."

"Lovely," she said. "For a brief while. And men do arrive here in such extraordinary, stage-managed ways. Their planes land in the desert. Or they appear, having walked for miles, with heat exhaustion. Nobody comes in a little air-conditioned blue car, like you."

I put down my glass, and the robot manifested and refilled it, precisely to the delicious ratio of before, spooning in the diamond ice with a silver scoop.

She said, "You've come at exactly the right moment."

I looked at Mary Sattersley. She had been beautiful, and she still was, but in that different, lunar way that older women have who are comfortable with time. After all, I did envy her. She had a grace not given to everyone. Not given to me. When I was her age, I'd be too fat, and – ridiculous opposite – too hard. I'd cut and dye my hair. The menopause would make me cry for all the unwanted children I'd never had.

"The right moment being because you're pregnant," I stated.

"The analysis predicts that I'll give birth tonight."

Outside in the court, the cheetah had fished up a drowned mauve lily. It padded in across the tiles, the flower in its mouth. It gave the flower to Mary Sattersley, then jumped up beside her. The cheetah lay with its head in her lap, underneath the mound of her belly. She stroked the cat gently, and it purred.

"Your animals are magnificent," I said.

"Thank you. I think so. They understand what you say, incidentally."

I drank the new vodka. "Can you prove that to me?"

"Yes." She leaned to the cheetah. "Look up at our visitor."

The cheetah turned its plush yellow head. It looked at me.

I said, firmly, "What's your name?"

Mary Sattersley interposed. "They don't talk. The jaw and throat aren't constructed correctly. And they have no names. It isn't necessary. They don't use mine."

I frowned into the cheetah's eyes. I said, "Then how do I know?"

"A simple request," she said.

So I said to the cheetah, "Close your golden eyes."

The cheetah closed its golden eyes.

"Open them."

They opened.

It was too little, and she knew it, but she began again her stroking. On her smooth hand that was no longer young, but shaped by some secret artistry, one small emerald shone. Who had given her that? Or was it only hers?

Francis Arlin had written a book about her. It was presented as fiction. Later, the revelation. At first no one believed this. And then, they said that he was mad. It was a sensation for half a year. No one could find her or get near her. If I had tried, during that era of fame, would the gate have stayed shut and the vodka unpoured? Anyway, I had been ten years old.

"At first," she said, "it was very strange for me, too."

"It must have been."

"Oh yes. Obviously strange the obvious way. But I don't mean that," she said. "I thought about my own name and it made me nervous. Stupidly so. It has no bearing. The Christian religion is to do with men."

I said, slowly, "You don't like men. I mean, you like them for sex. But not otherwise."

"When I was younger," she said, "I was terrified. But now, they arrive like lights, and vanish like shadows."

I thought, *She hasn't met Mr. Right.*

But – how could she?

The cheetah slept, and her hand with the emerald lay idly on it. A possessive hand that yet had no power or wish to control. If it liked, would she let the cat kill me?

My glance went back to her belly.

"Do you know?" I said.

"No. It doesn't matter."

I said, flatly, "Suppose it's only a child?"

Mary Sattersley laughed for the third time. "I want to rest now. The machine will take you down to the bathing pool. You can swim if you care to. There's a panther there. You won't mind? He likes the water. Dinner will be about seven-thirty."

"You're being very nice, very accommodating," I said.

"Yes. I'd like you to see. No one ever has. Francis was too afraid."

"Is there someone…?" I said.

"The machine has all the skills. But it's never very difficult."

She got up, and the cheetah slipped from her, and then followed her out of the room. The youngest, maybe?

When I too got up, the machine took me away through the garden to the swimming pool, where the panther lay on a long blue rock.

I said, to the panther, "So you don't talk. Make a noise, then."

And the panther made a low humming sound, and its tail lashed once. I had not been polite. It proved, ultimately, nothing.

I dived into the royal blue pool and swam, up and down, with the vodka ahead of me, as if my soul had inched out of my body.

When I woke under the awning the panther had gone, and the robot had arrived to inform me that I had half an hour before dinner.

In a guest room that had been put idly at my disposal, I washed, and combed my hair, darkened my eyes and put on lipstick. There were guest playthings everywhere, nail-buffers, hand soaps, deodorant and powder and perfume. I used my own things.

The machine took me down to a lagoon-blue room with russet walls. There were curios on tall dark cabinets, shells, and pieces of rock that looked like uncut jewels. The windows had pale green and blue panes, an abstract design, like water.

A marble table had been laid, and Mary Sattersley was already seated there, eating some little nuts on a wooden dish. There were none of her cats in the room; I thought probably they had been shut out to put me at ease. Or, she had conferred with them and requested that they stay away.

The meal was simple enough. A chilled fish soup, smoked chicken and green salad in a cream dressing, bowls of strawberries and cherries, brie and Stilton with slices of apple. Massive white candles burned high over our heads. The plates were clear glass incised by patterns of flowers, through which showed the blue veins of the tabletop. The glasses were midnight blue that made the wine look green.

I didn't drink very much. Surely I had to keep a clear head.

As we ate, it was she who interviewed me. She asked me about cities, summer beaches, politics, the world. She listened curiously, as if to an interesting traveller's tale. None of it was real or serious, to her. I almost laughed myself, describing to this woman a stormy flight on an airplane, a day at the races.

When we reached the fruit and cheese, the robot came and poured us some white brandy. She tasted that too. She had eaten sparingly, but drunk generously. It seemed not to affect her. She knew what she was doing, presumably. She had ostensibly given birth at least nine times.

She said then, "You can ask me anything you want. You've been very patient."

There was only one question: Is it a fact? Irrelevant to inquire. It could not be. She was insane. That was the interesting thing, the nature of her madness.

I said, "I'd like to know, if you'll tell me, how it began."

"Very straightforwardly. Or do you mean why? I don't know. Something in me, it has to be. But I think too it was because my life altered so suddenly. I was able to become myself."

"I'd like to hear about that, then."

She told me she had been herself an unwanted child. There was no permanent father, and later one of the substitutes abused her. After this she was put into an institution. She said that she would sleep with any boy or man who demanded it. She imagined sex was expected of her. Her first sexual experience, with the abuser, was at eleven years. Until the age of twenty-five, she slept with quantities of men. No harm ever came to her, and she was never pregnant, although mostly she took no precautions, even as an adult, because the six-monthly pill made her sick, and other methods repelled her.

To support herself amid the desperate, tiresome world she subsisted in, she worked as a clerk, waited tables, sold gas, wrote advertising slogans. Her schooling had been sketchy. She told me without rancour she had learned very little, and now knew only the strangest matters which came from reading disparate books. She was within yet without the world. She did not resist it, made no complaint, attempted no escape. She looked for nothing. At night she would eat some ready meal, and drink a beer, and curl up on her mattress on the floor of the one-room apartment. She watched the neons on the ceiling until she slept.

Mary Sattersley told me she had never been afraid or unhappy. She had enjoyed the smallest things – sunlight on a wall, the smell of fried potatoes, a glass of beer, the sudden colours of human eyes and fruits.

When she was twenty-five, the miraculous story-book event

happened. An old man stopped her on the street, got out of the big black car and touched her arm. He wanted to sleep with her. She assented. She always had. It had never occurred to her that she was beautiful, beautiful enough to be causing this, to light such a fire. They went to a hotel, a very opulent hotel, and here they drank champagne, and she bathed in a coffee brown tub as large as her room at home. His lovemaking was quite strong, and quite violent, not sadistically so, but in the way of compulsively squeezing and biting, and it left her bruised, but she took no notice of that. A month later, when the bruises had faded, the letter came that informed her this urgent old man had died, and that she was to have some money, rather a lot of money.

In the smart steel office thirty floors up, they talked to her, in detail, about him, her rough lover; but she barely listened. Since she had always accepted everything as it came, she accepted the miracle also. At the door, the lawyer announced, casually, that the old man had confided Mary put him in mind of a lioness or tigress. That this was her type; what had drawn him on the street. She did not immediately associate the words with herself. Just as she did not truly assimilate the facts of her fortune.

But soon her life was changed. Others seemed to want to direct for her the course she should now take, and as always she went along with the imposition. There was a vast house, the first of several, that were accumulated for her. There were accessories, and, even then, mechanical servants.

"I came to live," she said, "very quickly, in such a different way. I took to it very easily."

She said she did not realise that it had changed her for several weeks, and by this time she had discovered too that her benefactor had left her one other appurtenance. She was pregnant.

She meant to see a doctor. But time went by. She had understood that she would have nine months, or thereabouts. On a night in the fourth month she went into labour. She was not frightened, only in pain. She merely let it happen.

"That was the first," Mary Sattersley said.

"So, it was his child. Didn't you think that it was because of him…?"

"Oh no," she said. "I knew that it was because of me. Everything had changed and so enabled it to happen. Besides; a year later, I slept with another man, a young man I met sometimes in the town, and it was all the same."

"You kept it secret," I said.

"Yes, but the young man was Francis Arlin. He saw them, afterwards."

"And he believed you. Why," I said, "would he? You said he was too frightened – to watch it happen."

She smiled. She said mildly, "I don't know why he believed me. It could have been a trick, couldn't it? With all this money – I could have managed it all without trouble."

"Then he wrote his book."

"Yes, and I had another house found for me. Finally this one. It seemed the wisest course."

"But now I'm to be your witness."

"Yes," she said, on a long, intense sigh, and she looked at me with a sort of infinite pleasure. "It's lovely," she said, "that someone will know. Not like poor Francis."

"But what do you expect," I said, "from me?"

"Nothing. Nothing at all."

The candles had burned down half their length, and getting up slowly, almost lasciviously, she went to a pair of windows and opened them wide.

Outside, the night filled the veranda of her house.

As I had predicted, the sky was massed with stars. There was not a sound.

"In about an hour," she said, "it will begin."

The robot took the empty plates from the marble table. I listened to the silence, in which the sputter of the candles was like some secret tongue.

She said, "You'd better come to the room with me. Then you can be sure none of it is false."

Nothing made her uncomfortable, my eyes on her nakedness, her heaving belly, the parting of her body.

Nothing. Not even the squalid truth, whatever that would turn out to be. I felt a flicker of fear. But it was too late now.

She had selected a room on the upper story. There was a big old bed, from under whose white sheet hung down an underlay of plastic. The windows stood open to the garden, the desert and the stars.

Into the bathroom she went with the machine, and there was running water.

When she came back, her hair was down in long grey ropes. She was already unclothed. I looked and saw the plump sag of her full breasts, and the belly – certain now and very real, hard as one of the creamy nuts she had eaten before dinner. This was not faked, could not be. I could see the life moving inside it, ripples of preparation.

Her face already frowned with pain, and sweat ran down her forehead, cheeks and neck.

"Quick tonight, I think," she said.

She lay on the white bed and the machine bent over her to arrange her with smooth metal paws.

I sat in the chair that faced the bed. I wanted to be anywhere but here.

Yes, it must be that she would give birth. And then, my God, what would she do? What would she say? But I recoiled too from the idea of the wrinkled infant sprung on its cord. I had seen these things before. I was filled by terror, panic. This ordinary horror, this mundane wonder, which all my life I had and would refuse.

Did she kill them then, and the machine dispose of the evidence? Next the call to some obliging and illegal precinct that would supply her need.

I drank my brandy. I tried to make it last.

She talked to me sometimes, even then, quite softly, now and then breaking off to whimper. She spoke of the other births, their speed or tardiness, the easiest and worst. Then she spoke of the results, the gold and ebony and carnelian and jasper that had been wrung from her womb. She spoke proudly, lovingly, like any fond mother.

The room soon smelled of blood and intimacy, and through the coolth of the air-conditioning and the low desert night, feverish wings of heat, her heat, beat up and down.

The machine performed careful, efficient necessities, nothing drastic. Apparently, everything went to plan.

I've written of many occurrences. Now I have to relate this. At about twelve o'clock, Mary Sattersley cried out and began to push from her core an envelope of diaphanous stuff which broke and flowed away. From this membrane presently tumbled the child. It was wet and dark, almost earless, helpless, and blind.

I saw it taken up and thoroughly cleaned with materials laid ready, and then the robot put it on the woman's breast.

Mary held her baby with wordless contentment. She made to it little crooning noises. She offered to the velvet of its mouth her ripe oval breast.

The child suckled.

While this went on, the machine cleared everything, and washed the mother nimbly. A white sheet was pulled up across her body.

Her head turned then, and she looked at me with tired glad eyes.

"Do you want to come closer and see him?"

"No, I can see."

She said, "There's nothing to be afraid of. It must be natural. It happens."

I did not go to her, to verify what I could plainly make out. Instead I crossed to the windows and looked down. On the veranda they were standing. The panthers like black velour, the yellow cheetah and the tawny lynx, the tigers and the leopards. There were ten in all. Their eyes caught the lamps of the house, their house, and shone and blinked.

The new one was sleeping now, snoring faintly, on his mother's chest. The fur, as it dried, was rising up in orange nap. His stripes were woolly, blurred. When grown a little, he would play with the others on the lawns, among the palms and vines, the tiger cub.

I said, "But I can't report this. No one would credit this. I'm not going into the hell Francis Arlin made for himself."

Mary Sattersley said, "I think that's sensible."

Then the machine came to show me back to the guest wing, but instead I went down through the house and out on to the veranda, where the big cats glanced at me and away. There was no need to tell them anything. They gleamed in the lamplight and the starlight like effigies in a dream.

The gate let me out at a request, and I walked up to where my car was parked. I released the door and got in and sat there for the rest of the night, sometimes looking up at her house, where the lamps were eventually extinguished, even in the upper rooms.

PINEWOOD

Author's Note: A poem written in my early twenties gave rise to this short tale. Either from past lives or the memory of DNA, we seem to know very well emotions never yet experienced, and, glancing back at your prophecies, you may sometimes award yourself eleven out of ten.

Clear morning light slanted across her face and woke her. She turned on her side and murmured: "David. David, darling, I think it must be awfully late."

Receiving no answer, she opened her eyes. The other side of the bed was empty, and the little clock on his side table showed half past ten. Of course, he had woken when the alarm went off, as she never did, and left her to sleep. The clock's little round face, like cracked eggshell, ticked with a menacing reproach. She had always been certain it disliked her, in a humorous rather than a sinister manner, because she never responded to its insistent morning screams, and when David was away on business, forgot to wind it up.

Beyond the bright window the pines rubbed their black needles against the autumn wind. She shivered as she sat up in the bed. The Gothic trees disturbed her, a stupid notion for a woman of thirty-seven, she told herself.

Dear David. She brushed her teeth with swift meticulous strokes. He alone had never minded about her sluggish waking.

She examined her eyes and her throat in the harsh light, bravely. Not so bad. Not so bad, Pamela, for the elderly lady you are. She smiled as she ran the bath, thinking of her anxious questionings, her painful jokes: "I'm too old for you, darling, really. People will ask you at parties why you brought your mother..." In reality she was three years David's senior. And the batch of youthful snaps: "Oh, but I look so young in these..." He was good to her, sensing the nervous, helpless steps she took toward that essentially, prematurely female precipice of age – the little line, the grey hair. He told her all the things she wanted to hear from him, all the good things, and never seemed to find her tiresome. He had always had a perfect patience and kindness toward her. And she had always known that she had been unusually lucky with this man. She might so easily have loved a fool, or a boor, and found out too late, as had Jane, or her sister Angela, a man with no ability to imagine how things might be for the female principal in his life – a lack of comprehension amounting to xenophobia.

Sitting in the bath she had a sudden horror that this was the day for Mrs Meadowes, the cleaning lady. A twice-weekly visitation of utter cleanliness and vigour, she nevertheless doted on David, and, naturally, bullied Pamela. Frantically Pamela towelled and scattered talc. She never seemed to know where she was with Mrs Meadowes. Her days and times of arrival seemed to be in constant flux. And now, come to think of it, Pamela remembered she was to meet David for lunch.

She grasped the phone and dialled the Meadowes' number. An incoherent child answered, presently to be replaced by a recognised contralto.

"Oh – Mrs Meadowes, Pamela Taylor here – I'm dreadfully sorry, but I simply couldn't remember – is it today you're coming? Or is it tomorrow or something?"

There was a pause, then the contralto said carefully: "Well, dear, I can fit you in tomorrow. If you like."

"Oh, good, then it wasn't today. Thank you so much. Sorry to have bothered you. Goodbye."

There had been something distinctly strange about the Meadowes phone call, she thought, as she ate her grapefruit. Probably something to do with that appalling child. She switched on the radio. She caught a news bulletin, as she always seemed to. Somewhere a plane had crashed, somewhere else an earthquake – she switched off. Angela had frequently told her that she should keep herself abreast of the news, not bury her head in the sand. But she simply could not stand it. Papers depressed her. They came for David, and when he forgot to take them with him to the office as he always seemed to nowadays, she would push them out of sight, bury them behind cushions and under piles of magazines, afraid to glimpse some horror before she could avert her eyes.

David teased her a little. "Where's the ostrich hidden my paper today?"

As she constructed her peach-bloom cosmetic face before the mirror, she thought of Angela, vigorously devouring black gospels of famine, war, and pestilence with her morning coffee. James liked her to know what she was talking about at their dinner parties. He rated a woman's intelligence by her grasp of foreign correspondents and yesterday in parliament. It was in a way rather curious. Angela had met James in the same month Pamela had met David.

She took the car with her into town, a feat she performed with some dread. David was a superb and relaxed driver, she by contrast sat in rigid anxiety at the wheel. Her fears seemed to attract near disasters. Dogs, children, and India rubber balls flew in front of her wheels as if magnetised, men in Citroens honked and swore, and juggernauts herded her off the road. Normally she would take the bus, for David often used the car, but today it lurked in the garage, taunting her, and besides she was pushed for time.

She reached the restaurant ten minutes late, and went to meet him in the bar, but he had not yet arrived. Bars were unfortunate for her, and alone she shunned them. David said she had a flair for being picked up; men who looked like Mafiosi would offer her martinis, and all she seemed able to do in her paralysed fright was apologise to them. She left the bar and went into the restaurant and ordered a sherry at her table.

The room felt rather hot and oppressive, and all the other tables were filling up, except her own. She drank her sherry down in wild gulps and the waiter leaned over her.

"Would madam care to order now?"

"Oh – no thank you. I'm sorry, you see, I'm waiting for my husband..." She trailed off. A knowing and sombre look had come over the man's face. *Oh, God, I suppose he thinks I'm a whore too.*

She took out a cigarette and smoked it in nervous bursts. She could see another waiter watching her from his post beside a pillar. *I shall wait another ten minutes and then I shall go.*

It was fifteen minutes past two when she suddenly remembered. It came over her like a lightning flash, bringing a wave of embarrassment and relief in its wake. Of course, David had told her very last thing last night that the lunch would have to be cancelled. A man was coming from Kelly's – or Ryson's – and he would have to take him for a working snack at the pub. She felt an utter fool. Good heavens, was her memory going this early? She almost giggled as she threaded between the tables.

She shopped in the afternoon and ate a cream cake with her coffee in a small teashop full of old ladies. She had bought David a novel, one of the few Graham Greenes he hadn't collected over the years. She had seen for some time that he was having trouble with his present reading – the same volume had lain beside the round-faced clock for over a month.

The journey home was relatively uneventful. At the traffic lights a boy with a rucksack leaned to her window. She thought in alarm that he was going to demand a lift, or else tell her in an American voice of how he had found Jesus in San Francisco, but, in fact, he only wanted directions to Brown's the chemists. It seemed such a harmless request it filled her with incongruous delight. Purple and ochre cloud drift was bringing on the early dusk in spasms of rain. With a surge of immeasurable compassion she offered him, after all, the lift she had been terrified of giving. David would be furious with her, she knew. It was a stupid thing to do, yet the boy looked so vulnerable in the rain, his long dark hair plastered to his skull. He was an ugly, shy, rather charming student, and she left him at the chemists after a ten-minute ride during which he thanked her seven times. It turned out his mother was Mrs Brown, and he had hitched all the way from Bristol.

After he had gone, she parked the car, and went to buy fresh cigarettes. Coming from the tobacconists, she saw the cemetery.

She had forgotten she would see the cemetery on her errand of mercy. It was foolish, she knew, to experience this 'morbid dread', as Angela would no doubt put it. It was, nevertheless, a perfect picture of horror for her – the ranks of marble markers under the orange monochrome sky with rain falling on their plots and withered wreaths, and down through the newly turned soil to reach the wooden caskets underneath... She experienced a sudden swirling sickness and ran through it to the car. Inside, the icy rain shut out, she found that she had absurdly begun to cry.

"Oh, don't be such an idiot," she said aloud.

She turned on the car's heater, and started vigorously for home, nearly stalling. She was much later than she had meant to be.

There were no lights burning in the house, and she realised with regret that he would be late again. She coerced the unwilling car into the garage and ran between the rustling pines. She clicked a switch in every room and resuscitated the television to reveal three children up to their eyes in some form of super sweet. Their strawberry-and-cream bedecked faces filled her with disgust. She had never liked children, and never wanted them. She paused, her hand on the door, a moment's abstracted thought catching at her mind – had she failed David in this? She could remember him saying to her as she sobbed against him: "I only want you, you know that, and nothing else matters."

That had been after the results of the tests. In a way she felt she had wished herself into barrenness. She thought of Angela's two sons, strapping boisterous boys, who went canoeing with their father, and brought home baskets of mangled catch from a day's fishing, and spotted trains, and bolted their food to get back to incongruous and noisy activities in their bedroom.

"A man needs sons," Angela had once said. "It's a sort of proof, Pamela. Why don't you see a specialist? I can give you the address."

But then Angela and James had not slept together in any sense for ten years, Pamela thought with sudden, spiteful triumph, and it had always been a doubtful joy to them. She remembered David's arms about her and that earthy magic they made between them, an attraction that had increased rather than diminished.

The phone rang.

It made her jump.

"Oh, damn."

She picked it up, and heard, with the relevance of a conjuration, her sister's cool, well managed tones.

"Oh, hullo, Angela. I don't want to be a cow, but this really is rather a bad time – I was just about to start dinner..."

"Pamela, my dear," Angela said, her voice peculiarly solemn, "are you all right?"

"All right? Of course I am. What on earth...?"

"Pamela, I want you to listen to me. Please, my dear. I wouldn't have rung, but Jane Thomson says she saw you in Cordell's at lunch time. She says, oh, my dear, she says she saw you waiting for someone." Angela sounded unspeakably distressed. "Pamela, who were you waiting for?"

Pamela felt a surge of panic wash over her. "I – oh, no one. Does it matter?"

"Darling, of course it does. Was it David you were waiting for, like the last time?"

Pamela held the phone away from her ear and looked at it. There was a bee trapped in the phone, buzzing away at her. She had always been terribly afraid of bees.

"I really have to go, Angela," she shouted at the mouthpiece.

"Oh, Pamela, Pamela," Angela said. She seemed to be crying. "Darling, David can't come back to you. Not now."

"Be quiet," Pamela said.

The bee went on buzzing.

"Pamela, listen to me. David is dead. Dead, do you hear me? He died of peritonitis last July. For God's sake, Pamela…"

Pamela dropped the phone into its receiver and the buzzing stopped.

The dinner was spoiled before she realised how late he was going to be after all. He had told her the conference might run on, and not to wait up for him. She waited, however, until midnight. Upstairs, she took the book from his bedside table and replaced it with the Graham Greene – it would surprise him when he found it.

She hated to sleep without him, but she was very tired. And she would see him in the morning.

Outside, the pines clicked and whispered, but she did not listen.

NIGHTSHADE

ONE

It was seven o'clock; the sun was dying on the sea. The water, like the sky, was glazed by a smoky glare, which diluted at its edges before smashing itself delicately on the beach.

The house stood on the highest point of the cliff overhanging the bay, the shoreline, and the wide sea falling away before it into the mouth of the sunset, the levels of the city falling away behind into shadow.

The house was sealed from the city by a high wall, reminiscent of a jail, broken only by a pair of oriental wrought iron gates. The wall mostly shut off the elevation of the cliff, and the induced gardens which clothed it, yet a scent of roses, oleanders, peach and lemon trees filtered occasionally into the streets below. Rising from the gates, a hundred shallow stone steps, indented at their centres as if from age and great use, led in four tiers to the house. On each landing stood two marble columns with horses' heads.

The house itself had a strange decaying look, the stucco of its balconies and arches purplish-brown as if steeped in incense, erupting into growths of vine and tamarisk.

The first lamps and neons were spangling across the city to the south. The polarised windows of the house, losing the stain of the sun, became black.

Sovaz stood at the window, telling the chain of pearls like a rosary, listening to the sounds that her husband made, putting on his clothes in the dressing room. Such immaculate, precise sounds: now the rustle of the linen shirt, now the icy clink of a cufflink from its onyx box. Presently he came into the room.

"You aren't dressed yet."

"No."

"It's very dark in here."

Kristian touched the discreet electric bell. The door opened almost at once and the black girl, Leah, crossed the room and let down the drapes of the three tall windows without a word. Light came obediently, spreading from the master switch at the touch of Kristian's hand. Sovaz' suite was mainly black, the lamps gold or green silk with crystal pendants on jade stands. A scented joss stick was burning in an antique bowl of bronze.

Sovaz glanced aside at Kristian in his perfect white dinner clothes, the little cold fires of emeralds winking on his cuffs. He was forty-eight: a very handsome man of excellent physique, his hair a rich blue-black which led women who had failed with him (most women) to suppose aloud that he had it dyed. His face was arrogant, remote. His eyes, a light but definite blue, seemed extraordinarily intent by contrast with the eyes of Sovaz which, even as she looked at him, appeared unfocused. She stood in her slip, playing with the pearls absently.

"Leah," Kristian said, "help my wife with her dress."

The black girl lifted the dress from the bed and quickly, deftly, slipped Sovaz into it. Like the room, like Leah herself, the dress was black.

"Were you intending to wear those pearls?" Kristian said. "Where are the rubies? They would be more suitable."

"If you think so," Sovaz said.

Leah, who had already opened the ivory box, brought the rubies and proceeded to fasten them in position. Sovaz let go the chain of pearls; they fell into the rugs. (Leah bent immediately to retrieve them.) Sovaz went to the arrangement of mirrors. She touched hesitantly at her neck. "I look as if I had had my throat cut."

"If the rubies don't please you, then wear the sapphires. You have plenty of jewels."

The black girl, her tasks accomplished, perambulated silently about the room and out of it. Sovaz stared after her with that remarkable, apparently abstracted gaze.

"Yes, I do, don't I?" The door was shut. Sovaz returned to her own image and extended the tip of one finger to her reflected face. "So white."

"You should use your sunlamp."

He himself was tanned to a healthy, satiny finish, like wood, from use of a lamp. She, who lived mainly by night, sensed her element. The sunlamp obscurely frightened her; she was psychologically afraid it would scorch her blind. She did not answer but leaned to adjust the low neck of the black lace dress, then picked up a lipstick and slowly coloured her mouth.

"Why do you burn this disgusting cheap rubbish?" Kristian said. He reached in and extinguished the joss stick.

"They sell them in the night market on the quay," she said irrelevantly.

He took out his cigarette case and lit a cigarette.

She had bought the joss sticks in the city three months before, the last night she had spent with her last lover to date, a boy twenty-two years old. Sovaz was twenty-five; the ages of her lovers had ranged from twenty-three to nineteen. There had never been anyone older. These amours did not offend or distress Kristian; if anything, they fitted into his scheme of things, as a hobby which kept the woman in the background of his life. Always, though indirectly, he vetted the young men. But their high standards of physical perfection, their sound health and good manners were symbols for him, for others, of his own opulence and taste, not pleasures he sought for her. The wife of Kristian might have only the best.

He himself had not been to bed with her in four years. She had never interested him particularly except for a week or two at the start of their marriage, when she was virgin, novel, and unexplained. Now she was a convenience and an ornament, a showcase for his wealth and aesthetics, like the carious grandeur of the house.

They had been married for seven years. She was the daughter of a friend, a librarian and scholar, a man a few years his senior, to whom Egyptian and Greek manuscripts were brought for translation.

Kristian had seen the girl reading under a green and red stained window, the panes casting gems on her white skin, and her black hair down her back. Her eyes were so large, like coals, her body slender as a stalk, with a woman's breasts. He had been stirred by that picture. He did not know what she was reading but had hoped for some of the father's intellect in the child. She disappointed him. She gorged herself mainly on bizarre modern fantasies by writers with inelegant names, among the gracious ancient dusts of the great library.

The old man (Kristian composedly thought of him in this way; although virtually contemporaries, physically they were quite unlike) became sick, and tuberculosis was diagnosed. He refused to leave his books to be cured, dismissing medicine as preposterous.

"I shall soon be better," he would say. Kristian found his illness distasteful, like a bad smell. Presently the old man's lungs haemorrhaged, and he died. Kristian, going to witness the aftermath, now acceptably clean and sterile, found Sovaz wandering like a lost pet animal among a welter of stacked furniture. The old man had died a pauper. Everything would go to bury him and to settle his debts.

Kristian found the mess agitated him, a last unhealthy odour. He paid off the debts and took the girl into his house. Despite her vulgar leanings, the vile books and records she brought with her, her presence did not jar. She did not, for example, cry. She seemed a void that might be filled. He became fascinated by the task of remodelling her, forming her into his own creation.

She was not precisely rebellious, but he found he made no headway. The culture he wished to impose slipped off her surface.

One night she found sleeping tablets in his dressing room and swallowed most of them. It was only three months since her father had died. She was eighteen.

At least nothing about the affair had been public. Kristian's valet, finding her with the last tablet clenched in her hand, had forced an emetic between her teeth, and compulsorily brought her back to life. Five days passed before Kristian could bring himself to see her, however. When he did, he was startled by her quality, like a rare porcelain. She sat behind the house, looking out over the garden and the sea, the warm night wind, perfumed with jasmine, lifting up strands of her dark hair and setting them down again.

He had not expected to find, after the sordid thing that had happened, something so exquisite.

"I imagine you want me to go," she said. "I shall."

And again he sensed in her the unfilled, empty room.

"My dear child, where do you propose to go to? You are quite untrained, unfit for anything, except possibly for factory work or prostitution."

"That, then. Does it matter?"

"I doubt very much if you would enjoy either. The work is hard and wages low."

"I shall have to bear it then, shan't I?"

He felt a flicker of alarm. It was no secret she had been with him, here, in this house. If she deliberately left him for the filth, petty crime and squalor of the back alleys and doss houses of the slums, she would leave a smear of this dirt on his own life.

"I suggest you think again, Sovaz. You're not a little girl. You have a brain, I believe. Attempt to use it."

He did not keep a watch on her then. Before dawn she was gone.

It had taken him three days to find her. Tenacious as a lover, he had gone to a great deal of trouble and expense to do so. His hands were clammy with a dungeon sweat. He was afraid the besmirching quicksand had already swallowed her. Prescott, the Englishman, had finally hunted her down.

Evening on the quay, the wharves rife, active. A stink of rotting fish, oranges, cheap hashish, the rancid oil in the lamps bobbing and coruscating their moons on the glutinous black water below. Men waiting, smoking and spitting, alert for work on the smacks of the midnight fishermen, the pleasure craft with their fringed canopies. Kristian's valet pushing open the canvas door of a leprous overhanging tenement. A whore putting her hands on him, Kristian striking her off; some trouble with the pimp, settled by Prescott. The long climb up the broken stairs, the tang of urine on the treads, fumes of inferior opium and zombie laughter from small black holes passing as rooms.

It was the attic, rafters sloping, lamplight and waterlight cast up on them, and a battered chaise-longue, where a girl was lying, smoking a green cigarette. It took Kristian some moments to realise this was Sovaz. Her hair was bleached, her eyes sticky with mascara.

Prescott and the valet drew back beyond the door. Kristian crossed to the open window, and turned, staring at the creature which confronted him.

"You look already like a hag seventy years old," he said, "riddled by disease and sick with opium. Is this the life you prefer?"

She murmured: "The madam is bringing a man here. Of some importance, she said. She has told him I am fifteen, but well developed for my age."

"No doubt."

"You had better be going, Kristian. You might meet him on the stairs otherwise."

"How many men?" he asked abruptly.

She started. "Do you care? Oh, none so far. This will be the first."

"Get up at once," he said, "you're coming with me."

"Leave me alone. You don't want me," she said bitterly. Her eyes were very dull.

He tapped his fingers impatiently. He wore gloves.

"Get up," he repeated, "or I shall have Prescott fetch the police."

"I have chosen what I want."

"You talk like a melodramatic schoolgirl."

"You know," she said, meeting his eyes suddenly, "that I am in love with you. You, for your part, have scarcely ever exchanged a word with me that was not a criticism or an instruction. I am sorry to have failed your ideals so dreadfully. I am certain you see I can't possibly return with you. Now go. Please."

Outside a man was strolling by, harnessed with cages full of twittering birds.

It had not before occurred to Kristian that the young girl might think herself in love with him. Yet she was impressionable and without anchor, the logic of it struck him now. Love. A clinging, cloying emotion. He found it almost offensive to be the object of her desires. If she had said she passionately admired him it would have been different. But love – it was too familiar of her, impertinent almost.

Nevertheless, the filthy room, the weird light and smells, the hopeless laughing and twittering of the damned below, snapped his nerve. He must get out and she with him, for she had come to belong to him – her ingenuous confession only branded her more irrevocably his property.

He went to her and pulled her up. Even in her tart's costume she was beautiful. At first, he thought she would lean on him and be still, quiescent as before. But abruptly she began to fight him, using even her nails and teeth, putting him in mind of a white fox one of his father's gamekeepers had once trapped, which had immediately gnawed through its manacled foot in order to be free.

Kristian began to sweat in earnest. The situation became immense and intolerable. Already his face and neck were streaked by her nails; disgusted panic took hold of him.

"Stop it," he rasped, afraid to speak more loudly for the valet and the agent outside the door. And then, uttering the first promise that came to him to quieten her: "I intend you to be my wife."

The effect of his words was not as he expected. Though she ceased fighting, she began instead to laugh.

Nevertheless, he was able to propel her slackening body to the door.

"As I thought," he said coldly, "there has been some mistake."

The two men accepted the ridiculous statement without comment. The woman and her customer were late in coming, it seemed; they passed no one on the stairs, but got down to the limousine without incident.

Prescott stood at the street corner watching them drive off, his eyes impersonal behind green-tinted glasses, his hands thrust deep in the pockets of his rumpled jacket.

As a boy, Kristian had been brought up on his father's large European estates. It seemed to him in retrospect that those years were very nearly perfect. He had not precisely loved either father or mother, but he had respected them, a fastidious man of great erudition and intellect, a woman of elegance and finesse. It was easy to recollect the huge white house, burning from within all the long hot nights of summer, the indigo sky, the coloured lamps flickering across the slowly moving couples on the lawns, the black swans sleepless on the lake. To remember also the hunting parties at dawn, his father a faultless shot, and the beautiful guns, clammy with the dew, and the white brandy in the silver hip flask burning on his throat. In those years, life had been confined to certain compartments, each item in its place, ready to be taken up when needed, to be replaced when finished with, like ornaments from a box. Times for dinner engagements, for shooting, for riding, for music, for literature. Everything was there to hand. Even women, if he wished for them, would come discreetly to his room, ask nothing except to please him, and never importunately, departing when he desired, gracefully and without question.

The estates were a kingdom of sorts, in some ways rather more. His father presided at curious little courts of justice set up to contain disputes among the tenants and workers of the land. It was tacitly understood, too, though never demonstrated in Kristian's time, that the power of life and death belonged also to his father. There were a couple of stories, one being that three months before Kristian's birth his father had hanged a persistent poacher, the other that once, years earlier, he had shot a stranger caught at midnight trespassing in the grounds.

In this environment and from this soil Kristian grew, observing the feudal pyramid at its most explicit all about him, the workers beneath, the landowner above, and, elevated just beyond the rest, the images which represented God.

For religion, like everything else, had its seasons and observances. Though it was quite clear to Kristian from the earliest that his father did not believe a godhead to exist, the symbol and the ritual – the motions of the censers, the candles and the exquisite singing – these were all-important. At forty, the milk-white faces of the icons still stirred in Kristian cool thrills of pleasure, and the light through coloured windows. It was too intimate a delight to be shared with any rude intrusive deity.

Perhaps there had been a half vision in Kristian's subconscious of the milk-white face of Sovaz lit similarly by coloured windows, as he had once found her beneath the panes of the library. Nevertheless, he was inspired to marry her in the office of a registrar with a handful of acquaintances looking on, the only hymn the distant external wailing of a street musician's flute.

That marriage. It had surprised everyone.

When he brought her back to the house from the tenement attic her laughter had been stopped. Indeed, he did not see her laugh much after, except sometimes, now and again, across a room full of guests and smoke. He had her hair dyed to its original shade; her face wiped clean in readiness for expensive cosmetics. She was now extremely docile. Kristian discovered in himself a sudden quickening, almost of desire or lust. He had rescued her, barely in time, from the filth of the waterfront night, from the nights of disease, ugliness and ennui which would inevitably have followed. Had rescued himself, more important, from a foul memory, a stinking leper of a ghost in every angle of his house that she had occupied.

Just over a year later, when all vestige, even all travesty of communication had flickered out, she told him.

She had begun to paint by then, small exact paintings which he abhorred for their theatrically gesturing participants and their raw colours. Moths were fluttering like rain against Sovaz' lamp as he came out of doors to smoke his Turkish cigarette. Sovaz, looking up from her canvas, had said: "Didn't it occur to you, Kristian, how lucky it was we never met the madam and her customer on the stairs, when you came for me that night?"

He did not wish to speak of it. "I don't recall the night in question."

"The night you found me on the waterfront, I told you the

madam was bringing a man up to me. Do you remember now?"

"There is no point in discussing this."

"I lied to you," Sovaz said.

He did not turn but kept his eyes on the descent of the gardens and the black sea below.

"Wasn't that foolish of me?" Sovaz murmured. "I thought it would force your hand, make you aware of me in spite of yourself, if you imagined that I'd despaired enough to do that – but really, the moment you came into the room I guessed it would be useless. I should never have told you that lie. Are you disgusted at my deceit? Disgusted enough to divorce me?"

"I suggest this conversation has come to an end," he said. He finished his cigarette. "You understood, I thought, that divorce is out of the question."

She said nothing, but, taking up her brush again, began to work upon her picture.

Presently he went inside.

Sovaz had remained at the mirrors, still fingering the rubies round her throat. It was extraordinary to Kristian that she should use on her canvases such garish hues, when she would only clothe herself in black or white, and baulked even at the coloured jewels in her box.

He said: "I'm going down. I suppose you will be following shortly."

"Yes. Of course."

"Very well," he said. He went out.

In the dressing room she could hear the valet busy among Kristian's things, setting them out, pure as brides, for his return.

Beyond the blinded window came the eternal soft disintegrations of the sea.

TWO

Prescott, finishing his drink alone on the terrace, saw the young American come out of the open double windows leading from the ballroom, and take a swift surfacing deep breath of night air.

Prescott automatically ran over him a quick, mercilessly thorough glance. The Greek pearl merchant's *protégé*, some youthful itinerant New Yorker named Adam Quentin. Mikalides, it seemed, had at some time known (in whatever sense) the American's mother. Finding Quentin adrift on the unsafe currents of the city, he had taken him up, and now brought him here with an intention as transparent as when he praised his latest pearl.

How old was the boy? About twenty, probably. What you expected perhaps of a young American male, lean, athletic, gold-coloured skin and sun-bleached hair and eyes, very white teeth, and too broad-shouldered to look particularly elegant or at ease in a dinner jacket. His clothes were correct but had a look to them that suggested to Prescott they might have been hired for the occasion. There was no cunning in the boy's face. He stood at the balustrade, clear-eyed and ingenuous, for either he was an opportunist like the Greek, or else naive.

Prescott had already inadvertently memorised the face. He now found it turned to him.

"Good evening," Prescott said.

The American smiled.

"It's a beautiful night," the young man said softly.

Just then the Greek, pausing at the threshold of the room, called the boy back to him like a man whistling a dog.

Prescott put aside the feeling of compunction that had come on him. No doubt he would be seeing something of Quentin in the future.

The Englishman set down his glass and left the terrace for the garden. A few couples were strolling in the dark. Their different accents and the scents of their cigarettes and perfumes came drifting across the ambience of the lemon trees.

It was indeed a beautiful night, but not an extraordinary night, for mostly nights were beautiful in this climate.

A man and woman passed him, going towards the terrace, their arms lightly linked. Prescott paid little attention to them; the woman's soft voice, a snatch of French: *"Je veux aller a la plage..."* Only the flash of the small diamonds in her ears recalled Sovaz to him, for Kristian's wife must by now be on the stairs.

The marble staircase cascaded, shining, down into the old ballroom, between ranked candelabra. The space below was full, as it was always full on the occasions of Kristian's receptions and dinners, and men and women had also placed themselves at various junctures on the stairs, falling apparently unconsciously into the harmonious shapes the room seemed to expect of them.

Long ago, Sovaz had wondered that he should invite so many people, permit even, though at the reception only, the uninvited companions of guests to invade his sanctum. Yet nothing could touch the house, the great jewel box lying open and all the jewels laid out. The enchanted visitors, like ghosts, went swiftly by, unable to dirty or profane with their insubstantial hands and voices, until only the house remained.

Sovaz came along the wide gallery and set her foot on the topmost stair. It was ten minutes before nine, ten minutes before the dining room would be thrown open, the room in which at all times, other than these, Kristian dined alone. She had come late, yet she paused and looked straight down the dazzling vista of the staircase to the spot where Kristian was standing. Sovaz took little notice of the group about him, a swarthy Egyptian, a tall woman with hair the colour of ice, one or two others. Although no longer aware of Kristian as an object of love or desire, she had remained, nevertheless, acutely aware of him as a live presence. She knew that immediately he saw her he would approach her, take her arm and lead her among his guests. He would expect nothing of her save the gracious manners and mannerisms he had seen to it she practised. Envious and evaluating, the eyes of his guests would follow her wherever she went.

She was noticed now. Heads were turning to look at her black and white figure and the scarlet glitter round her throat.

Like blood, she thought again, suddenly, for no reason. *Priceless life blood. I'm bleeding to death.* And just then she caught a fragment of conversation, someone nearby speaking analytically of a murder in the city.

She came down the stairs, and Kristian moved to take her arm. Once, six years ago, at the theatre, when his slightest touch still had the power to excite in her the most extreme of emotional and physical reactions, he had taken her arm, and she had undone the diamond brooch from her shoulder and, pretending to place her hand over his, had thrust the pin deep under his thumb nail. He started violently; his mouth whitened from the pain. She thought he would curse or strike her, but he did nothing, said nothing, waiting even until their party was seated before staunching the surprising flow of blood with his handkerchief. When some acquaintance leaned across to inquire what had caused the wound, he said, "I can't imagine." Returning alone together to the house an hour before dawn, he said to her, "You were careless this evening. Don't let it happen again."

The Egyptian had kissed her hand. They were passing on. Other lips on her skin, other faces and other names floating like the thickening light of the room across her eyes and mind. She was now so adept that she could react perfectly to them, and at the same moment stay within herself, looking out, through their transparent bodies. Afterwards she would remember neither what she had done nor what she had said to them.

At the far end of the room the great windows which gave onto the terrace were wide. The moon was snowing on the sea.

Suddenly a black shape appeared between the windows, extinguishing the moon like an eclipse. Sovaz glanced up. Kristian stood talking at her elbow to Mikalides, the man who controlled half the pearl fisheries based on the waterfront.

"Madame Sovaz is welcome to call at my office on any evening she cares to name. I can show her the queen of our recent catch – a large pale green pearl with, nevertheless, a peerless orient." The shadow still blotted out the moonlight. A man. A man too tall and too slight to be Prescott.

"Why not pay Thettalos a visit, Sovaz? It would be a pity to miss something so rare, wouldn't it?"

"Oh yes," she said automatically. "If you think so."

The shadow moved, turned a little. The brightness of the room passed like a summer lightning across his face, and was gone. She caught only an impression, like a plaster mask, no detail except a pair of eyes, very dark, like her own, looking directly, demandingly, at her. At once a burning electricity ran up her spine and spread across her shoulders. She did not know why. Then the path of the moon was clear again on the water, and the shadow had stepped aside into the night.

She felt a violent prompting to run to the windows, go out, shouting into the darkness: "What do you want?"

But she found she was instead being given the hand of a very beautiful young man, with a gentle uncertain American voice.

"Are you sure, Madame Sovaz," Adam Quentin said to her, "that there hasn't been some kind of a mistake?"

"I don't think so," she said.

"But surely, Madame Sovaz, to seat me next to you. Do you think someone has the places mixed?"

"Why should I think that?" she said.

"There must be thirty people here more important than me. It looks like some kind of a mistake."

"Well, we shall have to make the best of it."

He smiled sideways at her, grateful, perhaps, for her tolerance. Sovaz marvelled absently at his wonderful teeth, so even and so white. She made conversation as a sleepwalker takes steps, but more proficiently.

"I guess I'm nervous," he confided to her. "I quit my job in New York about a year ago. I've been travelling since then, living pretty rough."

She smiled. "What an adventurous thing to do."

"No, not really. I wanted to write a book..."

"Yes?"

"But I never did get the ideas together..." Aware of the writer's compulsive urge to communicate his dream, which threatened to overwhelm him like an attack of coughing, he broke off and began to eat the *consommé*.

"Forgive me, but you are so very young, aren't you?" Sovaz murmured, touched in a sentimental way by his youth, to which she had abruptly become sensitive.

He flushed faintly. "That sounds kind of strange, Madame Sovaz."

"Why should it?"

"Well, you don't seem much older. You couldn't be."

"How chivalrous, Mr Quentin."

"Please call me Adam. I'm not trying to be chivalrous."

"Then how very charming of you."

He glanced at her, his eyes wide, bemused by the poised denying quality of her voice, the careful sophisticated utterances of a woman of forty.

Servants slipped between them, removing their plates. The wine had gone to his head; he sensed something without understanding it and dropped his eyes. The rubies round her neck cast a transparent fiery mesh across the curves of her breasts, which were pulsing very slightly to the beat of her heart. The surreal atmosphere of the dinner seemed every moment to grow stronger, like the scent of jasmine now pervading the whole house. He stared at the fresh course that was in front of him, and, like a swimmer way out of his depth and valiantly drowning, he began to eat.

Poor boy, she thought mechanically.

Thettalos Mikalides, seated lower at the long table, had stolen a look at them. The pearl merchant was also a pimp. But it did not matter.

Her eyes moved along the length of the table. Few of the people in the ballroom for the reception had been invited for the dinner, the scalpel of Kristian's snobbery. For example, the shadow she had seen between the windows had not materialised into a dinner guest. Some stranger, he too had been exiled and was already gone. No doubt she had imagined the demand in his eyes.

When the meal ended, people drifted in twos and threes from the table.

The young man, who had grown silent and constrained – what had they said to each other all this while? – now stood up. She lifted her head and saw Kristian, the icy-haired woman still at his side. Sometimes Kristian showed an interest in other women, though never for very long.

"I have arranged for you to visit Thettalos tomorrow, Sovaz. Have the pearl if you want it." Kristian turned to Quentin. "I wonder if you would do me a very great service. I am unable to take my wife to the theatre tomorrow evening."

Sovaz heard the boy stammer slightly, trying to be courteous and gallant, not knowing how to refuse.

"Thank you," Kristian said. "I shouldn't like Sovaz to have to miss the play. I'll see the tickets are sent round."

Sovaz began to walk slowly through the room, into the ballroom, letting Quentin follow at his own pace.

Reaching the terrace windows, she hesitated.

The night was cool, smelling of darkness, yet below, the jagged glitter of the broken moon persisted on the water, and for no reason she stared about her at the empty space, before crossing it. She set her hands on the balustrade and gazed away from the sea. To the south, a million lights lay like fallen stars across the city; sometimes the wind would bring a distant twang from the bars, or the mooing of car horns.

The American emerged suddenly from the ballroom behind her and, as if unable to withstand the cliché, cleared his throat.

"It's very kind of you," she said, "to agree at such short notice.

I hope you had made no other plans."

"No," he said. He came forward, searching her face, troubled. It was a look she had grown accustomed to. It filled her with boredom and obscure pity. "If you'll excuse me, Madame Sovaz, I'd better leave now."

"So early? A shame. But I shall see you tomorrow evening, shan't I, Adam?"

"I guess you will."

She held out her hand to him. He looked at her hand, then came to her and took hold of her fingers. He was a little drunk. She only said: "Yes, you're so tanned. I think I should burn dreadfully if I stayed in the sun so long."

"Is this some game?" he whispered, bending over her through the moonshade of the jasmine plants.

She said nothing.

"You're so – and you act like you were some rich old woman – and your husband asking me to take – what the hell does he know about me?"

"Quite enough, I imagine."

"Yeah. So I gather. I didn't believe this."

"Oh, didn't you?"

His face was stiff and angry. Perhaps it was his good looks that somehow saved him from seeming absurd to her.

"Please don't distress yourself," she said. "All you have to do is stand me up."

"And then what? Someone else?"

He dropped her hand and his whole body tensed for some wild action.

She smiled and glanced away.

"Perhaps, Adam, you should go now," she said. "Don't try to be generous to me. Don't think about it anymore. I shan't expect to see you tomorrow."

She could hear the unspoken words hovering on his mouth, then a group came strolling onto the terrace from the golden room, talking, bringing with them the scent of Turkish tobacco and patchouli. The young man turned and immediately left her.

She felt a dragging downsurge of disappointment. Possibly it was the certainty of success which so depressed her spirits.

She let go of the balustrade and began to walk along the terrace to the spot where steps led down between the oleanders.

The group of men and women were murmuring and laughing together, discussing Strindberg. She understood that once she had descended into the dark, they would begin to discuss her with equal posturing vehemence.

Yet what could there be of interest to say about her?

The house, its sounds and lights, faded behind her. The garden closed her round. A melancholy night fragrance clung to every leaf and stem. Her mind emptied itself. She could hear the sea breathing on the beach below, and between each breath a resting soundlessness.

It was midnight.

By three o'clock the house was void of its guests, and the tide coming in to shore.

On the seaward perimeter of the gardens, a narrow oriental iron gate stood open in the high wall, and steps fell down the cliff to the shoreline.

Sovaz was walking on the beach.

The sound of the returning tide had strangely alarmed and aroused her.

The moon had set hours before. The water was impenetrably black except where its breakers hit the rocks like the unravelling silver fringes of a great shawl. The shore became a bowl of silence. The city and the house ceased to exist.

She walked eastwards, holding her evening shoes in one hand.

The beach below the house was for several miles generally deserted, only police patrols going by at irregular intervals. She had never encountered them. She might have walked till dawn. She had done so before.

But instead she made out a woman's long scarf trembling in short eddies along the water's edge towards her.

Sovaz stopped still. The scarf, moving as if half alive in the night wind, was somehow threatening. She drew away as it slithered by. Then, looking up, she saw the outline of a woman and a man stretched together on the ground, curiously unified by the darkness both with each other and with the surrounding sand. She thought they were making love; their stillness undeceived her. Only the woman's long dress was fluttering with the same motions as the scarf.

Precisely at this moment the man raised his head.

His eyes were for an instant glazed and withdrawn, seeing nothing, but Sovaz knew him at once. The sense of recognition had nothing to do with his physical appearance, which she had scarcely registered.

The starlight was very dim. It faded yet did not clarify the shadows. The pale elliptoid of the man's face, turned up to hers, so resembled a mask that at first the painted quality of the mouth did not surprise her. Then, she saw it was blood.

As his eyes focused on her, she made an instinctive attempt to avert herself, uselessly, for immediately her image seemed to have been snapped into storage in the brain behind his eyes, as if she had touched the tripwire of an automatic camera.

Everything had taken place in silence, the great sea-silence on the shore. Even now, she felt no impulse to cry out.

She began to take irrational paces backwards, towards the surf. The man watched her, making no move.

Their recognition was now mutual and significant.

The sea, reaching for her, laved her feet suddenly with cold. She ran.

She did not, somehow, expect him to follow. He did not. But the shadow had fallen on her so that where she fled it fled with her, ubiquitous as the night.

She reached the cliff steps and began to stumble up them. She had lost her shoes, the hem of her dress was torn and clinging cold. Finding the wrought iron gate, she clutched it, and, having got inside, thrust it shut, bolted it, and lay against the frame.

What now? she kept thinking shapelessly. *What must I do now?*

She forced herself to go through the garden, up the avenue of lemon trees towards the house.

Finally, she was on the terrace. She was trembling to such an extent she could not at once push open the unlocked windows. Her whole body ached, as if from fever.

The ballroom was empty.

One of the candelabras still sluggishly burned halfway up the marble staircase.

She began to climb the stairs, slowly. Great festoons of solidified wax poured from the candelabra. Something about the wax nauseated her. As she passed them the last lights smoked out.

"Leah!" she called or thought she did. Her voice made no impact on Kristian's house, and the black girl did not answer.

She came into the gallery and paused with her hand against the wall. She felt intolerably ill and listless, as if in the grip of *mal de mer*.

The doors of the library stood ajar.

Sovaz went to the doors but did not go in.

The aroma of Kristian's books was powdered thickly on the air. Everything was dark, except for the open windows where the balcony hung at the far end of the room. A lamp flickered there among the rustling vine.

The woman with the winter hair was leaning at the rail, as Kristian caressed her. There was no urgency or apparent pleasure in his movements, or in hers. The connoisseur, a statuette of valuable jade in his fingers.

Now, for the first time, the need to scream aloud overcame Sovaz. She could make no sound.

She turned away from the library doors and moved quickly towards her own, feeling her way with her hands.

Her room was empty, the bed opened, the lamps shining in their green and golden shades, her combs and brushes and cologne laid out for her, everything unchanged. Beyond the wall, in Kristian's dressing room, the accessories would lie in ranks, like well drilled soldiers. The first time he had been with a woman after their marriage, she had gone into his dressing room and smashed the mirrors and the bottles, torn open the drawers and chests and torn out the pages from the books lying by the window. The library had been locked, otherwise she would have gone there too. Yet he never spoke to her about what she had done. The valet had replaced the articles as if by magic.

Now, she did not think to go near Kristian's rooms. She went into her bathroom, turned on the taps of the bath and tore off the lace dress and silk underclothes and left them lying under the roaring, steaming water.

And, staring down at the swimming garments, she expected blood to run out of them.

Presently she turned off the taps and went through again to lie on the bed. Reaching out, she touched the master switch and blackness flooded her eyes.

She was floating, disembodied.

She had felt this sensation before, seven years ago, when she had swallowed all the sleeping tablets in Kristian's bottle, this same unanchored lightness. Who would find her this time? This time, surely, no one.

THREE

Sovaz woke in the heat of late afternoon.

Already the room was becoming real, her vision sharpening. Too late to sleep again. She leaned from the bed and pressed the bell. Would Leah come? Last night she had called Leah, and Leah had not answered - no, that was absurd. Of course Leah would come.

The door opened. The black girl came through.

"Leah, please open the windows and see to the blinds. Then run a bath."

At the inrush of air, perfumed faintly from the garden flowers below, the room seemed to hollow out. Sovaz sighed, lifting herself up in the bed. She could hear the black girl doing something to the bath, a sound of sodden garments dripping. Sovaz got to her feet and put on a wrap of Chinese silk, and seemed to activate, by doing so, a little gold and crystal clock which chimed thinly: four thirty. She crossed to the arrangement of mirrors.

Her face surprised her. There were still traces of cosmetics on her lips and eyes. She leaned forward, and saw, between the black silk revers of her wrap, the scarlet drops of the rubies lying on her throat.

Sovaz stood back. Her eyes widened.

"Leah!" she screamed out. "Leah! Leah!"

The black girl came running.

"What is it, madame?"

"Leah!" Sovaz screamed. She threw back her head.

"Madame – what's wrong? Have you hurt yourself? Madame…"

The girl sprang at her and took Sovaz' shoulders in a practical, restraining grasp. Sovaz was trembling convulsively. She ripped at the jewels around her neck. Leah, moving to help her, undid the clasp efficiently and in seconds.

"Get rid of them," Sovaz said. She had stopped screaming and shut her eyes.

"I'll put them in your box, madame…"

"No. I told you to get rid of them. I don't want to see them again. Do what I say."

Leah's face was impassive. She slid the gems into her pocket. She would take them to Kristian.

In the silence Sovaz heard the sea break on the shore. She sat down, and the horror went out of her abruptly, like a gush of blood. She did not open her eyes.

"I'll bathe now," she said, very evenly. "I can manage, thank you, Leah."

She sensed the girl hesitating, distrusting her.

"I shall want orange juice, fresh figs, black coffee. In half an hour, say." Her incongruous normalcy seemed to reassure Leah, or at any rate to bribe her. Sovaz heard her turn and go out.

Sovaz rose, remembered to open her eyes, went into the bathroom. The drowned clothes had been removed; the bath was filling. Sovaz stood staring down into the water until it brimmed over and ran out upon the floor.

At half past five Sovaz entered Kristian's library. This time he sat alone, reading, in the chair of Italian carved mahogany.

"Kristian," she said.

He did not look up.

"The limousine is waiting for you," he said. "Don't forget you are going to look at the Greek's pearl. I hope Mikalides has now provided his young friend with a better dinner jacket."

She had forgotten the pearl, that she was going to the theatre with the boy, Adam.

"Kristian, last night a woman was murdered on the beach."

He did not immediately reply. His distaste at discussing such a topic hung thickly in the room as the odour of books. But he was not surprised. It was his habit to glance at the evening papers, a dutiful, contemptuous glance. If death was in them, he would have seen. Presently he said, "So I believe."

She said slowly, "A man cut her throat. No, it was worse than that. I think he was drinking her blood. There was blood on his mouth."

"Not a subject to deliberate on, do you think?"

"I saw it," she said.

She checked at once. It was too unequivocal. She should not have put it in this way.

After a moment, he did look up at her. His face was blank. "Saw what, Sovaz?"

"I saw the dead woman on the sand, and the man lying on her. His mouth was covered in blood; I thought at first he was hurt. Then I saw her throat. I ran back to the house. He didn't follow me, though he was here earlier, before dinner. I came to tell you, but you weren't alone."

His expression did not change. He said nothing.

A thrill of pure horror went through her.

"Kristian, what am I to do?"

"Do?" He set aside the book. "You will go down to the car, and Paul will drive you to Mikalides' office. When you have looked at the pearl you will meet the young American and go to the theatre."

Sovaz swallowed and said, "You don't understand me. She was lying on the beach and the man on top of her. I thought they were making love – but the blood... I was walking, Kristian, do you see? And I found them..."

"This will stop, Sovaz. Do you expect me to believe this rubbish? You came here last night, and I was with a woman. I am sorry you were distressed, but you are not a child. Now you have heard a news bulletin and made up a ludicrous fantasy. What do you suppose you will gain by it?"

"But it's true," she said, "it's true."

"You forget," he said, "there have been other occasions on which you have lied to me."

She pressed her palm over her mouth.

Kristian had turned away from her to open the balcony windows, as if her words had introduced too much carbon dioxide into the air.

"You had better be going," he said, "otherwise you will be late."

She stood inside the doors of the library.

She thought: *Perhaps I heard some radio in the house, half awake, perhaps I fell asleep again. Perhaps I dreamed it. No,* she thought, *perhaps I invented it, and now believe it to be true.* Her mind seemed full of shadows. She searched them. Yes, there was the long scarf blowing on the rim of the sea, and there was the woman on the sand, and the creature crouched over her. Now he looked up, and now – the plaster mask face, the bloody mouth, the optic discs, and yet...

Remembering the landmarks of the man's face, she could not recapture his appearance.

She had not known him by his looks; he was collective, symbolic. He had no face, after all.

In the gallery she experienced again the urge to scream. She leant against the cool wall, and presently the spasm passed. She began to walk on.

She had forgotten where she was going, but Kristian's chauffeur, Paul, was waiting for her; he would know.

Outside the house, the mature sunlight fell over the garden walks, the parched stone of the hundred steps, the chess piece statues.

The chauffeur handed her into the limousine.

The quay at this hour was mostly deserted. A fisherman sat mending his net, the idle ships rocked indolently at their moorings. The ceiling of mazarine sky phased to lilac on the horizon like the smoke from the distant burning galleys of some antique war. The American, Quentin, leaned at the rail in his sun-bleached denims – the uniform of the youthful foreigner – watching a great black beetle creep along the deserted road from the north. He had been scribbling notes; now, diverted by the limousine, the paper hung dead in his hand.

A block away, the limousine went sliding down among a complex of side streets. Pushing the incomplete notation (the description of a woman) into his pocket, the American followed.

The car had slowed to a disdainfully careful pace. Its windows were of a black-green vitreous, impenetrable. He had never seen Kristian's car, neither been told its make, yet he had known it at once. It was inevitable that the rich aristocrat should possess only such a car, of a gliding, subtle oiled quality...

Now it had moved aside into the open space before the pearl merchant's offices. The engine stopped.

Adam too stopped, watching the car. His guts tightened. A chauffeur appeared from the front of the limousine and opened the left-hand door.

The woman got out. Her hair was long and very dark, loose on her shoulders. She wore a white voile frock, no jewellery.

The chauffeur stood back against the car. The woman began to walk towards the buildings. The little embryonic breeze of sunset fluttered her filmy dress and hair, making her look weightless, incorporeal.

Adam started after her. He passed the chauffeur, but the man's eyes did not follow him, the face betrayed neither interest nor boredom.

"Madame Sovaz."

She halted at once and turned. At first, she seemed to look

straight through him, as if she were indeed a ghost, or he. Then her eyes apparently focused. Adam felt himself flush. She appeared bewildered, genuinely at a loss. She did not quite say: "Who are you?" It was not pretence, or any kind of cruel playfulness. He was startled.

He drew the two theatre tickets from his shirt pocket, as if to identify himself. Her eyes went down to them then up again to his face.

"Last night," he said, "your husband asked me to take you to a play – I said a few things I wish I hadn't. Look, I just brought you the tickets. They came round by mistake, I guess."

"Adam," she said.

"I'd like to apologise to you," he said. "Would it do any good?"

"Adam," she said again.

The breeze still moved her hair and dress. It blew across the space from the buildings to the giant lizard of the limousine, unchecked, except where it encountered their two bodies.

Her face, though beautiful and beautifully made up, was grey, her large eyes leaden. Six months ago, sick with food poisoning in some nameless hospital, he had seen this same look of blind struggle in the eyes of amnesiacs or men dying of cancer. As then, he was consumed by sensations of helpless frightened horror. He could not see how he could go to her aid, and he was half afraid to touch her.

"Something's wrong, Madame Sovaz?"

She stirred. She smiled at him. She was attempting, listlessly, to reassure him.

"Oh. Just the heat. I can't bear the heat." Still with the smile nailed on her mouth, she turned away towards the limousine. "I don't think I'll bother with Thettalos' pearl. Kristian wants me to have it anyway. Paul!" she called.

The chauffeur discarded his pose and came over.

"Please go up for me and say I should like the pearl. My husband will see to it. Then take the car back to the house."

The chauffeur gave a little bow and went wordlessly off.

"Do you drive, Adam? Of course, all Americans drive."

He was choked by the need to undermine this dialogue and come at the truth. He discovered himself saying, with atrocious banality, "I haven't got a dinner jacket."

"It doesn't matter. It will take twenty minutes to get there, by the hill road," she went on. "Will that be all right? The performance begins as the sun goes down, doesn't it?"

He said, "You want me to come with you."

"Why not? Oh, yes. Of course you must come." Her eyes flashed a desolate brightness.

He felt a child in her presence, nine years of age, and she an old woman. He was presented with a frightful vision of Miss Havisham in *Great Expectations* screaming, her swirling white bridal dress alight, and he trying to beat out the flames, while the disturbed beetles and spiders ran away over the floor.

Driving northeast through the outskirts of the city into the hills, they sat unspeaking, the American turning the wheel in his hands, she lying back on the dusty seat of the ramshackle little hired Ford, the voile dress spreading round both their feet and the gears of the car.

The road ascending was crowded by olives growing on the slopes, a landscape now darkening as the sun sank. By contrast, the whole sky, even the east, was vivid with an exceptional bronzed red.

The theatre was constructed in the old style, weathered by sun and rain and by the emotions of joy and tragedy conjured on the stage at its core, travelling up its tiers like thrills along a complex series of nerve endings. It appeared to be and felt of enormous actual age. Though in fact, built ten years before, time, as if recognising a good copy, seemed to have consented to the deception. On the top terraces of cheaper seats, men and women clustered like pigeons over bottles of wine, baskets of cheeses, figs and sausage, and children ran about like dogs. The spell of the play was not yet cast on them, the occult masked figures on the skene below, the voices of gods and doomed kings manifested by loudspeakers with terrifying intimacy even on the highest benches.

Kristian's tickets of course belonged to those rows where men in evening clothes smoked cigars and women with diamonds in their ears murmured over fans and programmes. Adam Quentin, feeling conspicuously undressed-up, took the seat beside Sovaz. He was appalled and fascinated that they should be sitting to watch a play by Euripides with all this burden of unsaid things between them.

A gong roared somewhere beneath the stage. Immediate soundlessness responded from the upper tiers. Prepared for magic and superstition, the opening of hearts and minds was almost audible. Below, the intellectuals composed themselves differently, stubbing out their cigarettes.

The palace of a Hellene king, a ruined altar with smoke stirring on it. Quentin saw Sovaz' eyes abruptly flicker, as if in recognition.

The *Bacchae*. It would be performed in its intended Greek, so he would pick up one word in ten. Three years since he had read the play in translation, a minute here and there, in a drawing office in New York.

A flute sounded in the sunset's scarlet stillness. The god was coming. The young man felt the atmosphere, with no warning, overwhelm him. He dimly realised the unfruitful communion with the woman beside him had quickened and made him ready, on these chill and flame-drunk hills.

The sun left the incredible sky. Soon the evening would creep down the slopes to follow Dionysos, the shadow precious to his worship, and torches would flash, and Selene's altar-fire spring up. The god would come to the city of Thebes to establish his divinity. The Theban women, who had scorned and refused his gift of wine, he would send mad to the hills, to dance with wild beasts and to rend cattle with their teeth and nails. Pentheus, the king, who would attempt to imprison and humiliate him, Dionysos would send after them to spy on their rites, where, discovered, the king would be torn to pieces, and Agave his mother would wrench off his head.

He came out with a deadly grace, an animal tread. The god. A sigh like a gust of wind surfed across the benches.

The masks were in the true style, very lifelike. Dionysos' face, framed by supernatural hair, jet black yet somehow catching a gold highlight on every grape-cluster of curls, seemed living, though exalted. A pale, beautiful, unhuman face, matching exactly the almost naked body, dark white and slender, which, even in its fawnskin loincloth, breastless and male, was oddly hermaphrodite, an enticement to either or any sex.

The demon.

Sovaz sank back against the seat. The world seemed to go from under her.

Dionysos. The features, which in her memory comprised no face, came suddenly together. A white mask with kohl-ringed, impenetrable eyes, its lips stained with wine, or blood.

The headlights burst on the road before them. Objects seen beside the road, trees, walls, the abandoned corpse of a motorcycle, appeared to leap forward at the window.

Suddenly Sovaz put her hand on Quentin's arm.

"Stop the car."

She did not speak loudly, her touch was light, almost impersonal, yet a surge of adrenalin shot through him. He found he had jammed on the brakes as if a man had run into their path.

The car stilled about them with small subsiding noises. The night came closer. Crickets ticked in the grass. He switched off the headlamps. He heard the door open, the rustle of her dress as she got out. Presently, opening his own door, he too came out and stood on the slope. He caught a glimpse of her face, pale as the dress, expressionless yet intent, before she turned. She began to walk up the slope. He followed her slowly, his mouth very dry.

Wild olives clambered and clustered. Sovaz stopped in front of him. The shadow of the leaves, dappling her, gave her frock the strange look of a leopard skin, a Bacchic image, a maenad. As he came nearer, she moved round and caught his hand. Her own was icy and narrow.

"You're cold," he said, acutely aggravated at the idiocy of his own remark.

"Yes."

She stood staring up at him. Her eyes did indeed contain terror, he could see it now.

"Do you want to go back?" he said hesitantly.

"Where? To Kristian's house? No."

Her hand slipped from his. She began to unbutton his shirt, then slid her arms about him. The touch of her cold, cold fingers burned on his skin. But her mouth, following, was warm.

"Adam," she said to him, as if to be certain who he might be. Her whole body was trembling. He caught her need inevitably, abruptly, like catching fire. Shadows, grass, the smoke of her hair; the dark roped them together inexorably. Yet, even as she clung to him, there seemed no energy in her, no fierceness or real intention. Lying down with her, the folds of her dress spread away from them over the uneven ground, shifting slightly in imitation of their movements. Her hands clutched his flesh in a drowning, strengthless motion, she cried out softly, and let go. She was one of those women who in orgasm seem possessed by a devil, which expels their reason, shakes and worries at their bodies.

When, in a few moments, she opened her eyes and gazed at him, it was with a dull, amazed and bewildered expression.

"And so you see," she said, as if they had been speaking of it all along, and had paused only briefly, perhaps to admire the view, "that everything you accused me of on the terrace, everything you thought of me, was quite correct."

His own eyes were wide open on her, by contrast very clear.

"Sovaz... that doesn't matter anymore."

"Poor Adam," she said.

"Sovaz..."

The wind brushed over the tops of the olive trees.

She shut her eyes. She lay void and joyless. The clamour of panic had faded. Now only the white mask hanging in her brain, the beautiful god with his dark gifts of blood and wine, and the human youth shipwrecked on her body, and the whisper of the wind in leaves.

At about four thirty in the morning, strolling across the sprawling waterfront night market, Prescott found Adam Quentin seated on a bench beneath a canvas awning, among a row of derelicts smoking the cheap hashish sold on the quay.

Prescott sat down opposite and pushed away the old man who came immediately scampering to him, offering a pipe and squeaking.

The rest of the market, having scented the dawn like a scurrilous and night-preying animal, was now in the process of packing itself up and sliding away down into the rat-hole crevasses of the city to hide from the sun. Lamps guttered out. Men cried hoarsely to one another. Canopies were dragged free and folded, charcoal stoves extinguished, goods thrown back into crates. All along the shore the pleasure boats were returning stealthily, black-winged across the moonless water, like vampires seeking their tombs. Only here and there the occasional island of humanity still unstirring – the brothel door, the booths of the opium eaters, the sellers of night flowers, the astrologer beside his crackpot telescope and tarot cards, placidly chewing a lemon.

Adam looked up. The fact of seeing the Englishman did not appear to disturb him.

"This isn't the place for you," Prescott said quietly. "Here you will be cheated, robbed, probably followed afterwards, attacked or even killed. It's a popular theory that certain kitchens in the vicinity obtain their meat from dubious quarters."

Adam laughed.

"I can recommend several establishments," Prescott said, "where you would be safe, and where the quality of the goods is also above reproach."

"Great. I guess the price matches the goods."

"Yes. We'll come to that presently. I'm surprised you've chosen this form of amusement. Have you enjoyed yourself?"

"I surprised myself," Quentin said. "It's been a surprising night. No. It's been a night that was surprisingly unsurprising." He looked at Prescott. "Is that what I mean? No, I didn't enjoy it."

A man next to the American muttered and spat on the ground. Prescott spoke to him in the slum argot. The man's gaze darted and watered.

Prescott rose and pulled the boy up, unresisting, by the arm. They walked into the wider open streets north of the market.

The boy was unused, Prescott imagined, to the unclean mixed hashish of the old Arab's stall. His eyes were swimming and dreamlike.

"What time is it?" he asked, without interest.

"Almost dawn. Where are you living?"

Adam leaned against a peeling wall. "I forget. Nowhere special." His eyes swam leisurely across the sky. The eastern edges of faint clouds were beginning to become visible. "You're the rich man's agent, my mother's Greek jockey says. Did you follow us tonight?"

"Follow? Whom?"

"You know damn well whom. Who. Sovaz. You're paid to keep tabs on her for him, aren't you?"

"Did Mikalides say that too?"

"Maybe he did."

"Then maybe he was right."

"And now your boss told you to keep me out of trouble. Oh, man, I can believe it."

"I am authorised to offer you a sum of money," Prescott said. "Your inclination may be to refuse it, but you should consider first. The companion of Kristian's wife will need ready cash. She's used to the best."

Adam Quentin, still staring up at the sky, said, "He's very

generous, your *master*."

"Not exactly. You must remember the lifestyle Madame enjoys; people know whose wife she is. Her reputation is valuable to him."

"Caesar's wife," Adam said. "But not above suspicion."

He eased himself from the wall and began to walk on, unsteadily.

Prescott was oddly struck by the curious gracefulness of the young man's naivety. Here was a creature which was still openly amazed, moved, wounded by what took place about it, the somehow tragic aura of the young. A quality Sovaz had never possessed.

"I shan't bother Caesar's wife any further. So forget the money. And forget seeing me to my door, will you?" Adam said abruptly, "In the morning I think I'll take the goddamned train out of this place."

Prescott fell out of step with the young man, allowing him to proceed alone.

The sky above the hills was turning to the colour of steel.

How many of Sovaz' lovers had behaved in this fashion? Perhaps a third. Some actually escaped the city, then came back, like the addict.

Prescott was not generally given to flights of fancy, yet in respect of Sovaz, highly coloured images sometimes suggested themselves to him. He supposed he too was not quite immune to the perfume, like that of some poisonous night-growing plant, that clung about her. He still vividly remembered finding her in the tenement attic, lying on the rotting French sofa, her hair burned a chemical yellow, her eyes eaten by night. In some extraordinary way she put him in mind, as she lay there, of a succubus, or the *rakshas* of Indian mythology. A stupid notion. She was then a pathetic and inexperienced young girl, without hope or common sense.

Dawn had not yet touched the house, or the sea.

Behind the sightless windows, the woman was lying on her bed, Stravinsky playing from the gramophone, the dark discordant harmonies washing over her, as the tides below washed over the rocks and sands and other detritus of the beach.

Presently the record came to an end, though the turntable continued to revolve with the mindless beat of a mechanical heart.

Sovaz opened her eyes. The room was all shadow, only the faint smoke rising from the joss sticks burning in the bronze bowl.

She lifted herself on one elbow. Across the room, catching the angle of the mirrors, she saw her own face looking back at her, a mask, set with two black glass gems to give an illusion of sight. She touched at her face with her hand. Her eyes fell on the array of combs, perfumes, the crystal tray with its boxes of powder and sticks of kohl, the ivory jewel casket.

Sovaz left the bed. She crossed the room (her feet were bare; the thick carpet had a feel of life, the pelt of some creature, lying supine). She set her fingers on the clasp of the ivory box. Heat burned up in her as she did so. She drew back her hand.

She went out into the gallery. The house was breathing to itself like an animal.

The smell of the library in the dark was heady, despite the open window. The balcony lamp was extinguished, yet there was light in the sky, for the room faced eastwards.

In the rack of carved cedarwood stood the evening papers, neatly folded by Kristian's valet. Each sunset they were removed and replaced by fresh ones.

Sovaz picked up a paper, turned it to the east.

A woman had been murdered on the beach. The time of death was estimated at about three o'clock in the morning. She was twenty-nine years old, the wife of a minor official attached to the French consulate; she had had many lovers and was not particularly discreet. Her throat had been slashed, but she had not been robbed, the little diamonds were still in her ears and the garnet rings on her fingers. There was no sign of a struggle, or of sexual assault. The police patrol had found her. There had been in the city an identical case two months before, unsolved. And earlier...

The light, falling on to the paper, was turning molten now.

Below in the garden, birds were singing.

Sovaz wrenched the page out of the paper.

Going back to her bedroom she lifted the needle from the record. She opened the jewel box and placed the sheet of newsprint, folded very small, in the lowest compartment.

She felt exhausted and did not properly know what she was doing. She took up the silver-backed brush and began to use it on her hair. There was light now too in the western windows.

Somewhere in the city the American boy was walking or sleeping. She remembered now, only faintly, the wild olive grove in the hills. She did not at all remember parting with him, his eyes painfully searching her face for clues, the limousine materialising from shadow, the swift drive along the shore road.

She did not want to sleep, could not bring herself to it.

There was fresh blood inside the jewel casket.

The black girl, presumably on Kristian's instructions, had replaced the rubies in the box. Sovaz lifted them out.

Holding the necklace in her hand, she left the room a second time, went down through the house, descending blindly the marble stairway into the ballroom, opening the doors of the terrace, and stepping out.

The scent of the sea, overriding the scent of the garden trees. She reached the narrow Moorish gate and thrust it wide. Below, the beach, the agate layers of water, stained now by the rising sun. At the horizon, like a flock of black gulls resting on the waves, the boats of the night fishermen.

The dawn with its floods of light and colour, its avowal of radiance and heat, made her afraid. The shrill birdsong was full of menace. She flung the rubies from her – down, beyond the steps, towards the beach, out of sight.

The sea would take them away with the tide. Or some urchin searching for crabs would grab them up. You could not throw out rubies on the perimeter of the hungry city and hope to find them again. And yet, the small diamonds in her ears, the garnets on her knuckles... Perhaps it might have been better, driving on the fringes of the slums, to have tossed them into some filthy court, and seen the beggars and the sick tear themselves and the necklace apart.

There was a man standing among the lemon trees.

Her heart leaped up, choking her. She stumbled. He came quickly and caught her arm. It was the Englishman.

"Are you quite all right, Madame Sovaz?"

"Yes, thank you. Perfectly."

There was something she must eventually ask the Englishman. What was it? It had to do with Kristian's dinner party, the moon-drenched terrace.

The Englishman held open the nearest terrace window for her.

"Thank you," she said, and passed through, out of the rays of the sun.

FOUR

One warm evening, when he was twenty-three years old, Kristian had seen his parents' car plunge off a mountain road and fall three hundred and eighty feet into the ravine below.

They had been going to the theatre, he behind in the second car with various acquaintances, his father and mother alone in the first, the chauffeur left behind and his mother at the wheel. She had been wearing, he recollected after, a frock of amber silk, an Egyptian jade scarab ring on her right hand. Her thin mocking figure elegantly imposed on the last traces of the sunset, the cicadas buzzing, the darkening whiteness of the house against the backdrop of the great estate. She had said, he remembered, that she did not particularly want to see the play.

There had been no warning. The Daimler was perhaps half a mile ahead of them, going quite fast. The final orange flash of the sun swelled like a spotlight across the road. Abruptly the great car seemed to swerve, as if at some unexpected obstacle, then swung on in a fluid motion, a sort of horrid gracefulness, crashed through the railing and was gone.

The second car braked at once and disgorged its passengers in time for them to see the last of the Daimler's spinning descent. A ghastliness of predestination seized Kristian; the space of seconds seeming almost a full minute before the vehicle made impact below, those moments of time during which the occupants of the car still lived, screamed in the extremity of terror or possibly even hoped for some reprieve. Presently the car struck the rocks. Another instant of stasis followed. Then the explosion of the petrol tank, the blot of sound and colour on the porous paper of twilight. While figures ran back and forth along the road, Kristian sat beside the railing on the ground, watching the pyrotechnics alternately flare and fade, like a sleepy eye on the gathering night.

Later he learned that his mother, at the time of the car accident, was dying of cancer. There was, after all, no inanimate obstacle on the mountain road from which she might have swerved. Certainly, no small animal life would have disorganised her progress; once, driving back from a shooting party, proudly yet negligently displaying her bag, she had added: "I have also littered the road with dead hares and foxes." Kristian came to believe that his mother had chosen not to wait. The burning petrol took on fresh symbolism. She, in her beautiful clothes and jade jewellery, lying in the Daimler like a warrior in his finery and chariot, her consort, either willing or unwilling, consumed at her side. He could visualise her, indeed frequently did so, letting go the wheel, her hands in her lap, perhaps smiling.

In the muddled aftermath of the 'accident', Kristian discovered grey-faced grey men like gathering ravens at his door. His father's debts were numerous. Like all men who live hour by hour by means of their own reputation, he had left only chaos and unfinished business behind him. It became clear that the northern estates must be sold. Walking about the grounds, in those last days, among the vast stretches of pines, beside the lake, through the familiar house with everything now stacked up in crates or masquerading under sheets, the death which had precipitated it all became of necessity elevated, unique.

Finding one night the empty bottle of sleeping tablets in his dressing room, Sovaz hidden away, the valet wiping his hands on a towel, Kristian had fallen prey once again to a compulsion which he did not recognise. He must in some way elevate, he must simultaneously eradicate and deny, the thing which repelled and drew him. Experiences are initial: whether exact or distorting, all later situations are only mirrors of what has gone before.

Kristian wrote his signature over the final batch of letters. His secretary, a self-effacing young man, took up the correspondence neatly and silently and went out.

The previous night, coming back to the house at about midnight, Kristian had heard the gramophone whispering softly through the walls of his wife's bedroom. Both doors were shut. The music moaned, the records were occasionally changed or else played over and over. Sometimes water ran into the bath. Once Leah had been called to fetch her the fruit and black coffee that Sovaz habitually took on rising. Yet Sovaz lay on the bed, the turntable of the gramophone whirring ominously, the cigarette box half empty, a scattering of sketches for some new painting cast indiscriminately about the floor like fallen leaves. The black girl was not adequate to the task of describing to Kristian the subject matter of these drawings. She imagined she had seen one or two of an animal resembling a panther running with a white cloth draped loosely across its body. Despite her lack of descriptive power, a faint look of fear came over the black girl's face when she spoke of this, a fear so subterranean that she herself did not seem to be aware of expressing or even feeling it.

Sovaz had now been shut in her suite for thirty-nine hours.

Kristian rose. The items on the escritoire were meticulously arranged, the inkwell of black onyx, the Persian paper knife which had once actually tasted blood when some woman of past acquaintance – this time not Sovaz – had picked it up and flung it at him in a cataleptic fit of rage. The blunt little point, thrown with such force, had torn through the sleeve of his shirt and nicked his flesh before it fell back exhausted on the rug. The woman had fled. Going upstairs to change his shirt, he had discovered the empty tablet bottle lying face down among his brushes, and presently his valet had come through from Sovaz' bathroom, a towel in his hands.

Now, mounting the stairs, Kristian was not unaware of a distasteful unease building in him with each step. For six years his wife had been unassertive. Yet suddenly, once again these curious and hysterical lies, this demanding seclusion. The little bottle reappeared with a sharp perfection of detail in his mind's eye.

Prescott had told him the American boy had taken the train inland. Perhaps this might be the root of her behaviour, only some trite quarrel. A small package had come for her this evening and been left with Kristian's mail beside the fresh newspapers in the cedarwood rack. The valet had mentioned to him that, on removing the papers yesterday, he had discovered a page had been torn from one of them.

Outside her door, Kristian waited a moment. The gramophone, not playing yet still active, throbbed. He did not like her records: Stravinsky, Kodaly, Prokofiev – these seemed to pierce his ears like burning wires – neither Rachmaninov, whom he found impure and cloying.

He knocked. She did not answer. He tried the door, which opened.

She lay on the bed, smoking. The room was wreathed in smoke, smoke from her cigarette, smoke from the burning joss sticks he abhorred. She had on no make-up, which had the peculiar effect of making her appear excessively young to him, and yet, about the eyes, very old. She had lost weight. He did not like this look of her.

"Are you unwell?"

"Yes. But it's nothing."

"Do you want me to telephone Florentine?"

At the mention of the little doctor, she abruptly laughed, but almost at once was again lifeless. She made a small loose gesture with one arm.

"If you like. But it isn't at all necessary. I shall be perfectly all right tomorrow."

He caught sight, through the half open bathroom door, of steamless water held unused in the bath. He crossed to the gramophone and, lifting the needle, set the arm on its rest. One of the drawings Leah had reported lay on the table.

Kristian took up the sketch. A panther, caught in the midst of a statuesque static leap, filled in jet black with a heavy and merciless lead pencil. The lack of subtlety that always offended him in Sovaz' paintings prompted him to discard the paper at once. Nevertheless, he became aware that the white cloth Leah had described as draped across the animal's back was in fact an unconscious woman, her head dangling, her tangled hair trailing on the ground.

"I have something for you," he said, producing the small package. "It came with this evening's mail."

"Oh, leave it there," she said, immobile, uninterested. "I'll open it later."

As she spoke, the crystal clock suddenly sang out eight chimes like a tiny soprano.

The voice of the clock galvanised him. He set the package down beside her and was turning to go out, when she asked abruptly, "Who brought this?"

He glanced back at her. She was all at once sitting up, holding the thing, unopened, in her hands. She looked excited, feverish. "I don't know. Why not unwrap it and find out?"

Perhaps the American had sent her some cheap, paltry and emotional token. Yet she did not undo her parcel.

Kristian opened the door.

"Please," she said, "wait a moment."

He paused impatiently.

She pulled at the paper ineffectually. It appeared to come away only in despite of her. Her face, which had been white, now burned as if a fire was concealed in the wrapping. Sovaz thrust the contents, the paper, everything, from her. Blood seemed to splash out onto the black carpet. A pool of rubies. He knew them immediately and crossed to the bed.

"He was watching," Sovaz said. "He saw me. He's sent them back."

"What are you talking about?"

"The necklace. I threw it away, threw it down on the beach."

"You're talking nonsense," Kristian said, "I don't understand you."

A small fragment of paper still adhered to the coverlet. Kristian picked it off, for he could see a single line of writing on it. The words were part of a quotation from Virgil: *Nos cedamus Amori* – we must yield to love. He held it out to her. When she would not take it, he let it fall beside the jewels on the carpet and went out.

Going into the library, he closed the doors, and presently telephoned Florentine.

The doctor arrived at the house in the late afternoon. As on previous occasions, the hundred steps had left him breathless. In his black coat and white shirt, both still formally buttoned despite the heat and the climb, holding the apologetic cliché of his bag beneath one of his short arms, he resembled perfectly a penguin.

There was a tired gentle eagerness about the doctor, a nervous compulsion to ease pain, alleviate fear. He seemed to beg his patients to get well, if only for his sake. Standing in the foyer, upon the tessellated floor, it was plain that Kristian's house overawed him, not by its wealth or magnificence, but because of the emotions and aims so apparent in it.

Ushered by the black girl into the bedroom of Kristian's wife, oppressed by the sombre furnishings, the sombre sunlight soaking through the polarised windows, Florentine's psyche responded nevertheless to the isolated figure of the woman seated there. Her white silk robe, the loose hair, seemed to increase her appearance of youth and defencelessness. The doctor found himself falling into a stance – half avuncular, half conspiratorial – which he adopted with sick children.

"Well, Madame Sovaz. And how are you feeling today?"

"Quite well. It was nothing at all. A migraine."

"Ah yes, but they can be unpleasant. Have you had any vomiting?"

"No. I am quite well. I can't imagine why Kristian should call you."

"A husband worries."

Silence greeted this.

She let him take her arm and wind around it the serpent he used for checking blood-pressure. Unexpectedly she laughed.

The little doctor smiled at her encouragingly, cocking his eyebrows, asking to be let in on the fun.

"I was only thinking," she said, "how absurd it was that you should suppose Kristian might worry about me."

Dr Florentine dropped his eyes, embarrassed, and was unnerved to see suddenly that she wore about her throat the mesh of rubies Kristian had told him of.

He took her pulse; her flesh was cold. She seemed too entirely relaxed, relaxed to an extraordinary degree, as if drugged. Peering into her eyes, he was reminded of an oriental belief that women have no souls. Discouraged by this idea, which sprang from racial memories he at all times attempted to suppress in himself, the doctor packed up his bag and perched before her, with his prescription pad.

"Well, I don't think there's anything much the matter. These tablets should help."

"In what way?"

"Oh," he dismissed the question softly, "a mild stimulant, nothing drastic." He finished writing and pretended to have trouble with the spring of his pen. "I'm so glad that you recovered your jewels, Madame Sovaz."

"Yes. It was very lucky."

He waited, but she said nothing more. He put away the pen and glanced up at her. The alteration in her demeanour was strikingly obvious after her lassitude.

Her cheeks were slightly flushed. Her hands, formerly loose on the arms of her chair, were twitching. She was a young girl of seventeen, a virgin, or a woman pared of her youth, unloved and unkindled for seventeen years, seeing her lover advancing for the first time towards her bed. On her face there was briefly such an amalgam of vulnerable innocence, fear, longing, bewilderment and desire, that a complementary sweat started out on the doctor's forehead.

"And did you really throw such lovely things down to the beach?" he asked her, with the rusty playful air he used sometimes on the very old, unbalanced and ailing, in his care: *Did you really swallow all those pills? Did you really poison the concierge's little dog, after she had been so kind to you?* The usual response – "I *did*, I *did*" – was not forthcoming.

Sovaz' face paled serenely. "How strange you should think that."

Kristian had told him what she had said. In Kristian's opinion, she had no doubt mailed the rubies to herself, including the note – written in a palpably invented hand. Understanding that he had been employed more as detective than physician, the doctor now did detect, in her cool denying volte-face, the sinister rational stealth of the truly insane.

A little later, standing in Kristian's study, he observed painfully, "I don't think I am qualified to treat this condition."

Kristian's cold face made Dr Florentine afraid in a general, unlocalised way – perhaps of inhumanity.

"This is a confidential matter," Kristian said. "I don't intend it to go further than yourself."

"Well, of course, I am always discreet – it is my duty to my patients to be so. But the sort of attention your wife may need…"

Kristian was not listening, only politely waiting for him to finish. Dr Florentine began to say the things Kristian would tolerate from him. *A clockwork mouse,* he thought. *He winds me up, I must perform as I am meant to.* The key in his back was real enough: Kristian's generous promptness in the matter of bills, his donations. *One of my few paying patients.* Well, if one could not live by bread alone, certainly one could not live without bread. But what should he say? *Love your wife. A* simple cure, as possibly the cure might be for sclerosis or cancer, once it was discovered.

Going down between the savage horses' heads of the stairway, he saw again the scatter of leaves across her black bed, which he had surreptitiously observed as he moved about the room. Press cuttings concerning a murder, smudgy photographs of a stretcher, the Frenchman weeping and trying to shield himself from the flashing eyes of the cameras – it was the killing of the Gallier woman on the beach.

So many cuttings.

In her current mood, the crime might have obsessed her for any number of reasons. Perhaps she was afraid. Near the edge of the bed lay a sketch, unfinished. It filled the doctor with a sense of enormous horror, a horror he could not translate at all into cohesive thought. The drawing, surely, was a sibling to the cuttings. A leopard straddled a gazelle, tearing at its flesh. Underneath had been written the word μαινάς (maenad).

The bar was hot and humid, alive with the buzzing of flies, the cursing of a card game, the ineffectual noise of two electric fans whirring in a trance from the ceiling. The girl who had served him his drink had chattered to him with a spontaneous bright chatter, like a little bird. Her English, obviously learned from tourists, was spoken with an unintentional accent as American as his own. She was a pretty gentle girl, a girl plainly not of the city. Ten years, maybe, before the city stripped her down to greed, vulgarity, envy and despair, ten years or five, or two, or less. Yet now she fluttered her eyes at him sweetly. Adam Quentin, longing to become involved in the mayfly tragedy of her life, could think only of Miss Havisham in the crumbling white dress, Miss Havisham with her vampire eyes, not sweet at all, only starving. This girl's eyes were also black, yet a superficial warm blackness, a shallow river, containing uncomplex instincts, quite animal, even understandable.

And yet, when he stood up and left her, he saw on those eyes the first stoical scars, the adult tiredness...

The number of the house he had seen about a week ago in Mikalides' book of numbers, which the Greek carried with him as a magician carries his trick cards, and for similar reasons of deceptive magic.

Adam telephoned. Then, the receiver clicking in his hand as if with radioactivity, depressed the cradle.

The girl, polishing glasses at the bar, no longer watched him. Adam took up the receiver a second time, dialled, and presently stood once more waiting, at a loss. A servant answered.

"...Madame Sovaz..."

"Who is calling, please?"

"My name is Quentin. Q-U..."

"One moment. I will see if Madame is able to receive your call."

Three days. He had taken the inland train. He had worked one day at erecting administrative buildings of white cement like guano, on the river. He had worked one day at unloading the cargoes of fish, oranges, melons, the tourist-bait of enamelled blue alligator skins, the aphrodisiac tusks of rhino. The second night, lying with a girl, empty of anything except Sovaz – the smell of her, the touch of her flesh, her hair, her premature oldness, her cold hands and burning mouth, her vacant hungry eyes. Again, the train. The night train. Families asleep, children sobbing fitfully, rattling into the city over tracks reverberating like machine guns.

The telephone clicked against his ear.

"Adam," the telephone said.

He could only stammer. He had not, after all, expected her to speak to him.

The line was poor.

"What?" he asked her.

"Help me," she said faintly. "I'm going mad," she said. It was only a whisper. "I must leave here – help me – help me…"

"Sovaz? You know I'd do anything…"

"No. You won't do anything. No one can help me. Why did you call?"

The line blanked suddenly out and began to sizzle. She had cut him off, or else her handsome pale-eyed husband, intercepting, had cut them off, or else the erratic wires had played a joke on them, or else the city had abruptly broken in two, and one half, crowned by Kristian's house, had vanished into the sea.

He dialled again, then hung up. He went to the bar and stood there, indecisively.

"You want another beer?" The girl looked out from her tired dark eyes. She no longer flirted with him. He had been appraised.

"No, thanks."

He went out.

He began to walk along the shore road. He did not want to. His muscles ached; his belly was leaden.

The sun lay smashed on the water. A meeting of flame and liquid that produced no smoke. Eastwards the sky spread great lammergeyer wings. He could reach the house in half an hour.

He felt no pity for her. He was apprehensive of her. And yet her voice in the telephone, the voice of a terrified old little girl, impelled him towards her as if by sorcery.

The day fell below the sea. A torchlight redness faded over the waves, leaving them the colour of the night. The crickets began their eerie irritation in the scrub at the roadside. Two or three battered cars passed him, going south, and a donkey cart loaded with pale flowers.

Finally, he was staring up at the facade of the enchanted castle, lowering above its prison wall.

The shadow of it, the scents of its garden disturbed him, but he had expected nothing else. Waiting to be admitted, he noted his own shabbiness, impartially. Like an armour the stained denims, the bleached shirt, a charm to keep him safe from the spell of the house.

Presently, all the lights sprang into golden life along the four tiers of steps. He could see now the chess piece marble horses snarling on the landings among the vines. A faceless man – truly, all Kristian's servants seemed faceless, or robots – came down to the oriental gate.

"Madame Sovaz is expecting me," Adam Quentin said.

The lie, unpremeditated but obvious and essential, seemed to release him from heavy chains. The dehumanised servant stared for a moment out at him through the iron lattice, then activated the electric switch in the wall. The password presumably was correct. The gates slid open.

Adam stepped through, waited for the servant to close the gates, then followed him up the hundred steps into the house.

The scent of jasmine clung in the foyer, reminding him of the dinner party. After her entreaty to him, he half expected some hint of upheaval or of fear to have manifested itself. Seeing nothing out of place, nervousness overtook him, some unease that he had imagined the swift, half inaudible torrent of her words, or misunderstood some flippancy.

At this moment Kristian emerged to his left from between a pair of polished wood double doors. Rather than reinforcing, by his arctic faultlessness, the illusion of balance, his presence seemed to Adam Quentin to make entirely possible Sovaz' hysterical anguish.

Kristian overawed him, as he overawed and intimidated most of those he met.

"You have come to see my wife," Kristian stated.

"That's right. Do you think you can stop me?"

"I see you are in melodramatic mood, Mr Quentin. Of course, I have no such intention. Why should you imagine that I have?"

Kristian moved aside, graciously motioned Adam to step into the room behind him.

"Like you told me, I'm here to see your wife," Adam said.

"But first I should like a moment of your time. If you would be so good."

Despite everything, Kristian's impeccable manners overpowered him. Adam Quentin's age sat, in that moment, so lightly on him that he felt almost unborn. He went past the older man, into the room. It was so obviously Kristian's, the Persian rugs, the escritoire with its onyx penholders, a case of silvery duelling pistols and other guns, an icon with a white unliving face. Adam seemed to discover himself suddenly standing in the midst of it all like a bedraggled beaten dog.

Kristian had come in, closing the doors behind him.

"Now, Mr Quentin. I believe you telephoned my wife earlier tonight. Am I correct?"

"Why ask? I reckon you must know what goes on in this house."

"Yes, Mr Quentin, I do. Which is quite reasonable, do you not agree, since it is my house?" Kristian paused. "I may assume, I think, that your conversation gave rise to some concern. Which is why you have come here so promptly."

Adam found his responses could only free themselves through a defensive angry boorishness, which in its turn further disabled him.

"I only know she wanted to get out of this goddamned place."

"As you say, Sovaz may wish to spend a few days in other surroundings. Are you willing that she should also spend them with you?"

Aware of being manipulated, Adam said nothing.

"You are grudging of your time, Mr Quentin. If you answer my questions as I ask them, you would waste a good deal less of it."

"OK. Yes. I'm willing."

"Good. In that case, I recommend that you return tomorrow. I shall by then have made all the necessary arrangements."

"What the hell are you talking about? If she wants to leave, it's now…"

"I doubt it. I believe you will be sleeping in a dosshouse in the slums. Did you intend to take my wife there?"

"You surely know everything, don't you?"

"I know enough, Mr Quentin. Let me suggest you do as I say. By tomorrow afternoon I can provide you with a car, accommodation, and money."

"I don't want your money."

"Probably not. But I am merely providing for my wife's comfort, which you, you recall, are unable to do."

"Perhaps she feels the same way I do."

"Yes. Perhaps at the moment she does. I suggest therefore that you tell her the money and car are a loan from Mikalides. Also the beach house you will be taking, about forty miles outside the city."

"All right. I'll go along with it for what it's worth."

"Splendid," Kristian said, without inflection.

"And now I want to see her."

Kristian opened a box of Chinese jade and extracted a cigarette which he slowly lit, by this gesture finally demonstrating his power over the American, who stood intolerably still and silent, as if turned to stone, during the procedure.

"Yes, Mr Quentin. As I assured you earlier, I shall not attempt to prevent you. But I would point out that my wife is at present in an unsettled state of mind. She is a highly-strung woman, a victim of her temperament. It will be good for her to get away for a while. However, since you can as yet do nothing, does it occur to you that to return tomorrow, with every means at your disposal, would be better than simply to exacerbate her mood unnecessarily tonight?"

Adam felt a wave of guilty release sweep over him. He would not after all have to see her until the following day. He cleared his throat.

"Do you know something," he said, "you make me sick."

Kristian's cold face did not change. Only the cigarette smoke moved past his eyes as he exhaled. "Regretfully, Mr Quentin, I find your opinion of me entirely immaterial. And now, I would not dream of detaining you further. My chauffeur will see that the hired car reaches you, also the money I spoke of, and any essential documents."

Adam turned towards the door. "Does it strike you she might not come back to you?"

"No," said Kristian, "it does not."

"You didn't buy her," Adam said, "like the furniture."

"Oh, but that is exactly what I did," Kristian said. "And like my beautiful furniture, my beautiful wife fully understands and appreciates her position in my house, whatever notions she may entertain from time to time. She is playing with you, Mr Quentin. And the pure and doubtless estimable ideals of your youth and inexperience are blinding you to that salient, unalterable fact."

At midnight, lying awake among the ranks of restless, groaning or snoring men, his fellow occupants of the run-down *dortoir*, Adam felt this conversation turning like a great wheel in his head. He was indeed sick, sick to his stomach with a depressive dread. Like a fly caught in a web, struggling in the sticky substance over which it has no control, for which it can find no name, but which it vaguely ascertains means death.

The spitting and farting and weeping prayers of the human creatures about him were all that stood between him and the day, and the woman.

Kristian entered her room this time from the dressing room and found her seated in a chair. She had, as usual, the unawakened look so familiar to her. Ashtrays were littered with dead cigarettes. He noticed with distaste that her hands, normally exquisitely manicured, were yellow with patches of nicotine.

The interview with the American had also been distasteful, unpleasant. Never before had it been necessary to spend so much time on one of Sovaz' amusements. The telephone conversation had been reported to Kristian by his valet, a silent third party on the line.

"Sovaz," Kristian said, "please get up. I want you to come downstairs with me."

It surprised him when she did at once as he said. She had looked immovable. As she rose, the silk robe slipped away from her left shoulder. Against the whiteness of her skin, through the darkness of her hair, he glimpsed the bloody fire about her throat. She drifted to the mirrors and stood, apparently aimlessly, before them. Then took up a slender phial of scent and began to dab it on her flesh.

Kristian went out of the bedroom door into the gallery. Presently, she followed him. He saw that, despite her acquiescence, she carried in her hand one of the grey press cuttings from her bed.

Below, Kristian opened the doors of polished wood for her. She went inside and stood, much as the American had done, roughly at the centre of the room. In fact, what he had to say to her would have been said as well in the black chamber above, yet he felt a compulsion to speak to her away from the fumes of a room choked with her mental smoke as well as that of her cigarettes.

The study, his room, seemed able to hold her at bay.

Without asking her, he poured a little cognac into a glass and gave it to her. She lifted the glass and drank.

"Sovaz, you can't possibly continue in this way. You are making yourself ill."

She said clearly, "Oh, yes."

"I should like you to go away for a few days. Longer if you wish. 1 think it would do you good. The young American was here earlier. I believe he has some plans for you both."

"And do you have no plans for me?" she said.

"I plan that you should regain your health and your self-control."

"Do you?" she said. She smiled at something her blind eyes were seeing. Then the smile slid back into her mouth like a snake. "My father," she said, "never imagined he could die. He thought all the while he would get better."

Kristian turned away from her to light a cigarette and noticed the stub of a previous cigarette.

"The night he died," Sovaz went on, "there was a storm. He must have been calling to me, and I didn't hear him for the rain. When I went in, it was only by chance, because I had seen his lamp was still burning. He was working on a translation of Plato, but there was blood all over the page, the book, the top of his desk. I ran to him and he caught my hand. He looked terrified. But he only said very calmly, 'I think I'm rather worse tonight. Will you go to the doctor's house and ask him to come?' I let go his hand and rushed out, but I heard his head fall down on to the papers before I reached the door."

"This is pointless, Sovaz."

"Yes," she said, "quite pointless. I shall, naturally, do whatever you say. When am I to leave?"

"Tomorrow."

"And when do I come back?"

"When you are ready."

"Suppose," she said, "that I never come back to you."

"I don't think that you will be so foolish."

"I am foolish enough to stay, why not to go? Why," she said softly, "why didn't you let me go when I was able?"

"If you are speaking of divorce..."

"No. That would be very stupid of me, wouldn't it?"

He glanced at her, but her eyes still seemed blind, yet a polarised blindness, appearing dark only to those who stood outside.

She said: "Kristian, I opened the door and there you were. Everything was in crates and boxes. I had to sell all his books, and I thought I would be jailed because there wasn't any money left... I thought I should have to steal food, and they would catch me... And I opened the door and there you were."

He said: "I think you should go upstairs."

"Yes," she said, "of course."

She turned and went without another word. But he saw that she had left lying on the rug the grey press cutting.

Kristian retrieved it. A cold feverishness had come over him; he found he was repelled even by an object she had been holding. He saw for a second the headline as he balled the cutting in his hand. Igniting the desk lighter, he set fire to the smudgy wad, and let it fall into an ashtray to burn. It was a dramatic gesture, a gesture alien to him.

The paper flared with a cleansing flame. It reflected brightly in the case of pistols, as the rising sun had once reflected on the beautiful guns, and the birds had rained from the sky, and the deer crumpled with the grace of ballerinas between the tall stalks of the pines.

FI♀VE

The slender white sports car sprang eagerly southwards. Leaving the cement towers, the minarets and spires of the city behind, it rattled down the shore road, between landward banks in mourning with cypress groves, and the tumbling western edge, which in places dropped sheer to a glittering afternoon sea.

The road, tortuous, caked red or white with powdered clay, owed its existence to various empires. The Persians, the Romans, the Americans had all had a hand in it. It was a polyglot, mongrel construction, an aggressive bastard of a road, and given to practical jokes (a dead cow lying around the bend feasted upon by clouds of flies, a flock of ragged sheep spilling across between broken fences from one field to another, an abandoned cart on its side).

Old farms dotted the eastern heights. Goats galloped away, pretending that the car was still a unique anachronism on this ancient time-locked landscape – that, meanwhile, swarmed at certain periods of the year with cars and buses fleeing from the summer heat of the city, and which had burst consequently into little red gas stations like an eruption of acne.

The slender vehicle was open, a golden young man driving it, a black and white woman at his side, partly concealed beneath a wide-brimmed, black straw hat.

The journey was not long. They did not speak.

The robot chauffeur had handed to him relevant keys, receipts, a manilla packet. Sovaz had appeared on the steps, moving between the chess pieces like another chess piece, the Black Queen, in her inky frock and hat, a trailing of black and white chiffon about her neck.

She looked altogether too dramatic, coming towards him, and he had a ghastly sort of Sunset Boulevard impression of her, an aging insane actress, dolled up to the nines. It was a shock to see, when the sun struck suddenly on the triangle the hat left free of shadow, how young she was.

He said to her awkwardly, "Do you have everything you need?"

"Yes," she said, "thank you."

Two small suitcases, packed by her maid, lay already in the boot.

He opened the door for her. She got in. Claustrophobia welled in his chest as he shut both of them together into the car, despite its state of rooflessness.

He was near to hating her, for he hated himself. He could not even now comprehend how he had become entangled in this incredible act. Somehow the train had run away downhill before he could get out. Now, left clinging to its trembling superstructure, he could only stare about him at the fall in disbelief.

He was to say Mikalides had lent him money and a villa so that they could be together. No doubt, other men had absorbed Kristian's money without reluctance and lied graciously when needful. Yet surely she must know? It was obvious she had only come with him because Kristian had so instructed her. That he, Adam, had only come to take her because Kristian had so instructed *him*. Of her earlier cry for help nothing seemed to remain. She was polite and soulless. The situation was laughable, pathetic and revolting.

She sat beside him and said nothing. They were two strangers summoned to a hanging. There seemed to Adam no way out of it.

The quality of the afternoon altered. Veils of heat obscured the sinking sun. They drove through a little town with the obligatory number of gasoline pumps, a cafe or two and tiny shadowed shops and alleys. The road ran up then down. In the hot grey dusk, bumping along a track between the dunes, they reached the white beach house so carefully indicated on the chauffeur's map.

The breakers buzzed softly far out on the shore.

The interior of the villa was neatly designed, the walls regardlessly whitewashed. It was an acceptable, almost elegant setting, though not imaginative. A pang of reluctant admiration went through Adam, for it was so very much what the Greek merchant would have arranged for him, as he had arranged the evening clothes to be worn to the dinner party.

A freezer lurked in the stone-flagged kitchen; its gut stuffed with food. Green and gold idols of wine and spirits glinted in a wooden comb. A woman and her husband from the town came and went in the day, he had been told, to clean, and to prepare meals if necessary. Everything had been taken care of. Even a cold supper had been set out for them beneath covers, which neither approached.

Now the sound of the car had left them, as once before, their silence seemed to grow. The dull resonance of the sea, muffled by a sky of low cloud, did nothing to dispel it. Sovaz sat in a high-backed chair, motionless and unspeaking, still in her Swanson-Garboesque hat.

His mind went back to a beach party three years before on Long Island, trying to warm itself at those red fires, now ashes, among the beer cans, now further wreckage polluting the Sound, and the tanned young bodies and thoughtless, hopeful, silly, happy laughter, now stifled forever by experience. He extracted a bottle of wine from its melting ice and opened it.

"Do you want a drink?"

"Why not?"

The words fastened in his brain like a code of conduct. Why not? Why not?

He handed her a glass of the wine and drank his own rapidly. Very quickly it warmed him. He felt a surge of anger and dislike.

"Well, here we are," he said. He poured himself another glass and sat facing her. "Why don't you take off your hat, Sovaz? There's no sun in here. I can't see you."

"Does it matter?" she said.

"Sure it does."

She put up her hand and drew off the hat, then held it on her lap with the untouched wine.

"Do you remember what you said to me," he said flatly, "when I called you at the house?"

Her eyes flickered and dilated.

"That was stupid," she said. "I don't know why I should have said such a thing."

"You said it because you meant it."

He felt something at her confusion, for he could see he was confusing her. Mixed together in him now were interchangeable desires to help or harm.

"Sovaz," he said, "stop running away from it, whatever it is. If you tell me, maybe we can work something out."

"I was foolish to speak to you as I did. You can do nothing."

"OK," he said, "OK, Sovaz, if that's what you want."

He got to his feet again. He took up the half empty wine bottle and its companion from the table and went straight out of the villa onto the beach.

The sea was stealthily abandoning the shore. He walked after it, a bottle in either hand.

He finished the first bottle and slung it out to sea.

He was, after all, leaving her. He could travel all night and fetch up God knew where and get some train and beat it, and this time not, oh Christ, not come back. He pulled the loosened cork of the second bottle. *Dionysos,* he thought, *god of wine.* He had eaten nothing all day and was already drunk.

Abruptly there was a noise of war in the sky overhead.

Lightning shrilled across the ribbing of the waves. Rain fell to meet them.

All at once he visualised her seated alone in the beach house while the storm tore at it. The cold water slapped him across the face as if trying to sober him. "Help me," she had said to him. He recaptured suddenly how she had clung to him in the wild olives, how she had looked in the aftermath of sex, as if she had fallen from a great height and lay dashed on the ground. A wash of pity did after all well up in him.

He turned and half ran up the sand to the villa.

The room was deserted. Her hat lay on the ground where she had let it fall, the wine stood pristine in her glass on the table.

"Sovaz!" he shouted.

She did not answer.

He went to the wooden stairway and ran up it. A whitewashed

225

bedroom exploded in the bomb blast of the lightning.

He went through the door. She stood brushing her hair at a glass, long rhythmic strokes.

He said hoarsely, "Didn't you hear me calling you?"

She turned. She seemed strangely puzzled.

"The rain," she said, "I didn't hear you above the rain."

The relief of finding her, engaged in such a relatively normal action as brushing her hair, made him feel ill. He leaned by the door and waited for the feeling of illness to abate. The storm was already dying but lightning still flashed on and off inside his head.

Then looking at her, he saw the most extraordinary phenomenon of weeping he had ever witnessed. For her wide-open eyes seemed to fragment in tears, and the tears themselves gushed forth like the water that falls from the urns or breasts or dolphins' mouths of fountains.

At sunrise the tide returned gently to the beach. The waves, each overtaking the other, ran up into the morning, and opened in slow platinum fans, like the glissandi of successive harps.

Dawn woke Sovaz, dawn softly rupturing the parchment blinds of the villa windows. Opening her eyes, she was for a moment unnerved by the pale window spaces, by all her surroundings.

She lay quite still, faintly hearing the harp notes of the waves, and watching their reflective patterning cast upwards on the ceiling by a freak of angle and light. Memory came into her conscious brain in similar gentle rushes, one upon another, and, like the beach, she received them.

How strangely easy it was now to look back into yesterday, at all she had felt and done, unmoved, as if looking at some other person. But then, each sleep being a sort of death, each waking therefore a definitive of birth, yesterday's Sovaz was indeed no longer herself. That woman, sloughed like the skin of a snake, might be observed without prejudice. The new Sovaz, reincarnated, was at her beginning.

Never before had she experienced this sense of absolution and hope. A creature of night, she had seldom woken to sunrise.

Yet something in her warned her how fragile the moment was. She lay still, afraid of cracking the delicate glass that encased her.

Yesterday she had been an old woman.

She had moved through a terrible timelessness, that anaesthetic suspension which before had sometimes overcome her for an hour or so, which all at once had swallowed her whole. Events and people had beaten on her numbed flesh and spirit like hail on stone. She did not precisely know what had happened to release her. A storm – she had begun to cry. She had not cried, had she, for seven years.

Then the presence of the young man made itself known to her. Of his troubled and uncertain comforting she was not conscious, nor of his murmured entreaties that she stop crying, tell him what was wrong, let him in some way help her.

The last orchestral violence of the storm faded over the sea. The storm of her pain faded also. Soon the need to comfort and be comforted exchanged itself in both of them and merged with an inevitable progression. Not speaking, they made love, and presently slept, only to wake again to each other thirstily at intervals through the black, sea-breathing night, sleeping still locked, as if they were indeed only a twin machinery of desire. In this manner, she lost her identity, her sense of past or role. She woke at dawn, the old skin seeming sloughed, to a day seen through crystal, a day for the moment novel as the first morning of the world.

Later, the light upon the blinds turned golden.

Sovaz rose on her elbow. She had fallen asleep once again. The magic of the dawn was over; now she could move without shattering the glass – the warmth of the sun had melted it.

Adam lay, still asleep, turned on his side towards her. She studied him gravely, as if seeing him properly for the first time.

Sleep had both accentuated his youth and curiously dispensed with it. He too had a timelessness. She was put in mind of the marble statues of renascent Italy, the slumbering heroes carved on mausoleums. Having accepted sleep in its aspect of death this did not chill her.

As she leaned looking at him, as if responding to her mood even in sleep, he opened his eyes. At once he smiled at her.

"Sovaz..."

She put out her hand and stroked his hair, and he lay, still smiling, his eyes shut in pleasure at her touch.

She lay down and drew him into her arms. His sleepy happiness seemed to soak into her, by a method of osmosis.

He turned suddenly and sat up, looking down at her as she had looked at him.

"You are so beautiful," he said to her, "and you look like you were about fifteen years old."

He seemed as if about to speak to her with an earnest seriousness from which she withdrew.

"Adam," she said, "open the blinds, the sun is so lovely, and it's not even hot yet."

A shadow crossed his face. Then he grinned and swung out of bed. The blinds flicked their tassels like the tails of obedient horses and ran up the windows.

He stood looking out at the sea and sky.

Watching him, the play of gold on his blond hair and amber skin, entranced by his physical splendour and prepared abruptly to adore him for it, she felt young indeed, perhaps for an instant even as young as he had said.

With all her lovers she had sought youth. Thinking it to be their youth she sought, she herself felt, with each of them, far older than she was. The image of the rich and desolate matron with her creased skin, her toppled breasts, and her gigolo, lay always in her mind's eye. She had seen these women years before through the green and ruby windows of the great library, walking in the squares below. Painted wizened monkeys with their handsome boys strolling like expensive dogs at their sides. Now an emerald monkey, tapping her cigarette on its green metal case, now a scarlet dog rearing acrobatically on its hind limbs to light it for her.

It had never occurred to Sovaz, until this moment, that it was not after all the youngness of her lovers that attracted her to them. It was her own youth she hankered for, freely expressed, untrammelled, in their bodies. She was a victim of the bizarre juxtaposition which made a woman imagine she had fallen in love with a man, when in fact she had actually fallen in love with the masculine facet of her own self as projected in this man's image. The heart of the timid and puritanical virgin was inflamed by the daring and libidinous pirate in the universal myth. But the cutlass thrust through his belt was as much the symbol of her own unrealised potential, of the castration of her mental bravura, as it was the emblem of the male phallus. In reality she did not yearn for the pirate's embrace, she yearned to *become* the pirate. The frigid strength of Kristian then was something Sovaz had not worshipped but jealously burned to possess for herself. For herself the anchor of his wealth, his iron and impervious will, what she saw as his emotionlessness. Kristian would always perhaps be her torment. She could not devour him.

But Adam, Adam who, more than all the others, was her beauty, her sweetness, her youth, Adam it seemed she could love, at least for a little space.

The woman came from the town. They heard her, in a hoarse voice, singing snatches of *Tosca*.

When they went down, she brought them hot rolls, peaches, and fresh coffee, to a table laid for them on the veranda. The man, whistling tunelessly, had begun to clean the white sports car. He gnawed used matches as he worked and, occasionally emerging to cross in front of the veranda to the side door of the villa, would grin at Adam a macabre grin of filbert teeth and matchsticks protruding between them like the limbs of tiny prey.

The beach house, in the honey sun, was warm and friendly, the stretching glittering sand like powdered topaz, the surf rolling in, in lazy gusts of white smoke and blue fire.

Sheltered by a bay, the villa was remote, without another habitation nearer than two miles away. The shore blazed, deserted under the sun. After they had walked leisurely along the rim of the sea for a while the house was out of sight. Adam discarded his clothes and swam out into the silken water.

Sovaz, who could not swim, seated herself. The sand was voluptuously warm, even so early. The sun, the caress and colour of it, soothed her, seemed to penetrate into her bones. She stretched and dreamed in it, unafraid. And although she had put on again the black straw hat, the black and white chiffon was now tied about it. She wore a knee-length white dress, which also left her throat and arms bare.

(She did not recall how Leah had taken off the rubies in her black bedroom, and then locked them in the ivory box. How Leah had looked doing it, how she, Sovaz, had stood in petrified terror at this omen. No doubt Kristian had given instructions. Before she had gone to meet Adam, almost inadvertently – for she was then still a stone with only hail beating on it – she had bound her neck with the chiffon, rather tightly, as if to staunch a flow of blood.)

It was easy to follow Adam's progress through the sea. He was gold, the water cobalt. The simplicity of it pleased her. Shortly she saw the gold flash as he turned and came back to her.

Wading up out of the waves, metallically naked, he resembled something archaic and fabulous.

He lay down beside her on the beach, shading his eyes with one hand.

"It must be wonderful to swim so strongly," she said.

"It's great. Why don't I teach you?"

"Oh no. I should be dreadfully afraid."

"That's OK. It's easy when you know how."

"You learnt when you were a child, I expect."

"It doesn't make any difference, Sovaz. I wouldn't let you drown."

She smiled drowsily. Although envious of his ability in the water, she had basically no desire to emulate him.

"No. I enjoyed watching you."

"You should have thrown me a stick," he said, with an unexpectedly acid humour.

He drew her into his arm and her heart began at once to drum excitedly as her skin encountered the texture of his, for she was adoring him. Each new mannerism which she had not seen before, each new message of his thought, seemed wonderful to her. They made love in a languorous slow motion induced by the sun and the rhythm of the sea.

Looking down at her afterwards, he noticed the absence of that expression of bewilderment – of fright almost – that he had seen on her face the first time.

He touched her cheek gently with his mouth, and she smiled. Her eyes were closed against the sun, the hat fallen away, the ebony glissade of her hair spread like an enchanted net on the sand.

It was impossible to associate with this day the day which had preceded it. Even less than she did he understand what had broken the spell on her. Some old guilt and pain, this much he had guessed, had been expunged in tears. All dread of her had vanished with her alteration. Now he felt only her warmth, her actual youth, what seemed to him her profound and innocent sweetness, those things which, as she had vaguely known, sprang from her chameleonism, her ability to become a mirror. Kristian, when he thought of him, was even more a figure of sick disgust. Kristian was the sorcerer. He wanted to free her from Kristian. Adam was impulsive with this desire, yet the calmness of the day somehow restrained him. There seemed time for everything.

About two o'clock they walked down the baked road to the little town and ate omelettes and wine at one of the cafes whose tables now sprawled in the open under *eau-de-Nil* umbrellas. When they had finished eating, they progressed carelessly and unhurriedly about the winding streets. On the highest level of the town, they found a market with goats and sheep in pens and bright birds in cages. The heat of the day had come and fell in white squares between the stalls.

Sovaz paused among tubs of hyacinths and other flowers, fingering their clusters lightly. Adam instinctively recognised the ingenuous almost naive signal of a woman who has no money of her own but for whom everything she requires is bought. So he bought her flowers, though not with Kristian's money.

Sovaz fastened the stems of the yellow and blue flowers into the band of the scarf so that the heads spilled along the brim of her black hat. She laughed as she did so, as a child laughs. She did indeed look very young, he thought, the same age as himself. He caught her hand and they walked on, palm to palm, as any pair of lovers might have done.

They talked a good deal. At least, he talked, and she responded, prompting him. She did not seem to want to talk about herself, only about him. He spoke of New York, the cryogenic winters, the dry-as-dust summer madnesses, the parties and the drawing office, his mother with her chain-smoking affairs, the unborn yet often conceived and aborted book. He was neither self-conscious nor flattered at being made to tell her all these things. It seemed natural that she should have the groundwork of his life upon which to stand when later she might wish to reveal her own.

He mentioned the incomplete notation he had written, attempting to describe her. She laughed again. Her face seemed all the beauty of the day held in crystal. He was, without understanding it, experiencing the joy of the artist who has made, even if inadvertently, something fine. For he had given her this life.

Abruptly the sun went down, dusk washed over the streets.

The sky was brilliant with enormous stars as they strolled back again, still hand in hand, towards the shore, and about the wild tamarisks at the roadside fireflies winked their tiny neons.

Nevertheless, with the resurrection of night, some indefinable unease stole over Adam.

They did not at once return to the villa, but moved slowly, following the pale contours of the beach. Suddenly she said: "Today has been wonderful, Adam."

"It isn't the last day," he said. "Sovaz," he said, "why do you stay with him, with Kristian? You can't live like that for ever."

The moment he had given in to the irresistible demand to say this, he regretted it. He saw everything at once in total proportion. He felt ashamed of speaking to her in such a way. She was a woman used only to certain modes of existence. He could not maintain her financial standards, had nothing to offer her. The atmosphere of the hothouse might limit the scope of the orchid but take it outside into the intemperate world and it would die. Truly, she *could* live like that for ever, and in no other fashion.

As for Sovaz, a strengthless exhaustion overcame her at the thought of leaving Kristian.

The exhalation of night pressed suddenly on her.

"Adam," she said, "why should Thettalos loan you a house?"

"What?" Startled by the unexpected question – he had been expecting almost any other reaction from her – Adam let go her hand.

"Thettalos would never do such a thing," Sovaz said. Her voice was light and cool. She stared out at the sea. "Why should he? He only aids and abets in order to win Kristian's approval and custom, and he would know there would be no need for you to ask anyone other than Kristian for money."

Adam swallowed. He was at a loss. Seeing she had realised the truth, it seemed better to concede the facts. In any case, it was such a stupid, irrelevant lie.

"OK, Sovaz. Kristian's renting the house. Does it matter now?"

"No, Adam. Of course it doesn't matter in the least."

He took her hand again. This time her hand was cold.

"Look," he said impractically, "tomorrow we could go some-place else..."

"Where?" she said. Her voice said, Kristian is here with us after all. He is, as I had always thought, omnipresent. Where could we go to escape him?

But Adam, Adam her youth – there was no strength to be found in him, no individual impulse of action. He, too, was part of Kristian's plan to be tidily rid of her until she might be purged and refashioned and returned to him in the mood of dull, bored serenity with which she left all her lovers. All. Adam only one with all the rest. Her dog on a leash. Whose wages were not even paid by herself, but by her husband.

Reaching the villa, they ate a little of the cold food laid out for them, drank the wine, and later went to bed and made love together. Yet it was all done in an oddly wooden and desultory manner. They were trying to continue, unchecked, the happiness of the day, but now their actions had become imitative.

The tide retreated from the shore, and Sovaz, who did not often recollect her dreams, dreamed vividly a dream which woke her.

In the dream she had already woken.

The room was a black box, the windows oblongs of paler black, casting no light inwards, and she was alone. Around the house she heard soft footfalls circling on the sand.

In the way of dreams, not meaning to, she found herself at a window, looking out. The scenery was altered. The beach house – if house it still was – was perched on the crest of a sweeping broken hill, a hill roped with vines and ivies. The sky above was no longer black, but black-red, a sky of funeral fires; and green smoke, like the smoke of a volcanic altar, was rising up into it in places from fissures in the ground. On this ground were also other things. Euripides' bacchantes had recently passed this way in their frenzy, leaving the earth littered with the ribs of cattle and flags of flesh caught on trees.

Directly below the window a panther was feeding. As she glanced down at it, it raised its head. Its stare was blindly seeing as the lenses of cameras, its mouth was full of blood; yet blood which had crystallised, full of rubies.

She felt no particular fear. Perhaps something other than the dream woke her, for she opened her eyes with none of that frantic struggle which accompanies the escape from nightmare. However, conscious now in the dark room, the dream still jewel-bright in her brain, she was at once overwhelmed by a nameless instinct that drove her out of bed and towards the window.

She released the blind, and there lay the blue-grey beach, the blue-black sea, the sky of stars.

The surge of her body settled. She stood at the window with an inexplicable sense of unfulfillment. Then came a sound from the back of the house – a sound like an animal's large pad descending on the sand. It struck her nerves; a silver chord ran over her. She thought: *I am afraid.*

She ran back across the room yet halted at the door. She did not even recognise her fear. She felt the bemused and fascinated horror of vertigo, the abyss at the bottom of the height drew her, and she caught involuntarily at the walls to save herself.

"Adam!" she cried, but she did not really remember him at all.

Her movements had already disturbed him. As she discerned that morning, he was aware of her even asleep.

"What is it?" he murmured.

"He has followed me here," she said, still holding to the walls, still gazing sightlessly down the dark stairway.

"Who? Who did, Sovaz?"

"He's outside now," she whispered.

In her mind she was seeing the surrealist black panther. She imagined it prowling across the veranda, slipping from shade to shade, stealthy as the night itself. Nevertheless, despite the waves of confused hysteria now converging on her brain, she knew perfectly well and with a deadly logic that the demon was real enough, and very near.

Adam had risen and was tugging on clothes swiftly.

"Calm down, Sovaz. I'll go and see. You know, perhaps it's nothing."

Deep inside her (lost, unattended) a small nerve throbbed at his gentleness to her with a returning remorseful gentleness that was almost pity for him. He brushed her cheek with his finger, and then went by her, going down the stairs noiselessly. Passing the table in the living area below, he took up, with an off-hand and surprisingly brutal resourcefulness, an empty wine bottle.

"Stay there," he said. "I won't be long."

She saw abruptly that he must open the house door. This thought terrified her. Only the shadow of the night was so far in the villa but open the door and night's black face would peer round it.

The vampire, assuming the form of mist, could slip in through the slightest crack and materialise. And yes, the demon had been a vampire, for he drank the blood of his victim as he lay on her as if in the act of love. She wanted to scream out to Adam, to stop him, but already he had done the thing she dreaded. The door stood wide a moment then folded shut.

She was alone in the black house with her terror.

Of course, it was so simple. He had been watching her, she had always known it. He had returned the rubies as proof. (How could she have put him from her thoughts?) She had witnessed his crime. He must kill her. And how easy for him to follow her here, and what better spot than this, the isolated villa lapped by the sea and the dunes, only a beautiful boy to protect her, one who picked up a bottle to defend himself, without cunning...? Sovaz ran from one end of the room to the other and back once more, in a trap. Yes. Perhaps she was trapped.

She stood quite still. Her whole body was pulsing, electric. It was no longer fear she felt, but a more ancient and more complex emotion, the extreme abandon of something hunted.

If the murderer, (yes, yes, call him that, though he was also the demon, the magician), if the murderer had waited outside in the shadow, why could he not similarly wait until Adam had moved off a little way, searching, then slip into the villa, come softly up the stairs to her.

She pressed herself against the wall and began to slide herself down it and down the unseen steps. If she could reach the side door she could run out, she could cry for help across the desert of the sands to the waste of the sea, and perhaps be heard.

Adam Quentin walked quietly around the house, then along the beach a little way. He was not, in fact, particularly uneasy. His itinerant life about the vitriolic slums of this and other cities had partly revived in him those primitive senses geared to deal with danger, and these same senses relayed no warning. The night seemed to offer nothing except its perpetual air of menace.

At first, he believed she had imagined the intruder. Then her words *He has followed me here* struck him with a certain symbolism. She had been reservedly distressed since his admission that Kristian had after all financed him. Possibly a phantom Kristian stalked round the villa for her. This idea gave birth to another. Standing on the empty beach, he recalled Kristian's agents, the Englishman Prescott, the other men who discreetly followed Sovaz wherever she went about the city, to observe and report on her movements. It was feasible that she had seen such a man patrolling on the sand, incautious under the unlit windows.

The thought gripped Adam with a sudden fury. He envisaged at once a traditional carbon-copy spy lying on the dunes, perhaps with binoculars. The untroubled tenderness of the morning, their lovemaking on the beach, the gentle afternoon, all reduced by the professional outlook of the watcher to the insipidity all sentiment assumes when divorced from motive.

Adam looked around him.

About two hundred yards away, on an upper level of the beach, he could suddenly make out the ill-defined shape of a car without headlights. Adam swore softly.

It was rough going here, the sand slid from under his feet like silk. A little track came meandering down from the road and the car was parked just off it, among the drily whispering tamarisks. The stillness as well as the darkness of the vehicle impressed Adam as he came nearer, so that he moved more cautiously. Eventually he had come close enough to see in.

Inside the car a man and woman were embracing frenziedly, writhing and entwining in total silence and with a faintly ludicrous concentration, as if afraid that, should their attention be permitted to wander for a moment, they would lose the thread of this physical conversation.

So much for Kristian's agent. Crazy to suppose he would be in the first parked car... A sense of foolishness came over Adam, also of slight shyness. He did not like to see his own sexual passion translated by the antics of others. Turning, fortunately unseen, he quickly and quietly moved away.

He had abandoned the quest. Reaching the level sand, he began to run back towards the house. He realised now he must have been gone almost half an hour, leaving her alone and distraught, as once before.

There were, even now, no lights in the windows. The door was shut, as he had left it.

As once before. As once before, the room was deserted, and the stairs.

"Sovaz!" he called, as once before. She did not answer.

He ran up the stairway. This time she was not in the bedroom.

He went over the villa methodically, turning on all the electric lights. Presently he discovered the side door standing open. He searched and found an oil lamp in the stone kitchen, lit it and went outside.

The shadows fled back in groups like black animals which had crept up to the house but retreated from fire.

Where was she – where had she gone? Purely instinctively he recognised the fear which had driven her into the open – his eyes ran automatically over the track which led from the villa back to the road. From the head of the track was visible the dull haze of neon still lingering over the town. Had she fled that way for comfort?

Adam left the lamp and hurried up the track, for some reason ignoring the possibility of using the sports car, and, feeling the hard clay of the road finally under his feet, he began to run in the direction of the town.

He ran for nearly a mile, then stopped. Sweat dried his shirt to his body in patches. He had been looking out for her at every step. But he could never hope to find her like this, it was too slow. He must go back for the car after all. (Something about the idea of the car repelled him; he pushed this from his mind.) Besides, maybe she had returned to the house.

He trudged towards the shore, weary with anxiety. He felt a child and was disgusted by the childish sick fear that threatened him.

It was about three o'clock when he reached the beach house. He went in and called her name, but perfunctorily, without much expectation. Unanswered he went for the car.

It would not immediately start. It too seemed reluctant to take the journey, and, fractious, obstructed him. At last the motor engaged.

Glancing over his shoulder as the car moved up the track, he noted incongruously that he had left every light in the beach house burning brightly.

When she reached the smaller door of the villa, opened it, and stood there, confronted by the night, Sovaz had ceased to exist.

The night was cool and black. It inspired ancient fears and joys. These feelings had always been present in her, though her method of living stifled even while it encouraged them. Now, through a process of dreaming, terrors and events magnified to terror, the inner elemental genius which was not Sovaz, but Sovaz deprived of all human conditions and desires, pared to the psychological and spiritual quick, emerged suddenly in the cold water of darkness and took possession of her shell of a woman's body.

If she felt anything at all, it was a sensation of release. As for fear itself, she was no longer afraid. What had driven her to flight now seemed unremarkable, almost normal. As when she had first run away from the murderer on the beach, the whole night was imbued with him, so that he was quite inescapable. And like the gods, he only asked for her consent, her surrender.

Yet she did not really think anything or know what she did as she stepped out onto the sand drifts.

The landscape was full of unexpected forms – black birds or animals of shadow, while smoking tinsel galleys floated in the sky or on the sea.

Reduced to an ultimate in symbols, she followed at first a natural depression in the dunes, then, coming on the track, she followed this up to the road and so went along that, towards the dim phosphorescent glow above the town. The glow represented Destination, the trackways and the road a means of getting there, but these things were merely occupations. For she was offering herself, unprotected, vulnerable in her robe of white Chinese silk, to the night and the demon.

She could not have said what she anticipated – the knife, the Shadow – she did not know how death would divulge himself or how she would greet him. She was trembling, vibrating with a wild excitement. Every touch of the air on her skin, every breath of wind that lifted her hair, was in itself a kind of ecstasy.

Her bare feet (she had cut them on stones and not noticed) walked briskly. Shortly she passed through the little town where another woman had sat beneath the umbrellas with flowers in her hat. The streets were now mostly deserted. A few dreary neons stared from the exteriors of bars. From a dark archway a chewing man came out and stopped to gape at her. She had all the appearance of a sleepwalker, or even a devil, so much so that he did not even lurch across to her to seize her arm as he might ordinarily have done with a stray woman seen on the night road. (About an hour later, a young American in a fast, white car would come by, and give him money for this information.)

Sovaz went through the town following the road, and, because nothing had happened, continued on the other side of it.

The sea sounded very close on her left, though she was not aware of it. It threw itself against the rocks below with titanic explosions, as if trying to attract her attention. Hereabouts the great slopes began which fell down sheer beyond the railing – to the sea at high tide, or else to this vast lashing cauldron of rock and spray.

The wind blew up from the sea.

Coming from the town, Adam drove slowly, with a painful discipline, knowing she was probably ahead of him on the road. Reaching the first of the horrific roadside drops, his guts seemed to rise up and slam him in the chest, thinking of her wandering by in the state the opium-eater had described. Of course the man was drugged, yet his hallucinatory representation of the dark-haired woman in her thin white robe seemed, rather than to exaggerate, to strike the very essentials of her condition.

His hands sticky with sweat, Adam drove on at the same agonising snail's pace.

Then he saw her. She was quite unmistakable, picked out by the headlights, walking at the very centre of the road. He managed to overtake her smoothly, pulling up ahead of her, getting out of the car and going back without moving too fast. She looked as though she were dreadfully shocked. Something must indeed have happened at the beach house after he had left her, yet there had been no sign of intrusion or violence.

Although she did not look at him, she had stopped still. Going up to her so carefully, in a rigour of tension accentuated by finding her, he abruptly recalled any number of the cheap horror movies illicitly seen in his childhood, lovely zombies in fluttering graveclothes, *décolleté* heroines lured from their beds by vampires.

"Sovaz," he said, unsteadily.

Her eyes were totally unfocused, yet she gave a brief, polite little smile. He wondered whom she might be seeing in her brain that she greeted with such civil uninterest. He could not believe himself so entirely demoted. With a gradualness that made his arms shake, he reached out and took hold of her.

"Come to the car, Sovaz."

She allowed him to direct her, quite docilely. He caught sight of her feet, the blood on them, and set her like eggs inside the vehicle and shut the door before he got in beside her.

A wash of desperate confusion went over him. There was no room to turn the car, only the steep bank going up on the right, the roaring descent on the left, crashing adjacent to his window. He saw he must go on in this same direction until he came to a wider and less perilous stretch of road.

He started the engine and began to drive swiftly north.

The road hugged itself to the flank of the up slope, as if afraid of the sea below. Sovaz seemed to be staring out at it. All at once she said, with a sharp insistence, "No."

"What, Sovaz? Don't be scared, it's all right."

"No," she said again, "I won't go with you. Let me alone."

She screamed, a prolonged and terrible scream, and, turning towards him, began to scratch at his face.

Insurmountable horror attacked him. He put up his right arm to defend himself. She was no longer human. Her mouth and eyes were enlarged and quite mindless. He had a leopard locked in with him. Then, slashing at him with her left hand, she clutched and scrabbled with her right at the door.

"Sovaz!" he shouted.

He was trying to thrust her away and hold her in at the same time, while with the other arm he attempted to steady the car.

At this moment the road, swirling around a bend, presented one of its practical jokes. A broken cart – perhaps even one they had passed earlier on their journey south – with a great sugaring of smashed glass about it. The sports car shot forward and ploughed through the cart, the glass... Sovaz' door gave as if at a signal. Adam wrenched about involuntarily, instinctively, to snatch her back. Simultaneously a glass dagger stabbed into the front nearside tyre, which blew with the sound of a gunshot.

The car spun left on the impetus of its three remaining tyres. It spun against the railing, which capitulated without protest. The car leaped forward and was for a moment apparently poised in stasis on the starlit sky. Below, the sea gnashed its jaws hungrily.

Adam Quentin, flung sideways across the seat, the sleeve of his denim jacket now uselessly caught on the wheel, thought in a blazing jumble of emotions for which no words were possible, thought, as primitive man or as babies did, in pictures – but only for an instant, or perhaps twenty instants.

The car fell, still spinning, towards the explosions of rocks and sea.

Sovaz, lying on the road just clear of the cart and the broken glass, raised her head at the enormous boom of thunder that burst below, louder even than the waves.

A glare kicked up against the night.

Sovaz pulled herself to the shattered railing to look down at it, a huge chrysanthemum of flame alight on the rocks, the petrol burning blue and green on the water.

SIX

The house, caught in the last resinous light of the afternoon, had taken on the inanimate and empty look it frequently acquired by day, its blindness of windows unlit, the vines resembling cuttings of dark paper. It had seemed to the doctor, as he struggled up the steps towards it, like some great sarcophagus, to enter which inevitably invited a curse.

Dr Florentine was afraid of the woman, or, more accurately, of the condition in which he would find her. Kristian's note had been concise but unrevealing. Although additionally the limousine had been sent for him.

Kristian's valet ushered him into the study. The room was burnished with the unearthly sheen that invaded the whole house during the late afternoon and sunset, through the polarised windows. It was hard to tell anything about Kristian in this mezzotint, and yet it seemed clear to the doctor that he was changed.

"Please sit down," Kristian said to him, and the quality of voice and manner were certainly the same.

Dr Florentine sat; his short penguin flippers folded neatly over his bag.

"I had better put you in the picture, hadn't I?" Kristian said. "My wife has been involved in a car accident, last night to be exact. She was driving in company with a friend," (the word was spoken quite implicitly), "on the shore road about twenty-five miles south of the city. There was a wreck of some sort. I gather the young man swerved to avoid it and lost control of the car. The passenger door seems to have given way; my wife was discovered lying at the side of the road, unhurt. Her driver, however, had no time to get clear of the car before it broke through the railing. There is nothing that side except the sea, and rocks when the tide is out."

"Dear God, how terrible," the doctor murmured. The permanently unhealed wound of his compassion received this fresh pain with dismal fortitude. Through it, he was able to wonder briefly at Kristian's exactness in describing the accident, even to details which did not concern Sovaz, all reeled off in that impersonal, almost casual fashion.

"My wife, although uninjured, is deeply shocked as you will

imagine," Kristian said to him. "Which is my reason for troubling you."

Again, the doctor strove, half unconsciously, to detect behind Kristian's voice the motives and intents that moved him. It was not love or concern for the woman he lived with in this house, merely he wished her, like an expensive piece of precision machinery, to function. *It is a watch-mender not a doctor you require,* Dr Florentine thought, yet with no anger. He got to his feet. "Very well. I will do all I can. But as I have said before…"

"And as I have said before," Kristian interposed smoothly, "I intend the matter to go no further than yourself."

The doctor spread one flipper as if to balance himself on the ice of Kristian's indifference. "But Madame Sovaz is…"

"Is in need of your attention. You underestimate yourself, my dear doctor. You should have more faith in your own skill."

So the doctor arrived once more at the threshold of the black bedroom, and thought, *I've been putting this off. What shall I see now?*

The black girl opened the door to him. Her expression was enigmatic. He glanced hurriedly about and discovered Sovaz beside a half open window. She was seated in her silk wrap, her face bowed, intent as a child's, over a drawing. The memory of the other drawing he had seen accosted him – the leopard and the deer, with its obscurely dreadful label μαινάς. The grey autumn leaves of her press-cuttings, he noticed, had been removed, tidied or destroyed.

"Well," said Dr Florentine, "well, well." And he went towards her briskly, as if stepping quickly under a cold shower.

She suffered his examination – this time more thorough and thus more complex – in a dreaming silence, a rapt inattentive submission not unlike her demeanour during the previous visit. Yet, as with Kristian, there was something altered, something not as it had been. Despite her appearance, her pulse was quite rapid. She seemed, but no longer was, apathetic. He recalled the extraordinary reaction that had come over her before in his presence, the look of waiting and anticipation, of frightened desire and longing which had so unnerved him.

The maid was clearing the drawing out of his way before he could examine it, as if instructed. He was not certain of this, but it added to his sense of unease. He found too in Sovaz evidence of some drug, possibly Nembutal, probably administered to her last night as a sedative. This also somehow hinted at a form of coercion, of a jail. Kristian had mentioned no sedative to him.

Physically, she was sound enough, by some miracle. Only the hidden region inside her skull seemed full of abrasions and plagues.

The driver of the car – what was he to her? A lover, surely, no less. And she said nothing, did not, when he probed with his awkward questions, respond at all. Yet she was no longer shocked as far as he could ascertain. Not even mildly so.

"I'm sorry to hear that your companion was killed. At least it would have been mercifully quick," he eventually wildly said, attempting to unlock whatever strictures held back her emotions.

But quite calmly, and with surprising cruelty, she answered, "How is it possible to know? It may have seemed longer to him. Poor boy," she added, but remotely, indifferently.

Packing his bag, the doctor found himself abruptly transported backwards in time. He recalled the old scholar, Sovaz' father, discovered smiling in the public surgery among the human wreckage, a small leather case of manuscripts tucked between his knees, and the sadly inadequate sentence, (a sentence indeed in every sense), "I am having some bother with a cough."

At first, suspecting cancer, Dr Florentine had treated him with a painful kindliness, which shortly became nearly jovial when tuberculosis was instead diagnosed. For this a complete cure would almost certainly be possible, at the worst the progress of the illness could be arrested. Presently the doctor became aware that the scholar would not accept the cure. This was madness. The scholar shook his head.

"No, no, it's not feasible. I cannot give up the time. My work – do you know, only yesterday I received by post, from America, a request for a fresh translation of certain portions of Plato's *Republic*..."

"Either you will spare the time from your work now, in order to get well," the doctor said, "or you will have no time left to spare for anything. You must understand this. Now..."

"No, no," the scholar said again. "You see, I have many debts, yes, this is true, I am not ashamed. They are, shall I say, honourable debts. My work is more expensive than people suppose. And like you, I suspect, my dear Florentine, I don't always collect my fee. And there is my daughter, my Sovaz – how can she support herself while I am in some clinic? She's still such a child. That is my fault, I admit as much. I have made her as unworldly a being as myself...

No, no, I must go on with my work for her sake, do you see? And I shall soon be better. I have not rubbed shoulders with these philosophers for nothing – the cure is in my hands, and in the impartial hands of the gods. I must show them I am worthy to be spared."

There had flashed then across the doctor's mind, as suddenly as it did now, the remembered vignette of Sovaz as he had briefly glimpsed her at fourteen. Passing below on his way to assist at a birth, he had glanced up and seen a face like a cameo, set in the high twilit window of the scholar's house like a picture in a dark frame. There drifted down from behind the picture the scratchy recorded notes of a Khatchaturian piano concerto, which mingled eerily with the sullen pipes of snake charmers in a neighbouring street. Having met her earlier in company with her father, Dr Florentine raised his hand in greeting, for she seemed to be watching him. Yet even then her eyes were fixed inwards, she had not noticed, and he, feeling all the unaccountable foolishness of one who makes such a gesture in error to a stranger, passed on. The child, a male, which he delivered that night, was still born. Malignant superstition had inextricably connected the dead baby with the girl hailed in the window. The doctor hated the roots of superstition in himself which refused to wither, just as he hated the superstitions of his patients which caused them to lay filthy and tetanus-conveying relics on their sores, and to practise contraception by means of a small scrap of cloth pasted over the navels of their women during intercourse. Nevertheless, now as then, he fell prey to the evil djinn. The boy baby died because the doctor had looked up at the girl's window; the girl's father died because he must keep her safe from the world. And yesterday a young man drove through a railing and down onto the broken rocks, and she was left beside the road unharmed…

No, all this was stupidity. He snapped shut his bag. He must speak to Kristian again; it was essential that she receive help of some kind other than his own. Perhaps a psychiatrist could unravel those areas of shadow in her skull. Certainly, little Dr Florentine could not.

As he was going towards the door, he noted the black maid standing before the mirrors, Sovaz' drawing held defensively close, yet at such an angle that it was reflected in the glass behind.

Dr Florentine checked. He turned aside and held out his hand. "Please. You will let me see that."

A ripple of unmistakable fear went over the black girl's face. Dr Florentine saw at last it was the drawing itself she feared and therefore attempted to hide. She gave it up, however, immediately.

After a moment the doctor looked back at Sovaz. She had risen and was standing at the open window, her eyes staring blindly outwards.

"And what's this?" he asked her.

"Oh, that," she said. And unexpectedly her head turned, and she was looking straight at him, holding him in a clear and perfect focus as if in the sights of a gun. "I am working on a painting taken from the *Bacchae*. Dionysos revenged himself on the king of Thebes, Pentheus, by sending him to spy on the maenads. I expect you recollect the story."

"No. I don't remember," the doctor said slowly.

"Why, the women found him and tore him to pieces. Because he had come between them and the god, do you see?"

Dr Florentine discovered that his hands were shaking. Like the black girl, he was experiencing a completely instinctive revulsion, though the picture itself, which showed the king in the grip of the shrieking women, was horrible enough. Setting the paper carefully down, he went out and stumbled along the gallery, clutching his bag like an amulet.

He had recognised again in her logical voice the cunning of the insane. And at the last moment her eyes had fastened on him so sharply. He realised now what had been wrong when he had spoken to Kristian in the study. For that Antarctic and pitiless gaze had been today vacant and blurred over as the eyes of the woman had always been in the past, and suddenly were no longer.

The sun stood on its own fiery tail just above the purple water. The magnificence of its display was not quite lost on the Englishman. As he crossed the terraces of the garden, he paused to regard it, his hands in his pockets, yet not bothering to remove the tinted glass from his eyes that distorted all the colours.

As he watched, Prescott heard a woman's voice call his name from the avenue of lemons. He turned at once, and saw Sovaz in a long, white frock, the girl Leah waiting about three yards behind her. He walked towards them.

"Good evening, madame."

She seemed unusually alert. The sun flamed on her face like the glow of a great fire, but her eyes, though narrowed, were intent.

"There is something I have been meaning to ask you," she said.

He waited. He thought she would refer to the previous night, the blazing car on the rocks below, his own treatment of her, her inertia.

She said: "The last dinner party my husband gave at this house – do you recall?"

"Yes, Madame Sovaz. I think so."

"Perhaps you were on the terrace outside the ballroom – at about nine o'clock?"

"Yes, madame. I was there until about nine. Then I went round to check the lawns, as I usually do."

"On the terrace," she said, "did you notice a man? A tall slender man, very pale, handsome, with dark hair and eyes?" Her own eyes as she said this narrowed to slits.

"No, madame, I don't recollect seeing anyone like that."

She drew in a breath. "Please think," she said. "I am certain you must have seen him there."

"Perhaps, if you could tell me who the man is."

"I don't know his name. A guest at the reception, but not for dinner."

Prescott looked at her implacably. The only man he had seen on the terrace had been the American boy, the golden boy now ash and charred bone. He had thought at first she had been going to speak of Adam Quentin.

"Possibly," she said, "he may have been with a woman – a woman with diamond earrings and garnet rings and a long evening scarf – a French woman."

At once there rose from Prescott's adhesive mind the briefest of images – the dark garden, and the white flash of diamonds in a woman's ears catching the light from the open terrace windows, a scatter of words: *...A la plage... je veux aller a la plage...* "On second thoughts, madame, I passed a man and a woman as I was coming away from the terrace. The woman, if I remember, was dressed as you describe."

"And this was all you saw?"

"Yes, madame."

She smiled, but not at him. The conflagration in the sky still dyed her pale face like a blush of shame or delight. "You think that she was a French woman?"

"Yes, madame. At least she was speaking French."

"Good," Sovaz said clearly, as if congratulating him. "Thank you," she said. She turned and moved back towards the house, and the black maid turned also and followed her.

Prescott drew from a crumpled pocket a crumpled pack of cigarettes and lit one. The peculiar conversation had stuck in his throat. They had not often spoken together, he and Kristian's wife, yet they shared a curious intimacy – the night years before when he had found her in the tenement on the quay, last night when he had found her lying at the edge of the road watching wide-eyed the burning thing below, its light reflected on her face as the sun had reflected on it here in the garden – these dialogues of darkness had tangled their lives together in a violent wilderness of actions.

The sun now threw itself beneath the ocean, symbol of death, of bright young lives snuffed out, and whom the gods loved, no doubt, died young indeed. And somewhere out there the ashes of the young American were blown by the sea currents in and out the fabulous caves, the mouths of fishes, and the scorched human bones drifted with the scorched bones of the car to the bottom, to lie among the bones of galleys, Roman legions swept away by naval wars, Greek merchantmen, Egyptian pirates, all turning to coral, suffering their sea-change, full fathom five, in a company unhindered by racial discrimination or the divisions of time.

At 4 am, Prescott, as a matter of routine, had come cruising by the beach house, driving from the direction of the town. As soon as the road dipped, he saw the lights, and shortly he made out also that the door which gave onto the veranda was standing wide open, while a single lamp burned like a marker on the sands. Coming closer, he noted the absence of the white sports car from beside the villa.

Prescott parked his own vehicle and went down the beach and into the building. The first examination was slight, for he merely wished to ascertain the presence either of the boy or of Kristian's wife. Both were gone. The house had taken on necessarily a slightly Marie-Celeste quality, the open doors and burning lights, the lamp outside on the beach, and upstairs, the bed pulled open. Judging the direction the white sports had taken from the scuff of its treads on the verge, Prescott reversed his car and drove back towards the town, and consequently through it, travelling north.

He was taking the road at an average speed with already several of the huge drops behind him, when he became aware of a dull fluctuating colour, now orange, now blue, to the left, slightly ahead, and below. Coming round a bend, the headlamps broke over an upended cart and the diamante glitter of glass; next a stretch of mashed and mutilated railing. He stopped the car at once, got out and, going to the railing, looked down.

The returning tide had already partially smothered the flames, although at intervals, between the inrush of surf, small oases of fire reasserted themselves.

No sense of shock or horror came over Prescott. The nacre of experience had long since hardened on his inner skin. Only disgust rose in his belly.

He had assumed that both of them had gone with the car onto the raw teeth of the sea. For Sovaz he felt only a mocking ghost of pity. It was the boy he visualised, the boy's broken limbs barbecued down there in that gape of spume and night. It came to him that he had been a little in love with the boy, or the idea of the boy, his youth. Not in love to any sexual or even sensual degree, for these titillations of the flesh had long since become a superfluity to Prescott's inartistic and sufficient body. It was what he himself had outgrown, or never possessed, attributes he had perhaps cynically observed, attributes now obliterated by gravity, fire, and flood, which now assumed an almost unbearable poignancy.

Then, half turning, Prescott caught sight of what he took in a moment of furtive incomprehension to be some extra merchandise from the fallen cart, a white shape lying just across the gap in the shattered railing.

But the fire leapt again below. Prescott saw the shape emerge on the light, the black foliage of hair, the glowing face made predatory by the movements of the flames. Sovaz.

The disgust in Prescott changed to a sort of loathing. The sensation had no basis in any kind of logic. Therefore, he found himself unable to reason it away. He crossed to her and asked matter-of-factly, "Are you hurt?"

Like a fish in a net, she flopped onto her back and stared up at him. She said something.

"What?"

He leaned closer. He realised she was speaking in Greek, one word over and over: "μαινάς, μαινάς, μαινάς."

He knelt down beside her and felt her over for broken bones. He had become conscious of the lucky solitude of the road and accepted the need to hurry. She seemed sound so he pulled her up. She gave a laugh then, a mindless yet lilting laugh.

"Shut up, you bloody bitch," Prescott told her, and dragged her to the car and pushed her into the back where she fell down as limply as a swathe of white silk. But he did not trust her, for as she was she might be capable of anything. He went round to the boot of the car and presently returned with a coffee flask. He offered her a capsule – she only turned her head away. He took hold of her and forced the capsule brutally into her mouth and followed it with the coffee. She responded to this treatment with total obedience. The swallowed capsule did its work rapidly. Soon she slept.

Prescott returned in the car to the beach house and parked a little way down on the track. This time he laboured methodically, tidying the house, packing the clothes of Kristian's wife, and separately those things of the boy, even making the bed, rinsing and stacking away the cutlery and china they had used, removing all trace of their presence. There would, naturally, be other forms of tidying to be done, by means of telephone and chequebook, once he had contacted Kristian.

As a matter of course, Prescott checked that nothing had been stolen from the villa while it stood empty, glancing especially into the unlocked travelling jewel case. The most precious items, the rubies, emeralds, sapphires and diamonds, that marked, like inexorable sparkling milestones, the seven birthdays that Sovaz had experienced as Kristian's wife, these had been omitted by Leah, as always on similar occasions of Sovaz' absence with a man. Only a scatter of little silver and gold ornaments remained, and one long string of pearls, a gift of her scholar father. Beneath the pearls was lying a closely folded square of newsprint. Prescott took it up and opened it carefully, in the line of his inquiry. A fragment of white paper fell out into his hand. It bore some Latin scrawl to which he paid no attention. Neither did he spare more than a glance for the piece of newsprint. That she should keep among her jewels the description of a murder was unsurprising to him. The memory of her sick, half-mad, merciless face had hinted at all manner of extremes. He replaced the cutting and the scrap of Latin and shut the case.

Shortly, the villa put to rights, Prescott turned off the electricity and closed the door. He carried the bags to his car and, getting in, drove north while the dawn swept unsparing light over the land.

Standing smoking, he became aware that the two women, one all white, one all black, were poised like a couple of gulls high above him on the upper terrace.

Prescott looked back. The maid, of course, had halted because Sovaz had done so. Sovaz herself was gazing out towards the far edge of the shore where the sand ran after the retreating tide. Prescott, turning again, followed the direction of her eyes.

The short half-light had begun, dissolving contours, the darkening water ebbing before it. What was the woman searching for down there in the dusk?

Suddenly Prescott made out the figure of a man standing quite still on the glistening abandoned ridges of the sand. Seen from this height in this uncertain afterglow, it was impossible to tell anything of much significance about the figure. Only its complete immobility was apparent, an immobility that somehow conveyed a sense of waiting.

A man waiting for his girl perhaps – the beach was mostly very private. (*Je veux aller a la plage.*) The French woman had wanted to go to the beach. Prescott glimpsed again the diamond flash of her earlobes; her arm linked with that of a masculine companion. He had not paid much attention to them, just two shadows, that brilliance of a jewel, the words...

A circuit in Prescott's brain engaged.

The diamonds, the beach, the garnets, the French woman, the oblong of newsprint between his fingers unintentionally photographed by his retentive brain: Madame Gallier, the twenty-nine-year-old wife... French consulate for three months.... sadistic and apparently motiveless killing... diamond earrings and three garnet rings were found intact on the ears and fingers of the dead woman... police discovered Madame Gallier's body on the beach at dawn...

The woman Sovaz had described to him, the woman he had glimpsed in the garden, had been the Gallier woman, arm in arm with a man. *Je veux aller a la plage.* If it had been her murderer with whom she had been walking, then he had taken her to the beach as she wished, and there he had cut her throat.

And what did Sovaz know about him? Why did she question Prescott?

Prescott sifted facts automatically. If Madame Gallier had been invited to the reception, some police inquiry at the house would have been inevitable; those hours had been her last. There had been no police. Thus, it was the man, the unknown murderer, who was the invited guest, bringing with him, as so many reception guests were apt to do, the one permitted companion. This time the precious cold adornments of Kristian's house had been bait to snare the killer's victim. He had shown her – pathetic little social climber, wife of a nobody at the consulate, sporting her tiny gems – the rich man's house. Then on the shore, the knife's edge.

Did Sovaz understand this? Her description of the man, unlike her prosaic description of Madame Gallier, was self-consciously romantic. And in her jewel case she carried the details of his crime, like love letters or pressed flowers. Once more he saw the drained hunger of her face, the brimming hunger of her eyes, lit by the fire (the sun, the burning car) beneath. Yes. She would understand everything.

The Englishman turned again sharply, but the white gull and the black had vanished into the house. Crushing his cigarette underfoot, he noticed that the occult figure had now also vanished from the darkening beach below.

Tonight, there were white roses on the long table, selected, as were all other flowers ever impaled on the cruel metal quills within the porphyry bowls, for their lack of odour. It had been a habit of his mother's, which Kristian had observed throughout his life, not to mingle the scents of a garden with those of a dining table. Yet the eternal smell of the jasmine still drifted in the room.

Kristian seated himself at the table's head. Directly opposite him but some twenty yards distant, a place had been laid, as always, for his wife. This was the place which, during Kristian's dinner parties, she would occupy in her elegant black or white frocks of guipure lace, hand painted silk, or gauffered Egyptian linen, with flashing lanterns of faceted carbon or corundum at her wrists or throat or ears. For six years, apart from the occasions of the dinners, and although her place was invariably laid, Sovaz had eaten no meal in this room. She and Kristian had never discussed the matter, for, having long since exhausted the topic of the disease, its symptoms were of little interest to either of them.

It was half past nine. The servants were already busy with the wines and hovering like silent wasps about the silver. The doors opened suddenly.

An instant of total pause overcame the room. Even the precise hovering of the wasps was momentarily checked. The cessation of the slight breeze created by their movements caused even the tulip-headed flames of the candles to straighten.

Sovaz came through the room. She walked easily yet decisively. A wasp hurried to her chair, drew it out for her. Kristian came slowly, belatedly, to his feet. She sat. He sat.

She wore a white dress, but not the rubies — somehow he had expected her to wear the rubies — only emerald ear pendants and a great cameo ring.

He was unnerved, agitated by her presence. She appeared calm, yet very certain. It seemed to him he had never before encountered her in this mood. He was confronted by a stranger. After what had happened to her, after the outpourings of the little slum doctor, he had expected everything of her but this. His aesthetic dread was replaced merely by a new and more specific one. He did not trust her. Only the refuge which the presence of his servants afforded him steadied his hand on the glass.

"Good evening, Sovaz," he said presently. "This is an unusual pleasure."

"Isn't it?" she said. "But I thought tomorrow it might be more interesting to dine in the city. What do you think?"

"Whatever you like, of course," he found himself saying.

"I mean with you," she said, "or do you have a previous engagement?"

He set down his glass. She had grown rather thin, a curious El Greco elongation was apparent in the lines of her. It seemed wise to be careful of her mood, although he had never troubled before.

"No," he said, "I think that should be possible."

Her eyes were brilliantly fixed on him. "I shall look forward to it, Kristian. Will you mind if I buy a new frock?"

Aside from these few sentences, they ate in silence.

The Englishman had telephoned about an hour after dawn. His explanation had been succinct, everything became clear at once, yet not quite everything, for it had seemed at first, as it had seemed to Prescott himself, that both the American and Sovaz were dead.

Immediately the vision of the car had shot into Kristian's mind, the spinning tyres, the shattering burst of the railing, the vehicle poised above the brink, the descent, the vast explosion of sound and light and flame on the darkness. In those seconds he had seen Sovaz at the wheel of the car, her hands in her lap, smiling her arrogant greeting to death, shortly cremated like the warrior, her consort, willing or unwilling, consumed at her side. Next moment, Prescott's voice, travelling along the wires, was speaking of the unconscious drugged woman lying in his car. The American of course had been driving, Sovaz had somehow fallen to safety. Sovaz could not, in any case, drive. Her passage to oblivion had lain in the mouth of a little bottle.

Kristian had avoided seeing her on her return. He had left instructions with Prescott, Leah, and finally with Florentine. With everybody. And now, his first sight of her, this metamorphosis, suggesting to him what they should do together with their social hours, precisely as he had seen his mother do with his father over half his lifetime before. An unreal death. A resurrection.

As she toyed with her sorbet, Kristian rose and went out and up to the library, where soon after the Englishman came to find him, and was told, through the medium of Kristian's valet, that whatever his business was it must wait until the following evening. Impartial, Prescott went away.

The limousine passed, like a black leopard on wheels, with a soft predacious purring, through the terracotta afternoon of the city, pausing here and there to make its kill, (the bloody corpse of a dress carried away to be devoured), or to lap gasoline into its vitals.

From the body of the leopard, like a dark intention, at intervals, issued the black girl. She moved with a stately and imperious rhythm. Wardress and maid, she betrayed nowhere her unease – except in her eyes, held wide open. The first errand was the most diabolic, the argument with the jeweller, settled when he came out to the car.

In a salon fanned by the electric zephyrs of the wind machines in the walls, Sovaz submitted her body to highly paid slaves. Each had a mask-face of white enamel with red lips and, as they bent over the gold or black or green-white flesh of the women in the cubicles, these masks cracked into charming smiles spiked with the teeth of lynxes. Sovaz said nothing to these maenads, but the symbol was not lost on her. She was at peace beneath the deft hands of the hairdresser, the manicurist, the cosmetician with her box of paints.

Sovaz emerged into the dusk, her face, between the black grape clusters of her curled hair, now also enamel, kohl and flame, the tips of her white hands hennaed. She herself went this time into the jeweller's shop.

"Is it ready?"

"Yes, madame. I've followed your instructions, though I was grieved to do such a thing."

"Your grief is unimportant to me. Please let me see."

The jeweller produced for her a damask tray.

She probed among the gems to be sure he had done, after all, as she had told him. The great rubies, each now severed from each, fell individually between her fingers.

"Excellent," she said.

"I'm glad you think so, madame. To destroy such a necklace was…"

Sovaz took up in her white and scarlet hand the central pendant of the dismembered mesh and held it out to him.

"Take this to console you."

"Madame, how can I…? You're joking with me."

"Don't be foolish. If you like I will make out a statement to the effect that it is a gift."

"No, madame." The jeweller's eyes flicked rapidly about the shop as if seeking help from his cases.

"Very well. If you prefer."

She slipped the jewels carelessly into her purse, but, going out, let fall the pendant on the road, where it lay like a highly coloured sweet dropped by some child.

In the black bedroom the dress was taken from its wrappings. Sovaz stepped into it. In the mirrors she watched as Leah drew the zipper like a thin silver snake up her spine, then stood back, waiting with dilated eyes at the foot of the bed. Posed like this, the black girl reminded Sovaz for an instant of the painting by Gauguin entitled *The Spirit of the Dead Watches*, which, as a child, had exerted over her an influence of fascination and terror.

The clock spoke in its delicate *castrato*.

It was nine in the evening. Sovaz took up the new scent she had chosen at the salon and applied it to her skin. She poured the contents of her purse into the little evening bag. The severed rubies collided like smashed glass. She stood before the mirrors and placed the long chain of pearls around her neck, touching their round white bodies with her fingers.

"There's no need for you to wait up for me," she said to the black girl. "Go to bed or go out. Whichever you wish."

She moved to the window, and here also, though dimly, was reflected a drowned and darkly glowing image of herself. Now she could hear the sea fall distantly against the shore below, and cheated, hissing, slide away. She could smell the faint drifts of the jasmine, rising like smoke. Tonight, all things had a curious, marvellous savour, all these ephemeral things, for this was the last night of the world. She pressed her hand against the inky glass. Yes – yes – tonight… A surge of almost intolerable excitement rose in her throat.

In the pane she saw her own elliptoid face, the black holes of eyes, the scarlet mouth.

Sovaz stood at the window, telling the chain of pearls like a rosary, listening to the sounds that her husband made, putting on his clothes in the dressing room. Such immaculate, precise sounds; now the rustle of the linen shirt, now the icy clink of the cufflink lifted from its onyx box. Presently he came into the room.

"You're dressed already."

"Yes. I've been listening to you next door. It was amusing."

She glanced at him. He looked, she saw, (saw clearly in the bright dissection which infused her vision), tired and strained. His face was pale. He had not used the sunlamp today probably. As if she had been half blind for years and suddenly put on spectacles, she observed, with a kind of delirious surprise, the lines of age which had gathered in his face, the cobwebs at the corners of the eyes which themselves seemed sunken. She stared at the elegant lean line of him beneath the beautiful dinner clothes – she had not seen his body for five years: what had happened to it? An old man had come into her room. Exultantly she smiled at him.

"Do you know, Kristian, I find you, at this moment, perfectly ridiculous."

She measured delightedly how he controlled any reaction he might have felt at her words. To seem ridiculous was perhaps the worst fate for such a man. Rather burn in fire. She laughed.

"You have changed your mind, then," he said.

"Changed my mind?"

"You prefer to remain here tonight."

"No," she said. "Much as you would like to, no." She went towards the door. "Let's go down."

He stood quite still a moment; his eyes fixed on her. "Is that the dress you bought this afternoon?"

"Yes."

"It's the first time I have ever seen you wear red."

She wanted to dance along the gallery, every sedate step she took tried to contort her mouth into fresh excited laughter. *Slow steps now, slow careful steps, or you will leave the rich old man behind with his wallet.* She felt free as fire in her red frock, she felt like a whore who loved her work and flaunted herself at the night, neoned in diamonds: HERE I AM. This man, this old man with his finicky ways, had been her lord, her master for seven years. Well, now her master was exchanged for a god of night, a prince of darkness, a destiny. She could therefore no longer bow herself like grass before the man. These desires which had possessed her always, the ultimate need of submission, slavishness, which her nature carried, those aching, agonised and wondrous chains which had held her at Kristian"s feet in misery, had now accepted the ultimate soil which occasionally finds out the ultimate seeds. The Devourer would have her. To him she gave homage. Kristian had become necessarily superfluous, his dominance, beside the other, absurd. She took vengeance on the dethroned monarch.

Kristian also was witnessing the change. He could hardly avoid it. The blood-red colour of her dress, the ornate styling of her hair – these alone were unique. Even the perfume radiating from her flesh was different, as if her chemistry were altered. Her manner startled. She was liable to do some monstrous thing – he had been vaguely aware all day that he was dreading this dinner alone with her.

Having some business to attend to in the city, he had found himself, at its conclusion, within walking distance of the great library. A compunction drew him towards it. The scabrous bronze *daevas* that dwelt in the foyer glared from their protuberant eyes. The dusts, the shafts of dusty light were unaltered. He did not comprehend what had taken him there until, crossing between the brooding wooden stacks, he had come to a window seat dappled over by the jade and ruby glass of the pane behind. A girl was sitting here, about seventeen or eighteen years old, a slender girl bent to a book, her black hair down her back. The vision was so perfectly reproduced, so uncanny, that he froze before it. The girl, sensing his presence, glanced up and, liking the look of him, flushed slightly and smiled. A compulsion to run away gripped Kristian as he stood there. The smiling girl he barely noticed, for it was the other, earlier girl he was seeing, who had looked up into his face coldly, vacantly at first, a welling of concentration gradually gathering in her eyes. He had made a journey through time.

Presently, outside in the caustic heat of the afternoon, he sat on a marble bench where sometimes the octogenarian intellectuals of the library came to sit. Perhaps the old man, the librarian and scholar, her father, had sat here too, hugging to him his case of translations and his deadly little cough.

SEVEN

The restaurant, though impeccable, was one Kristian had never before visited. Somehow it had seemed essential to take her to some place where, even should he be recognised, which was quite probable, he would not be known as a regular patron, so that no dossier of evidence would wait on him, no knowledge of his likes and dislikes, of previous solitary dinners or dinners with certain women not Sovaz. More important, that there should be no expectation that he would return thereafter. He had robed himself in an aura of incognito, actually mostly ineffectual, so that whatever might occur, he could absent himself from the scene of the crime.

Their table was discreet, another precaution. But Sovaz was faultlessly decorous in her scarlet dress, yet somehow always smiling, almost laughing.

The meal progressed. She ordered dishes different from his own, as if on purpose. Also, pointedly, the most expensive dishes, which she then played with as a well-fed domestic cat will play with a mouse it has caught.

Once, about eighteen years before, he had begun a liaison with an impoverished actress, because she was beautiful and seemed to possess that quality of soullessness which, for some reason he had never troubled to question, attracted him. She, on a visit such as this to some expensive eating house, had done exactly as Sovaz did now, asking for gold bars to be put on her plate, to show her independence, that she was *using* the rich man. A pathetic charade; she was already in love with him and shortly lost his interest. In the case of Sovaz, however, Kristian was aware of a difference.

Presently she asked for champagne.

This seemed to him, more than all the rest, offensive, bourgeois, indiscriminate. He told her, dispassionately, what she should drink instead. She had always obeyed him. This time she laughed exuberantly, as if at some delicious joke, and, calling back the waiter, ordered for herself.

As the man went away, Sovaz opened her evening bag and took something out which she laid on the table.

"Look," she said, smiling.

Kristian sensed unerringly that the moment had come. It was an effort to control his alarm. "What is that?"

"A ruby. Part of a necklace you gave me." She opened the mouth of her bag farther and let him see the contents. "I took it to a jeweller today to have it broken up into individual stones. At first he wouldn't. Then he couldn't. But I persuaded him. I expect you will get the bill tomorrow. Tomorrow," she added, and her eyes clouded over sightlessly, but not for long. "What do you say?"

"Am I supposed to say something?"

"You are supposed to say: 'I am gravely disappointed in you for making so infantile and melodramatic a gesture'."

He wondered if she could see the sudden tremor in his hands.

The waiter returned. For a few moments they discussed the wine. When this was settled, Sovaz took up the jewel and placed it within the waiter's reach.

"For you," she said, "a ruby. For bringing me my champagne."

The man was uncertain. He glanced at Kristian.

"Yes. Take it," Kristian said, feeling it imperative that he speak.

"But, monsieur, if it is a…"

"Thank you," Kristian said. "We require nothing further for now."

The waiter, nervous, suspicious, picked up the red drop from the cloth, turned and made off. Meeting another of his tribe, he stopped him. Soon heads swivelled like clockwork.

Sovaz smiled again and drank from her fizzing glass.

"Do you want to leave, Kristian?" she murmured. "I'm not ready to leave. I shall scream at you at the top of my voice if you suggest it. Or do you believe I wouldn't? Try me."

He found himself confronted suddenly by his mother, his terrible mother who so far he had always managed to escape by the original means of demanding that her attributes be expressed by those unable to do so. Her smooth steel, her frigid fire, her elegant destructiveness, her cruel, charming, remote dominance which had held his father impaled on a female phallus of self-sufficiency. The woman who had actually driven her husband down to his death with her, not from a sense of need or histrionics, but simply because she found him so unimportant that she could not be bothered to thrust him out of the car.

"We will leave when you are ready," Kristian therefore said to Sovaz. He felt dizzy, almost unwell. He knew the horror of a man in a gas-filled room who fears he will faint before he can break down the door.

But, meeting no opposition, she was prepared to leave after all. She abandoned a further ruby on the table, dropped one with the skill of a perverse pickpocket into the dinner jacket of a man going by in the foyer, let one fall on the pavement outside. Kristian was paralysed. He did not dare to remonstrate. This was what she had reduced him to – he did not *dare*.

Paul handed them into the limousine.

They drove slowly across the city. It was almost midnight, but traffic was still heavy. The icon face of Sovaz flashed on and off like a neon in the headlamps of passing cars.

Sovaz opened the window and cast out at the sides of the road a trail of rubies. She did it in a neat calculated manner. The exercise finished, she turned to him.

"Poor Kristian," she said, with practically genuine sympathy. "After tonight I shall be very docile. You will have no further worries about me."

He had no notion what to say. The rest of the journey was made in silence.

As they went up through the gardens towards the house, she paused at each landing to touch, almost experimentally, the chess piece marbles. They reached the wide doors and went in. Her face had taken on, most unexpectedly, a gentle yielding look.

"I am going up now," she said quietly. "I may take a walk in the garden later, then I shall go to bed. Good night."

She started to mount the stairs, then halted and looked back at him. Her eyes went over him, head to foot, next over the things surrounding him, the inanimates of the hall. A puzzled frown appeared between her eyes, then smoothed itself away. She turned and walked on up the stairway, the red dress pulsing on the shadow above long after the gleam of her hair and flesh had been extinguished.

Kristian moved heavily towards his study. He felt the need to be among his own things, the mementos of the great estate. Yet, as he crossed the tessellated floor, he saw Prescott politely awaiting him before the double doors.

At each step she thought, I shall never do this again or I shall only do it one time more.

And in the gallery, she thought, *How insignificant all this is, the house, the ornaments of the house.* And yet they were beautiful too, ephemeral, bathed in the fascinated glare of terminus.

Reaching her room, having shut both doors which led into it, she unzipped the red dress and took the string of pearls from her neck, and put them both away. The girl, as she had instructed her, was gone, yet everything lay to hand. Sovaz bathed once again, scented herself, and sat before her mirrors, her combs and paints laid out before her.

She was now completely calm, yet there was so much time to waste: three hours at least before the house was safe and Kristian either absent or shut in the library.

A sort of nostalgia was coming over her, as if she were about to go travelling far away.

She did not anticipate death. As on the shore road she visualised neither the stroke nor its consequences. Certainly, she did not see as far as extinction, the end of life. She foresaw – and this only with her body – the ecstasy of utter submission. And since it was to a god that she was offering herself – will-less, welcoming – she herself seemed strangely deified. As the sacrifices of pagan festivals walked with dignity and joy towards their destiny, so she walked now in her instinct, and the people showered her with flowers and begged for her holy blessing as she passed.

The rubies, scattered about the city, were a sort of symbol of this blessing. But also they were a message, a signal to the god. It did not really matter where she laid them; being ubiquitous, he could look down from the stars, out of the eyes of a cripple, or a banker, or a *maître d'hôtel*, and see at once what she had done, what she was saying to him. Since the first, she had vaguely understood he had been holding back only for this, her free surrender. *Nos cedamus Amori.*

As she stared pensively into the glass, picturing the mask of her own face which represented the Dionysos mask of the god, she recognised the great power the god had vested in her. Had she not destroyed the young boy, the American, in her fury at his intrusion, the coitus interruptus of her vision on the road? Yes. *She* had caused the car to swerve, to plunge. Like Agave, she had torn her Pentheus to shreds when he threatened the rite of love. Never had she felt such power in herself, such assurance, coupled so strongly with the knowledge of yielding and abnegation.

The little clock struck one, then two. The sea also struck its hours on the beach below. She retouched her lips and eyes meticulously and examined her hands to which the effects of the manicure still adhered. At last she took from the closet the black lace frock, now faultlessly cleaned and repaired, and put it on. A communion, uncommon to her, had sprung up between her fingers and her flesh.

She was like a very young girl discovering her body for the first time, adoring it, striving to please it, this temple of her emotion, which because it was lovely, desirable, was also magic.

Presently she opened the windows wide.

He would see the light, the one who waited for her, as she for him, on the shore.

Warm night winds like the wings of birds filled the room, lifting her hair, disturbing the sheaf of drawings stacked neatly by the gramophone. She crossed to the bronze bowl in which she had burned joss sticks, an activity she recalled with wistful tolerance, the amusements of a child, and took up a box of matches. She struck a match and, selecting a drawing, she crumpled it and fed it to the flame, letting the paper fall into the bowl to burn and adding fresh ones instantly. Soon, gorged with its meal and made adventurous by the wind, the little fire shot up like the watchlight of an altar.

Perhaps he could see that too.

Fantastically aware of all her movements and her acts, Sovaz became for herself a sorceress who had created fire.

Not once did she look at the drawings to see what they might represent. It no longer mattered, for the internal theatre, like

Kristian, was now superfluous. She had become at last her own canvas.

Prescott observed Kristian as he stood beside the case of guns, with the impartial evaluating composure so easily construed by others as good-mannered obedience. It was, after all, a part of Prescott's job to present himself in the guise of an intelligent dog, the kind that will carry things in its mouth and shake hands. Nevertheless, left to harden now for so long in this mould, he had actually lost interest in the ruthless vivisections of humanity which he still automatically carried out. The sort of scorn that Kristian and men of his class and type inspired in him in no way influenced Prescott's attitude or work. He waited patiently therefore for Kristian to digest what he had told him of Sovaz, as he had once waited seven years before.

Finally, Kristian spoke to him. "You say the man has been to this house?"

"Yes. I have the guest list with me, the list from the last reception and dinner. I've been making inquiries, and I think I have located him." He held out the list and indicated the spot so Kristian could see it.

"I don't recollect the name," Kristian said.

"An invitation at the request of someone more important, perhaps," Prescott suggested.

"Perhaps." Kristian seemed preoccupied. "You assume my wife is in danger."

'Inevitably, if this man is the murderer, and I have good reason to think he is. Madame Sovaz has extended her friendship to him, clearly without realising what he will be bound to do to her. He is a compulsive killer. Given the opportunity, he will not be able to resist cutting your wife's throat. Precisely as he did the throat of Madame Gallier, and possibly the throats of other women in the city."

Kristian took from a jade box a cigarette and lit it with the concentration of a man unaware of his surroundings. "Why do you imagine he will come here tonight?"

"I've been talking to Leah. Madame Sovaz has been making certain preparations. As far as I can see, she will go down sometime tonight and open the small gate that gives onto the beach. That is the way he will gain admission, then up through the gardens, into the house about three o'clock or half past. The servants are either in bed or out at that time. She will reckon on your being in the library."

Kristian sat slowly down. His eyes were blank. Surely, Prescott surmised, he also guessed the nature of Sovaz' interest. Prescott had spoken at some length with the black girl and with the chauffeur, Paul. He had built up a bizarre picture of Sovaz' behaviour over the period of time following the night of the murder. The press cutting, the drawings, the rubies, her apathy, her sudden decisiveness, her conversations with the doctor... all the paraphernalia of some unbalanced infatuation. This was what the American boy had become part of, her madness. Almost certainly what had killed him. Prescott felt no compunction to save the woman – it was merely part of his job to do so. As with Kristian, his personal feelings would not intrude.

"You have not contacted the police," Kristian said.

"Naturally I informed you of the matter first."

"Good." Kristian rose and crossed to the case of guns. "These pistols are in perfect working order. I shot with them only a few days ago."

A glimmer of amusement lit deep down in Prescott's brain. The feudal aristocrat, absolute law on his own land. Kristian, bemused by his wife's madness, took refuge in his own past. Quite clearly, with these exquisite and perfectly kept weapons, they were about to gun the murderer down, the police business to be delicately settled afterwards, for those legendary strings-which-might-be-pulled were always available to the city rich. In some alley tomorrow night, a whore would perhaps stumble over the corpse of a man, or in a week some fishing boat would bring up a green and bloated fish from the bay.

Kristian, as he took out the pistols, examined and presently loaded them, felt a soothing sense of purpose come over him. He had handled these guns, or their fellows, so often. The reassuring psychometry of well-known possessions. There was no need after all to analyse, to enter the cloud of confusion that had swept through his brain. He had become aware, though only in the farthest pit of his consciousness, behind all the thousand veils with which human beings conceal their own impulses from themselves, of the true possibility of Sovaz' death. He feared her, he hated her, he despised and shuddered at her monstrous attachment to his life, yet he was magnetised, he had known as much from the first moment of seeing her. She was *his* devil. The eternal presence which he must dominate and have no interest in, in order to achieve his sense of self, which in turn burdened him with its indispensability. And, like all addicts, he scented destruction with hungry terror. She must not die. Yet if she should... Not the independence of suicide. The helpless victim of a murder which he himself could permit.

It was half past two. He went with Prescott silently and in darkness down the stairs, across the ghostly ballroom, through the windows (open), and so onto the terrace of the house. Turning aside into the shadow of the jasmine, they saw her coming up the avenue of lemons towards them in her black lace frock.

She was touching the flowers as she came, lightly. She looked very young, very knowing, wary as an animal picking its way towards the house. She had a rose in her hair, a red rose. There was something horrible, obscene about her, like the stench on the breath of the beautiful vampire, unlooked-for poison. Both men felt it yet would not feel it; for their different reasons rejection of the Gothic and the primeval was instantaneous. She slid in through the double windows.

"She's been to the gate," Prescott said softly after a minute had gone by. "This is the way he'll come."

So they waited, ready to ambush death with their silver pistols.

The wind was not blowing from the city tonight with its freight of car horns, trains, music. There was only the flash and murmur of the tide. Prescott noticed that Kristian had put on gloves, as he had done on entering the slums seven years ago.

Then a step fell, like the drip of a tap – huge in the silence between the phrases of the sea.

Prescott glanced at the luminous dial of his watch. Five minutes to three. A shadow appeared through the lemon trees, following the path she had taken. What signal had been given him? Perhaps her lighted windows – lights now out – or some signal to him as he stood on the beach. Or probably he had come before and tried the ornamental gate, finding it always locked, tonight ajar.

The shadow moved, not with particular stealth or grace, rather clumsily in fact. The shade of the garden made identification impossible. Prescott had earlier suggested activating one of the master switches of the ballroom which lay beside the windows, flooding the area outside with light, and so apprehending the intruder by means of surprise. Kristian had ignored the suggestion, determined, Prescott supposed, to shoot the man.

Now the visitor, skirting the oleanders, began to climb the steps. He was ungainly, the foliage rustled. Prescott was reminded of a rat scuttling over a wharf among old paper and rinds. He anticipated some cue from Kristian; nothing came. The man entered abruptly into the black of the house. Kristian also was invisible and unmoving. Prescott had neither premonition nor suspicion. He only saw the chance of the man's escape, the work botched – he moved from concealment, disengaging the safety catch of the pistol as he did so.

A voice, out of the shadow ahead, the murderer's, high-pitched, anguished. A crack like the snapping of a bone followed, the safety catch of Kristian's gun. Prescott saw the perfect tailor-made stance of the professional shot, outlined only by starlight, as Kristian fired directly into the unseen area ahead that was a man.

Sovaz lay across the bed in the black night-silence. Every line of her was quiescent, only the pulse in her throat, a drum under her skin. The Sleeping Beauty in the Dark Tower. Lying, as if spent, still the sum of her was gathered, she was immensely aware of the huge inky womb in which she floated, of the approach of waking, the savage kiss.

Now he was in the ebony garden among the skulls of flowers, now perhaps in the shimmering ballroom. A pale electric current ran in her veins. Each step she had taken, he now took, noiseless, drifting like unheard music towards her through the dumb pyramid of the house. Now on the marble stairway, between the icicles of the candelabra. He came to her so slowly. An unbearable excitement murmured in her which only the touch of him on her in the black unseen could satisfy. She did not need to see him, knew him, could superimpose his image on the blindness of the room, white, gold, black, scarlet. The god.

Suddenly there was a crack of enormous sound. It pierced her stillness, raped her silence. She started up on the bed, staring sightlessly about. Having dismissed civilisation and its concepts she could no more remember how to draw the drapes from the windows, turn on the light, than she could recall such things existed in the elemental world to which she had given herself up. So she crouched on the bed in the attitude of a cat or an ape confronted by the inexplicable sorcery of mankind. Shaken from her dream she was not, even so, awakened.

Some time passed. She did not register time as such. All at once she heard a footfall in the gallery outside.

Now she felt fear, extreme fear, ecstatic. She flung herself down in an attitude of abandonment, trembling and writhing, her mouth parted, her teeth set, her eyes shut.

A hand fumbled at the door. She uttered a little whimpering plea and spread her arms wide. The door opened.

She felt his presence in the room with her. A great wave, a sea wave gushed through her. She stretched herself, arching her body. Suspense, stasis.

"Sovaz," a voice said.

She could not answer. Only the anguished entreaty of her straining flesh responded.

"Sovaz," the voice said, more insistently, "the man was very dangerous. I don't think you can have realised. We discovered who he was and waited for him downstairs."

She twisted, struggled against some invisible restraint. Her eyes opened. She knew the voice, the man. She gave a sort of hoarse inarticulate grunting sound.

The gallery outside was pitch dark, no light had come into the room. She could not see. As he came nearer, she could only smell the odour of smoke from the pistol.

"I am afraid I had no choice but to shoot him," Kristian said.

Neither could Kristian see her very well. He stood in the room tiredly. The hidden urge in him had never reached fruition, he did not know it. He had not switched on the lights.

Sovaz sprang from the bed across the floor to her husband. She gave a series of screams that were heard throughout the house, as not even the pistol shot had been. She hurled herself against him, gripping him with legs, feet, teeth and one arm, in an embrace like love, and, snatching with her right hand at the pistol he had retained in his gloved fingers, she thrust the muzzle against his chest and pulled the trigger.

The second bullet was ejected in a shattering spasm and muffled roar of noise. He made no sound but jerked like a marionette between her limbs. A convulsion went over her that seemed to uproot her heart, her lungs and her brain from her flesh.

She slid down him, and as she let him go, he also fell.

She was kneeling on the floor above Kristian's dead body, her hands and the front of her dress sticky with blood, the pistol in her lap, when the Englishman ran up the stairs, along the gallery and into the room.

Hearing the cries, the unexpected second shot, Prescott ran upstairs and, reaching the bedroom, immediately depressed the master switch of the electric light.

He saw at once that Kristian was dead. Sovaz seemed to be dying, rocking limply in her bleeding gown. Then she raised her head and looked at him.

Her face was white, but her wide eyes were completely intelligent, rational. Despite the unnerving scene, she was in full possession of herself. It seemed to him he had never seen her so before.

"I thought," she said quietly, "that Kristian was the killer, coming for me. It was dark, I couldn't see. I was terrified. I somehow got hold of the gun and fired it into him."

"The man used a knife, always," Prescott said.

The murderer, impregnated by Kristian's bullet, huddled on the floor of the ballroom. A small body, its spine curved like a clerk's, and with receding hair, totally nondescript save for the stiletto in the pocket, so unlikely, yet highly polished for his victim, as a man might polish his shoes before visiting his mistress. He was not as Sovaz had described him. Even in the dark, it would be hard to mistake Kristian for such a creature.

"Prescott," Sovaz said casually, "I suggest that I confided in you a fear that the murderer might have armed himself with a gun in addition to the knife, and that this is why my husband fired on him so arbitrarily in the garden. I suggest that, hearing Kristian's shot, I was in terror that my husband and not the killer had been harmed. I suggest that, hysterical with panic and seeing a shadowy figure enter my room, I attacked it wildly, with such tragic consequence. Your supporting statement will be useful but is merely a formality. As you know, the police can be perfectly accommodating, particularly since my husband's money will devolve on me. I can pay to retain my good name. I shall also, in future, be paying your wages, your deservedly high wages. Unless, of course, there is some mistake about this dreadful business in which case no one will be able to pay you."

She stood up now, imposing, in her dress of lace and blood.

Prescott, seeing only the transformation, the result, could have no inkling of the vast cataclysm which had brought it about. She had been Agave, she had torn Pentheus and, in a metaphysical completion of the Dionysiac rite, she had devoured him. Prescott felt all the ancient erosion of his cowardice. It disguised itself as flights of fancy that women, particularly Sovaz, had always sparked off in him. And cowardice nodded his head to her, puppet-fashion. In fact, he bowed it.

"Yes, madame. That makes sense."

"Very good," she said.

Downstairs he could hear the muted hubbub of the emergent servants, the flat voice of Paul taking charge, while somewhere out to sea, the requiem of a lost ship added its note to the night.

Sovaz glanced aside at the curtained window, as if the noise of the ship held some significance for her. Her face was arrogant, remote to a point almost of unworldliness, yet entirely sane. Her eyes seemed extraordinarily intent by contrast with the eyes of Kristian, glazed and unfocused bits of lapis lazuli in his death-mask on the floor.

As he looked at her in that split second, it seemed to Prescott that she, like the *rakshas* of Indian mythology, had acquired the ability to take on another form.

Kristian's.

Author's Note:

Although set 'somewhere' in the Mediterranean, and 'sometime' in the late Sixties (probably) Nightshade was and is what I would class as a contemporary novel.

But then again ... It certainly has some exotic and wildly fantastic elements.

There is the Dionysus theme: this god, generally dismissed as the deity of wine - he is much more - has always intrigued me. The master of inner terrors and truths, the breaker of chains, his power passes through the freeing medium of drink, or any strong excitement, including madness.

There is, too, the character of the anti-heroine, Sovaz.

Elizabeth Taylor, surely one of the most beautiful women in the world, is proof that a beautiful human being may also possess great talent and character, and a fully operational soul. And yet I confess a fascination with those great beauties, male and female, who are, operationally, soulless. One glimpses them now and then, usually briefly. What, if there is no warmth, is making them tick? What, aside from beauty, has vampirised them? Some of this I have tried to investigate in the form of the pale, red-lipped icon of Sovaz.

WHY LIGHT?

Part One

My first memory is the fear of light.

The passage was dank and dark, and water dripped, and my mother carried me, although by then I could walk. I was three, or a little younger. My mother was terrified. She was consumed by terror, and she shook, and her skin gave off a faint metallic smell I had never caught from her before. Her hands were cold as ice. I could feel that, even through the thick shawl in which she'd wrapped me. She said, over and over, "It's all right, baby. It's all right. It will be OK. You'll see. Just a minute, only one. It'll be all right."

By then of course I too was frightened. I was crying, and I think I wet myself, though I hadn't done anything like that since babyhood.

Then the passage turned, and there was a tall iron gate – I know it's iron, now. At the time it only looked like a burnt-out coal.

"Oh God," said my mother.

But she thrust out one hand and pushed at the gate and it grudged open with a rusty scraping, just wide enough to let us through.

I would have seen the vast garden outside the house, played there. But this wasn't the garden. It was a high place, held in only by a low stone wall and a curving break of poplar trees. They looked very black, not green the way the house lamps made trees in the garden. Something was happening to the sky; that was what made the poplars so black, I thought it was moonrise, but I knew the moon was quite new, and only a full moon could dilute the darkness so much. The stars were watery and blue, weak, like dying gas flames.

My mother stood there, just outside the iron gate, holding me, shaking. "It's all right... just a minute ... only one..."

Suddenly something happened.

It was like a storm – a lightning flash maybe, but in slow-motion, that swelled up out of the dark. It was pale, then silver, and then like gold. It was like a high trumpet note, or the opening chords of some great concerto.

I sat bolt upright in my mother's arms, even as she shook ever more violently. I think her teeth were chattering.

But I could only open my eyes wide. Even my mouth opened, as if to drink the sudden light.

It was the colour of a golden flower and it seemed to boil, and enormous clouds poured slowly upward out of it, brass and wine and rose. And a huge noise came from everywhere, rustling and rushing – and weird flutings and squeakings and trills – birdsong – only I didn't recognise it.

My mother now hoarsely wept. I don't know how she never dropped me.

Next, they came out and drew us in again, and Tyfa scooped me quickly away as my mother collapsed on the ground. So I was frightened again, and screamed.

They closed the gate and shut us back in darkness. The one minute was over. But I had seen a dawn.

Part Two

Fourteen and a half years later, and I stood on the drive, looking at the big black limousine. Marten was loading my bags into the boot. Musette and Kousu were crying quietly. One or two others lingered about; nobody seemed to grasp what exactly was the correct way to behave. My mother hadn't yet come out of the house.

By that evening my father was dead over a decade – he had died when I was six, my mother a hundred and seventy. They had lived together a century anyway, were already tired of each other and had taken other lovers from our community. But that made his death worse, apparently. Ever since, every seventh evening, she would go into the little shrine she had made to him, cut one of her fingers and let go a drop of blood in the vase below his photograph. Her name is Juno, my mother, after a Roman goddess, and I'd called her by her name since I was an adult.

"She should be here," snapped Tyfa, irritated. He too was Juno's occasional lover, but generally he seemed exasperated by her.

"Locked in that damn room," he added sourly. He meant the shrine.

I said nothing, and Tyfa stalked off along the terrace, and started pacing about, a tall strong man of around two hundred or so, no one was sure – dark-haired as most of us were at Severin. His skin had a light brownness from a long summer of sun-exposure. He had always been able to take the sun, often for several hours in one day. I too have black hair, and my skin even in winter, is pale brown. I can endure daylight all day long, day after day. I can *live* by day.

Marten had closed the boot. Casperon had got into the driver's seat, leaving the car door open, and was trying the engine. Its loud purring would no doubt penetrate the house's upper storey, and the end rooms which comprised Juno's apartment.

Abruptly she came sweeping out from the house.

Juno has dark red hair. Her skin is white. Her slanting eyes are the dark bleak blue of a northern sea, seen in a foreign movie with subtitles. When I was a child, I adored her. She was my goddess. I'd have died for her, but that stopped. It stopped forever.

She walked straight past the others, as if no one else were there. She stood in front of me. She was still an inch or so taller than I, though I'm tall.

"Well," she said. She stared into my face, hers cold as marble, and *all* of her stone-still – this, the woman who trembled and clutched me to her, whispering that all would be well, when I was three years old.

"Yes, Juno," I said.

"Do you have everything you need?" she asked me indifferently, forced to be polite to some visitor now finally about to leave.

"Yes, thank you. Kousu helped me pack."

"You know you have only to call the house, and anything else can be sent on to you? Of course," she added, off-handedly, "you'll want for nothing, *there*."

I did not reply. What was there to say? I've 'wanted' for so much *here* and never got it – at least, my mother, from *you*.

"I wish you very well," she coldly said, "in your new home. I hope everything will be pleasant. The marriage is important, as you're aware, and they'll treat you fairly."

"Yes."

"We'll say goodbye, then. At least for a while."

"Yes."

"Goodbye, Daisha." She drew out the ay sound: and foolishly through my mind skipped words that rhymed – fray, say... prey.

I said, "So long, Juno. Good luck making it up with Tyfa. Have a nice life."

Then I turned my back, crossed the terrace and the drive, and got into the car. I'd signed off with all the others before. They had loaded me with good wishes and sobbed, or tried to cheer me by mentioning images we had seen of my intended husband, and saying how handsome and talented he was, and I must write to them soon, email or call – not lose touch – come back next year – sooner... Probably they'd forget me in a couple of days or nights.

To me, they already seemed miles off.

The cream limousine of the full moon had parked over the estate as we drove away. In its blank blanched rays I could watch, during the hour it took to cross the whole place and reach the outer gates, all the nocturnal industry, in fields and orchards, in vegetable gardens, pens and horse-yards, garages and work-shops – a black horse cantering, lamps, and red sparks flying and people coming out to see us go by, humans saluting the family car, appraising in curiosity, envy, pity or scorn, the girl driven off to become a Wife of-Alliance.

In the distance the low mountains shone blue from the moon. The lake across the busy grasslands was like a gigantic vinyl disk dropped from the sky, an old record the moon had played, and played tonight on the spinning turntable of the earth. This was the last I saw of my home.

The journey took just on four days.

Sometimes we passed through whitewashed towns, or cities whose tall concrete and glass fingers reached to scratch the clouds. Sometimes we were on motorways, wide and streaming with traffic in spate. Or there was open countryside, mountains coming or going, glowing under hard icing-sugar tops. In the afternoons we'd stop, for Casperon to rest, at hotels. About six or seven in the evening we drove on. I slept in the car by night. Or sat staring from the windows.

I was, inevitably, uneasy. I was resentful and bitter and full of a dull and hopeless rage.

I shall get free of it all – I had told myself this endlessly since midsummer, when first I had been informed that, to cement ties of friendship with the Duvalles, I was to marry their new heir. Naturally it was not only friendship that this match entailed. I had sun-born genes. And the Duvalle heir, it seemed, hadn't. My superior light-endurance would be necessary to breed a stronger line. A bad joke, to our kind – they needed my *blood*. I was *blood*stock. I was Daisha Severin, a young female life only seventeen years, and able to live day-long in sunlight. I was incredibly valuable. I would be, everyone had said, so *welcome*. And I was *lovely*, they said, with my brunette hair and dark eyes, my cinnamon skin. The heir – Zeev Duvalle – was very taken with the photos he had seen of me. And didn't I think *he* was fine – *cool*, Musette had said: "He's so *cool* – I wish it could have been me. You're so lucky, Daisha."

Zeev was blond, almost snow-blizzard white, though his eyebrows and lashes were dark. His eyes were like some pale shining metal. His skin was pale too, if not so colourless as with some of us, or so I'd thought when I watched him in the house movie I'd been sent. My pale-skinned mother had some light-tolerance, though far less than my dead father. I had inherited all his strength that way, and more. But Zeev Duvalle had none, or so it seemed. To me he looked like what he was, a man who lived only by night. In appearance he seemed nineteen or twenty, but he wasn't so much older in actual years. Like me, a new young life. So much in common. So very little.

And by now *I shall get free of it all*, which I'd repeated so often, had become my mantra, and also meaningless. How could I *ever* get free? Among my own kind I would be an outcast and criminal if I ran away from this marriage, now or ever, without a 'valid' reason. While able to pass as human, I could hardly live safely among them. I can eat and drink a little in their way, but I need blood. Without blood I would die.

So, escape the families and their alliance, I would become not only traitor and thief – but a murderer. A human-slaughtering monster humanity doesn't believe in, or does believe in – something either way that, if discovered amongst them, they will kill.

That other house, my former home on the Severin estate, was long and quite low, two storeyed, but with high ceilings mostly on the ground floor. Its first architecture, gardens, and farm had been made in the early nineteenth century.

Their mansion – castle – whatever one has to call it – was colossal. Duvalle had built high.

It rose, this *pile*, like a cliff, with outcrops of slate-capped towers. Courtyards and enclosed gardens encircled it. Beyond and around lay deep pine woods with infiltrations of other trees, some maples, already flaming in the last of summer and the sunset. I spotted none of the usual workplaces, houses, or barns.

We had taken almost three hours to wend through their land, along the tree-rooted and stone-littered, upward-tending track. Once Casperon had to pull up, get out and examine a tire. But it was all right. On we went.

At one point, just before we reached the house, I saw a waterfall cascading from a tall rocky hill, plunging into a ravine below. In the ghostly dusk it looked beautiful, and melodramatic. Setting the tone?

When the car at last drew up, a few windows were burning amber in the house-cliff. Over the wide door itself glowed a single electric light inside a round pane like a worn-out planet.

No one had come to greet us.

We got out and stood at a loss. The car's headlamps fired the brickwork, but still nobody emerged. At the lit windows no silhouette appeared gazing down.

Casperon marched to the door and rang some sort of bell that hung there.

All across the grounds, crickets chirruped, hesitated, and went on.

The night was warm, and so empty; nothing seemed to be really alive anywhere, despite the crickets, the windows. Nothing, I mean, of *my* kind, our people. For a strange moment I wondered if something ominous had happened here, if everyone had died, and if so would that release me? But then one leaf of the door was opened. A man looked out. Casperon spoke to him, and the man nodded. A few minutes later I had to go up the steps and into the house.

There was a sort of vestibule, vaguely lighted by old ornate lanterns, beyond that was a big paved court, with pruned trees and raised flowerbeds, and then more steps. Casperon had gone for my luggage. I followed the wretched sallow man who had let me in.

"What's your name?" I asked him as we reached the next

portion of the house, a blank wall lined only with blank black windows.

"Anton."

"Where is the family?" I asked him.

"Above," was all he said.

I said, halting, "Why was there no one to welcome me?"

He didn't reply. Feeling a fool, angry now, I stalked after him.

There was another vast hall or vestibule. No lights, until he touched the switch and greyish weary side-lamps came on, giving little colour to the stony towering space.

"Where," I said, in Juno's voice, "*is* he? He at least should be here. Zeev Duvalle, my husband-to-be." I spoke formally. "I am insulted. Go at once and tell him..."

"He does not rise yet," said Anton, as if to somebody invisible but tiresome. "He doesn't rise until eight o'clock."

Day in night. Night was Zeev's day, yet the sun had been gone over an hour now. Damn him, I thought. *Damn* him.

It was useless to protest further. And when Casperon returned with the bags, I could say nothing to him, because this wasn't his fault. And besides he would soon be gone. I was alone. As per usual.

I met Zeev Duvalle at dinner. It was definitely a dinner, not a breakfast, despite their day-for-night policy. It was served in an upstairs conservatory; the glass panes open to the air. A long table draped in white, tall old greenish glasses, plates of some red china, probably Victorian. Only five or six other people came to the meal, and each introduced themselves in a formal, chilly way. Only one woman, who looked about fifty and so probably was into her several hundreds, said she regretted not being there at my arrival. No excuse was offered, however. They made me feel like what I was to them, a new house computer that could talk. A doll that would be able to have babies... yes. Horrible.

By the time we sat down, in high-backed chairs, with huge orange trees standing around behind them like guards – a scene on a film set – I was boiling with cold anger. Part of me was afraid, too. I can't really explain the fear, or of what. It was like being washed up out of the night ocean on an unknown shore, and all you can see are stones and emptiness, and no light to show the way.

At Severin there were always types of ordinary food to be had – steaks, apples – we drank a little wine, took coffee or tea. But a lot of us were sun-born. Even Juno was. She hated daylight, but still tucked into the occasional croissant. Of course, there was Proper Sustenance too. The blood of those animals we kept for that purpose, always collected with economy, care and gentleness from living beasts, which continued to live, well-fed and tended and never over-used, until their natural deaths. For special days, there was special blood. This being drawn, also with respectful care, from among the human families who lived on the estate. They had no fear of giving blood, any more than the animals did. In return, their rewards were many and lavish. The same arrangement, so far as I knew, was similar among all the scattered families of our kind.

Here at Duvalle, we were served with a black pitcher of blood, a white pitcher of white wine. Fresh bread, still warm, lay on the red dishes.

That was all.

I had taken proper Sustenance at the last hotel, drinking from my flask. I'd drunk a Coke on the road, too.

Now I took a piece of bread and filled my glass with an inch of wine.

They all looked at me. Then away. Every other glass by then gleamed scarlet. One of the men said, "But, young lady, this is the best, this is *human*. We always take it at dinner. Come now."

"No," I said, "thank you."

"Oh, but clearly you don't know your own mind…"

And then *he* spoke. From the doorway. He had only just come in, after his long rest or whatever else he had been doing for the past two and a half hours, as I was in my allotted apartment, showering, getting changed for this appalling night.

What I saw first about him, Zeev Duvalle, was inevitable. The blondness, the *whiteness* of him, almost incandescent against the candlelit room and the dark beyond the glass. His hair was like molten platinum, just sombreing down a bit to a kind of white gold in the shadow. His eyes weren't grey, but green – grey-green like the crystal goblets. His skin after all wasn't that pale. It had a sort of tawny look to it – not in any way like a tan. More as if it fed on darkness and had drawn some into itself. He was handsome, but I knew that. He looked now about nineteen. He had a perfect body, slim and strong; most vampires do. We eat the perfect food and very few extra calories – nothing too much or too little. But he was tall. Taller than anyone I'd ever met. About six and a half feet, I thought.

Unlike the others, even me, he hadn't smartened up for dinner. He wore un-new black jeans and a scruffy T-shirt with long torn sleeves. I could smell the outdoors on him, pine needles, smoke and night. He had been out in the grounds. There was... there was a little brown-red stain on one sleeve. Was it *blood*? From *what*?

It came to me with a lurch what he really most resembled. A white wolf. And had this *bloody* wolf been out hunting in his vast forested park? What had he killed so mercilessly – some squirrel or hare – or a deer – that would be bad enough – or was it worse?

I knew *nothing* about these people I'd been given to. I'd been too offended and allergic to the whole idea to do any research, ask any real questions. I had frowned at the brief movie they sent of him, thought; so, he's cute and almost albino. I hadn't even got that right. He was a *wolf*. He was a feral animal that preyed in the old way, by night, on things defenceless and afraid.

This was when he said again, "Let her alone, Constantine." Then, "Let her eat what she wants. She knows what she likes." *Then*: "Hi, Daisha. I'm Zeev. If only you'd got here a little later, I'd have been here to welcome you."

I met his eyes, which was difficult. That glacial green; I slipped from its surface. I said quietly, "Don't worry. Who cares?"

He sat down at the table's head. Though the youngest among them, he was the heir and therefore, supposedly, their leader now. His father had died two years before, when his car left an upland road miles away. Luckily his companion, a woman from the Clays family, had called the house. The wreck of the car and his body had been retrieved by Duvalle before the sun could make a mess of both the living and the dead. All of us know, we survive largely through the wealth longevity enables us to gather, and the privacy it buys.

The others started to drink their dinner again, passing the black jug. Only one of them took any bread, and that was to sop up the last red element from inside his glass. He wiped the bread round like a cloth then stuffed it in his mouth. I sipped my wine. Zeev, seen from the side of my left eye, seemed to touch nothing. He merely sat there. He didn't seem to look at me. I was glad of that.

Then the man called Constantine said loudly, "Better get on with your supper, Wolf, or she'll think you already found it in the woods. And among *her* clan that just *isn't* done."

And some of them sniggered a little, softly. I wanted to hurl my glass at the wall – or at all their individual heads.

But Zeev said, "What, you mean – this on my T-shirt?" He too sounded amused.

I put down my unfinished bread and got up. I glanced around at them, at him last of all. "I hope you'll excuse me, I've been travelling and I'm tired." Then I looked straight at him. Somehow it was shocking to do so. "And goodnight, Zeev. Now we've finally met."

He said nothing. None of them did.

I walked out of the conservatory, crossed the large room beyond and headed for the staircase.

Wolf. They even *called* him that.

Wolf.

"Wait," he said, just behind me.

I can move almost noiselessly and very fast, but not as noiseless and sudden as – apparently – he could. Before I could prevent it, I spun round wide-eyed. There he stood, less than three feet from me. He was expressionless, but when he spoke now his voice, actor trained, I thought, was very musical. "Daisha Severin, I'm sorry. I've made a bad start with you."

"You noticed."

"Will you come with me – just upstairs – to the library. We can talk there without the rest of them making up an audience."

"Why do we want to? Talk, I mean."

"We should, I think. And maybe you'll be gracious enough to humour me.

"Maybe I'll just tell you to go to hell."

"Oh, *there*," he said. He smiled. "No. I'd never go there. Too bright, too hot."

"Fuck off," I said.

I was seven steps up the stairs when I found him beside me. I stopped again.

"Give me," he said, "one minute."

"I've been told I have to give you my *entire* life," I said. "And then I have to give you children, too, I nearly forgot. Kids who can survive in full daylight, just like me. I think that's enough, isn't it, Zeev Duvalle? You don't need a silly little *minute* from me when I have to give you all the rest."

He let me go, then.

I ran up the stairs.

When I reached the upper landing, I looked back down,

between a kind of elation and a sort of horror. But he had vanished. The part-lit spaces of the house again seemed void of anything alive, except for me.

Juno. I dreamed about her that night. I dreamed she was in a jet-black cave where water dripped, and she held a dead child in her arms and wept.

The child was me, I suppose. What she had feared the most when they, my house of Severin, made her carry me out into the oncoming dawn, to see how much if anything I could stand. *Just one minute.* What he had asked for too, Zeev. I hadn't granted it to him. But she – and I – had had no choice.

When I survived sunrise, she was at first very glad. But then, when I began to keep asking, *When can I see the light again?* Then, oh then. Then she began to lose me, and I her, my tall, red-haired, blue-eyed mother.

She never told me, but it's simple to work out. The more I took to daylight, the more I proved I was a true sun-born, the *more* she lost me, and I lost her. She herself could stand two or three hours, every week or so. But she *hated* the light, the sun. They *terrified* her, and when I turned out so able to withstand them, even to like and – *want* them, then the doors of her heart shut fast against me.

Juno hated me just as she hated the light of the sun. She hated me, *loathed* me, *loathes* me, my mother.

Part Three

About three weeks went by. The pines darkened and the other trees turned to copper and bronze and shed like tall cats their fur of leaves. I went on walks about the estate. No one either encouraged or dissuaded me. They had then nothing they wanted to hide from me? But I don't drive, and so there was a limit to how far I could go and get back again in the increasingly chilly evenings. By day, anyway, there seemed little activity, in the house or outside it. I started sleeping later in the mornings so I could stay up at night fully alert, sometimes, until four or five. It was less I was checking on what went on in the house-castle of Duvalle, than that I was uncomfortable so many of them were around, and *active*, when I lay asleep. There was a lock on my door. I always used it. I put a chair against it too, with the back under the door-handle. It wasn't Zeev I was worried about. No one, in particular. Just the complete feel and atmosphere of that place. At Severin there had been several who were mostly or totally nocturnal – my mother, for one. But also quite a few like me who, even if they couldn't take much direct sunlight, as I could, still preferred to be about by day.

A couple of times during my outdoor excursions in daylight, I did find clearings in the woods, with small houses, vines, orchards, fields with a harvest already collected. I even once saw some men with a flock of sheep. Neither sheep nor men took any notice of me. No doubt they had been warned a new Wife-of-Alliance was here and shown what she looked like.

The marriage had been set for the first night of the following month. The ceremony would be brief, unadorned, simply a legalisation. Marriages in most of the houses were like this. Nothing especially celebratory, let alone religious, came into them.

I thought I'd resigned myself. But of course, I hadn't. As for him, Zeev Duvalle, I'd been 'meeting' him generally only at dinner – those barren awful dinners where good manners seemed to demand I attend. Sometimes I was served meat – I alone. A crystal bowl of fruit had appeared – for me. I ate with difficulty amid their 'fastidious' contempt. I began a habit of removing pieces of fruit to eat later in my rooms. He was only ever polite. He would unsmilingly and bleakly offer me bread and wine, water... Sometimes I did drink the blood. I needed to. To me it had a strange taste, which maybe I imagined.

During the night, now and then, I might see him about the house, playing chess with one of the others, listening to music or reading in the library, talking softly on a telephone. Three or four times I saw him from an upper window, outside and running in long wolf-like bounds between the trees, the paleness of his hair like a beam blown off the face of the moon.

Hunting?

I intended to get married in black. Like the girl in the Chekhov play, I too was in mourning for my life. That night I hung the dress outside the closet, and put the black pumps below, ready for tomorrow. No jewellery.

Also I made a resolve not to go down to their dire dinner. To the older woman who read novels at the table and laughed smugly, secretively at things in them; the vile man with his bread-cloth in the glass. The handful of others, some of whom never turned up regularly anyhow, their low voices murmuring to each other about past times and people known only to them. And him. Zeev. Him. He drank from his glass very couthly, unlike certain others. Sometimes a glass of water, or some wine– for him usually red, as if it must pretend to be blood. He had dressed more elegantly since the first night, but always his clothes were quiet. There was one dark white shirt, made of some sort of velvety material, with bone-colour buttons... He looked beautiful. I could have killed him. We're easy to kill – car crashes, bullets – though we can live, Tyfa had once said, even a thousand years. But that's probably one more lie.

However, tonight I wouldn't go down there. I'd eat up here, the last apple and the dried cherries.

About ten thirty, a knock on my door.

I jumped, more because I expected it than because I was startled. I put down the book I'd been reading, the Chekhov plays, and said, "Who is it?" Knowing who it was.

"May I come in?" he asked, formal and musical, alien.

"I'd rather you left me alone," I said.

He said, without emphasis, "All right, Daisha. I'll go down to the library. No one else will be there. There'll be fresh coffee. I'll wait for you until midnight. Then I have things I have to do."

I'd got up and crossed to the door. I said through it with a crackling venom that surprised me, I'd thought I had it leashed, "*Things to do?* Oh, when you go out hunting animals and rip them apart in the woods for proper fresh blood, that kind of *thing*, do you mean?"

There was silence. Then, "I'll wait till midnight," he flatly said.

Then he was gone, I knew, though I never heard him leave.

When I walked into the library it was after eleven, and I was wearing my wedding dress and shoes. I told him what they were.

"It's supposed to be unlucky, isn't it," I said, "for the groom to see the bride in her dress before the wedding. But there's no luck to spoil, is there?"

He was sitting in one of the chairs by the fire, his long legs stretched out. He'd put on jeans and sweater and boots for the excursion later. A leather jacket hung from the chair.

The coffee was still waiting but it would be cold by now. Even so he got up, poured me a cup, brought it to me. He managed – he always managed this – to hand it to me without touching me.

Then he moved away and stood by the hearth, gazing across at the high walls of books.

"Daisha," he said, "I think I understand how uncomfortable and angry you are—"

"*Do* you."

"—but I can ask that you listen. Without interrupting or storming out of the room…"

"Oh for God's—"

"*Daisha.*" He turned his eyes on me. From glass-green they too had become almost white. He was flaming mad, anyone could see, but unlike me, he'd controlled it. He *used* it, like a cracking whip spattering electricity across the room. And at the same time – the *pain* in his face. The closed-in pain and – was it only frustration, or despair? That was what held me, or I'd have walked out, as he said. I stood there stunned, and thought, *He hurts as I do. Why? Who did this to him? God, he hates the idea of marrying me as much as I hate it. Or – he hates the way he – we – are being used.*

"OK," I said. I sat down on a chair. I put the cold coffee on the floor. "Talk. I'll listen."

"Thank you," he said.

A huge old clock ticked on the mantlepiece above the fire. Tock-tock-tock. Each note a second. Sixty now. That minute he'd asked from me before. Or the minute when Juno held me in the sunrise, shaking.

"Daisha. I'm well aware you don't want to be here, let alone with me. I hoped you wouldn't feel that way, but I'm not amazed you do. You had to leave your own house, where you had familiar people, love, stability—"

I had said I'd keep quiet; I didn't argue.

"…and move into this fucking monument to a castle, and be ready to become the partner of some guy you never saw except in a scrap of a movie. I'll be honest. The moment I saw the photos of you, I was drawn to you. I stupidly thought, this is a beautiful, strong woman that I'd like to know. Maybe we can make something of this pre-arranged mess. I meant make something for ourselves, you and me. Kids were – are – the last thing on my mind. We'd have a long time after all, to reach a decision on *that*. But you. I was... looking forward to meeting you. And I *would* have been there, to meet you. Only something happened. No. Not some compulsion I have to go out and tear animals apart and *drink* them in the forest. Daisha," he said, "have you been to look at the waterfall?"

I stared. "Only from the car... "

"There's one of our human families there. I had to go and—" he broke off. He said, "The people in this house have switched right off, like computers without any electric current. I grew up here. It was hell. Yeah, that place you wanted me to go to. Only not bright or fiery, just – *dead*. They're dead here. Living dead. *Undead*, just what they say in the legends, in that bloody book *Dracula*. But I am not dead. And nor are you. Did it ever occur to you," he said, "your name, *Daisha* – the way it sounds. *Day* – sha. Beautiful. Just as you are."

He had already invited me to speak, so perhaps I could offer another comment. I said, "But you can't stand the light."

"No, I can't. Which doesn't mean I don't *crave* the light. When I was two years old they took me out, my dad led me by the hand. *He* was fine with an hour or so of sunlight. I was so excited – looking forward to it. I remember the first colours..." He shut his eyes, opened them. "Then the sun came up. I never saw it after all. The first true light – I went blind. My skin ... I don't remember properly. Just darkness and agony and terror. Just one minute. My body couldn't take even that. I was ill for ten months. Then I started to see again. After ten months. But I've seen daylight since, of course I have, on him, in photographs. I've read about it. And music – Ravel's *Sunrise* from that ballet. Can you guess what it's like to long for daylight, to be – *in love* with daylight – and you can never see it for real, never feel the warmth, smell the scents of it or properly hear the sounds, except on a screen, off a CD – *never?* When I saw you, you're like that, like a real daylight. Do you know what I said to my father when I started to recover, after those ten months, those thirty seconds of dawn? '*Why,*' I said to him, 'why is light my enemy, why does it want to kill me? *Why light?*'"

Zeev turned away. He said to the sunny bright hearth, "And you're the daylight too, Daisha. And you've become my enemy. Daisha," he said, "I release you. We won't marry. I'll make it clear to all of them, Severin first, that any fault is all with me. There'll be no bad thing they can level at you. So, you're free. I regret so much the torment I've unwillingly, selfishly put you through. I'm sorry, Daisha. And now, God knows, it's late and I have to go out. It's not rudeness, I hope you'll accept that now. Please trust me. Go upstairs and sleep well. Tomorrow you can go home."

I sat like a block of concrete. Inside I felt shattered by what he had said. He pulled on his jacket and started towards the door, and only then I stood up. "Wait."

"I can't." He didn't look at me. "I'm sorry. Someone – needs me. Please believe me. It's true."

And I heard myself say, "Some human girl?"

That checked him. He looked at me, face a blank. "*What?*"

"The human family you seem to have to be with – by the fall? Is that it? You want a human woman, not me."

Then he laughed. It was raw, and real, that laughter. He came back and caught my hands. "Daisha – my *Day* – you're insane. All right. Come with me and see. We'll have to race."

But my hands tingled, my heart was in a race already.

I looked up into his face, he down into mine. The night hesitated, shifted. He let go my hands and I flew out and up the stairs. Dragging off that dress I tore the sleeve at the shoulder, but I left it lying with the shoes. Inside fifteen more minutes we were sprinting, side by side, along the track. There was no excuse for this, no *rational* reason. But I had seen him, *seen*, as if sunlight had streamed through the black lid of the night and shown him to me for the first, light that was his enemy, and my mother's, *never* mine.

The moon was low by then and stroked the edges of the waterfall. It was like liquid aluminium, and its roar packed the air full as a sort of deafness. The human house was about a mile off, tucked in among the dense black columns of the pines.

A youngish, fair-haired woman opened the door. Her face lit up the instant she saw him, no one could miss that. "Oh, Zeev," she said, "he's so much better. Our doctor says he's mending fantastically well. But come in."

It was a pleasing room, low-ceilinged, with a dancing fire. A smart black cat with a white vest and mittens, sat upright in an armchair, giving the visitors a thoughtful frowning scrutiny.

"Will you go up?" the woman asked.

"Yes," Zeev said. He smiled at her, and added, "This is Daisha Severin."

"Oh, are you Daisha? It's good of you to come out too," she

told me. Zeev had already gone upstairs. The human woman returned to folding towels at a long table.

"Isn't it very late for you?" I questioned.

"We keep late hours. We like the night-time."

I had been aware that this was often the case at Severin. But I'd hardly ever spoken much to humans; I wasn't sure now what I should say. But she continued to talk to me, and overhead I heard a floorboard creak; Zeev would not have caused that. The man was there, evidently, the one who was 'mending'.

"It happened just after sunset," the woman said, folding a blue towel over a green one. "Crazy accident – the chain broke. Oh God, when they brought him home, my poor Emil—" Her voice faltered and grew hushed. Above also a hushed voice was speaking, barely audible even to me. But she raised her face and it had stayed still rosy and glad, and her voice was fine again. "We telephoned up to the house and Zeev came out at once. He did the wonderful thing. It worked. It always works when he does it."

I stared at her. I was breathing quickly, frightened. "What," I said, "*what* did he do?"

"Oh, but he'll have told you," she strangely reminded me. "The same as he did for Joel – and poor Arresh when he was sick with meningitis—"

"*You* tell me," I said.

She blinked.

"Please."

"The blood," she said, gazing at me a little apologetically, regretful to have confused me in some way she couldn't fathom, "he gave them his blood in drink. It's the blood that heals, of course. I remember when Zeev said to Joel, 'it's all right, forget the stories – this won't change you, only make you well.' Zeev was only sixteen then himself. He's saved five lives here. But no doubt he was too modest to tell you that. And with Emil, the same. It was shocking." Now she didn't falter. "Zeev had to be here so quick – and he cut straight through his own sleeve to the vein, so it would be fast enough."

Blood on his sleeve, I thought. *Vampires heal so rapidly ... all done, only that little rusty mark...*

"And my Emil, my lovely man, he's safe and alive, Daisha. Thanks to your husband."

His voice called to me out of the dim-roar of the water-falling firelight, "Daisha, come up a minute."

The woman folded an orange towel over a white one, and I numbly, speechlessly, climbed the stair, and Zeev said, "I have asked Emil, and he says, very kindly, he doesn't object if you see how this is done."

So I stood in the doorway and watched as Zeev, with the help of a thin clean knife, decanted and poured out a measure of his life-blood into a mug, which had a picture on it of a cat, just like the smart black cat in the room below. And the smiling man, sitting on the bed in his dressing gown, raised the mug, and toasted Zeev, and drank the wild medicine down.

"We're young," he said to me, "we are both of us *genuinely* young. You're seventeen, aren't you? I'm twenty-seven. We are the only actual young *here*. And the rest of them, as I said, switched off. But we can do something, not only for ourselves, Day, but for our people. Or my people, if you prefer. Or *any* people. Humans. Don't you think that's fair, given what they do, knowingly or not, for us?"

We had walked back, slowly, along the upper terraces by the black abyss of the ravine, sure-footed, omnipotent. Then we sat together on the forest's edge and watched the silver tumble of the fall. It had no choice. It to fall, and go on falling forever, in love with the unknown darkness below, unable and not wanting to stop.

I kept thinking of the little blood-mark on his sleeve that night, what I'd guessed, and what instead was true. And I thought of Juno, with her obsessive wasted tiny blood-drop offerings in the 'shrine', to a man she had no longer loved. As she no longer loved me.

She hates me because I have successful sun-born genes and can live in daylight. But Zeev, who can't take even thirty seconds of the sun, doesn't hate me for that. He... he doesn't *hate* me at all.

"So, will you go back to Severin tomorrow?" he said to me, as we sat the brink of the night.

"No."

"Daisha, even when they've married us, please believe this: if you still want to go away, I won't put obstacles in your path. I will back you up."

"You care so little."

"So much."

His eyes glowed in the dark. They put the waterfall to shame.

When he touched me, touches me, I *know* him. From long ago,

I remember this incredible joy, this heat and burning, this refinding *rightness* – and I fall down into the abyss forever, willing as the shining water. I never loved before. Except Juno, but she cured me of that.

He is a healer. His blood can heal, its vampiric vitality transmissible – but non-invasive. From his gift come no substandard replicants of our kind. They only – *live*.

Much, much later, when we parted just before the dawn inside the house – parted till the next night – our wedding day – it came to me that if he can heal by letting humans drink his blood, perhaps I might offer him some of my own. Because my blood might help him to survive the daylight, even if only for one unscathed and precious minute.

I'll wear green to be married. And a necklace of sea-green glass.

As the endless day trails by, unable to sleep, I've written this.

When he touched me, when he kissed me, Zeev, whose name actually means Wolf, became known to me. I don't believe he'll have to live all his long, long life without ever seeing the sun. For that was what he reminded me of. His warmth, his kiss, his arms about me – my first memory of that golden light which blew upwards through the dark. No longer any fear, which anyway was never mine, only that glorious *familiar* excitement and happiness, that *welcomed* danger. Perhaps I am wrong in this. Perhaps I shall pay heavily and cruelly for having been deceived. And for deceiving myself, too, because I realised what he was to me the moment I saw him – why else put up such barricades? Zeev is my sunrise out of the dark of the night of my so-far useless life. Yes, then. I love him.

ABOUT THE AUTHOR

Tanith Lee (1947-2015) was born in London. Because her parents were professional dancers (ballroom, Latin American) and had to live where the work was, she attended a number of truly terrible schools, and didn't learn to read – she was also dyslectic – until almost age 8. And then only because her father taught her. This opened the world of books to her, and by 9 she was writing. After much better education at a grammar school, she went on to work in a library. This was followed by various other jobs – shop assistant, waitress, clerk – plus a year at art college when she was 25-26. In 1974, her career as a writer was launched, when DAW Books of America, under the leadership of Donald A. Wollheim, bought and published *The Birthgrave*, and thereafter 26 of her novels and collections.

Tanith was presented with a Lifetime Achievement Award in 2013, at World Fantasycon in Brighton. During her lifetime, she also received the World Horror Convention Grand Master Award, as well as the August Derleth Award and the World Fantasy Award for short fiction (twice).

In 1992, she married the writer-artist-photographer John Kaiine, her partner since 1987. They lived on the Sussex Weald, near the sea, in a house full of books and plants, and never without feline companions. She died at home in May 2015, after a long illness, continuing to work until a couple of weeks before her death.

Throughout her life, Tanith wrote around 100 books, and over 300 short stories. 4 of her radio plays were broadcast by the BBC; she also wrote 2 episodes (*Sarcophagus* and *Sand*) for the TV series *Blake's 7*. Her stories were read regularly on Radio 4 Extra. She was an inspiration to a generation of writers and her work was enormously influential within genre fiction – as it continues to be. She wrote in many styles, within and across many genres, including Horror, SF and Fantasy, Historical, Detective, Contemporary-Psychological, Children and Young Adult. Her preoccupation, though, was always people.

PUBLISHING HISTORY OF THE STORIES
(from printed publications in the English language)

Huzdra: *The Year's Best Horror Stories: Series V.* DAW Books, 1977. Ed. by Gerald W. Page. *Nightshades: Thirteen Journeys into Shadow,* Headline 1993.

A Wolf at the Door: *A Wolf at the Door and Other Retold Fairy Tales.* Smon & Schuster, 2000. Original anthology, ed. by Ellen Datlow & Terri Windling. *Dark of The Woods: Fairy Tales for Modern Times.* Aladdin Paperbacks, 2006, ed. by Ellen Datlow and Terri Windling

Venus Rising on Water: *Isaac Asimov's Science Fiction Magazine (No 176),* October 1991. *The Mammoth Book of Vampire Stories by Women,* Constable Robinson, 2001, Caroll & Graf 2001, Skyhorse Publishing, 2017, ed. by Stephen Jones.

The Puma's Daughter: *The Beastly Bride: Tales of The Animal People,* Viking, 2010, ed. by Ellen Datlow and Terri Windling.

The Return of Berenice! *nEvermore! Tales of Murder, Mystery & The Macabre: Neo-Gothic Fiction Inspired by the Imagination of Edgar Allan Poe,* Edge Science Fiction and Fantasy Publishing, 2015, ed by Nancy Kilpatrick and Caro Soles.

Sea Wharg: *Full Moon City,* Galley Books, 2010, ed.by Darrel Schweitzer and Martin H. Greenberg. *The Year's Best Dark Fantasy & Horror 2011,* Prime Books, 2011, ed. by Paula Guran.

Table Manners: *Immortal: Love Stories with Bite,* Borders Exclusive [in conjunction with Teen Libris], 2008, Benbella Books, 2009. ed. by P.C. Cast & Lean Wilson.

The Werewolf: *Worlds of Fantasy and Horror. Vol 1 No 3, Summer 1996. Weird Tales, Summer 1994-Summer 1996,* Wildside Press, 2003, ed, by Darrell Schweitzer. *Curse of The Full Moon: A Werewolf Anthology,* Ulysses Press, 2010, ed, by James Lowder.

The Janfia Tree: *Blood Is Not Enough: 17 Stories of Vampirism,* Morrow 1989, ed. by Ellen Datlow. *Nightshades: Thirteen Journeys into Shadow,* Headline 1993. *A Whisper of Blood: A Collection of Modern Vampire Stories,* Fall River Press, 2008, ed. by Ellen Datlow

Tiger I: *Asimov's Science Fiction. Vol 19 No 15 (No 240),* mid-December 1995. *Isaac Asimov's Mother's Day.* New York: Ace, 2000, ed, by Gardner Dozois and Sheila Williams, *Tempting the Gods: Selected Stories of Tanith Lee,* Wildside Press, 2009

Pinewood: *Whispers. No 21-22 (Vol 6 No 1-2),* December 1984. *The Year's Best Horror Stories: Series XIV,* DAW Books, 1986, ed, by Karl Edward Wagner. *Horrorstory Volume Five,* Underwood-Miller, 1989, ed. by Karl Edward Wagner. *Nightshades: Thirteen Journeys into Shadow,* Headline 1993.

Nightshade: *Nightshades: Thirteen Journeys into Shadow,* Headline 1993.

Why Light?: *Teeth: Vampire Tales,* Harper Collins, 2011 ed. by Ellen Datlow and Terry Windling. *The Year's Best Dark Fantasy & Horror,* Prime Books, 2012, ed. by Paula Guran.

BOOKS BY TANITH LEE

Series

The Birthgrave Trilogy (The Birthgrave; Vazkor, son of Vazkor
[published as Shadowfire in the UK], Quest for the White Witch)
The Blood Opera Sequence (Dark Dance; Personal Darkness; Darkness, I)
The Flat Earth Opus (Night's Master; Death's Master; Delusion's
Master; Delirium's Mistress; Night's Sorceries)
The Lionwolf Trilogy (Cast a Bright Shadow; Here in Cold Hell;
No Flame But Mine)
The Paradys Quartet (The Book of the Damned; The Book of the Beast;
The Book of the Dead; The Book of the Mad)
The Venus Quartet (Faces Under Water; Saint Fire; A Bed of Earth;
Venus Preserved)
The Vis Trilogy (The Storm Lord; Anackire; The White Serpent)
The FOUR-Bee Series (Don't Bite the Sun; Drinking Sapphire Wine)
The S.I.L.V.E.R. Series (Silver Metal Lover; Metallic Love)

Novels and Novellas

34
The Blood of Roses
Companions on the Road
Days of Grass
Death of the Day
Electric Forest
Elephantasm
Eva Fairdeath
The Gods Are Thirsty
Kill the Dead
Heart-Beast
A Heroine of the World
Louisa the Poisoner
Lycanthia
Madame Two Swords
Mortal Suns
Reigning Cats and Dogs
Sabella
Sung in Shadow
Vivia
Volkhavaar

When the Lights Go Out
White as Snow
The Winter Players

Young Adult and Children's Fiction

Animal Castle (picture book)
The Castle of Dark
The Claidi Journals (Law of the Wolf Tower; Wolf Star Rise,
Queen of the Wolves, Wolf Wing)
The Dragon Hoard
East of Midnight
The Piratica Novels (Piratica 1; Piratica 2; Piratica 3)
Prince on a White Horse
Princess Hynchatti and Other Surprises
Shon the Taken
The Unicorn Trilogy (Black Unicorn; Gold Unicorn; Red Unicorn)
The Voyage of the Bassett: Islands in the Sky

Story Collections

Blood 20
Cold Grey Stones
Colder Greyer Stones
Cyrion
Dancing in the Fire
Disturbed by Her Song
Dreams of Dark and Light
Fatal Women
Forests of the Night
The Gorgon
Hunting the Shadows
Nightshades
Phantasya
Red as Blood – Tales from the Sisters Grimmer
Redder Than Blood
Sounds and Furies
Tamastara, or the Indian Nights
Space is Just a Starry Night
Tempting the Gods
Unsilent Night
Women as Demons

TANITH LEE TITLES PUBLISHED BY IMMANION PRESS

The Colouring Book Series

Cruel Pink
Greyglass
To Indigo
Ivoria
Killing Violets
L'Amber
Turquoiselle

The Blood Opera Sequence

Dark Dance
Personal Darkness
Darkness, I

Novels and Novellas

34
Ghosteria Volume 2: The Novel: Zircons May Be Mistaken
Madame Two Swords
Vivia

Collections

Animate Objects
A Different City
Ghosteria Volume 1: The Stories
Legenda Maris
The Weird Tales of Tanith Lee
Venus Burning: Realms: Collected Short Stories from 'Realms of Fantasy'
Strindberg's Ghost Sonata and Other Uncollected Tales
Love in a Time of Dragons and Other Rare Tales

Of Interest to Tanith Lee Enthusiasts…

Night's Nieces

This anthology is a tribute to Tanith Lee, comprising short stories written shortly after her death by some of her writer friends to whom Tanith was a profound influence and inspiration: Storm Constantine, Cecilia Dart-Thornton, Vera Nazarian, Sarah Singleton, Kari Sperring, Sam Stone, Freda Warrington and Liz Williams. With an introduction by Tanith's husband, the artist John Kaiine. Illustrated throughout by the contributors and with photographs from Tanith Lee's personal collection.

IMMANION PRESS
Purveyors of Speculative Fiction

Venus Burning: Realms by Tanith Lee

Tanith Lee wrote 15 stories for the acclaimed *Realms of Fantasy* magazine. This book collects all the stories in one volume for the first time, some of which only ever appeared in the magazine so will be new to some of Tanith's fans. These tales are among her best work, in which she takes myth and fairy tale tropes and turns them on their heads. Lush and lyrical, deep and literary, Tanith Lee created fresh poignant tales from familiar archetypes.

ISBN 978-1-907737-88-6, £11.99, $17.50 pbk

A Raven Bound with Lilies by Storm Constantine

The Wraeththu have captivated readers for three decades. This anthology of 15 tales collects all the published Wraeththu short stories into one volume, and also includes extra material, including the author's first explorations of the androgynous race. The tales range from the 'creation story' *Paragenesis*, through the bloody, brutal rise of the earliest tribes, and on into a future, where strange mutations are starting to emerge from hidden corners of the earth.

ISBN: 978-1-907737-80-0 £11.99, $15.50 pbk

Voices of the Silicon Beyond by E. S. Wynn

Vaetta is not human, but far more than a mere robot. Her world is overcrowded, it resources at breaking point. The humans who govern this parallel Earth need a solution to these problems. Then a strange, androgynous visitor appears from an inexplicable portal to another world, also seeking help. His world is sparsely populated, following the demise of humankind and the rise of a civilization known as Wraeththu. Vaetta is chosen to scout this new world and begin preparations for invasion, but what waits for her on the other side of the portal doesn't make sense to her, until a fatal meeting through which she discovers a history with far-reaching implications covering all realities. (A novel set in Storm Constantine's Wraeththu Mythos.)

ISBN: 978-1-907737-97-8, £9.99, $14.99 pbk

http://www.immanion-press.com
info@immanion-press.com

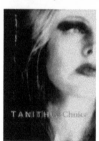
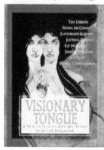